THE INVITATION

Reaching out to where it had stood, Jamie felt only darkness. Nothing remained but the image retained on his retinas. He stood perfectly still, as one might who felt he had made a fool of himself among strangers. Then his fear came back.

It had been the same figure: like a man, but not a man, wrapped in the cerements of the dead. And this time, behind the burial cloth, he had seen a decomposing face. Only one eye had been open, glowing fiercely, like an ember. The pupil had been a pinhole, the nose long and narrow, the mouth wide and full, smudged against the transparent ivory linen that covered it.

Grotesque as it was, Jamie knew the face. He recognized it a moment late, as a man lifting a candle in the dark would realize a moment late that he was looking into a mirror....

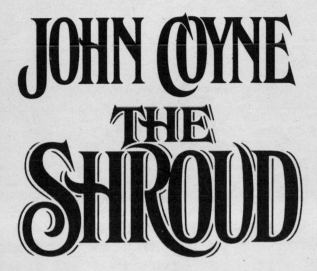

JOHN COYNE
THE SHROUD

BERKLEY BOOKS, NEW YORK

THE SHROUD

A Berkley Book / published by arrangement with
the author

PRINTING HISTORY
Berkley edition / July 1983

ISBN: 0-425-06243-0

A BERKLEY BOOK® TM 757,375
The name "BERKLEY" and the stylized "B"
with design are trademarks belonging to
Berkley Publishing Corporation.
PRINTED IN THE UNITED STATES OF AMERICA

For James E. Cronin
Founder of
The Writers Institute
Saint Louis University

CHAPTER ONE

December Twenty-fourth, Evening
Feast of Saint Gregory of Spoleto

Mary Margaret O'Donnell knelt before the nativity crib and mumbled. Then, as the wind howled around her, she crossed herself and began the Apostles' Creed. She could no longer remember the entire prayer, so she kept repeating the first few lines: "I believe in God, the Father Almighty, Maker of Heaven and Earth. And I believe in Jesus Christ, His only begotten Son."

Her bones ached from the kneeling. She felt the pain in her joints, in her left hip where a cop had kicked her that fall, chasing her from LaFayette Park, but she offered up the suffering, making it a special penance for her sins. One less day in hell, she thought, dimly recalling how as a little girl she had said dozens of rosaries, offering them up to God for plenary indulgences.

Then her memory gave out completely and she only stared at the nativity scene. It was well past midnight in LaFayette Park and in the swirling snow the light of the streetlamps was dim. But the outdoor crèche had been carefully spotlighted and

Mary Margaret could see every detail of the life-sized figures of Joseph, Mary, and the Christ Child. "So beautiful," she muttered, and her gray eyes glittered with tears. "So real, all the little animals, the sheep and shepherds, and, oh, look at the Wise Men with their camels! All of them in Bethlehem to praise dear sweet Baby Jesus. Oh, dear Lord of heaven, I love you." Her tearful voice cried out in the dark empty park.

In the late night silence, no one heard or noticed the bag lady kneeling at the deserted crèche. She was swathed in layers of old clothes. A long wool coat was pulled over sweaters and skirts, and her face and head were wrapped up in a babushka. Surrounding her were half a dozen shopping bags that she kept pulling closer, as if for comfort.

Mary Margaret no longer knew why she carried these bags. When she first arrived in the city she had had a suitcase, but hadn't been able to remember her name or where she was from. In summer she slept in the park, and in the winter she slept in the doorway of the nearby Cathedral. When she could, she sneaked inside.

She glanced furtively around, looked across the wide avenue at the huge Cathedral. Once early that night the sexton had chased her from the church. He had spotted her in Our Lady's Chapel unwrapping a sandwich she had salvaged from the trash can, and he had swooped down, yelling like an Apache, and sending her scurrying. She had barely had time to gather up her bags and get out the side entrance.

She had stood awhile on the north porch, begging money from the few parishioners that passed her on the way to Midnight Mass, but then it had begun to snow. The large, wet flakes stuck to her cloth coat and seeped through the worn soles of her shoes. Within minutes she had lost all feeling in her feet. She had left the Cathedral and stumbled across the street. There was no one on the avenue. Not many people still lived downtown by the river, and only at Christmas did they come in from the suburbs to hear mass at the city's old Cathedral.

Now, kneeling before the crèche in the park, Mary Margaret O'Donnell began to cry. She was unaware of the tears. They ran the length of her rough, red face, washed the dirt from her cheeks in warm rivulets. She had fallen recently and been beaten by a gang of kids. They had found her sleeping in the doorway of a vacant tenement and pounced on her shopping bags, searching for money. She had tried to fight them off, but they had beaten her face and knocked her unconscious. The cuts had healed, but her lips and cheeks were still bruised and puffy from the attack, and she was now more afraid than ever of strangers, of people who came close to her. She didn't wash. She had learned that no one came near her when her body stank.

Mary Margaret heard a car door slam in the distance. She ignored it. The park was safe after dark, she knew. No one, not even the police, came there late at night. Besides, she was having a good time watching the Holy Family in their Bethlehem stable.

She heard footsteps next, heavy boots crunching the deep snow. Her heart stopped and she clutched her clothes. Someone was approaching, coming toward the Christmas crèche. She didn't look up. It was better if they couldn't see it was a woman. He was close now; she could see him from the corner of her eye. Tall and dressed okay, in a black overcoat. He was no cop, that was sure, and no bum either. He knelt down beside her, before the Holy Family. She edged away on the makeshift kneeler.

He shifted over, moving toward her. Mary Margaret fumbled in the pockets of her old coat. She had a small knife somewhere, a kitchen knife she had lifted from someone's garbage.

"Wait," the man said. He reached out and touched her lightly.

Mary Margaret knocked his hand off her arm and swore. "Keep away," she told him. She grabbed her shopping bags and stood up, backed away from the lighted crèche.

"Oh, now, Agnes," he said, standing, following her.

"My name isn't Agnes!" she shouted, spinning away from the man in the deep snow.

"Here now, don't worry." He grabbed her again, seized her arm this time and held her.

This time she swung at him with both hands, doubling her old fingers into one small fist. She wasn't afraid of him. She could take care of herself, but then she felt the soft cloth over her mouth and nose and she couldn't breathe anymore.

• • •

The light was in her eyes. A bright light. She squirmed and tried to sit up, to get away from it, but she couldn't move. She was tied down flat, and her arms were at her side.

She was sick. Something had made her nauseous and involuntarily she vomited on herself, retched her trash-can sandwich onto her face and neck. She turned her head sideways, away from the mess, and saw him coming at her with the needle.

"I haven't got no money," she cried out. "I haven't a thing, dear God, only these old clothes, a few scraps of paper, some pictures of my mommy and daddy. They're dead. They're all dead now."

"Easy, Agnes," he whispered, coming out of the darkness.

She pulled up her thick legs and tried to kick at him. She realized she was on a wet rubbery sheet, tied to a table. The place was damp and her body was shaking from the cold and her fear.

"Please, don't," she asked, and in that small corner of her mind where some sanity still remained, Mary Margaret knew that he was going to kill her.

She felt the needle, felt the sharp, painful jab at her neck, and she gasped, gargled one last breath. And she didn't care, didn't fight the man, and for the first time since she had come to the city, Mary Margaret felt warm and safe and secure. She was indoors now, out of the snow, and she wept softly as the liquid spread through her body, found her aching heart, and stopped her life.

CHAPTER TWO

December Twenty-fifth, Morning
Feast of the Nativity

Christmas.

"Bah, humbug!" The young priest smiled. He couldn't quite pull it off. He loved Christmas, especially on such a lovely, snowy dawn. He sat in the bay window of his bedroom in the rectory, staring down onto Church Drive, the short, residential street that dead-ended into the parking lot behind the Cathedral.

"Merry Christmas," he whispered experimentally. He sipped his herb tea and yawned. He was tired, yet he was too excited from his long night with the Cardinal to sleep.

The view from his third-floor window wasn't beautiful— burned-out lots, abandoned brownstones, the panorama of urban decay. But it had been snowing since before midnight, the large, soft flakes softened the landscape, made the shabbiness almost quaint.

All that bothered him on this Christmas morning was that so few people had come out for Midnight Mass. Despite all his telephoning, the arm-twisting of the Holy Name Society, the special bus for the Knights of Columbus and their families, the huge Cathedral had been only a quarter full. Well, there had been the snow, he reasoned. He couldn't have predicted a storm. Of all the goddamn luck.

He could still see the Cardinal's face as he stepped from the sacristy and saw the half-empty church. He had really wanted to pull it off for the Cardinal, especially since the Boss was celebrating the High Mass himself, and had even come early to have Christmas Eve dinner at the rectory with him and Monsignor O'Toole.

"I haven't forgotten you two," the Cardinal had said, pushing away from the dining table. "I think of this old Cathedral as our missionary effort, and you as my Maryknolls down here among the poor." Then he had smiled and nodded around the table at the half-dozen other priests he had brought along with him from the Chancery—uptown priests, the kind who did important jobs in the archdiocese and never paid a sick call.

It was a big festive occasion by Cathedral standards—too big, in fact, for the rectory's housekeeper, Mrs. Windmiller. She hadn't been able to manage for so many, especially since the menu the Cardinal had requested was complicated and unfamiliar.

So a delegation from Christ the King parish had come to the rescue—younger, suburban women who had taken enough cooking classes to manage *saumon en croûte* in a watercress sauce. The homemade mayonnaise had been a drop too oily, but the Cardinal had overlooked it, beaming at the women as they assembled in the kitchen doorway for their moment with His Eminence. They wore their best Sunday dresses, and Christmas corsages on their aprons.

The Cardinal said grace after the meal, then stood to address the room. He was good at these after-dinner talks, and they all knew it. Already several of the priests were leaning back, crossing their legs, smiles of anticipation on their faces as they glanced about.

It was an old act. The young priest had seen the Cardinal this way a hundred, a thousand times before. It was something he'd missed, all those years in Rome after the seminary, and it was one of the best things about being back. He could remember sitting on the older man's knee when he was just five years old and the Cardinal—then just a parish priest—had been playing Santa Claus. The young priest smiled in spite of himself, remembering.

Then later, when he'd been in high school, and later still at the seminary, the same easy routine: the slight pause, the shuffling in the pocket of his black suit coat for a cigar. Always a little stage business of unwrapping a thick Havana. "I have a connection," he said, as he always did, winking. He took his time, knowing how the priests would wait for him. Everyone, always, waited for His Eminence.

"I guess you know," he began slowly, holding the unlit cigar in his left hand, looking at each one in turn, the women in the doorway as well, seizing each one for a moment with his brilliant blue eyes, "why I wanted to come down to the old Cathedral and spend the day with Monsignor O'Toole and this young—" A smile caught at the corners of his mouth, swept across his face like a sunrise. "—this young *máisdèen.*"

They all laughed at the Irish expression, and Monsignor Kane even led a brief moment of spontaneous applause. The Rosary Society smiled, too, but more uncertainly. They glanced among themselves, not quite sure what the Cardinal had said.

Sitting at the right of His Eminence, the young priest could feel himself blush, and he realized again how much he loved this man. The Cardinal had raised him, trained him, and brought him back home. Now all the young priest wanted was to do his best, to be of service.

"You're aware, I'm sure," the Cardinal continued, "that we celebrate two birthdays this Christmas Eve." His voice picked up its cadence and broke quickly over the audience. He had stepped back slightly from the table, planted both feet as if to defend that corner of the room. He was large and imposing, a block of a man with a massive head, stout neck, and a square, solidly built body. He looked as if he had been chiseled whole from hardwood.

"Our faith is renewed and enriched tonight as we celebrate the birth of Our Savior. Tonight Christ is born once again in a cold manger in the town of Bethlehem, the son of Mary and Joseph."

His Eminence paused, searched their faces with his blue eyes. His voice had softened and his thick brogue lilted like a lyric. "Remember tonight at Mass that the priest's life is the most humble of all. Remember who we are: priests, shepherds of God's flock. We are the link with the centuries of Christians who have carried the good word forward, from one generation to the next, kept alive this flame of hope and everlasting redemption." His hands swept out, blessing them, drawing them closer, as if into an embrace.

The Cardinal stopped and before they could prepare, changed tones, said offhandedly in mock seriousness, "The second birthday we celebrate tonight is only slightly less auspicious." A roar of applause greeted his words. Again the young priest felt everyone's eyes on him.

His Eminence remembered his cigar then and used the moment of laughter to light it. A thick cloud of smoke rose above his gray hair like a halo.

"And how old would you be tonight, Father?" the Cardinal asked innocently, looking down at the young man.

"Thirty-two, your Eminence."

"Thirty-two?" The Cardinal repeated. "Thirty-two, you say? Well, you're making me an old man, Jamie. Are you sure about that figure?" He glanced sideways at the other priests. "I mean, Jamie, you never were much good with numbers."

More laughter and applause. And now, Jamie knew, the Cardinal would tell the story.

"I was still in the seminary myself," the Cardinal continued, speaking slowly, as if he had all the time in the world, "and was helping out down here at this old Cathedral for Christmas. Of course, in those days this was quite a parish. There were half a dozen young priests, all kept busy morning and night, and grateful for another pair of hands.

"It was Christmas Eve, a snowy one like tonight, and I was coming home from visiting the sick. The priest I was accompanying had gone on to see his own family, and I had walked back alone along McCarthy Avenue, then crossed over at Benton Place. Where they built the A&P, the one that burned down during the riots." He gestured, making sure all the priests knew exactly where he meant.

"I had come along Church Drive and was going up the side steps of the Cathedral when I heard this baby crying." He stopped then. He always stopped at that point, the young priest knew, to build suspense. When he continued, his voice was hushed, as if the events that followed were truly miraculous.

"It was a windy night and blowing snow. I wasn't sure at first if it really was a child, and not some small animal caught out in the cold. Or maybe nothing at all. I stood there on the steps, nearly knee deep in snow, and listened.

"I wasn't sure which direction the crying had come from; the snow was whirling about me. I was cold and damp myself, and thinking only of getting inside and dressing for Midnight Mass. Then I heard this cry again, and I knew for certain it was a child."

He stopped again. The young priest glanced up and saw His Eminence tending to his cigar, flipping a thick, perfect ash into the saucer of his cup. He was the only one smoking. The priests, all silent around the table, stared up at him and waited.

"I heard the cry only once more," the Cardinal whispered in his deep confessional tone, "and I could tell the infant was growing weak. With each cry it was losing strength. I got down on my knees—my hands and knees—because I couldn't see otherwise, what with the blowing snow—and I began to crawl around the steps, feeling my way in the drifts.

"I searched the length of those side steps until I got to the corner, the niche to the right of the entrance, where the statue of Ignatius Loyola stands—or did, until it was vandalized. And there I found a child, wrapped up literally in swaddling clothes."

He stopped again. The cigar had gone out. He held it motionless in his thick fingers, not moving, not speaking. The young priest noticed the women, riveted in the doorway. Unlike the priests, they had never heard the story before.

"We saved that child," the Cardinal went on, still speaking slowly and thoughtfully. "I got the baby to the convent next door and with the help of the good sisters and the late Doctor Senese, God rest his soul, the little boy was saved. Doc Senese told me the baby would have lived only a few minutes more in that freezing cold. It was, you know, as if a tiny kitten had been tossed into the snow. The child was less than six hours old.

"We never found the mother. Some poor helpless woman, I'm sure, overwhelmed by it all and thinking she had nowhere to turn for help. Perhaps she had planned to leave the child in the vestibule, where it was warm, but was frightened off at the last minute by people passing. I don't know." He shook his head as if still seeking the reason.

"I searched for her afterward, asked around in the tenements along the Parkway. We always thought she might be German. It was 1950 and MacPatch, as some of you may remember then, had a small German community, refugees from the war. But I never found her. Never found any trace of her." The Cardinal sighed.

"But the child lived," he said quickly, summing up. "The child lived with us at the orphanage of Saints Peter and Paul, and later went to our prep school and the seminary. He grew up, we can truthfully say, within the warm embrace of Holy Mother Church. The good sisters wanted to call him Nicholas, as it seemed he was our Christmas gift, but I thought it was more appropriate to name him after the saint who watched over him in the niche. That is, after Saint Ignatius."

The Cardinal turned toward the young priest. "Father James Ignatius," he announced, "my own son, I might claim, if I wasn't so modest." He winked at the gathering. "And if I could be sure he wouldn't someday disgrace me." The room broke into laughter.

The young priest could feel the Cardinal's hand on his shoulder, the strong fingers gripping him tightly. He did not look up as the Cardinal said, "And I think if we can get the good ladies from Christ the King to join us, we owe this fine young fella at least a chorus of Happy Birthday to celebrate his day and wish him many happy returns. Monsignor Corboy, would you mind starting us out? We're not your fine citywide choral group, but we can, I believe, all sing loudly, if not on key."

The young priest stood and turned to the Cardinal. He was taller than the older man, but slender, and beside the bulky Cardinal he looked younger than he was, with his thick, unkempt blond hair, strong cheekbones, and pale blue eyes the color of a clear winter's sky.

"Thank you, Your Eminence," he said softly and moved to kneel, to kiss the prelate's ring, but before he could genuflect, the Cardinal pulled him into a tight embrace.

The outburst of affection from His Eminence surprised the gathering, momentarily silencing the priests. These men were not used to displays of affection; were, in fact, conditioned against behaving that way with each other. But the genuine love between the Cardinal and Jamie Ignatius touched them all and they burst into the chorus of Happy Birthday that the Cardinal had prescribed.

Now, hours later, Father Ignatius was still moved by the embrace. He could still feel his cheek being squeezed against the big man's shoulder, still smell the sharp scent of the other man's after-shave lotion.

In the semidarkness of his room, he glanced at the clock. Six. An hour before it was time for early Mass. In that time he had to dress and unlock the front doors of the Cathedral, but there was still time to meditate. Still he did not move.

He had begun to meditate a few years before, while studying in Rome, and he had found it a wonderful way to pray. When he first began he had read enviously of Saint Teresa of Avila who had fallen into raptures while meditating, losing all feeling in her body, all knowledge of her surroundings. He had prayed it would be that way for him, but now he was afraid.

Since returning that October to Saints Peter and Paul, his experience of meditation had changed. While contemplating Christ, he found himself reaching a place beyond reality, in a world beyond the physical. But it wasn't Christ that he was finding there.

Abruptly Jamie left the window and went to his bed mat. He had to keep trying. Not all of his meditations led to the experiences he had come to fear. And perhaps they were only sent to try him, to see if he would persevere. Well, he told himself, he would.

His bedroom had been redesigned for meditation. Its original furnishings had been heavy, dark furniture, walnut and mahogany from the turn of the century. In his first week he had moved all those pieces to the basement, painted the walls white, and moved in a thick mat for a bed. His desk consisted of two filing cabinets and a piece of plywood; a few plastic cartons served as end tables and bookshelves.

The white walls he had left bare, except for a single crucifix, and one picture portraying Christ in the Garden of Gethsemane. It had been painted by Duccio di Buoninsegna in the Middle

Ages, and he had found a reproduction one day in Rome, while sorting through the offerings of a flea market outside the Colosseum.

The painting showed Christ kneeling in the Garden, his white-robed body leaning exhaustedly against a rock, his eyes staring upward, while a dozen yards away Peter and the two sons of Zebedee slept peacefully, unaware of his torment.

In his bedroom, Jamie always felt good. The bareness of the walls, the silence and dark shadows, the absence of possessions, this he found comforting. He glanced at Duccio's painting and saw again the sorrowful figure kneeling alone against the rocks of the hillside. It was time now to reach out to Christ, through meditation.

"Lord, I have sinned against you. Lord, have mercy," Jamie whispered. Slipping off his shoes he sat down carefully in the center of the mat, crossing his legs and laying his arms on his thighs, opening his hands and turning the palms upward.

Jamie sat straight, his head held high, his eyes closed, beginning the process of calming himself, of slowing down his body. He imagined a cord of energy running from the base of his spine down through the brownstone rectory, down three stories into the earth, tying him tightly to the ground. He took his time, let the image develop, felt the tug of the cord as it pulled him tightly to the center of the world.

Slowly he began to count the exhalations of his breath, concentrating on that simple exercise, cleansing his mind. Over and over he counted from one to ten. A dozen minutes passed as he gradually disciplined his mind, moved his attention deeper and deeper into himself, went closer and closer to an awareness beyond sleep, reached for a state of rest deeper than dreams.

He thought of Jesus Christ. He let the name of God float in and out of his consciousness, let it grow fainter, let the word draw him into that space where he no longer realized he was meditating. Jesus, he prayed, you are truly present at my center, at the ground of my being. I love you, Lord, I am one with you in your love. Jesus, be my all. Jesus, draw me to yourself.

Ready now, he moved across that psychological ledge he feared, moved once again through silence and solitude to touch the darkness of his own soul. And then he asked God the only true question of his life: Who am I, Father?

The priest waited. Waited for that question to move him further, to let him slip beyond his consciousness, but nothing happened.

He began again, counted out his breaths, tried to slow down his body, put away his worries and reach in his mind, throughout his body, a peaceful, restful state. He gazed at the Duccio and thought of Jesus. He let the name of God float in and out of his consciousness, but still he could not relax, could not lose his self-control.

Jamie sat back, rolled off the mat. It was no use. He was too excited from the long evening with the Cardinal. Picking up his cup of tea he walked back to the bay window, stood looking at the falling snow.

The snow was still heavy, in the thin light of morning he could see it blow across the vacant lots, swirling, drifting, and settling on the brick rubble, the remains of the houses that had burned in the riots. The snow was so thick it distorted his view, and it was several minutes before he realized there was someone out there, someone wandering among the ruins. He leaned forward.

At that distance he could not tell if it was a man or woman. The figure was bundled up in overcoats, and stooped with the weight of two shopping bags. The bags dragged in the deep snow, leaving behind a path, like markings from a sled.

The person left the vacant lot and came toward the rectory, walking straight now, directly down the empty center of Church Drive. The short street was ankle deep in snow, and the lumbering figure plowed forward, coming closer to Jamie's building, the last row house before the Cathedral parking lot.

It seemed to be a woman. She was going for the church, Jamie figured, to find some warm corner. He had encountered shopping bag women before, and he knew he couldn't let her stay inside the Cathedral. The smell was worse than having a dead rat trapped in the walls.

It was better to stop her before she got inside. Perhaps he could get someone from the precinct to pick her up and take her over to the Community Center. They would delouse her, get her into clean warm clothing.

Still it tore at him, the sight of the pitiful creature stumbling through the storm. Yet there was nothing more that he could

do besides pray for her soul and see that she was cleaned up
and fed.

There were just too many of them in MacPatch. The river-
front parish was full of the city's castoffs: winos, derelicts,
runaway kids, the old and the infirm.

He looked out the third-floor window again. The woman
had reached the rectory and he pressed his face against the
glass to see directly below him. It was difficult: the swirling
snow, frost forming on the pane. He wiped his hand across the
window. The wind subsided for a moment and the shopping
bag woman was visible again. He saw how wretchedly she was
dressed, her head wrapped in rags with a baseball cap holding
it all in place, tied down around her ears with rope.

The snow had drifted and was knee deep in front of the
rectory. She was having difficulty walking, and the huge shopping bags were too much for her. She stumbled a second time
and fell forward into the drifts.

"Oh, Christ," he whispered. He would have to get her into
the rectory. She might die otherwise, freeze to death. But then
the woman rose up out of the drifts. She struggled to her feet,
fought her way another few steps.

Then she stopped, as if giving up, and the young priest
hesitated. He did not want to leave the window until he saw
what she would do next. If she collapsed he would wake Monsignor O'Toole and have the older priest help him carry her
into the rectory.

Jamie pressed against the windowpane once more to be sure
of what he was seeing. It was now daylight, the steely cold
light of dawn, and the street was no longer full of shadows.
The old woman slowly raised her head and looked up at him,
as if she had known all along that he was watching her.

Jamie saw then that he had been wrong. It wasn't a woman.
The wretched figure in the snow below the rectory was a man,
a disheveled creature with long hair, an unkempt beard.

Jamie knew him. He was willing to swear it. He pressed
his cheek against the cold glass, looked harder. The snow
picked up, blew in blinding swirls around the tramp, who kept
staring up, watching Jamie now, as if waiting for something
in the deep snow and freezing weather.

It took Jamie a moment longer before he recognized the

face. Stunned, Father Ignatius stood gripping the window frame, meeting the man's steady gaze with his own. Except for the beard, the man staring up at him could have been his twin. Stopping only to jam his feet into a pair of loafers, he slammed out of his bedroom and down the stairs, not pausing till he had reached the bottom of the three flights.

"Father Jamie!" the housekeeper scolded. She had come out of the front parlor, where she drank her morning cup of tea, to confront him disapprovingly. "What's the point of your taking the early mass if you're going to wake the Monsignor anyway with your clatter?"

"Mrs. Windmiller, I'll explain in just a moment," he said, easing himself around her as quickly as he could.

The housekeeper had come in the back entrance, so the three locks on the double front doors were still in place. By the time he had unlocked them and thrown the door open, the man in the snow was gone.

Father Ignatius squinted up and down Church Drive searching for a hint of which way to follow. But any traces the man had left were covered by the silent, drifting snow.

CHAPTER THREE

December Twenty-fifth, Morning
Feast of the Nativity

"A vision, perhaps, Jamie?" Monsignor O'Toole suggested, serving himself from the plate of scrambled eggs. "There was a saint in the seventh century, Saint Cuthbert, who as a child was watching his flocks in England and saw the heavy clouds part and then a multitude of floating figures, all of them shining. The next day he learned that a holy man from the abbey at Melrose had died. It was his soul that Cuthbert had seen, being carried to heaven by God's own angels. Would you care for more eggs, Jamie?"

The two priests sat away from each other, at opposite ends of the long dining room table. Usually they had their meals in the small alcove off the kitchen, but it being Christmas, Mrs. Windmiller had served them upstairs on the second floor, in the formal dining room they seldom used.

"I doubt if I'm saintly enough to be having miraculous visions, Monsignor."

"Well, which of us is, Jamie?" O'Toole replied, letting the young man's sarcasm pass.

The Monsignor's face was thin and elongated. As a young man he had resembled an El Greco, stylized and romantic, but he had aged poorly and now his features seemed mismatched. It had taken Jamie awhile to realize what was wrong. The face had no dominant feature; it had no real character.

"Did you see the man again?" O'Toole asked, peering over his glasses. Then holding his knife and fork like surgical instruments, he cut into the soft eggs. "Did you find him inside the Cathedral? You know how those tramps like to hide back there by the baptismal font."

"No, Monsignor, that's the whole point of the story. He simply disappeared. I ran downstairs and into the street and he was gone. The Cathedral was locked; I walked around and checked every door. He wasn't anywhere."

The Monsignor forked a small portion of scrambled eggs onto a thin slice of toast and bit into it. The crackling sound silenced Jamie, who returned to his own breakfast. The silence grew around them as the old man munched his food.

It was a shame he'd had to tell O'Toole, Jamie thought. The Monsignor had nothing useful to suggest. A vision in the snow, for Christ's sake. Jamie sighed and ate his food. But it was his responsibility to seek guidance from his superior, and to get his approval in advance for any course of action. That was part of the vow of obedience, and in theory Jamie saw its value in the subjugation of his own will to that of God, in the form of his superior. What tested the vow, of course, was having a superior like O'Toole.

"Did you ask Clarence about him?" O'Toole asked, after a moment.

"No, I didn't, Monsignor." If there was anyone even less likely to be helpful than O'Toole, it was the simpleminded sexton.

The Monsignor kept nodding, as if Jamie had agreed with him. He had lifted a corner of his large linen napkin and tucked it into his stiff Roman collar, letting the napkin fan out over his suit. Now he took one end of the linen and dabbed his mouth before speaking.

"Mary McGrath telephoned me on Thursday last and was nice enough to ask me out there for Christmas dinner. I told

Hilda to leave early. She has family, you know, out in Clayton. Cousins, I believe; they've invited her for the day. You have dinner plans yourself, I'm sure. . . ." The old man kept eating, avoiding Jamie's eye.

"Oh, yes, ah . . . I'm going out to dinner later."

O'Toole sighed, relieved, then went on chatting about Mary McGrath. She lived in Christ the King parish now, across the river.

"Mary's a Doyle. Her mother and father came to Saints Peter and Paul from Kerry. Mary herself was for years the president of our Rosary Society, and she stayed down here with us longer than most."

The old man kept talking but Father Ignatius was no longer listening. He had no Christmas invitation. Earlier that week the Cardinal had phoned and asked him uptown, but he had declined, not wanting to leave the Monsignor alone.

Well, it wasn't O'Toole's fault, Jamie thought. He should have investigated the pastor's plans in enough time to make his own arrangements. Yet he knew also that neither he nor the Monsignor really wanted to be left to spend the whole of Christmas Day in each other's company, alone in the rambling rectory.

"I'll tell Hilda then to be on her way." The pastor pushed back from the dining table. As he stood, he waved a brief blessing over the remains of breakfast, mumbling, "Thanks be to God for all His gifts."

Jamie scrambled to his feet, still holding a slice of toast in his hand.

"It's all right, Jamie. Finish your meal." The pastor walked quickly by and out of the dining room, but at the top of the curving oak staircase he hesitated. "Oh, we had a call, Jamie, while you were saying the seven."

The young priest looked toward O'Toole. The storm had cleared and daylight filled the front windows of the brownstone, silhouetting the older man and hurting Jamie's eyes as he looked that way.

"Someone from the Community Center," the Monsignor went on. "I left her number downstairs in the office. She wanted to know if one of us would stop by there later this afternoon.

They're having a Christmas dinner for the needy and she asked if one of us would come by and say grace. Seems quite a few of the homeless are Catholics.

"Would you mind then, Jamie? I'm sure they'd appreciate it, having a priest with them on Christmas Day." Knowing the younger priest's answer, O'Toole did not wait to hear it. He disappeared down the front stairs and Jamie could hear him in the hallway below.

Jamie let him leave. Smiling, he wondered if the old man would ever take up meditation in the hope of seeing Saint Cuthbert's angels. He could see O'Toole relaxing his mind and never returning to reality.

Not, he reflected, as he got up from the table and headed downstairs himself, that the pastor had much to do with reality as it was.

"Have you seen Clarence, Mrs. Windmiller?" Jamie asked, walking into the kitchen. The housekeeper had just arrived at the rectory in October, the same week he had, reassigned there from the Cardinal's residence where she had been second in command for as long as Jamie could remember. Now she had just him and the Monsignor to care for, and Jamie liked to think she was his ally.

"He came through here a few minutes ago, Father, on his way to the basement. I think he's down there now. Would you like me to fetch him?" She stood waiting, eager to do his bidding. She was a round, tiny woman, with plump features and the fine, translucent skin of someone who spent little time out-of-doors.

"Oh, no, Mrs. Windmiller. Why should you go up and down those stairs for me?" He walked around the woman toward the basement door. She followed him with her eyes.

"No trouble, I'll get him," she said quickly, wiping her hands on a dish towel.

"That's all right, I'll go down myself." He reached the basement door and pulled the knob. "It's locked," he said, surprised.

"Well, it's always locked, Father." She moved away from the sink, wiping her hands briskly. "That's the way the pastor wants it."

"May I have the key then?"

"You know, I don't think he's in the basement after all, Father. I think he must be over in the church. Let me ring up the Cathedral." She moved at once toward the intercom.

She was always so helpful that her sudden odd behavior was both annoying and perplexing. She was, he knew, intimidated by O'Toole, but hiding the basement key was silly.

"I won't say anything to the Monsignor," Jamie offered, making it easier on her.

"I don't know why he's so secretive about the basement," she whispered, moving slowly toward the kitchen drawer, "but he doesn't like even my going downstairs." She handed the small key over to him.

"Thank you, Mrs. Windmiller," Jamie said, unlocking the door. He knew the housekeeper wanted to talk about the pastor, to complain about his idiosyncrasies, but he had promised himself when he came to the parish not to get caught between them. This was his first assignment, but he had heard plenty of stories in the seminary and in Rome about how tempestuous a rectory household could be. "It's like a bad marriage," the Cardinal had once remarked, "except worse, because there's no divorce. It isn't easy getting rid of a housekeeper. There's always talk in the parish of why the woman is leaving."

"You won't be too long, will you?" Mrs. Windmiller asked. The tiny, stout woman stood at the top of the stairs clutching her dish towel.

"Only a minute."

He had never been downstairs before and was immediately surprised at how clean the basement was. The walls had been whitewashed and the wooden beams painted. In one corner he recognized the pieces of mahogany furniture that Clarence had brought down from his bedroom. Up against the back wall was a workbench with enough power equipment for a small shop. The rest of the space had been partitioned off, with one cubicle for the oil heater, another for a large storage refrigerator, and another for a supply of lumber. Jamie had not realized Clarence did any work down there.

"Clarence?" It was a low-ceilinged room, running the length of the building, and Jamie could not see to the far end, nor find the light switch. There was nothing he could do but move slowly toward the front of the brownstone, waiting for his eyes to adjust to the darkness.

Midway through the basement the atmosphere changed. The front half had not been remodeled and the moldy smell of decaying mortar filled his nostrils. He shuddered in the dampness and stopped walking. This end of the basement was creepy, and he didn't want to wander around.

"Clarence?" he said softly.

From the corner of his eye, he caught something move. He heard a quick rustle, then the sound of scurrying across the wet cement floor. Then a rat's fat body brushed against his leg and Jamie kicked out, sending the rat squealing through the air.

"Terrific!" Jamie sighed. He hated rats. In the dormitory of the orphanage, rats had nested in the walls during the winter and run across the wooden floors at night. He could still remember them clinging to the overhead pipes when he'd go into the bathroom late at night. They'd scurry wildly when the fluorescent lights blinked on, but the sight of their furry gray bodies, the flash of their teeth, always sent a shiver through him.

The young priest turned back to the remodeled end of the basement. He was moving back toward the lights when again he noticed movement in a dark corner. He jumped, ready to defend himself again, when he saw that it was a man, crouched down by the wall of the passage.

"Clarence?" Jamie asked.

At the sound of his voice the man straightened, moving toward him in the darkness. Behind him, Jamie saw, was a door, a small, wooden half-door that looked as if it might lead to a coal bin.

The man was too tall and slender to be Clarence, who was powerfully built despite his age.

"Monsignor!" Jamie exclaimed.

"Jesus, Mary and Joseph!" the old priest stumbled. "What are you doing here?" he demanded.

"I'm looking for Clarence." Jamie backed away as the tall priest moved into the newer section of the basement. When they stepped into the light, Jamie was surprised to see the priest carrying what seemed to be a case of wine. Even if only half full, the case was a heavier load than he would have thought O'Toole could manage.

"Clarence isn't here," the pastor said. He set the case down on the workbench and brushed cobwebs from his black suit. "I sent him to the Cathedral. You should have called him on the intercom."

"I didn't realize we had a workshop down here, let alone a wine cellar." Jamie kept talking nervously.

"There's a great deal about this parish that you don't know, Jamie," O'Toole replied. "Now who let you down here?" He looked stern.

"No one *let* me down here," Jamie spoke up. "I got the key from Mrs. Windmiller. You told me yourself to find Clarence and ask him about the tramp."

"I don't like people wandering around in here," the old man answered back. "You can see for yourself I have power equipment. A person could get himself hurt."

"I'm sure I won't," Jamie replied, trying to speak calmly. "I have no interest in your woodworking, or your basement."

He spun around and went upstairs, his footsteps banging on the stairs as he left. He had been rude, disrespectful to his superior, and he knew that later he'd have to apologize. But now he enjoyed the comfort of his anger. It was hard, he was coming to realize, to subordinate himself to the Monsignor, especially knowing that the old man had no real authority over him, and that their time together was drawing to a close.

CHAPTER FOUR

December Twenty-fifth, Afternoon
Feast of the Nativity

She was young, beautiful, and black Irish, Jamie saw.

She had spotted him at the entrance of the Community Center—hesitating, unsure of whom to approach—and came through the crowded room toward him, moving easily between the long rows of tables with the sureness of a woman who was accustomed to attracting attention. Her long dark hair was pulled back severely, making her look older, but Jamie could see that they were the same age, and that, for some reason, pleased him immensely.

"Thank you for coming by, Father," she said smiling.

"It's my pleasure. A Ms. Chase told me to ask for Maureen Sullivan."

"I'm Maureen, Father. Karel Chase is the director of the Center." She stepped back, as if to give him room to take off his coat, and stood piously with her hands linked together before her. She had green eyes, the color of bright patches of grass, and a long, narrow face. She looked, the priest thought, like an Irish Madonna.

When he had folded his overcoat across a chair he looked at her again and this time he smiled, saying with a mock brogue, "Now wouldn't you be Liam Sullivan's daughter?" He pronounced it "Lim," in the Irish way.

"Indeed I would, Father." A smile spread across her face and he found himself staring at her openly, as if dazzled.

"But I've never seen you at the Cathedral," he blurted out. "And I've been saying Mass there three months."

The bright green eyes cooled.

Bad move, Jamie realized at once. "Of course, you're not in our parish," he said quickly, letting her off the hook.

Maureen shook her head. "Oh, I'm in your parish, all right. Geographically, at least. I live a few blocks from the Cathedral, near Benton Place. But I'm not a practicing Catholic." She said it calmly, without a trace of guilt or anger, as if Catholicism was something she had left behind with other notions of her childhood.

Her directness impressed the young priest. He had encountered plenty of Catholics who had given up the Church, but usually they were abashed about it when priests were around, and muttered about "coming back someday."

"As you can see, Father, we're about to serve dinner," she went on. "I'll make a little welcoming speech and then introduce you for the blessing. I'm not sure how ecumenical you are, but we have a few Jewish people with us and lots of non-Catholic Christians. I know you'll want to take that into consideration."

She smiled, but the point was made. This was her Center and he was her guest. Nevertheless it surprised him. Women never presumed to put him in his place—not since he had begun to wear a Roman collar.

He nodded and glanced around, taking in for the first time the main room of the Community Center. Rows of folding tables and chairs had been set up, and what few pieces of furniture there were had been pushed back against the walls. It reminded Jamie immediately of the orphanage on holidays, when all of them were crowded into the main assembly room.

But instead of orphans, the Center was filled with the homeless, bag ladies and bums, street people, and the poor from the neighborhood. They sat quietly, expectantly, at the bare folding tables, many still wearing heavy coats and sweaters, with their paper bags of belongings pulled up under their feet.

"How do you stand this?" he asked, suddenly overwhelmed.

Maureen looked at him questioningly. Then, as she realized what he meant, the warm smile slipped away. "They're God's children, too, Father Ignatius," she answered coolly, and turning, walked off swiftly, leading him toward the main table at the front of the large room.

Jamie followed after, ashamed of himself, yet careful not to brush against anyone as he stepped carefully among the tables. As he neared the front someone reached for him, grabbed his hand as he passed, and without thinking he jerked back, pulled away from the old woman.

"Father! Father Ignatius! It's only me . . . Grace Keller." The fragile, apple-cheeked woman smiled up at him. She had taken off her coat but was still wearing a white knitted hat, a Christmas present, he was sure, that she had been wearing that morning when he handed out Communion at Mass.

"Miss Keller! I'm sorry, I thought . . . I . . . had caught my hand on something." He smiled and gave her his full attention, hoping to smooth over his awkwardness. "And what brings you down here with all these—" He caught himself, then left the sentence unfinished, hanging in thin air.

"Well, Maureen is my little niece." She looked around toward Maureen, who stood waiting behind the chair that would be his. "But I imagine you won't know that, being in Saints Peter and Paul for such a short time." She kept smiling, beaming up at him, and then she whispered, "And she asked me to come over here today. I really couldn't say no. She's such a dear, and she is so good to all these poor people." The aunt nodded slightly toward the crowded room. "We're going out later to Spring Valley. Maureen's older sister Nola lives there. She's married to Kevin Kennedy, Martin Kennedy's boy. He's with the city. In the mayor's office, would you believe?"

She looked at Jamie and winked, then glanced down the length of the long front table. "Well, you better go on now. I'm getting looks from herself. She's a real Simon Legree when it comes to running these affairs, but she's a darling and she takes such good care of me. I don't know what I'd do down here in MacPatch without her." A flash of warm tears watered the old woman's eyes. "And you're a dear man yourself, Father Ignatius, to come out in the cold on Christmas Day and say a few words of blessing over these poor people." As she took Jamie's hand and patted it, Jamie found himself staring down at her fingers. They were heavily veined, and bent with arthritis.

"I'll see you soon, Miss Keller. And you look terrific in that new hat of yours." He squeezed her hands and moved off.

"Oh, thank you, Father. Maureen made it herself. There isn't a thing that child can't do," she called after him, as if making a recommendation.

"Your aunt," he said softly, reaching Maureen at the head table, "she's some old lady. Full of life and goodness."

"Be careful, Father," Maureen said, smiling.

"Why? What do you mean?"

"She likes young priests and you're the first one the old Cathedral has had in years."

"Oh, I see." Jamie laughed, then said, "Well, I'll have to concentrate on you instead."

"How so?" Maureen frowned.

"Getting you back to church, among the faithful," he answered lightly. "If I have to say Mass at seven every day, the least I'm entitled to is a pretty face in the congregation."

"Your entitlements aside, Father, I don't think we have to concern ourselves with that possibility. I've gotten over all that—" Maureen was about to say "nonsense" but stopped, and looking out over the room of hungry people, said instead, "This is my church, Father Ignatius; these are my people. Now, I think we should start. I'm sure everyone is very hungry. For most of them, this will be their first real meal in weeks."

Jamie blessed the food and the people and spoke briefly, saying how pleased he was to be with them on Christmas Day. He praised them and the Community Center, and "good people like Ms. Sullivan."

The extemporaneous talk was for Maureen. Most of the old people, he could see, were not tuning in. They looked about, talked among themselves, and waited humbly for the warm food they had been promised. He finished by saying that he wouldn't talk any longer, since he was staying to supper himself and couldn't wait to get started. As he pulled out a folding chair and sat down the staff of the Center applauded, pleased that he had gone out of his way to be more than just perfunctory.

"Father Ignatius, it isn't necessary for you to stay. We have taken enough of your Christmas Day as it is." Maureen Sullivan was being sincere, and there was concern in her eyes. "You've been more than kind," she said.

He looked down at his dinner: a plate of turkey slices and mashed potatoes steaming under thin brown gravy. To him it was orphanage food, and the sight of it turned his stomach. Still he persisted, wanting her to believe he wasn't insensitive. He wanted, he admitted, for Maureen Sullivan to like him.

"As a matter of fact, I'm homeless today myself," he said, looking up at her. "There's just the Monsignor and myself at the rectory and he had a previous invitation . . ." Jamie let his voice trail off. Playing the poor waif again, he thought. Yet he did want her sympathy, her attention.

And he got it. He saw the concern flash in her green eyes, like a storm gathering.

"Of course," she responded, "I . . . we . . . would be pleased if you would join us." She took the chair beside him and addressed herself to the job of making conversation.

"I thought the clergy were on everyone's invitation list," she said. "When I was a child, and my father was alive, it seemed our house was always filled with priests having meals with us. Father Reilly, Father Whelan, Father Keane. . . ." She sighed, remembering.

"Well, times have changed," he said. "The old parish can't even afford the Monsignor and myself. The Cardinal calls us his missionaries, his Maryknoll fathers down here in the ghetto."

"And how is the Cardinal these days?"

"Oh, wonderful, as always. He was kind enough to come down yesterday and say Midnight Mass. Do you know His Eminence?" Jamie asked, stealing a glance at her.

"Yes, of course." She lowered her voice and did not look at him. "He was a friend of my father. This was years ago when he was just a monsignor. My father was very active in Saints Peter and Paul, president of the Holy Name Society, that sort of thing." She kept toying with her food.

"You don't care for the Cardinal, do you?" Jamie said suddenly. It was tactless, he knew, but she continued to surprise him. He had never met anyone before who disliked the Cardinal.

Maureen turned, confronting him directly. She was keeping herself under control, yet he could see the anger building, sweeping across her handsome face, coloring her cheeks.

"No, Father, I'm not a friend of your Cardinal."

Father Ignatius kept quiet. He picked up his knife and fork and made an effort to eat. He wanted to quiz her, to prove she was in the wrong, but she was too intimidating, and he realized he wouldn't be able to handle her.

His experience with women had been limited. He had grown up in a celibate world, raised by nuns, taught by priests, surrounded always by boys and men.

"I'm sorry I said that about the Cardinal," she volunteered after a moment. "I would appreciate it, Father, if you wouldn't repeat anything—"

"Oh, no, Miss Sullivan, I won't. I'm sure you have your reasons. Prince of the Church or not, he's only human and fallible." Jamie spoke quickly, hoping to sustain the conversation, to get beyond their many misunderstandings.

"I realize you're a friend of his," she went on, "and that he has taken special care of you."

"Why do you say that?" Jamie looked startled, as if she had guessed a secret.

Maureen smiled, amused by his question. "Father Ignatius, everyone in Saints Peter and Paul knows the story of you and the Cardinal. When I was a little girl in grammar school the story of how he found you on the steps of the Cathedral was one of my favorites. The nuns told it every year on the last day before Christmas vacation. It was part of the pageantry, as important as the nativity play. In fact, when I was in the sixth grade, the Cardinal himself told us the story. I can still remember him. He was a wonderful storyteller."

"He still is. He told that story again last night, to a room full of clergy. Sometimes I feel like a bar of soap; you know, being sold over and over again."

"I'm sorry." Spontaneously she reached out and touched his arm. The feel of her hand on his forearm sent a quick thin sliver of delight through his body. She spotted the flush on his face and pulled away.

"I'm sorry," she said again. "I should have realized this would be a sensitive topic with you. I didn't mean to take your part lightly, except that . . . everyone who grew up Catholic in MacPatch has heard about Jamie Ignatius. I mean, we *loved* that story! It showed us children that God did work in wonderful, mysterious ways. It made us all want to become nuns and priests."

"And now you no longer believe God works in mysterious and miraculous ways?"

She shook her head. "No, Father. Not when I see these old people, forgotten and left alone to die."

"And you've never stopped to think that perhaps you might be God's instrument—that *you* might be the miracle?" He was speaking softly, but there was a hard edge of conviction in his voice.

"No, Father. I'm here for purely selfish reasons—or at least I was at first. I'm getting my Ph.D. in parapsychology. My thesis is on the phenomenon of survival of bodily death. That's why I'm down here in MacPatch."

She nodded toward the crowded tables. "This is my research group, though they don't realize it. I came to the Center to find old people who wouldn't be dying in hospitals or nursing homes. I follow them through the last months of their lives; I interview them during their final days, and if I'm lucky, I'm with them when they die. I want to document any sort of resuscitation—you know, coming back to life after having experienced an 'afterlife' phenomenon. Unfortunately. . . ." She stopped then and stared off, looked across the large room.

"Unfortunately what?"

"Unfortunately for my research, I've become too involved to be scholarly." She shrugged. "I found I cared too much for them as human beings. I kept trying to improve their lot, find them shelter and food and help, and my research has gone by the wayside. It's no longer important to me when their 'spirits' or 'souls,' as you would say, leave their bodies. What is important is simply to keep them as clean as possible, healthy, and safe here in the Center, especially now."

"Why now?"

"Well, now that so many of them are turning up missing." She said it offhandedly, as if it were common knowledge.

"What do you mean, missing? I haven't heard about it. There's been nothing in the papers."

"I know. I went to the police myself but they wouldn't believe me." Her voice had softened and seemed less certain. "But who is to report them? No bodies are being found, no remains washed up in the river. Yet they're missing from MacPatch. I know by sight at least a dozen old homeless people who have disappeared from the streets. Gone without a trace."

"But why not assume they've just left the city? Wandered off, the way they wandered in. These people arrive without any family or friends, without a past. And most of them are deranged in some way, suffering from at least partial amnesia."

Maureen kept shaking her head. "What you say is true, but the workers at the Center know these people. We've followed them day by day through the summer and fall. Unlike you or the police, we know them as individuals—separate people with their own personalities, and not just so many stray cats and dogs. The police think there's such a lot of them out there that we can't possibly know if ten or twenty are missing. But we do know. We know that in November, shortly before Thanksgiving, they began to disappear from the city streets. They simply vanished."

"It's the weather. We had an early winter, as you know. They left town, went south. Look, they don't have anywhere to live, no homes, as you say."

"That's right, Father, no homes as *you* say." She dropped her knife and fork, as if too upset to eat any more.

"What? What are you getting at?" he asked, but knew instinctively what she was angry about.

"You have a huge empty convent over there on Twelfth Street, Father, as well as my old grammar school, Saint Aloysius, which is standing empty and boarded up. Both of those buildings could be used to house people, keep them safe and off the streets."

"Maureen, do you know what it would cost the archdiocese to open those buildings, refurbish them, turn on those oil heaters?" Jamie sounded alarmed just talking about it.

Maureen turned and stared at the young priest for a moment, then asked calmly, "And just what is Catholic charity for, Father Ignatius? Why have we been giving money all these years for foreign missions, for Catholic Relief, for Propagation of the Faith in countries ten thousand miles away, if we can't take some of it today and put it back where it came from? Here, the old neighborhood, MacPatch, the Irish ghetto?"

He opened his mouth to argue, but she was rushing on.

"Okay, most of the middle-class whites have gone. But there are still plenty of needy people here—old Jews living in those tenements; the homeless on the streets, living in the park; the blacks crowded into those ugly project buildlings; and the young men, the ones from the shut-down plants."

She gestured toward a table where several unshaven young men sat bent over the steaming food, eating silently.

"They grew up in this city but now they're out of work. They've lost their apartments and now they can barely keep themselves clean, much less be presentable enough to try out for what jobs there are."

"But you don't understand, Maureen—"

"I do understand, Father. They're not all Catholics. Oh, I understand all right. Let someone else take care of them. That's the Cardinal's plan, though you won't get him to admit it. So he stays uptown at the Chancery, driving down in his big black limousine on special feast days to visit his protégé. And you and Monsignor O'Toole stay safe in your ivory tower there on Church Drive; say your Masses for Aunt Grace and the handful of other 'respectable' Catholics remaining, and simply ignore the people crying out around you." She was trembling now in her rage and she turned away from Jamie, staring down at her plate while she tried to bring her temper under control.

"I'm sorry," said Jamie softly after a moment. "But you have to realize MacPatch has been caught up in a broad social change. You surely understand that. And whenever that happens, individuals always suffer. There's always some heartache, some tragedy for the people left behind."

Her head snapped around, a hard green gleam in her eyes. "Then begin here, Father Ignatius. Begin with *these* tragedies. Even Christ told us that much. The poor were his chosen people. Well, prove it! Open up your empty old Cathedral to the people in the streets."

"I can't," Jamie said. She would despise him, he knew, but there was nothing he could do, short of telling her the truth.

"And what's to prevent you? You don't have much to do at Peter and Paul. There are no grammar school children, no converts to instruct, no babies to baptize. And the Center would help. There's no one here who hasn't daydreamed about how we could use your buildings and resources. We could put together a solid program and present it together to the Cardinal." She was excited now, and eager.

Jamie shook his head again. "Maureen, believe me, His Eminence wouldn't accept it."

"How do you know?" she cried. "How can you be sure? You're the one who admires him so much—can't you even give him credit for being open to a good idea?"

"It's just too late," he said desperately. He would have to tell her; there was no other way. Even though the news was still confidential up at the Chancery; even though it would make trouble with His Eminence.

She searched his face for a moment. "Too late? What do you mean?"

He spoke calmly, now that the decision to trust her had been made. "You were right before, when you said there weren't many Catholics left here. That's why the Cardinal has decided to . . . follow his flock, so to speak."

"Follow the *flock?*" she repeated. "Perhaps you would translate for the laity, Father. What does that mean in plain language?"

"What that means," he said coolly, stung by her sarcasm, "is that we're pulling out. I've been sent here to put the books in order and sell off the property to the highest bidder. The Moonies, probably, or maybe Calvary Baptist. If I do a good job, this Cathedral will be closed by spring."

The rectory was silent, empty, when Jamie returned in the early evening darkness. He locked the door behind him and took off his overcoat in the foyer. He had worn his black suit to the Center, and now he tugged at the Roman collar, unbuttoned his shirt. It was stifling in the brownstone. As usual, he noted, the Monsignor had not turned down the heat before he left.

Jamie lowered the thermostat, then crossed the foyer and went into the parish office. Picking up the phone, he dialed in the dark.

"Chris?" His friend's voice sounded distant. "I didn't wake you, did I?"

"Oh, no, I'm watching the game."

"Game?"

"Football, Jamie. My God, you weren't that long in Rome."

"Yeah, well, I just got back. I'm not even sure what time it is."

"Where've you been—with *himself?*" He mocked the Cardinal's Irish brogue.

Still standing in the dark, Jamie grinned at the perfect replication of the Cardinal's tone. Chris Hanlon had mastered his imitation of the Boss back in seminary days.

"No. Community Center for the Aged. It's a MacPatch organization, mostly private. I went over to give a blessing."

"You're earning your pay down there, Jamie."

"Then I stopped by the orphanage for a couple of hours . . . saw the kids. I thought you might be there, actually. . . ." Jamie stopped talking, realizing how down he sounded. But he had hoped to see his friend and tell him about the tramp in the snow.

"I didn't get off the altar until after one. We had them lined up out to the street. And Fenwick is a great one for having all of us up on the altar, showing the flag, as it were. I didn't get to eat until two. What about yourself? You mean, you didn't go to the Residence at all?" Now he sounded curious.

"Well, the Cardinal was here for dinner last night, said Midnight—"

"Oh, yeah; I forgot. McDonough mentioned that yesterday. Well, where's O'Toole?"

"Out having dinner with the McGraths, in Christ the King; they lived down here before the riots."

"So you're wandering around that old place by yourself. Well, come on up. I'll call McDonough."

"How about a movie? Sissy Spacek in—"

"I saw it."

"Well, what about—"

"I saw them all, Jamie. Hey, look." He could tell Hanlon was trying hard. "I'll call around; we'll get up a poker game. It's the third quarter here. By the time you get uptown it'll be over and I'll put on a couple hamburgers. If you didn't eat with the Boss you probably didn't eat anything. Your housekeeper's off, right?"

"She's visiting some cousins across the river." Jamie stopped talking. From deep in the brownstone he heard something, an unexpected sound, and he spun around in the dark.

"Jamie? You there . . . ?" Hanlon raised his voice, questioning.

"Yes. I just heard something, that's all. It's nothing." He looked out the office window, toward the side street and the old Cathedral. Hanlon was making an effort, but it was clear he'd been happy watching his football game. And there was no way he could get up enough guys for a game on Christmas; he'd be on the phone all night.

"Look, Chris, I'm going to skip it. The weather is terrible. By the time I catch a bus uptown—"

"No problem; I'll come get you. Or Tom will. We have cars in our parish, Jamie. We're not on welfare at Saint Michael's." He laughed, trying to cheer up his friend.

"Thanks, but . . . look, the old man isn't around. For once I can get some work done."

"Jamie, take a break. It's the Lord's day."

"The Lord won't mind. I'll see you tomorrow anyway, right? At the orphanage. I'm teaching my new class at two, but we can play a little B-ball after."

"Jamie, I can't. Fenwick wants me on duty tomorrow. He's flying off to Florida on vacation, and I've got to drive him out to the airport. Call me after five. We can do something tomorrow night, okay?"

"I still want to see that Sissy Spacek movie."

"Okay, okay. Jamie, she's not your type. Besides, she's married."

"I can dream, can't I?" Jamie said.

"Not if they're wet dreams, laddie. So call tomorrow. Sure you don't want me to come down? I mean it's early. . . . Shit!"

"What's the matter?"

"Nothing. The Rams just fumbled. I'm about to lose five to McDonough."

"Listen, go back to the game. I'll catch you tomorrow."

Jamie hung up and again he heard something. He stood still, listened hard. In the few months he had lived in the brownstone, he had learned the sounds of the old building. This was new. Quietly, he stepped back into the foyer and stood there, listening, watching. To end his own anxiety, he quickly flipped on the foyer light, and then the one in the downstairs hallway. There was nothing out of order. He could see into the kitchen, see that the back door was closed and locked. He flipped off the light and went upstairs two steps at a time, as if rushing to the safety of his bedroom.

While the pastor wasn't about, and while the rectory was quiet, he wanted to meditate. He was unsettled—by the strange tramp he had seen that morning, and now this encounter with Maureen Sullivan—and the silence of the building would help him concentrate.

In his dark bedroom, he settled himself on the mat, his legs crossed, his palms upturned on his thighs. Tonight, Jamie told himself, his meditation would be successful. He would think only of Jesus. He would not be drawn the other way, into one of the trances that were leaving him so shaken and confused. The trances that both excited and appalled him.

Collecting himself, Jamie fixed his eyes on the Duccio, the portrait of Christ in the garden. He began the breathing exercises and started counting. But before he had even reached the number five he felt himself draw back, become conscious again of the huge old empty brownstone.

Had it been a sound? He wasn't sure. But in the next moment uncertainty ceased. Downstairs a door banged loudly, its sound clear and identifiable.

An intruder in the house. His Eminence had warned him about such incidents before sending him down to MacPatch. It was always dangerous here, Jamie realized, but he had only worried about the streets, about being caught outside at night. He had always assumed the rectory was safe, with its downstairs windows securely barred, its doors all double-locked. It simply wasn't possible to open one of those doors, he thought, not without using a jimmy.

Then he heard the footsteps. They were in the first floor hallway, and his heart caught in his throat like a gag. Whoever it was must have come up from the basement. Now he was walking down the long dark hallway toward the stairs.

Jamie jumped to his feet. He was afraid, but he could not just cower in his bedroom while whoever it was went from room to room, searching out the valuables. He couldn't let the thief steal the Monsignor's television, or take the silver chalices that were locked in the office, or destroy any of the church records.

Jamie's bare feet made only a soft, dull sound on the hardwood floor, and he kept away from the boards he knew were squeaky. From the bedroom door he tiptoed out into the hallway, then to the top of the stairs. Looking over the railing he peered three floors down into the darkness. No flashlight bounced off the hallway walls.

Perhaps it was the Monsignor, Jamie thought. He might have come into the rectory through the back door, then gone into the study. Clinging to that thought, the priest cocked his head and listened for the faint, familiar sound of the television.

More footsteps from below. Heavy, measured steps on the hardwood floor. It was definitely not O'Toole, then; his pace was more hesitant, slower. It had to be a thief. And someone who thought he was alone. He'd run, Jamie hoped, if he knew someone was upstairs.

"Who is it?" Jamie demanded. He could hear the fear and panic in his own voice.

The footsteps reached the foot of the staircase and started up, the stairway runner muffling their sound.

Impulsively, Jamie flipped on the third floor hallway light. For a moment it made him feel secure. He called out a second time and his voice echoed down the stairway. Then he started down, thumping each step, announcing his descent.

Outside the pastor's second-floor bedroom, Jamie looked over the railing once more, searching the deep darkness below.

The man was there. Jamie sensed him on the first floor landing, hiding, waiting.

"Yes? Who is it?" Jamie struggled to keep his voice under control. It could just be Mrs. Windmiller, he told himself, grabbing onto that unlikely thought. She might have forgotten something and come back. For a split second that notion gave him comfort, and then he turned the corner and looked down to the first floor landing.

It was there for only a moment, and for that moment his mind rejected what he saw. He had prepared himself—braced himself—for a man in cheap pants and a pea jacket, or some kid in blue jeans and gym shoes. And what he saw was so incongruous that his mind pushed it away, while his eyes held the image.

It had been a man. It *might* have been a man. A tall, thin figure dressed in gray robes. No, not robes, he realized, but a figure dressed in...cerements, the burial linens of a body wrapped for the tomb.

The shrouded figure had looked up at him, waiting, watching. Jamie had felt eyes on him. And then it had moved. It shifted position at the bottom of the stairs and the grayish-white burial linens swayed, as if touched by a cold breeze.

Terrified, Jamie jumped back from the sight, fell against the wall, upsetting a statue of Saint Rose of Lima as he crashed to the floor.

He lay there shaken, waiting for the shrouded figure to climb the steps, to come for him, but after a dozen minutes, when nothing appeared at the top of the stairs, he crept forward from the corner and looked down. The landing was empty, the shrouded figure was gone.

Another phantom in his mind. He stood and walked down the final flight of stairs, slowly making his way down the hall to the kitchen, switching on all the overhead lights as he walked.

There was no one in the rectory, nothing hiding in the corners. In the kitchen everything was still the same, except, he saw, for the basement door. In spite of the Monsignor's instructions it was unlocked, and stood ajar a few inches.

Possibly Mrs. Windmiller had left it open. Unlike him, she had a key. But the open door made him nervous all over again. The narrow crack and sliver of darkness below were ominous. He edged around the kitchen table, keeping his eyes on the door, half fearing, half expecting to confront the shrouded figure again, to have it suddenly appear to him. He moved closer, got within range, then leaped forward, slammed the door shut and fell against it, out of breath and trembling. Before he went upstairs again he shot the bolt.

CHAPTER FIVE

December Twenty-sixth, Afternoon
Feast of Saint Stephen

Father Ignatius was disappointed with the turnout. He had hoped more of the older boys would show up, but so far it was only a dozen junior-high kids who had assembled for the martial arts class. Perhaps it was because a priest was teaching the class. From his own experience at the orphanage, Jamie knew what the teenagers thought of priests and brothers, the clergy that ran the place. Yet he had hoped the course would give him an entree to the older boys, the ones who were the angriest and most troubled.

At the last moment, just before class began, a handful of older kids drifted in and sat in a cluster up on the bleachers. Jamie left them alone for the moment, but it was a good sign. He would talk to them later, after he had gotten the first class going.

He had the junior-high boys sit on the gym floor before him, but he raised his voice so that those in the bleachers could hear him easily.

"Tae Kwon Do is what this class is about," he began. "It's

a new word—less than thirty years old—but its meaning goes back in history for centuries. The word means: the art of hand and foot fighting. Yet really it means more than that. Tae Kwon Do is the scientific use of the mind and body in the methods of self-defense. When you finish this course, you'll be able to defend yourself against anyone, no matter who, no matter how much stronger he is than you. No one, I promise you, will be able to mess with you again, *ever!*"

He laid it on thick, making the martial arts sound vicious, and he watched with amusement as the eyes of the smaller boys widened with excitement. But it was more than the violence that was appealing to them, he knew. As inmates of an institution they were powerless; as children—and children without parents—even more so. Jamie wished he could defend each one of those little boys himself. The best he could manage was to teach them to do so.

"This martial art began in the sixth century, in Korea, with an elite fighting corps called the Hwa Rang Do. The rules were developed by a man named Won Kang, who was a priest. So it's not that surprising that a priest is up here now, teaching you guys Tae Kwon Do."

Two of the boys in front laughed at his little joke, then quieted when they saw no one else was responding.

"We'll go more into the history later, during the winter, but just a couple more points. Tae Kwon Do was first learned by westerners during the Second World War. It was used by our soldiers in Korea, and after that in Vietnam. Now, in this country, there are over a million people practicing this unarmed form of self-defense."

Jamie paused a moment, looked down at all their upturned, eager faces, and added slowly, dramatically, "And now *you* are going to learn this martial art—not because you want to hurt someone . . . but because you want to go to Hong Kong and make a million dollars as the next Bruce Lee!"

He grinned at the kids and several laughed and clapped, then jumped to their feet, ready to start. Jamie glanced over at the bleachers. The small knot of older boys was still sprawled out passively. Well, he thought, at least they haven't left.

"Stand back, okay, and let me show you a few basic moves . . ."

"Father Ignatius?" One of the boys spoke up. "How did you learn this stuff, being a priest and everything."

"I'm not sure really where I first got the idea of it...I mean, I read about it years ago, and started practicing here, right at the orphanage. And then when I was at the seminary, out in Rocklands, a few of us started to take a class. They all dropped out after a while, but I kept doing it, in case, you know, I met up with the likes of you." He winked at the circle of twelve-year-olds.

"Okay! The first move is the *Chunbi*, which means ready stance." Jamie stepped away and positioned his fists waist high, seven inches in front of his body, with his elbows turned outward. Then he set his feet apart the same width as his shoulders, and held his head erect. "From this position, all basic moves are begun and ended."

Moving suddenly, taking them by surprise, Jamie did the side kick, mid-section punch, the turning kick, spinning back fist, roundhouse kick, and side thrust. He moved smoothly from one position to the next, his bare feet slapping hard against the waxed gym floor, snapping out each kick and shouting as he cleared the air before the young faces.

It was not a demonstration for the purists, but he had wanted to be flashy. He wanted to impress the silent audience seated along the side. When he finished he was briefly out of breath, but he tried to conceal it, said evenly, "All right, let's form three lines and start working on the *Chunbi* stance."

Jamie did not press the younger boys. He let them practice the front snap kick before they were even close to ready, just so the first class would be fun. Halfway through the exercise, he wandered over to the bleachers.

"Well, what do you think?" he asked.

No one responded.

Jamie let their silence pass. He remembered how, as a teenager, he had prided himself on his sullenness. He looked over the boys spread out above him. Some of the group were white, some black, but all were dressed alike; all young James Deans in sneakers, jeans, old sweat shirts. It wasn't just poverty; they wanted to look sloppy. Jamie knew their routine, their disdain for authority. He had thought when he came back to the parish that he would be the one to break through to these boys, get on their side, but he had been wrong. They treated him like every other adult. It didn't matter that he had once been one of them.

"Want to give it a try?" he asked casually.

"Looks like a lot of shit work to me," one of the teenagers commented, not moving from his position.

"It's work, yes, but you come out of it really tough. You know how to defend yourself."

"I can defend myself."

"Well, come on, let's see. You and me . . . out here. Maybe we can both teach each other something."

The kid snorted, signaling the others to laugh.

"Hey, man . . . Father. I ain't into nothing physical, you know." The boy had the small eyes of a bully. Jamie was sure the younger kids lived in fear of him.

"Well, you said you could defend yourself." Jamie tried to keep his voice loose and friendly. He wanted to make contact, not create more trouble.

"Not with any of that judo shit. Who needs it, anyway? I've got—" He stopped, caught himself before he said more.

Jamie knew what he meant. Somewhere on his person the boy had a knife, stolen from the dining room and sharpened, transformed into a killing instrument.

Jamie backed off, let the conversation go. He wasn't proving anything today. Later, perhaps; another time. He held on to that small hope and walked back out onto the gym floor.

"That's very good," he told his class. "Now let me show you a little trick for keeping your balance."

When he looked again, the bleachers were empty. Jamie kept teaching. Tomorrow, he thought, it might be better. Tomorrow they might come again.

The rectory telephone was ringing when he got home and he rushed for it, tramping his wet boots across the foyer floor.

"Saints Peter and Paul. Good evening."

"Father Ignatius, please."

"Yes, speaking."

"Oh, Father. This is Maureen Sullivan . . . from the Center."

"Yes, Maureen." Jamie cradled the receiver between his

chin and shoulder and with his hands free began to unzip his
heavy parka.

"Father, have you heard tonight's weather report?"

"No, but I just came in and the weather's terrible out there."
He looked out the window and saw large flakes blowing in
thick blasts.

"We're due for another twelve inches tonight," she said. "If
that happens, what with the snow already on the ground, we're
going to have homeless people dying. Hardly anyone out on
the streets tonight will survive."

Jamie didn't know what to say. She sounded very certain.
"Well, Maureen, is there anything I can do?"

"I know you don't have a free hand on this, Jamie, but I
was hoping...if the Center supplied the cots and bedding,
could you house some street people for a day or two—at least
until I can get them placed with other agencies uptown? The
fire marshal won't let us take any more here at the Center."

"Maureen, I wish we could really, but where would we put
them? As you know, the convent and school buildings are
boarded up, and—"

"The Cathedral, Father. Downstairs. You have that huge
room where everyone used to play bingo."

The room was at the front of the church. Years before it
had been the parish hall, used for bingo and also to handle the
overflow crowd from the eleven and twelve o'clock Masses on
Sunday.

"I know it's a big favor to ask, but there's no room here.
What I want to do is go out in the Center's van, drive around
MacPatch, and pick up whomever I can find. On a night like
this, they'll come along with me. They won't want to stay out.
We've had five inches already since noon."

"I'll have to ask the Monsignor—"

"He'll only say no," Maureen answered quickly. "Isn't there
some way that we can just do it? I'm only talking about one
or two days. We'll do everything. Set up the beds. Bring them
food. I know that parish hall is empty. I bet it hasn't been used
in years."

Jamie didn't answer. He knew the room was never used.

"This is an extreme situation," Maureen kept urging. "No

one can remember a winter like this."

She kept talking, but Jamie did not need to listen. He knew Maureen was right. The pastor would never approve the plan. And there was no way he could conceal a room full of bums and shopping bag women in the basement of the Cathedral.

"I know this is difficult," Maureen was saying. "And I don't want to compromise you with Monsignor O'Toole or the Cardinal, but it's just so unfair . . . all that clean, warm space going to waste and these old people, and young ones too, left to die of exposure on a night like this—"

"I'll do it!" Jamie interrupted. "Don't worry about the Monsignor, or His Eminence. This is an emergency. And it's only temporary, a few days." He was talking himself into his decision.

Maureen sighed, relieved. "Thank you, Father. I knew you'd be on our side." Her voice softened, as if he had done something very special for her.

"And I'll go out in the van with you, too," he added. He could postpone Hanlon and Sissy Spacek. "You shouldn't be alone out there."

"Thank you, but one of the other women is going to come. It's not your responsibility, after all. It's mine."

"Why is it just yours?" he answered back. "MacPatch was my home too. And now it's my parish. I want to do something to help."

"All right, then," she said, "if you really mean it. Karel can take charge of setting up the parish room, and you can come with me. Thank you again. I'll be at your front door in half an hour. Okay?"

"Okay. See you soon."

As they hung up he wondered if he did mean it. Did he want to do something for the old neighborhood, or was it really for Maureen Sullivan?

The snow that hit the city that night was one of the worst winter storms of the century. An icy wind dubbed the Siberian Express blew Arctic gales across the river and into the downtown streets. In the old tenements of MacPatch the water froze and the pipes burst. Ice was everywhere, on the floors, walls, and windows. It drove people out into the streets and into the city shelters.

The Man in the Box was untouched by the raging storm. As the night snow fell he sat in his home, reading the morning newspaper by the light of a candle stub. The news was a day old, but days did not matter to him. What mattered was that today he had received the paper complete, all five sections, and neatly folded. He liked that. It was almost like having a fresh paper to read. A woman rushing to catch a taxi had dropped it into a trash can inside the Sears Building and the Man in the Box had retrieved it immediately, stuffing it inside his overcoat to keep it safe from the snow.

He had saved it until now, kept it dry until he had gotten back to his shelter. His home was two large cardboard boxes he had fitted together, and lugged across town until he found a hot air vent. Then he had tipped the boxes over, trapping the hot air. Now he had for himself a rectangular room seven feet square, warm as a sauna in the middle of the snowstorm.

The Man in the Box read the weather report first. Weather fascinated and frightened him. Living as he did, always in the streets, he came to know weather in his bones. The clock on the First Bank building told him the temperature, but otherwise he had a Farmer's Almanac view of the weather. Each morning early he'd walk across LaFayette Park, stand there in the open field and study the sky. He blamed the present icy temperatures on the hydrocarbons deposited in the atmosphere by the Mount St. Helens eruption the year before. "Red sky at morning, Shepherd's warning," he had announced two days before this snowstorm, standing alone in the deserted park.

Now he took delight in seeing his prediction confirmed, and he chuckled as he read reports on the temperatures across the Midwest. "... But numbing cold was the story in cities as far south as Nashville, where it was 11 below, posting a record temperature... in Eagle Rock it was 34 below, the coldest temperature noted by Marcia Graham in the twenty years she has been checking the weather in the Indiana Forest Service.... In Paw Paw, Michigan, I–94 was closed and about two thousand local homes were without power overnight."

The Man in the Box was pleased with his own accuracy,

but he went on skimming the paper, searching for the item that mattered most to him. He was looking for the list of deaths in the city.

The deaths worried him. They were his real source of fear. He knew people died on winter streets; he had found them himself, curled up on park benches, their black faces frozen to the wooden planks. Once he had tried to move a woman he found dead that way, and the skin had torn off her cheek like an orange peel. He shuddered just thinking of it. Still, he had to read the list: "Since Saturday, ten people have lost their lives in weather-related deaths in the city." He began to read the accounts of tenement fires, of snow shovelers having heart attacks, but he was searching for something else. He was looking to see if the paper mentioned the people who were missing. He didn't know their names, just their faces—men and women he knew well enough to offer a drag on his cigarette or a hit from a bottle of whiskey. But now they had vanished, disappeared from the park and side streets.

But no mention was made of them, of his friends who had lived on the streets, in the tin shanties under the bridge, in the burned-out buildings, and he grew tired of the newspaper. It was almost tropical inside the box. The blast of hot exhaust from the building steam system roared in his ears, swirled around him and made him sweat.

He had already taken off his heavy overcoat and shoes, set them to one side so that they could dry over the wide vent. He stripped off more layers of clothing, getting down to only a tee shirt and one pair of pants.

Then he crawled back to his shopping bags. It was time for inventory. Time to find out what he had to eat that night.

In one bag he found matches and an empty cat food can. He lit another candle stub and melted the wax onto the bottom of the can, securing the candle. Then he set the can down carefully beside the vent. Seafood Platter, he noted, reading the blue label. He had found the cat food the week before, in a garbage can off Olive Street. Six full cans had been tossed away with the stiff remains of a dead calico cat.

He had been careful of the cat, wary of touching it and contracting a disease. Pus and mucus had been frozen on the

cat's eyelids and against its tiny nostrils. The body had been
thrown away in a red-and-white supermarket shopping bag,
along with the six cans of food that the cat would no longer
need, and the corpse had quickly frozen, buried beneath six
inches of overnight snow.

The cat food had lasted the Man in the Box for a week. He
had eaten a can every night, warming the contents over the hot
vent. It wasn't bad, he thought. It wasn't bad at all. He just
couldn't think of the cat, its yellow eyes half open in death.
That put him off the food.

The Man in the Box searched through his food bag, picked
out two day-old sugar doughnuts and set them aside to eat.
They had been a gift that morning from the owner of the coffee
shop on West Pine, along with a small carton of milk. He
arranged the milk and doughnuts on the grille as if he were
fixing a place setting. Then he struck his hand deep inside the
food bag, felt around until he found a crumpled foil ice cream
wrapper. He took that out, smoothed it flat, licked it clean.

He looked back at what he had for dinner: a can of cat food,
the two sugar doughnuts, and a carton of milk. It wasn't bad,
he thought. It wasn't bad for a winter night.

"Look for cardboard," Maureen told Jamie. "They find big
cardboard boxes, like refrigerator cartons, and set them up over
hot air vents."

Jamie opened the side window to see better, ignoring the
wind that quickly numbed his face. In the driving snow it was
difficult to spot anyone and he had to keep brushing fat, wet
flakes from his mouth and eyebrows.

They had begun at LaFayette Park, circling it slowly, leaving the van only to pick up the two shopping bag ladies who
now rode in back. The first woman, whom Maureen knew
slightly from the Center, was too disoriented to understand the
danger and Maureen had had to persuade her with bribes of
chocolate candy. The second, who said her name was Laura,
had climbed in willingly, her face raw and cracking from the
cold.

So far Laura and the other woman were the only people
they had found. Maureen had wanted to go into the park on

foot, to search in the bushes and the hollow down by the pond.

"That's where they're hiding," she said. "I've got to go down and look for them."

"Maureen, you're crazy," Jamie had argued. Her determination alarmed him. "You know you should never go into that park, even in daylight. If you insist this has to be done, I'll go."

"You can't," she said. "If they don't know you they won't trust you. They'll just stay hidden, or run if you find them. Most of these people have at least seen me before, at the Center or on the streets."

"Then we'll go together."

Maureen shook her head and gestured to the two women in the back of the van. "You have to stay with them. Laura is okay, but the other one will climb out, wander off."

Your safety is more important than hers, he wanted to say, but Maureen's eyes forbade it. In her mind, the three women in the van were all equal, and Jamie was shamed that he, a priest, could not freely feel the same.

Instead he said, "But what about the others—the ones out on all the downtown streets? We could be out picking them up instead of my just waiting here while you wander the park for hours." It was a good argument, and they both knew it. Without answering she hit the accelerator and pulled away from the park, heading the van downtown.

"There's two!" Maureen said. She tapped the brakes and the van skidded slightly in the deep, soft snow. The streets hadn't been plowed, so she was keeping as close as she could to the center of the street.

"See?" She pointed. "By the building."

Jamie wiped the fog off his window and squinted. Now he saw them, two dark figures in the alley next to a deserted brownstone. They had started a fire in an oil drum and, as Jamie watched, one of the men wrested a two-by-four off the boarded-up window behind him and fed the lumber to the blaze. For a tramp, Jamie thought, he seemed pretty strong and fit.

"Trouble," Maureen said as she braked.

"I'll get them," Jamie said, zipping up his parka.

"I don't know. This might be more than either of us can

handle. Maybe I should just get the police for those two."

"You mean because they've been drinking?"

She nodded. "The police could park them both in Detox. Of course that's assuming I'll be able to locate a patrol car. They usually avoid MacPatch on nights like this."

"Okay. I'll get them." He pushed the door open.

"Father!" She reached over and grabbed his arm. "Don't get tough with them. If they won't come along, then leave them."

Jamie squeezed her hand and stepped down into the deep snow.

Maureen kept the motor running and the headlights on. In the arc of light she could see that the two men had ducked further back into the alley, so they were out of sight and watching as the priest approached.

Oh God, she thought. Maybe they would knife him once he got close, once he was beyond the light of the high beams.

He was at the curb now, in front of the brownstone. Snowplows had passed through hours earlier, piling the snow high against the sidewalk. Now it had frozen into an icy four-foot mountain that had to be scaled to reach the other side.

Jamie started up, groping for footholds in the polished surface. He had just reached the top when he slipped, plunging face forward toward the ground.

For a moment time slowed. Then he felt the impact, the bruising force of the packed-down, frozen snow against his cheek. He was flat on his face in MacPatch, the wind knocked out of him by the fall, and the drunks were coming at him.

Maureen saw them and jumped out of the van, tried to run through the knee-deep snow. It could happen so fast, she knew— a single knife thrust, or a broken bottle quickly twisted into his stomach. It would be over before she reached him, the tramps gone with his wallet and Jamie Ignatius dead, his blood pouring into the snow.

They had surrounded him. She saw them reach down, saw them grasp his shoulders. Then they had pulled him safely to his feet and all of them were lurching a little in the snow, and laughing. They held their bottle out to Jamie and slapped his back approvingly as he took it. Bits of their loud voices came back to her on the wind and she sank into the snow, weak with

the relief that followed fright. Unaware of her, Jamie stood
between the two drunks, laughing himself, gesturing, having,
it seemed, a good time.

"How did you talk them into coming?" she asked, when he
had settled the two men into the back of the van, then slipped
into the front beside her.

"Well, I lied a bit. I promised them a party in the parish
basement." He grinned. "They're old Knights of Columbus, it
turns out."

She grinned back. "You're incorrigible, Father. Is nothing
sacred to you young people?" Guiding the van back to the
middle of the street, she started toward Grand Avenue feeling
good, feeling invincible. Next they'd sweep down toward the
river, see if anyone was left out on Grand.

"Beautiful, isn't it?" Jamie remarked, looking ahead down
the long, empty boulevard. The city sloped toward the river,
fell away in gentle hills, and the streetlights made the wide
boulevard seem like an airport runway.

"Pretty, yes," Maureen said, but she wasn't watching. She
could feel the big van skidding again, gaining momentum as
it descended the steep hill. They were high enough to see the
lower end of the city, MacPatch and the Project, the high-rise
tenements across LaFayette Park. Beyond that was the bridge,
an elongated span of light crossing the river and disappearing
into the dark beyond the city.

"Pretty," she said again, as if to remind herself. The city
seldom was, not to her. "The snow does it," she said to Jamie.
"It takes a good foot of drifting snow to cover up the grime."
Behind them, the two drunks had begun to shout a chorus of
"Jingle Bells," which quickly developed into an argument about
the lyrics. The older drunk was gesturing wildly, and the whiskey bottle hit the floor with a crash, filling the van with fumes.

"Now you did it!" the younger man shouted.

"Should I do something?" Jamie asked.

Maureen glanced in the rearview mirror. "Shhh now," she
said quietly to the men. "We'll all be inside soon, and warm.
Let's think about Christmas—about good times we've all had."
Then, softly, she began to sing "Silent Night." They began to
sing with her, humming when they couldn't remember the

words, and by the time she reached the second chorus, they had both stopped singing and were nodding off to sleep.

"Nice," Jamie whispered.

"A few kind words always helps."

"No, it's more than that."

"What then?" She said it coolly, but she was curious. She found herself wanting to have impressed him.

"You have a real way with people. It's a gift."

"Not with everyone I don't. Not with the Cardinal, for instance, or any of his cohorts. Or don't you take that personally?" She risked a sideways glance and again the van skidded.

"Easy," Jamie said, grabbing the dashboard.

"Don't worry, I'll get you home alive." They had reached the bottom of Grand Avenue, the last of the old business sections before the waterfront, River Street, and the warehouses. "You didn't answer my question. We don't really get along, do we?"

It took him a moment before he said, "No, we don't, but that's for other reasons."

"Like what?"

"You know what." He spoke softly.

"No, I don't." She would force him to say it. She wanted him to give her at least that much.

"We don't get along because we're attracted to each other." He sounded annoyed and put upon, explaining.

"That's too simple. It must be more than that. It's my Irish temper, and your Teutonic ways."

"Who said I'm German? I'm an orphan, remember. Parents unknown."

"You look German."

"So? Tell me your position on blond hair and blue eyes." It was quiet in the long van; the drunks had fallen asleep and the women were silent. They could have been alone, two young people out on a snowy night, except for the stench from the street people and the broken whiskey bottle. Jamie cracked open his window to let in some fresh air, then turned sideways in his seat to watch her.

Maureen seemed impervious to the odors. Intent on her driving, she leaned forward, both hands on the wheel. She wore an old seal coat, the kind that must have come from a thrift shop, and around the cuffs the fur was brown and worn. Her face was wrapped loosely in a long, bright woolen scarf, so only her eyes were visible. She looked like a bandit.

"Jamie, stop," she said softly, not taking her eyes from the avenue.

"Stop what?" He leaned forward to catch her eye, to make her pay attention to him.

"Stop flirting, Father. It's unbecoming."

He fell back in his seat dramatically. "I work up the courage to declare myself," he said sadly, "and where does it get me?"

"It's not supposed to get you anywhere," she answered, looking at him now to make her point. "Father Ignatius, I know the seminary teaches you people that every female parishioner dreams of sleeping with her priest. It's the Catholic version of the Oedipus complex. But I've always been immune."

"Why? You don't think men wearing skirts are sexy?"

She didn't laugh, as he'd meant her to. "No, not sexy. Just dangerous."

At that, he had to laugh himself. "Now you're giving me too much credit. Even the Jesuits aren't dangerous anymore, much less little parish priests like me."

"On the contrary," she said. "You local types are the ones who control people's lives—women's especially. The Church is set up that way. Women can't be priests. They can't even be altar boys. Nuns are allowed to teach, but if you notice, they never teach theology. Priests come in special for that, because it's important. And instead of getting mad about it, the nuns giggle and flirt and practically curtsy the whole time the priest is there."

"Well, what's the harm in that?" Jamie asked, a little defensively.

"This isn't about sex," she said.

He looked blank. "Then what are we talking about?"

"Power, of course. The Church is just like the real world, Father Ignatius. The priests have all the power, so women find them attractive. It's like bosses and secretaries. The secretary idolizes the boss—not because he's gorgeous, or smart, or a fine person, but because he's got the power. And bosses encourage that, just as priests do, because it means the woman won't question anything he does. And she's certainly not going to make a grab at being a boss herself. See the parallel? Of course, priests have it even easier. A corporate vice-president might have to fuck his secretary every now and then, just to keep her interested, but priests don't even have to do that. They can just flirt with women, which is to say, patronize them."

"That's just not true," he said sharply. "You don't know what you're talking about."

"Don't tell me what I know!" They were both angry now. "I put in my time with priests. My father, the sainted Liam, sat at the dining room table night after night with them— Tommy O'Toole, and young Will Donohoe, and the man you call The Boss. He was just a monsignor then, attached to the Cathedral. They'd talk theology, and Aquinas, and all the learned doctors of the Church, while my mother fetched and carried for them. And when she had a moment free she'd catch up on the ironing she had to take in because Liam was too busy dreaming of heaven to hold a job."

"You can't blame priests because your father was lazy."

"In his heart my father *was* a priest. But it's not him I'm speaking of, Father Ignatius. Those men saw my mother nearly every day. 'Peggy Keller,' your Cardinal was always saying, 'you're a fine woman. Your husband is a lucky man.' And she'd duck her head and blush, and dream, I'm sure, of what life could have been if she'd married a strong, tough man like him. And he let her dream it. And the month my sister and I were sick, and things were really bad, she got up her courage and went to your Cardinal for help. He told her there was nothing he could do, short of giving her money from the collection plate, and that was for the missions. She didn't want him handing out *that* money, did she?

"And so she went away, and two weeks later, for my father's birthday, what did the Cardinal give him but Augustine's *The City of God,* bound in leather and the title printed in gold. And my mother kept that book on the mantel till the day she died."

Suddenly, as if to punctuate her point, she hit the brake hard, sending the van into a graceful, arcing skid that ended with a thump against a snowbank. Thrown against each other, the two drunks woke up swearing, not knowing where they were.

"All right, all right, I get it," Jamie said angrily. "But let someone else die for the Cardinal's sins."

Maureen was concentrating on the U-turn she was executing. "I just remembered someone who lives one block over."

"Why bother? If he's got some place to stay?"

"It's no *place*," she answered. "It's the Man in the Box. We've got to get him."

By the time they got there, the snow had almost claimed the box. One side had disappeared beneath a drift, and several more inches covered the top like icing. Between the blasts of air inside and the heavy, wet pressure outside, the box would never make it through the night.

"I'd better do this," Maureen said as they approached. Through a small opening at one end, where the cardboard fitted together, they could see flickering candlelight. "He knows me. He refuses to beg, so he's had to come to the Center from time to time, when he's flat broke."

The van reached the corner and Maureen paused, leaned forward to look for traffic on West Pine Street. "Anything coming on your side?" she asked. "I can barely see anything that way."

Again Jamie rolled down the window and stuck his head out to see. Even so, visibility was poor, the street illuminated only by the high, ghostly lights of the old-fashioned lamps.

"Nothing. Well, wait!" It was not a car, but he heard something in the distance, coming toward them up West Pine. He turned his ear that way and listened. He could hear male voices, shouts, and then he saw them.

Plowing through the snow on West Pine, taking command of the wide empty street, in full authority of their own strength was a gang of boys. Ten of them were spread across the street in one long flanking line, like a military parade, and behind were more teenagers, younger, less able to keep up the steady, demanding pace.

"Maureen, lock the door on your side, and let's get out of here." He reached back and pushed down the lock on the van's sliding rear door.

"Why? What is it?" She, too, heard the voices. In the empty street, in the silence that a heavy snowfall brings, the shouts sounded like a celebration, or a battle cry. Then she, too, saw the gang, advancing on them swiftly. She always made a point of not automatically suspecting strangers, but in the eerie, ill-lit street the hoods did look dangerous, with ski masks pulled down over their faces.

Panicky, she jammed the accelerator and the back wheels slipped on the incline. She pulled her foot off the gas and the van stalled. "Oh, good God!" She fumbled in the dark interior for the ignition key.

Jamie was watching the gang. They were an odd mixture of ages and colors, and the thought came to him that he knew who they were. He debated whether he should jump out of the van and identify himself immediately. His being a priest might make a difference to them. But best of all, he knew, would be to get away before they reached the van.

Maureen turned the ignition key and gunned the engine.

"Easy," Jamie instructed, "don't race it."

"I'm not!" she shouted, silencing him. The van crept forward across the intersection, going slightly uphill on the street, still skidding on the icy incline.

The troop of teenagers had stopped, as if on a signal, and gathered together in a tight circle. The younger kids, no more than eleven and twelve, stood on the perimeter, stamping their feet in the cold. Jamie could remember when he had been that same size.

Perhaps they would do nothing, Jamie reasoned. It was early. They couldn't have been out for long. Dinner was over at 7:30. It would have taken half an hour to get the word around the dormitory to assemble after Lights Out in the boiler room, more time to slip out singly and in pairs, like criminals breaking loose from jail. Jamie smiled, remembering.

"They won't bother us, will they?" Maureen asked. She had transversed the intersection and taken her foot off the accelerator to let the long van glide slowly to the curb, close to the Man in the Box.

"I'm not sure. Depends on how cold and bored they are. I think it's better if we just keep going without stopping."

Maureen nodded toward the corner. "I have to go get him first."

"No!" Jamie grabbed her arm. "He's warm enough. He'll ride the night out in there. Let's keep going."

Maureen studied his face for a moment, searched for the reason behind his urgency.

"They won't do anything to him, will they?"

Jamie shook his head, but watching his eyes Maureen saw his uncertainty. Without comment, she unsnapped her seat belt and reached for the door handle.

But before she could turn it, Jamie was out of the van and into the deep snow, shouting to her to stay there. The gang saw him, swerved in his direction, and advanced in a tight formation. Between him and them was the Man in the Box, secure and hidden in his warm, fragile shelter. He had to reach him first, Jamie realized.

Lifting his knees high, he attempted to run, but fell at once, brought down by the deep snow. On his feet again, he fought forward, struggling with each long step. He felt as if he were losing ground, as if the corner was receding in a snowy mirage.

He could see the gang was moving faster. They seemed stronger than he, and better prepared for the weather. Jamie was still ten yards from the old man when the gang reached the corner and, without faltering in its march, uprooted the box, tipped it over, tossed it aside. A blast of freezing wind caught the cardboard and it skipped away out of control, and there on the sidewalk, huddled shirtless over the hot vent, was the old man.

For a moment the boys seemed surprised. Then they jumped him, swarming over the crouched figure. The younger kids grabbed the shopping bags, shouting happily as they scattered his few possessions into the wind.

It was the older ones—the sixteen- and seventeen-year-olds—who went after the old man, kicking at him with their heavy boots.

"Stop!" Jamie shouted, and the punk-gang turned to look at him. "Leave him alone."

Now the game was defined. Instead of stepping aside, the boys tightened their ranks and linked arms. One kept beating the old man while the others confronted Jamie. In their ski masks they were as anonymous as executioners.

Scanning the line for a weak spot, Jamie assumed the *Chunbi* stance and set himself to attack. He had never practiced Tae

Kwon Do as anything but a sport, and he wasn't at all sure how effective he could be in a real fight, especially against so many.

As if accepting his challenge, one of the taller teenagers broke free of the line and came at him. As he went for Jamie, the priest moved, blocked the grab with his left arm, then leaped into the air and let go with a front kick to the boy's midsection.

Jamie's boots were too heavy; he couldn't get a full right leg extension, but he caught the kid in the hip and the two of them fell together into the deep snow.

Then the others were on him. One hit from behind, chopped the back of his head, and Jamie's fingers went numb. Then, once again, they formed their deadly circle and began to kick. The first blow struck Jamie in the kidneys; the second on his temple. Jerking his legs up, he pulled himself into a tight curl, hoping to protect his body.

A shout from one of the younger boys stopped them. The smaller boys had surrounded the van and spotted Maureen. They waved and shouted for the others, and the older boys abandoned Jamie, stepped over him, and ran for the van.

"Get out of here, Maureen!" Jamie shouted. He tried to stand but his knees wouldn't hold him.

With the same mindless singleness of purpose, the gang swarmed over the van, breaking open the doors, pulling the women and drunks out into the street. The two drunks tumbled from the back seat, swinging wildly at the boys, then falling into the deep snow.

Maureen had locked the front doors, but they came at her from behind, dragging her back over the seats. Jamie could see her struggling, fighting back, but they restrained her arms and legs and tossed her out to the others.

But Maureen was not their target. As Jamie regained his balance, he saw the kids were climbing into the van, slamming and locking the doors, and one of them had jumped into the front seat, started the engine. The long van skidded on the ice and sprayed him with icy slush as it pulled away from the curb and gained speed.

Jamie went after it, running by Maureen, racing as best he could on the icy street. The hard wind froze his open mouth as he gasped for breath, but he kept running. In the deep marks of the van's snow tires he found some footing, and he picked up speed, gained on the gang.

The van was fishtailing, swinging wildly as the teenage driver pumped the gas. Jamie sprinted once, lunged, and grabbed the rear door handle, swung his leg up onto the bumper, and pulled himself aboard. The bastards, he thought, now he had them. They wouldn't get away from him.

Then the rear door was shoved open, knocking him off the bumper, sending him sprawling out into the street, blood gushing from his nostrils. He rolled over as the van raced away, disappearing toward the river and the bridge out of town.

"Jamie! Jamie!" Maureen was crying, running toward him through the snow. She reached him breathless, crying from her fright and from the cold. Somewhere in the melee she'd lost her coat.

"Oh, God, you poor thing." The blood was running from both his nostrils and freezing on his lips. "You're hurt," she whispered, and carefully helped him to his feet, then bending down, retrieved his wool cap and shook it free of snow.

Without speaking, he took the cap and put it on her head, pulled it down well over her ears. Then he unzipped his parka and bundled her inside. Underneath he was wearing a pullover sweater that Mrs. Windmiller had knitted for him. The Irish wool was thick and unyielding, but still the icy wind knifed through.

"Jamie, the Man in the Box..." Maureen was crying as she led him down the street to where the old man lay motionless over the vent. He saw then that she had used her own fur coat to cover the tramp.

The priest knelt down beside him. The man was conscious, Jamie saw, and his bright eyes watched suspiciously as the young priest gently felt his body.

"You're going to be okay," Jamie whispered to the man. Then he looked up at Maureen. "Can he understand me?"

She nodded. "Yes, he understands." She turned away and Jamie could see she had begun to sob.

"I almost got everyone killed," she cried. "All those people have run off...Laura...all of them; I couldn't stop them.

And you were almost killed . . . And I lost the van. Oh, God! The Center can't afford another one."

"Hey, we're all right." Jamie touched her arm. "The old man is okay, really." He tried to sound encouraging. "You stay here, and I'll go telephone the Center. As for the people we picked up, they're no worse off now than they were before. And you'll get the van back. That's the easy part. Those kids will leave it when it runs out of gas."

"How do you know?"

"I know. That's what kids do when they rip off cars."

"But who are they?" she asked, calming down. She drew away from Jamie and shoved her hands into her pockets. "White and black teenagers together in one gang—that doesn't make sense, not here in MacPatch."

"Let's worry about that later," Jamie answered quickly, trying to get her off the subject.

"You know, don't you, Jamie." Something in his voice had alerted her, and she spun him around so he was facing her in the blowing snow. "Tell me," she demanded.

"They're from the orphanage. They call themselves the Altar Boys."

"Are you sure? I've never heard of them."

Jamie nodded, looked off toward where the gang had disappeared, and said softly. "I'm sure. I was one myself. I was once an Altar Boy."

CHAPTER SIX

December Twenty-seventh, Early Morning
Feast of Saint John the Evangelist

The rectory was dark as Jamie made his way down Church Drive. The unwritten rule of the house was that the porch light be left on only when the pastor himself was out. That was one of O'Toole's quirky ways of cutting costs, but not at his own expense.

In the hours since Jamie had shoveled, the steps had disappeared beneath the drifting snow, and he had to dig a pathway with his hands before he could try to reach the door. It was the final effort of an exhausting night, and once inside he collapsed on the wooden bench that stood in the foyer. If it hadn't been for the fire, he acknowledged, probably none of them would be alive.

Maureen and he had argued, at first, about who would set off to find a telephone. She had wanted to be the one to go, but only if he would take his parka back first.

"I'll stay warm by walking," she'd argued, "but without a coat you'll freeze to death, just sitting here."

"Then you stay and I'll walk."

"No, you're the one who has been beaten. Forget about chivalry. What good will it do us if you walk two blocks and collapse in a snowbank? Besides, I know the neighborhood better."

"Says who? The Altar Boys roamed this area when I was a kid, too, you know. Look, I'm not discussing this any longer. You stay with the Man in the Box; he knows you better. I'll walk until I find a phone and call the cops."

Or until my frozen feet drop off, he thought later, as he struggled up the icy streets. He didn't expect to find a public phone still functioning in MacPatch, so he walked uphill, toward the new business district, cutting through the back streets, taking what he thought was the shortest route. But in the icy wind he could barely keep his footing and for the first time he began to think that he might not make it at all. In half an hour he had gone only three long blocks. At this rate, he knew, the Man in the Box would die of shock and exposure before he could get help. And Maureen . . . Maureen could handle anything, he told himself, and bent his face down, pushed forward into the blowing snow and wind.

At the next corner he looked up to orient himself and it was then he saw it: a strange glow in the near distance, backlighting the driving snow. Shielding his eyes he squinted into the night, and when the wind shifted direction, he smelled the fire, realized that a building was in flames, one of the old abandoned warehouses of MacPatch. Twenty minutes later worried firemen were wrapping him in blankets, feeding him coffee. The captain radioed for an ambulance and Jamie was on his second cup when he heard its siren, knew Maureen and the Man in the Box were safe.

They had been lucky, Jamie now realized. One of the policemen who'd driven them back, a red-cheeked, pompous Irishman, had called it a miracle. Too exhausted to object, Jamie had simply nodded and kept quiet. He and Maureen had both gotten out at her apartment, at the corner of Benton Place and West Pine. They had said goodnight wearily, and he had walked the few blocks back to the rectory. They lived very near each other, he noticed.

Now he pulled himself up off the bench and began to strip. His sweater and jeans were frozen stiff, his shirt and underclothes soaked with perspiration. Naked, he felt warmer than he had for hours.

Leaving his clothes where they fell, Jamie headed for the stairway. As he reached the first landing the oil burner kicked on, then sent a blast of hot air rattling up through the pipes. The sound reminded Jamie of the old orphanage building. He had forgotten that clank-and-rattle, just as he had forgotten the Altar Boys.

Jamie shivered as he climbed. Some people, he realized, were comforted by night sounds, the settling of old wood, the subtle shifting of walls. It gave them a sense of security, especially on a winter night. They felt as if they were wrapped in a womb and they slept patiently, awaiting the delivery of morning.

But he had always been different—lost at night, vulnerable, caught up in the belly of a beast. The memory returned of how the older boys would come to them at midnight, when the nuns left the children's dorm. The little boys were usually afraid at night anyway—of the dark hallways, the tall, black-robed nuns, the alien sights and sounds of the institution. But the Altar Boys were much more terrifying. One could never be sure when they'd come howling out of the darkness, dressed as if for the altar in long, lace-trimmed albs and starched white amices, sweeping down on the smaller boys like rampaging ghosts.

He had wet his bed all that winter of his sixth year, but he had never squealed on his tormentors, no matter how the nuns scolded. The Altar Boys. They had called themselves that, and later, when he was eleven and had moved upstairs he had become one himself, and run wild at night wearing vestments stolen from the convent laundry.

Yet still he was afraid. Afraid of big dark buildings, afraid sometimes of the brownstone rectory. Jamie reached the top floor and walked back toward his room, feeling his way in the dark by touching both sides of the narrow hall with his fingertips. He kept walking, deeper into the dark, until he bumped against his bedroom door and went inside.

By the shadowy light from the street, he pulled out his bed

mat and settled himself down under heavy quilts. He was too
tired to wash, even to put on pajamas. He pulled the blankets
up close and sought a safe spot in the warmth of his mat. But
the old fear, like a low burning pilot light, burned at his memory. He was one of those, he thought, that Frost described as
"well acquainted with the night."

Yet now it was worse. Now he was seeing phantoms—first
in his trances, now on his own stairway. He tried to explain it
away—hallucination phenomena, stemming from his intense
meditation experiences. That was what a therapist would say,
and that was what he had forced himself to believe. But the
shrouded figure had been so real. . . .

Silly, he told himself. Crazy. He rolled over and closed his
eyes, determined to resist his fears. He pictured the Monsignor,
asleep downstairs. The pastor had lived most of his life in this
rectory and he slept soundly, knowing the building was safe.

Still.

Jamie opened his eyes in the dark. He identified the rectory's
separate sounds, listed them in his memory. He waited for the
oil burner to go on and the steam pipes to rattle. He knew the
sounds of pigeons on the roof, the cooing they made as they
huddled together under the eaves. In minutes he had proven
there was no sound he could not account for.

Still.

He would have to count himself to sleep, use meditation
technique to force the fear out. Slowly he began to count.
Beginning with his feet, he brought his body under control,
made his legs and thighs relax. Slowly, gently, he unwound,
calmed his racing heart, uncoiled the muscles of his shoulders.
He closed his eyes and, as if slipping off the bank into a pool
of water, he dropped down into the deep liquid. He counted
backward from ten, let the numbers drift off his mind until he
gently fell off to sleep.

"Father, you don't feel so good?" Mrs. Windmiller asked
in her warm kitchen the next morning. Jamie had come in
wearing jeans and a sweat shirt. He was unshaven and still
barefoot.

"I'll feel better once I clean up, Mrs. Windmiller. No, I'm

not sick." He smiled, to blunt her concern.

"You haven't slept, Father Jamie." The housekeeper stopped her preparations and looked at him again. "And I found your clothes a mess this morning, out in the vestibule."

"I helped out last night at the Community Center," he said quickly, reaching for the pitcher of orange juice on the table. "I got back late and I'm afraid I just let the clothes drop." He tried to pour himself a glass of juice but his fingers trembled, spilling it.

"Father! No, you are not well." The housekeeper laid a hand on his forehead.

"I have no temperature, Mrs. Windmiller. I'm fine. Really! I'm just exhausted, that's all. A long night out in the cold." Through the kitchen window he could see the Cathedral, the empty back parking lot. Clarence was crossing the alley from his apartment above the garage to the side door of the sacristy.

"Sit! Sit!" The housekeeper ordered. "Get some food into you. Eat!" She began rushing, presenting him with a bowl of cornflakes while she peeled bacon strips into the frying pan.

"All right!" Jamie laughed, cheered by her determination to fuss over him. Her warmth was enough to dispel the memory of any shrouded midnight figure. "Let me clean up, get some clothes on. I'll be right back." He glanced at the wall clock. It was already twenty minutes to seven. He would be late saying Mass, but it didn't matter. Not even the regulars would be in the Cathedral, not after last night's storm. It was certainly no day for the old ladies of MacPatch to be out in the cold.

But Jamie was wrong. When he began the Mass, ten minutes late, he saw he had an audience of one: Grace Keller. She was sitting alone in the front pew, the only person in the whole of the vast, vaulted cathedral.

He rushed through the service, finishing the low mass in fifteen minutes, then stepped down from the altar and approached the old woman. She had left her pew and was coming up to the altar rail.

"Miss Keller, I can't believe you're here. I'm sure God would have understood your missing Mass one day, especially a day like this. Now I want you to come back with me to the rectory and we'll have a cup of tea or something. Then I'll take you home. You shouldn't be out walking on these sidewalks." He shook his head and frowned, trying to look stern.

"Oh, good, Father. I was hoping to have a chance to speak with you." She sounded confidential.

"What is it, Miss Keller? Is there anything wrong?"

"Well, in a way, Father, yes. But here, you go and take off your vestments."

"Come with me into the sacristy, Miss Keller. We can talk while I change." He reached down to unfasten the altar railing gate.

"But isn't it against the rules, Father Ignatius? A lay person like myself in the sacristy?" She sounded shocked.

"Oh, no, Miss Keller, come along and don't worry." He took her by the arm. "It's perfectly all right." He was amused by her embarrassment. She was like many other Catholics, still awed by priests and their secret rituals, the elaborate vestments they wore. And that was how those Catholics preferred it. They liked a distance between themselves and the clergy. It seemed more religious that way, more of a mystery.

"I saw your niece last night, Miss Keller. She had me out looking for people." He kept chatting, explaining their adventure in the snowstorm, but not mentioning the Altar Boys or the Man in the Box. He slipped off the chasuble and stole, pulled the long white alb over his head. "Now what's the trouble, Miss Keller? How can I help you?"

"It's Maureen, Father Ignatius," she began carefully. She stood in the middle of the sacristy, tightly clutching her imitation leather purse. "I want you to talk to the girl."

Jamie stopped untying the long strips of the amice and stared at the older woman. "What's wrong with Maureen, Miss Keller?"

"Oh, nothing, really, Father," she said quickly. "But I was wondering if you might be able to do me a little favor." She said it slyly, as if trying to involve him in a conspiracy.

"And what would that be, Miss Keller?" Jamie answered, smiling now.

"Well, being a young person yourself, Father, I know you'd have a way of talking with Maureen." She kept glancing away, not looking at him as she spoke. "Maureen's a real saint for looking after these poor unfortunate people. But you know yourself she isn't going to meet anyone down here in Mac-Patch."

"Meet anyone?" Jamie slipped off the amice and folded it carefully. He was in street clothes now: an old blue button-down shirt, jeans, and running shoes. "Do you mean a boyfriend, Miss Keller?"

"Of course!" She seemed surprised he needed to verify it.

"But does she want a boyfriend?" he asked carefully.

"And why wouldn't she, Father?" The aunt seemed slightly indignant.

"I'm sorry. I didn't mean to imply anything. She just seems so committed to her work, so devoted to the Center, that I—"

"She's not a nun, Father."

"Yes, I realize that." He nodded his head a few times, demonstrating that he understood. "And what is it you'd like me to do about this, Miss Keller?"

"Talk to her, Father. Tell her how a girl her age should be having a husband, and a family. God himself wants us to have families, now doesn't he, Father? The priests and nuns excepted, of course."

"Everyone has his or her own vocation, Miss Keller. Perhaps Maureen doesn't feel she's called to the life of a wife and mother."

"Father Ignatius, I know what you're thinking. She's not really a good Catholic, so it doesn't matter to you what she does. But don't be too hard on her. I know the dear girl doesn't attend Mass, but that's more Liam Sullivan's fault than hers. He drove all those children away from the Church with his craziness. It was Peggy, you know, my sister, who managed to keep them normal. Their father read them the Bible at breakfast, can you imagine? It's a fine book, of course, the New Testament part, at least. But at breakfast, when you're half awake and trying to get a little cream of wheat before getting off to school? And then they had to go to Mass each day as well, and rosary at night before they went to bed. Well, the poor children were fed up before they even finished grammar school. And it's not Maureen's fault at all!" The old woman's face was flushed with anger and Jamie found himself backing up a few steps.

"Yes, I agree. You're perfectly right, Miss Keller," he said quickly.

"And then there was the DeSales boy, Michael." She shook her head, weary now.

"DeSales?" It was all new information to Jamie and he found he wanted to hear it.

"Michael DeSales and Maureen were friends . . . were a lot more than that, to tell you the honest-to-God truth, Father. They met at the college, Our Lady of the Snows, as it was called, City College they've named it now. But she met Michael there. He was older than her, been off to Africa with the Peace Corps for awhile. Did a number of things when he got back, but couldn't seem to get his life in order. Dom DeSales is his father. DeSales Insurance, Father, you know it, I'm sure. The Cardinal and Dom are the best of friends. Dominic and Liam were old school friends, as well. You've heard it all before, I'm sure." She waved her thin hand, dismissing the story, then returned to talking about Maureen.

"The boy, Michael, had gotten away from the Church when he was over there in Africa, and then when Maureen took up with him, well, you know, one thing led to another, and the next thing we knew—any of us—they were living together uptown, near the college, as close as two bugs in a rug.

"The girl was only eighteen, Father. She had been with the nuns all her life and she didn't know any better. She didn't have a mind of her own. The father drove her out of the house, and soon she met this Michael DeSales, and he was a fast talker, like his own father." Grace Keller shook her head, still distressed at the shame of it all.

"But this man is out of her life now, isn't he?" Jamie found that he was anxious to know that bit of information.

"Indeed! They had their outs and all of that is good and done with. It isn't Michael DeSales I've come to see you about, thank God. Good riddance to him, taking advantage of Maureen that way.".

They had reached the front steps of the rectory. Except for the footprints Jamie had left on his way to Mass that morning, they were a solid blanket of deep, crusted snow.

"Won't you come in, Miss Keller, and have a cup of tea?" he offered innocently.

"No, thank you, Father," she said firmly, casting an eye at the ski slope leading to the door. "I won't be that much of a bother. There's just the one thing I'd ask of you, Father: Get that girl out of MacPatch."

Seeing his surprise she rushed on. "There's nothing for her here, Father, and she's not getting any younger. She only stays down here because of me, you know. She comes and takes me to Devotions at night, stops by the apartment every day. Drives me out to Spring Valley to shop. You can't get decent vegetables over on West Pine, Father. Oh, she's a dear, but I won't have her waiting on me, wasting her life when she could be living somewhere better, maybe in one of those new apartment buildings the other side of Lindell, in Christ the King." She fixed Jamie with her eyes, as if daring him to disagree with her.

"You know, Miss Keller, Maureen is a very determined young woman," he began.

"Strong-willed, you mean," Grace Keller put in.

"You could say that, yes. And feeling as she does about the clergy, I'm just not sure how much I could influence her." He looked to the woman for a reaction, but it was as if she hadn't heard him. She had come to her priest for a solution and she wouldn't release him till she'd received one. Jamie began again.

"Miss Keller, what if you left MacPatch? Moved up to Christ the King yourself. That's Father Reed's parish; do you know him?"

The old woman shook her head. "I've lived my whole life here, Father. Everyone wanted me to leave in '68, after the riots, but I still had my job then, at the library on Pine Street. Now all I've got left is my house and that's not worth much, I know. No, I'll be in MacPatch till I die, please God. But not Maureen with me."

Again she looked at Jamie expectantly. Obviously Maureen had not told her about the closing of Saints Peter and Paul in the spring. Perhaps she had forgotten, but more likely, Jamie thought, she hadn't wanted to break the bad news now, not in the middle of the winter. Spring still seemed a long way off.

"I'll speak to your niece," Jamie capitulated. "I'll try to convince her that she could move uptown and still work in MacPatch during the day. That way she could still drop by and see you, help out if you needed anything. And uptown she would have a better chance of meeting someone nice. Or at least some women friends her own age."

The old lady brightened. "Oh, thank you, Father Ignatius. Maureen likes you, I know. She'll listen to a young man like yourself." Grace Keller was all smiles. "Just don't let her be putting you off, Father. She's not always easy to talk to, you know; sometimes she gets upset when people . . . make suggestions."

The thought of Maureen locking horns with Aunt Grace made Jamie laugh. "Don't worry, Miss Keller. I'll get on her case," he said firmly, then winked, the way he imagined the Cardinal might, to charm an old parishioner like her.

CHAPTER SEVEN

December Twenty-seventh, Afternoon
Feast of St. John the Evangelist

Organizing the parish accounts, Jamie reflected, was like trying to organize a plate of spaghetti. There was eighty years' worth of accumulated property in the rectory and Cathedral that he had to inventory and sell off. For the belongings already disposed of—a dozen patens, four gold chalices, three asperges, two lawn mowers, the official parish vehicle, and much more—O'Toole had filed only a handful of receipts. Jamie sighed, frustrated.

Still, the work had kept him occupied. He had stuck to it all morning, while the pastor celebrated the second Mass, ate breakfast, then retired for his early nap of the day. Now, when the pastor was stirring again, getting ready to come down for lunch, Jamie was heading upstairs to meditate. This schedule, he had found, was the best way of avoiding the old man for most of the long, quiet winter day.

Jamie settled himself on the bed mat, then took his first deep breath, concentrating on the simple, elementary exercise. He focused his thoughts, began to count, saying "One" on his first exhalation, "Two" on the next, and so on. Eyes closed, he counted to the number four, then began again. He set himself no time limit. His body, he knew, would tell him when he was ready to focus on the centering prayer, when he was ready to ask God once again: Who am I?

For the moment his task was simply to control his thoughts and feelings, to close out the world around him, the city streets and the rectory. Fixing his eyes on the Duccio, he drew all his thoughts within himself.

As he did he felt the bedroom melt away, felt his consciousness open inward. He tried to fill his mind with Jesus, but instead, as he had come to dread, he felt his being rushed toward that mysterious inner brink he feared. And then Father Ignatius was gone, spinning off into that vast space beyond time, beyond reason, beyond dreams.

The albino boy sat cross-legged in the dust outside the *wagana* hut. Thin, small, less than sixteen years old, he had arrived in the early hours before dawn and stayed the whole day, sitting in what little shade was cast by the tall, slender coconut trees. No one, not even the children who lived in the compound, had spoken to him. They did not even look his way, although an albino was an unusual sight: his hair silky yellow, his pinkish skin cobwebbed by dark reticulations; his eyes red and tender, often weakening in the bright Zanzibar sun.

The boy had found his way across the island at night, living off the fruit of trees, sleeping at the edges of compounds, and searching for the town of Zanzibar and the woman called Mameh Hodi.

His mother had sent him. She had told him of Mameh Hodi, of how when he and his brother were born, the *wamamavua* had come to her and said, "Woman, you have slept without a light and the devil has changed your child and given you two."

His twin had been killed by Mameh Hodi and buried in the bush beyond the Ngambo compound. But his mother had escaped with him to the city, to live there among Arabs until he began to dream, to scream out at night, to be haunted by nightmares of his brother.

"The *wamavua* will cure you," his mother had told him.

"In the village of Zanzibar, find the white flag tied to the hut. That is the house of the *wamavua*."

So now the boy sat before that hut, following the shadow of the sun across the compound, the circle of grass huts above the river, and waited for Mameh Hodi.

At dusk she came to him, stepping from her hut and crossing the compound to where he still sat crosslegged under the coconut trees. She was a fat woman who moved slowly, shifted her heavy weight with the grace and slowness of an elephant turning in the forest. His eyes followed her, for now that the sun had set he could see again.

"*Yambo?*" The heavy woman stopped a few feet from the boy and squatted in the dust, rocking back on the broad heels of her bare feet. An entire bolt of bright calico was wrapped about her body and she tucked it tight as she sat. She wore no headdress of colored silk, but her black hair was plaited tight into cornrows.

"*Yambo,*" the boy answered. "I am well."

"*Yambo sana?* Are you very well?" she asked, watching him closely. Her face was oval and plump as a plum, with a broad, flat nose, and fat, meaty lips. In one nostril she had hooked a thin band of gold.

"*Sana,*" the boy said, not looking up at the woman. He knew better than to catch her eyes.

"*Cano looloo?*" she asked. "The same as pearl?"

"*Cano looloo.*"

"*Cana marajan?* The same as coral?"

"*Cana marajan,*" he answered.

"*Cana thahub?* The same as gold?"

"*Cana thahub.*"

"*Cana fether?* The same as silver?"

"*Cana fether,*" he said.

She nodded and for a moment said nothing, only keeping her dark eyes fixed on the child.

"What are you called?" she finally asked.

"Zayidi."

"And your mother?"

The boy hesitated, afraid now to answer.

"Your mother is called Myana Maua, I am certain," the woman said.

The boy nodded, still not looking at the *wamavua*.

The old woman sat quietly. She knew why the boy had sought her, had known who he was from the moment he had entered the compound. She had always expected him, yet now she asked.

"Why have you come?"

"For you to dance the *nyange*," he whispered, then told her of his dreams, of the white figure that woke him at night, of the devil that made him thrust his hands and feet into the fire.

"It is not *Dumgumaru*, or *Tari*, or *Robamba*," she replied, naming the devils of Zanzibar. "Your mother slept without a light and the devil changed your skin. I killed your brother, and I would have killed you, too, but your mother ran away. Go back, walk into the water, or let the dogs of Zanzibar eat you. You are a dead man."

She spoke without anger, as if it were a fact to be accepted.

"Kill me now," he begged.

She shook her massive head. "You have slept with a woman." And when he did not deny her accusation, she went on. "I cannot kill anyone who has already become a man. You must walk into the sea or let the dogs feed off your flesh."

He felt her brown eyes on him, felt his own worthlessness, the shame of his white skin. He looked at her now, fixed his eyes on her smooth, rich face, as if petitioning her without speech.

"Go to the Arabs," she said at last, as if washing her hands of him. "Speak to Ahmed bin Ahman at Matony. Tell him you will sail to Africa and help him hunt for slaves."

His head shot up, and he gained hope.

"In the mountains beyond the Manganga you will find the M'Do tribe hiding in the forest by the river."

She broke off then, as if her words were a thin limb snapped from a tree. He raised himself off the ground, anxious to know more, but still afraid to question.

"Go to the Arab," she said again, pausing at the entrance to her hut, "and tell him the *wamavua* told you. In Africa," she warned him, "you will find your brother. Kill him and you will live." And then she squeezed herself into the grass shack, leaving him in the darkness.

• • •

The albino boy squatted in the bushes above the Zwoubo River, less than three hundred meters from the M'Do compound. He had led Sheikh Ahmed bin Ahman and his Arabs there, following the instruction of the *wamavua* woman. Now they waited.

"How long?" Ahmed asked, speaking to the boy in Swahili. He too squatted in the dry river grasses, holding his musket in his lap, concealing the heavy caliber handgun in the folds of his white *kanzu*. Looped over his shoulder was a cowhide whip.

"Sijui," whispered the boy. That was the truth; he did not know. The *wamavua* had sent him dreams, but they had revealed only the river bank, the *shamba*, and then the M'Do men walking single file on the narrow path down to the river.

"Bassi," Ahmed uttered, then turning on his heels he motioned toward the other Arabs, ordering *"Karibu!"* In the silence of the long grass, the three men moved closer to the Sheikh.

They, too, wore *kanzu*, the long white gowns made of Indian muslin, and carried loaded guns. Buckled around their waists were *jambia*, curved daggers.

The boy wore only a loincloth. It was made of unbleached calico, called *Amerikani* in Zanzibar because of the ships that brought the coarse fabric from that distant land. Sheikh Ahmed had given him the cloth when they left Zanzibar, tossing it to him as he crouched in the corner of the dhow.

"We will take the people of this *shamba*," the Sheikh told his men, speaking now in Arabic, "then separate them into gangs of six. Yoke the men with forked sticks. Tie the women together with rope, and you *mazungo*"—he called the boy by the Swahili word for white man—"herd the young ones together. If they run away into the bush, beat them with this axe. Kill the wild ones at once."

The albino boy gripped the axe handle, waiting silently. It would be daylight soon and he would have difficulty seeing. He feared the sun, as he feared the Sheikh, as he feared the blacks who soon would come down the trail to the river.

Already he could hear them further up the path, talking and laughing. Their voices carried through the jungle like the sound of birds singing. Ahmed bin Ahman glanced at the boy and nodded, his small eyes black as wet slate. He had been wise,

he praised himself, for listening to the *wamavua,* for taking
the *mazungo* with him to Africa. The boy had led them directly
to the M'Do.

Through the thick bush, Ahmed bin Ahman could see them.
They had reached the last rise of the slope and were moving
single file, like a herd of gazelle. Ahmed watched the happy
faces descend the slope. The men were first, a long row of
them moving quickly; he counted a dozen, then more. Warriors.
It would be too difficult, he realized. There were so many. He
would let them pass, then attack at the river, squeeze them
between the bank and deep water. He raised his arm to signal,
to call off the attack.

His sight blurred by the sun, all the *mazungo* saw was that
Ahmed had raised his arm. Leaping to his feet, he ran for the
path above him, swinging his axe and calling on Allah as he
broke through the underbrush.

Zoulu saw him first. The son of Sulu and Burkuloo caught
the flash of white skin coming up from the bush and lifted his
spear. Then he remembered what the wise man had told them:
of how the M'Do would someday meet a white creature in the
forest and this creature would carry them away in the air, fly
north to where the gods lived in the mountains of Kilimanjaro.

The M'Do warrior threw away his spear, fell flat on the
earth. Behind him confusion spread through the long line of
men. One bent down to speak to Zoulu. Others rushed forward
at the *mazungo,* who stood terrified, deserted by his band,
waiting to be overpowered.

At that moment Zoulu lifted his head and cried a warning:
"It is the white demon," he shouted. "The one of whom we
have been told."

Hesitant now, the M'Do warriors halted. For a few seconds
there was a silence, then a buzz of whispered consultations.
All at once, in unison, the warriors cast away their weapons
and fell to the dirt, paying homage to the pale-skinned boy.

In the next instant the Arabs were on them. Bursting from
the underbrush, Ahmed fired his musket. The blast blew a half-
dollar hole in the face of one M'Do, and sent some warriors
cowering. The albino realized that miraculously he had been
saved. His life was spared.

"The children!" Ahmed bin Ahman was shouting in Arabic,

and the *mazungo* remembered suddenly that this was his task— to shackle the children, to lash them together with thongs. They were the prize Ahmed most wanted: the girls, each good for twenty dollars in the port of Muscat; the boys just coming into their strength with a lifetime of work still in them.

The *mazungo* ran toward them. The youngest clutched at each other like monkeys, seeking comfort and protection. There was none. The albino grabbed the first child he reached, a girl of eight. Her thin arm was brittle in his grasp and she shrieked at the touch of the *mazungo*. She had never seen white skin before.

The boy looped the leather around her leg and grabbed the next girl, tying the two together in a tight bundle. Morning sunlight flashed through the thick jungle and the *mazungo* kept his head down, away from the brightness. Brandishing his axe, he grouped the children into a circle, then gestured for them to lie flat in the dirt until their turns came.

He thought they had all obeyed him. Then he heard Ahmed shout, his curses louder than the wails of the women. The albino whirled to look where the Sheikh pointed with his *jambia*.

It was one of the older boys, an M'Do of his own age. He must have inched his way to the edge of the path and now was half running, half tumbling down the steep slope that drooped to the river. The albino couldn't see the boy's face, but his body was strong and well formed; he would bring a fine price at the port of Muscat.

"Get him!" Ahmed shouted in Swahili, then lumbered up the path to guard the other children with his cowhide whip.

The *mazungo* skidded down the bank, scanning the bush for the M'Do boy. It was cooler in the trees, darker. The sunlight did not burn his eyes. He spotted the M'Do below him, slipping easily through the brush.

He knew what the M'Do's plan would be: to reach the water, to swim out beyond the bank, and let the current take him downstream. The M'Do people were like crocodiles, he had heard. They could live under water, in a dry den carved out of the shore. He had once been told of a woman washing clothes in the river—of how a crocodile had pulled her under and how she had returned the next day to tell the *shamba* of the palace beneath the water, where a tribe of slaves lived among the crocodiles.

Now both boys broke from the trees and the albino flung himself forward, tackling the M'Do from behind. Without turning, the African jabbed backward with his elbow, catching the *mazungo* on the chin. The pain was sharp and the albino lost his grip, then grabbed again. This time he seized the M'Do's knee and tripped him into the rushing water.

The *mazungo* shouted in Swahili for help. Why hadn't one of the Arabs followed him? He could feel his feet slipping in the river bottom. Still, he caught the M'Do's ankle and did not let go. The boy was a prize; the Sheikh would give much to the one who brought him back.

Both his hands now gripped the M'Do's ankle and he swore at the boy, trying to stop the African from pulling them both out deep. Unlike the M'Do, he could not swim. If the current took him he would drown, or worse, become food for crocodiles.

The M'Do found his footing in the mud and twisted his leg sharply, breaking free of the *mazungo*. Two fast steps, then he dove for the foaming, rushing water of the current.

Now the prize was lost. The albino watched him surface, watched for a moment as he seemed to bob in place, his leg caught, perhaps, in a tangle of bamboo roots. Then the M'Do screamed, jerked around, as if searching frantically for something. He cried out, yelled to the white boy, and reached back to grab the *mazungo's* hand.

For the first time the white boy looked into the face of the African. It was his own. The same broad, straight nose; the thick lips; the slanted, finely shaped eyes. Only the skin was different. Dark instead of pale, unblemished by reticulations. And his eyes. In his fear, the M'Do's eyes had gone as blank and dull as copper pennies. But this was the *mazungo's* face. As the *wamavua* had predicted, he had found his twin.

"Pull!" the African begged, shouting in M'Do. The word was lost on the *mazungo*. He saw only the brown ridge of the river crocodile as it broke the surface, and he pulled back from the grasping hand.

"Help me!" his brother screamed. But now it was too late.

Holding the boy's thigh in his vast jaws the crocodile swept by, pulling his prey into the deeper water. Then it sank, in one swift, smooth movement, beneath the boiling surface of the river.

The telephone was ringing. It pierced his ears, breaking through the trance to pull him back. James Ignatius opened his eyes and stared. He was like a child, waking frightened in a strange room.

On the muddy banks of the Zwoubo River the mazungo *found his footing and backed away. Flapping his arms wildly, as if to shoo off danger, he struggled back to shore, grabbing the roots of the bamboo tree to pull himself from the swift, muddy current. His toes dug into the dry earth of the riverbank. He was alive. He was safe. And he would remain so. He recalled the words of the wamavua: "In Africa you will find your brother. Kill him and you will live."*

Jamie struggled for his bearings. The white-walled room was his own; he knew that. And the telephone was ringing. He reached out and grabbed the receiver.

"Hello . . . Saints Peter and Paul," he mumbled.

"Father Ignatius?"

"Yes, speaking." Jamie shook his head, hoping to clear it.

"This is Maureen, Father . . . Maureen Sullivan."

"Oh, Maureen, I'm sorry."

He stumbled up the steep embankment. He could feel his own labored breathing, the thick wet leaves scraping his body.

"Listen, I tried to reach you earlier, to see if you were okay after last night, but the line was busy. And I wanted you to know, I spoke to Brother Raymond at the orphanage. He's going to try to find out which boys were out in the street last night."

"Father!" she interrupted. "Another person is missing."

"Are you sure?" he asked, then regretted it. He could hear her quick, impatient intake of breath. "Of course you are. How did you discover it?"

"There's this old man, Tony, who hangs out at the Center.

He's not feebleminded or crazy like so many of these people, and just a few minutes ago, he came screaming into my office, saying 'they' had taken his friend Joe. I know who he means. The two of them are inseparable, which is unusual; these people often get so deranged that they can't even really talk coherently to anyone. But since this was Tony I paid attention, even when he began to rant that 'they' were trying to take him away too.

"I went to the front windows of the Center to see what he was talking about. I thought it might be the cops. Down here, you know, they have the habit of just busting street people for the fun of it. But there were no cops. The streets were empty. Deserted, really, except for this one person. . . ."

"Yes?" he said encouragingly. She was hesitating as if the person were someone she had recognized, but was reluctant to identify.

"It was a tramp. A man I had never seen before, with long hair and a scraggly beard. But he wasn't old. He was a young man, and blond, and . . . he looked exactly like you."

"That's him!" Jamie shouted, excited that someone else had seen him.

"Who? Do you know him?"

"Well, I saw him. On Christmas morning I was awake very early. It was snowing, but I was looking out onto Church Drive and there was enough light to see—" He told her all of it—how, he had first taken him for a shopping bag woman, because of the hair, and then realized it was a man—a man who looked enough like him to be his twin. "When I got downstairs to the street he was gone," Jamie concluded. "I searched Church Drive, but I couldn't find any trace of him, not even footprints I could follow."

"I did the same thing! I went back inside for my coat, but by the time I got out front he was gone. Father, I want to track this guy down. He may have seen something—and if it's the cops who picked up Joe, then I want a witness to prove it."

"Wait! I think we should get together first. There may be some way I can help you. I'll come over to the Center—"

"No, thank you. It's hard for me to get away during the day." She paused, thinking, and then suggested, "I'm taking Aunt Grace to Devotions tomorrow evening. Is it all right if I stop by then, around six o'clock?"

"Good! Monsignor O'Toole conducts the Devotions, so we can talk here in private."

"All right, then. See you about six."

He hung up the phone. The room was cold and quiet again.

Jamie remembered the tropical heat, the pungent orchids and liana vines. Then the sensations faded and he was Father Ignatius, alone in his room, staring blankly at the Duccio.

"It's only yourself for dinner tonight," the housekeeper said. She smiled at Jamie as he came into the kitchen. "The Monsignor went off with Clarence while you were upstairs. He said not to wait for him." After all her years in America, she still pronounced her w's as v's. "I've made you some lamb chops."

"Oh, Mrs. Windmiller, you treat me too well." Jamie put his arm around her shoulder and gave her a quick hug. The housekeeper seemed even tinier next to him; her head barely reached his ribcage.

"You needn't go to such a fuss," he said, moving past her to take down a dinner plate. After a lifetime in institutions it made him nervous to have people wait on him, and this was one deal he had made with Mrs. Windmiller: He would set the table when the Monsignor was away, and help clean up the dishes.

"It's no work, Father Jamie. Especially compared to the Chancery, with all those parties and such." She shook her head and sighed at the recollection. "This is like a vacation."

"It is," Jamie agreed, setting some silverware beside his plate. "But you worked hard enough all those years for His Eminence. It's nice, isn't it, being down in Saints Peter and Paul with just the two of us?"

"Yah! Yah! For me and the Monsignor, fine. But it's no place for yourself. Not here. You need young ones. A big, important parish. Someplace nice." She waved her plump arm, indicating the suburbs beyond the river.

Jamie kept silent. He knew how the rectory housekeepers gossiped among themselves. A hint dropped to Hilda Windmiller about the imminent dismantling of her parish would reach the pastor of Saint Michael's by dinner tomorrow, ricochet off Christ the King at breakfast, and get back to the Cardinal over drinks forty-eight hours hence.

"Mrs. Windmiller, they're expecting another snowstorm tonight, three or four inches at least. Why don't you hurry on home now before the weather changes? Call a cab. We'll pay for it."

The housekeeper glanced out the kitchen window. Like all old people, Jamie sensed, she was frightened by cold weather—the deep snow, the treacherous ice. "Okay," he said quickly, "let's put everything back in the oven to keep warm, and I'll walk you home now."

"No, no!" she protested, waving off his suggestion. "It's only just around the corner. I go out the back and I'm home. Sit! Sit!" she ordered, then bent over the stove and took the lamb chops out of the broiler. "You need to eat. Here you are running around, saying early Mass, shoveling snow, fooling with those boys at the orphanage." She shook her head as she served him. "You work too hard, Father Jamie. You can't do everything."

"It would be much harder in the suburbs, Mrs. Windmiller," Jamie replied, beginning to tease her. "There'd be more parishioners, and that means more politics. More evening groups. A high school. Baptisms. Cana conferences for engaged couples."

"Yah, but you would have more priests, much help." She stopped talking. He knew she didn't want to mention the Monsignor, nor complain about him. Jamie didn't press her. It would be unfair to gossip with the housekeeper about O'Toole. The old man deserved better.

"But I wouldn't have such a nice home out in the suburbs, Mrs. Windmiller. Instead of this old brownstone, with the third floor to myself, I'd have to live in one of those Cape Cod rectories—you know, split level, with a rec room instead of a front parlor. No, I think I'd better stay here." He smiled up at her teasingly, but Mrs. Windmiller looked serious and displeased.

"You are so young; you do not know what is best," she scolded.

"What do you mean, Mrs. Windmiller?"

She did not look at him as she replied. "It will be best if you have a parish of your own. Not here. A *new* church." She spoke like a woman who knew a secret.

• • •

Leaving his dishes to drain at the sink, Jamie walked through the house to his third floor bedroom, shutting off lights as he went. Evenings were often like this—Jamie alone in the rectory while the Monsignor was off somewhere, visiting former parishioners who now lived out in the suburbs.

Jamie was thankful he didn't have to go along. He was learning that real friendship between priests and parishioners was rare. Most people felt uneasy having clergy in their homes and treated them like strange creatures, to be fawned over and catered to. Jamie found it embarrassing, even insulting. Still, he knew, most priests liked the special treatment. O'Toole certainly did. Jamie often went to bed, as he was doing tonight, with the porch light still lit for the pastor.

Footsteps woke him. Footsteps from the first floor, on the landing. He sat up in the darkness, alert to the sound. He could not move. His naked body was chilled under the heavy quilts.

The Monsignor, he thought. The Monsignor had just come home. Yet he did not believe this, even as he forced himself to stay calm, to be logical about the night sounds. He knew who it really was.

The footsteps kept coming, moving purposefully up the stairs. Jamie grabbed a pair of jeans from the chair and slipped them on. But this time he did not leave his room.

The heavy steps had reached the second floor. They went past the Monsignor's bedroom and kept coming, up toward the third floor. Jamie's heart muscle tightened, as if being squeezed by someone's strong fingers. He was holding his breath, waiting it out, but the intruder kept plodding on, as if from a long distance, as if he always knew his destination was the small room at the top of the stairs.

The footsteps stopped. Jamie sighed, exhausted by his fright. He knew where the figure was: down the hall, at the top step, blocking his escape. Jamie glanced around the room. There was nothing with which to defend himself. But what could anyone do, he wondered, against a shrouded shape that might or might not exist?

Forcing himself closer to the door, he leaned against the wood and listened. Only his heartbeat pounded against his ears. There was no sound at all in the hallway, no footsteps.

Perhaps this time it really was a burglar, Jamie thought. He visualized a man with a knife in his hand, creeping closer, hugging the wall, but he blocked that fantasy from his mind. He could not panic. Not now. He would only get himself killed if he did. He reached down and felt for the key in the lock, knowing already that there was none. He couldn't lock himself away from the intruder.

The steps began again. Slowly they moved down the length of the hallway, muted by the old, thin upstairs rug, but still loud enough for Jamie to track their steady pace, until they reached his door, where again they hesitated.

Waiting, he felt the pain of anticipated torture. His fingers had begun to tremble and as if to bring on the suffering, to get it all over with, he hit the light switch and pulled open the door, hoping that again it would vanish.

The hall was dark, and as Jamie's door opened the shrouded shape dissolved, as if overexposed to light. But he had perceived it before it vanished. The figure had been tall and pencil-thin, shrouded in ivory-colored linen.

Reaching out to where it had stood, he felt only darkness. Nothing remained but the image retained on his retinas. He stood perfectly still, as one might who felt he had made a fool of himself among strangers. Then his fear came back.

It had been the same figure: like a man, but not a man, wrapped in the cerements of the dead. And this time, behind the burial cloth, he had seen a decomposing face. Only one eye had been open, but it glowed fiercely, like an ember. The pupil had been a pinhole, the nose long and narrow, the mouth wide and full, smudged against the transparent ivory linen that covered it.

Grotesque as it was, Jamie knew the face. He recognized it a moment late, as a man lifting a candle in the dark would realize a moment late that he was looking into a mirror, seeing his own ghostly image.

CHAPTER EIGHT

December Twenty-eighth, Afternoon
Feast of the Holy Innocents

"And there's our young friend!" the Cardinal exclaimed, looking up from his desk. He spread his arms wide in welcome, as the monsignor who was his secretary stepped aside and admitted Jamie to the spacious office. "And how's our missionary today?"

The Cardinal did not stand, but did push his leather chair back from the desk, saying, "Hold everything for me, Bob. I've got to talk to Father James Ignatius for a few minutes." He thickened his Irish brogue and played with the young priest's name. He knew how Jamie hated attention, and his blue eyes flashed with amusement as he waved the young man toward the easy chairs arranged around a coffee table.

Jamie stepped carefully across the deep carpet. As always, the size of the office dwarfed him, made him feel his inexperience. He could not get used to such trappings. They made him feel uncomfortable, like wearing wool against his skin.

"Can I get you a nip of something, Jamie?" the Cardinal asked, heading for the mahogany cabinets. He was wearing his black cassock and he tightened the red silk sash as he walked. Always an imposing man, in clerical garb he seemed almost imperial.

"No, Your Eminence, thank you. If Monsignor O'Toole found liquor on my breath, I think he'd revoke my visa for uptown."

"Well, that's true enough." The Cardinal smiled, pleased that Jamie was approaching his difficult assignment with humor. Too few of the young priests had any.

"That was a fine job you did on Christmas Eve, Jamie." The Cardinal sat across from the young priest, setting down his drink and then arranging the folds of his cassock.

"I'm sorry it was such a failure," Jamie answered. He had long since learned that it was better strategy to come clean with the Cardinal at once; if you didn't, he'd eventually come and get you.

Pleased to see they were in agreement, the Cardinal waved off Jamie's apology. "You can't be blamed for the snowstorm, and besides, as I told you, it's difficult getting people downtown nowadays after dark. They're afraid, and frankly," he peered across at Jamie, as if looking over bifocals, "I can't blame them. The old city is dangerous, especially MacPatch. We're not getting out of Saints Peter and Paul soon enough."

"I met a woman on Christmas Day at the Community Center. Maureen Sullivan. Her aunt is Grace Keller, who lives on Pierce Street. I don't know if you remember her or not."

"Of course I know Grace Keller!" The Cardinal smiled, pleased at the mention of her name. "And I know this Maureen Sullivan as well. I was good friends with her father, Liam. We grew up together, for God's sake, down there in MacPatch. Your monsignor as well, though Tommy was well ahead of us in school. Liam should have been a Jesuit, but Peggy Keller fixed her cap for him, and he was a goner. They had eight kids. I do believe I baptized this Maureen. She was one of the last. She knows me, I'm sure."

"Yes, she does." The young priest hesitated, afraid the Cardinal would ask what Maureen had said about him. He was always curious about what the public thought of him, his popularity in the parishes.

"Is she still at Saints Peter and Paul?"

Jamie shook his head. "She's left the Church, she says."

The Cardinal snorted and leaned back in the the deep, soft chair. "Poor Liam, he must be turning in his grave."

"Well, aside from that, this Maureen hasn't turned out all that badly, your Eminence."

He had the Cardinal's full attention now, and nervously he went on.

"She's involved in MacPatch, working with all those old bag ladies and tramps at the Community Center. That's Christian action, don't you think—even if she doesn't attend Mass."

His Eminence raised his eyebrows. Slouched down in the soft leather, he kept his eyes on Jamie. "The board of that Community Center has been after me about opening up the old convent and school," His Eminence remarked. "Did Liam's daughter say anything about that?"

Jamie debated for a moment, then plunged ahead and restated all of Maureen's arguments. "What particularly struck me, Your Eminence, was her contempt for us. As far as she's concerned, the archdiocese has simply turned its back on the old and the poor." He did not ask anything directly, but knew that the Cardinal would hear the question in his voice.

"Lapsed Catholics," the Cardinal snapped. "They think they're so well informed and sophisticated. Does that girl have any idea of how much money this archdiocese puts into charities? Last year alone we looked after ten thousand families citywide." He raised his hand, as if holding off an attack. "Over sixty-one percent of my annual budget goes into charities, and that's not even counting the Catholic Relief Services or the Near East Welfare Association, or for that matter our schools, our hospitals, our churches!"

He shifted his large body and pointed back across the office toward his desk. "I just got the new five-year forecast from Budget and Finance and, Jamie, I'm telling you it's bleak." He shook his head. "There's a half dozen churches in the city that can't support themselves anymore, not even including you fellas at Saints Peter and Paul. We can't keep them all going.

Between ourselves, I'm closing Holy Child next fall. The city tells me the school building is unsafe, and we can't afford to upgrade it." The Cardinal sighed. "It doesn't matter, I guess. We don't have the children to fill the first three grades."

It was in moments like this, when the Cardinal was being candid, that Jamie caught a glimpse of the man's responsibility, the hundreds of thousands of people who depended on him to hold the archdiocese together, to keep the Church strong. A man like that would have no time for ghosts and shrouded figures, and no patience with any subordinate who did. Jamie realized then that he had wasted a trip uptown. He could never tell him.

"So you see, Jamie," the Cardinal went on, "when someone like this little smart-ass Sullivan girl comes along and says we're not doing enough . . . after all the work and money I've pumped into those neighborhoods. . . ."

"I'll tell her," Jamie answered quickly.

His Eminence waved off the suggestion, pulled himself up in his chair. "Ah, don't waste yourself arguing with the likes of her." Then he smiled. "And how's the work going? Can you get us out by the first of May? I promised those Moonies they could have the deed by the end of June."

"The books haven't really been kept up for some time," Jamie said carefully, not wanting to sound too critical. "And I'm having a little trouble with the Monsignor. He tends to get upset when he sees me sorting through the files." Jamie paused a moment, then said softly, "You have told him, haven't you? I mean, about closing down this spring?"

The Cardinal looked off. "I have, in a way. I haven't been blunt about it, because I didn't want to break his heart. Tommy's been at Saints Peter and Paul since my time down there as an assistant. He never wanted to leave MacPatch, even after the riots."

"Yes, I know, he's told me. Many times."

"I can imagine. Well, when you arrived there in October, your passport stamped with Rome and all, Tommy came to see me. The sight of the young face, I think, upset him. He thought he was being put out to pasture. The fact is, he should have retired ten years ago, but after the riots there wasn't much to do there, and I knew he wanted to stay. Even then, of course, it was clear we'd have to close the place one day.

Anyway, I told Tommy in so many words that changes had to be made—cuts in the overhead, that sort of thing. Adjustments. I said there were too many poor people in MacPatch and not enough parishioners putting their pennies in the plate on Sundays. He got the idea."

"I just don't want him to feel that I'm superseding him down there. I try to work on the books when he's not around, but since he hardly ever goes anywhere, that's not proving a very good system."

"Jamie, my boy, you're new to the life of authority, I realize, but you've got to learn that at times you have to step on a few toes. I'm surprised they don't teach a course in that in Rome." The Cardinal rose, tightening the cord of his cassock, and moved back toward his desk.

"It's one of the obligations of management," he went on, kept talking as he circled behind his massive desk. "I'm glad Tommy's giving you a bit of trouble, though. It's a good initiation for when things start heating up around here. As they will, of course." He smiled across the office at Jamie.

"You have something special planned, don't you?" Jamie asked, beginning to grin himself, falling victim to the Cardinal's teasing. He remembered coming home to the Residence on holidays from the seminary, and the pleasure His Eminence always took in keeping little secrets from him.

The Cardinal said nothing, just buzzed for his secretary to return, and winked his young visitor good-bye.

He couldn't keep his eyes off her. The cold night had brought out the color in her cheeks, and to Jamie she looked absolutely beautiful.

"You know," Maureen said, unwrapping her wool scarf to shake out her hair, "I've been walking past this rectory ever since I was a child, but I've never been inside before. I used to have fantasies about what it was like. And," she added, glancing about, "it's not really that forbidding. In fact, it's actually . . . charming."

"Well, thank you," he answered. "I can't really take credit, of course, since most of this was here since before I was born."

"How old is the house, actually?" Maureen took off her coat and shook the snow off the wet fur.

"About 1800, I think. Monsignor O'Toole knows for sure. The style of the house is basically Queen Anne, with a few Renaissance touches. There aren't many brownstones like this still standing in the city, especially down here by the river. Look!" He pushed back a sliding door to reveal the front parlor.

"My God, it's the twilight zone!" Maureen laughed, stepping inside.

"It's the black walnut," Jamie explained. "They loved those heavy dark woods."

"And gilded mirrors," Maureen said, nodding at the one over the fireplace. "Oh, and grape bunches carved into the wood." She kept smiling and shaking her head as she toured the room, spotting the carved wood molding that framed the doors and windows, and the elaborate plaster ornament in the center of the high ceiling.

"Why hasn't this house been kept up?" she blurted out, surprised by its shabbiness.

"No money, why else? Several years ago, though, the Cardinal offered to run a special collection drive to renovate the place and the Monsignor said no. He claimed the old house wasn't that far gone yet, and if the Cardinal wanted to be fundraising all the time he ought to go be president of Notre Dame and leave everyone else alone."

Maureen smiled. "Now I'm torn. This house deserves better, but I do love to hear that someone sent the Cardinal packing."

"Well, O'Toole is feisty, all right. He's been at the Cathedral since after the war, first as a curate and then as pastor. And he grew up here, of course, and went to old Cathedral Prep, my alma mater." Jamie shrugged. "He thinks he's a king, and MacPatch is his kingdom. The other day he got all upset just because I was poking around in the basement. Mrs. Windmiller does the best she can, but he's difficult."

"Mrs. Windmiller is here?"

"Yes, she came this fall. Do you know her?"

"She was a friend of my mother's years ago. I should say hello."

"She's not here. She went over to Devotions with the Monsignor."

Maureen smiled wryly. "Mrs. Windmiller always was one for the Devotions."

"Like your aunt."

"Yes, like Aunt Grace. I guess at a certain age Devotions become a comfort."

"I'd say at any age."

Maureen glanced at him. She liked him least when he felt he had to play the dedicated young priest. She wanted to shake him up somehow, to tell him that he was smug in the way of people who have a lot of book learning and no experience.

"What is it?" Jamie asked, seeing her eyes flare up.

She shook her head. It wasn't worth the effort. She had learned long ago that priests thrived on disputation. "What about this man in the snow?" she asked. "The one I saw outside the Center."

"Well, I've been giving that whole thing some thought, and now—well, I'm not so sure I want to tell anyone else about it." He thought again of the night before: the face outside his bedroom, the glowing eye. . . . How could he ever explain all that to her?

"Least of all the police, who might tell the Monsignor you were siding with the Center. Well, as long as that's clear, I may as well be going." She reached for her purse.

"Wait!" His arms shot out as if to restrain her.

She paused, then looked him over, held him at bay with her green, evaluating eyes.

"What is it, Father?" she asked.

"Please call me Jamie," he said. "That's what you called me two nights ago, when you weren't feeling so hostile."

"All right, Jamie, tell me. Why have you decided to keep quiet about what you saw?" She sat back and relaxed, showing him that he had her full attention.

"It's a long story, I guess, but . . . well, I meditate. As a way of praying. This is all rather new in the Church, in America, at least, but a lot of the younger priests do it. We think it's a way of really getting closer to God."

"Thomas Merton," Maureen offered.

"Yes!" Jamie brightened, seeing that she understood. "It was Merton, and some others, like Sister Suzanne Zawalich, a Belgian nun, who made meditation respectable in the West again. Up until about the sixteenth century, you see, priests and nuns had always meditated. But then came the Reformation, and the Counter-Reformation, and the Roman Church purged itself of a lot of old practices. Catholics came to think that meditation was strictly for Buddhists and other weirdos. It's only twenty years ago that Merton began to make contemplation popular again."

"So now it's very hip, very chic to meditate?"

For a moment he looked surprised at her attack, then hurt, then angry. He should have learned to hide his feelings by now, she thought, if not in the orphanage then in the seminary. But his emotions were displayed as if on billboards.

"I'm sorry," she said. "Please go on. Though I don't see any connection between Thomas Merton and this bum who looks like you."

"You will, I think. But let me tell you why I meditate. Not because it's fashionable—" Maureen glanced down, embarrassed—"but because I'm looking for something. Another monk, Hubert Van Zeller, wrote that it's only in solitude, prayer, and silence that a man can hope to see below the surface of things. That meditation is the only way for a person to find his true self. That's what I'm trying to do: find out who I am." He smiled awkwardly, not looking at her. "I mean, who I am in a spiritual sense." He paused, as if waiting for her next piece of sarcasm.

"I understand," she said, caught up in his intensity. Suddenly she felt close to the man, as if they were sharing an intimate moment.

"There's a special way of meditating," he went on, "that we call centering. The idea is to descend into your own deepest self and reach an awareness of God. It's usually done by repeating a single word—the name of Jesus, for example—loudly at first, then more softly, and more slowly, until finally you fall silent.

"I realize this might sound strange to you. It's not the kind of praying that the nuns taught us, is it? But if you can pull it off, this 'centering' prayer has a way of transcending the physical."

"What do you mean, exactly?" she asked.

"Well, sometimes it's taken me to what I call a fourth state of consciousness. I'm not awake; not asleep; not dreaming. It's something else—a fourth way of being.

"Lately, as I meditate more and more often, I find that I slip into this fourth state very easily, without having to concentrate very hard. And once I do, instead of falling silent I experience . . . events. And I don't know whether these events are really *real*, or something I'm experiencing on this subconscious, mystical journey."

"So what you're saying is, you're not sure you actually saw someone out there in the snow on Christmas morning?"

Jamie nodded. Now that he'd begun he wanted to tell her all of it—about the albino boy and his other trances; about the shrouded figure who also had his face—but he knew that would be a mistake. This was enough for now. He didn't want to frighten her away. And he didn't want to tell her while the trances and apparitions still terrified him.

"I understand now why you can't take this to the police," she said. "Is there anything else you'd like to tell me?"

"God, no," he said. "I'm sorry it took as long as it did. All this meditation stuff; what could be more boring."

"It isn't boring at all," she protested. "I mean, I'd like to know about . . . you." She stopped, surprised by her own admission.

"And I'd like to know about you, Maureen."

When he said her name the breath went out of her.

"There aren't many young people left in this parish," he went on, not wanting to upset her again about priests.

"Oh, I don't know, Aunt Grace is a bit of a swinger."

They both smiled, and he watched her: how just her presence brightened the room. It was partly the color of her clothes, he realized—her red wool sweater. But mostly it was the color of her face. In the front parlor, surrounded by the heavy drapes, the dark mahogany and damask furniture, she was a glowing candle. Her face shone. He found himself smiling simply at the sight of her.

Maureen reached down again and this time she did pick up her purse.

"Do you have to go?" He sounded disappointed.

"Devotions will be over and I shouldn't leave Aunt Grace waiting in the cold." She smiled and then glanced away, busied herself with bundling up.

"You haven't said what you think about the mystery tramp, my double," he said, following her to the door.

"I think Monsignor O'Toole is right. A vision." She smiled, to show she was joking, but she was the one who didn't want to talk about it. Father Ignatius could write off the bum in the snow if he wanted to, or put him down to a "fourth state" experience, but the man she'd seen outside the Center had been real. She was not one to have visions, she thought grimly, pulling on her gloves and opening the front door.

"It's time for you to start shoveling again, Father," she remarked. Another two inches of new snow had fallen on the stoop.

"Jamie," he reminded her.

Maureen looked up at him and their eyes met. This time neither of them turned away. The night was dark and only her profile was lit by the porch lamp. She seemed timeless, like a painting, a study in black and white and shadow. At the edges of his memory an image began to form, to float into the light of consciousness. He held his breath, tried to seize the fragment, to drag it into daylight as if it were a witness.

"All right," she said, ending the moment, "Jamie it is!" She nodded good-bye and set off, picking her way carefully down the stoop.

He watched her the length of the street, ignoring the cold and snow until she reached the parking lot safely, then disappeared.

He should have gone with her, Jamie thought. It wasn't safe this late at night. Still, he kept himself from grabbing a coat and chasing after her. Maureen wasn't one to appreciate protection.

In the front parlor he was surprised to find that he could smell her perfume. It hung in the warm air, the scent of flowers, of luxury, of a life unknown to him. He breathed in deeply, as if that way he might catch hold of her. As if that way she might release her hold on him.

This is wrong, he thought helplessly. He had already made his life's decision. His allegiance was given, and he was glad of it. As if to confirm that choice, he went into the office and back to work. He was preparing a list of questions for the pastor, regarding missing receipts, and the backlog of recent invoices on construction materials. As well as the paperwork on the parish car. Who had bought it and what had they paid? He would prove he could be the practical priest the Cardinal wanted him to be.

CHAPTER NINE

December Twenty-eighth, Night
Feast of the Holy Innocents

Grace Keller hunched her thin shoulders against the biting, bitter wind. Behind her, Clarence swung shut the heavy Cathedral doors and locked them. She stood alone on the top step searching for her niece. A few minutes before a dozen parishioners, all acquaintances of hers, had crowded the steps, and Mary O'Connor had stopped to ask, "Come along with us, Grace. Don't stand here. It's freezing cold and dangerous."

"Oh, I can't, Mary. Maureen will be along in a moment. Himself finished up a little early tonight." She smiled, but her eyes were tearing in the wind.

"At least he got it all straight tonight. Good Lord, half the time he doesn't seem to know what he's doing up there. The other evening, remember, he forgot this was Devotions, not Mass, and started reading a Gospel."

"Oh, Mary, you know the Monsignor loves his Devotions. He's been leading them as long as I can remember."

"Then he shouldn't be forgetting how it goes, now should he? Well, it doesn't matter. Come along; we'll be snowmen next if we stay here. Mark has his car at the corner."

"Really, Mary, I can't. Maureen is over at the rectory, seeing Father Jamie. She'll have a fit if she comes out and I've disappeared. Go along yourself, and say hello to Mark."

Grace waited alone. She stayed at the edge of the top step, in plain sight. If she stepped back, up against the church doors, she could shelter from the wind, but then Maureen might not see her. And she felt safer in the open. She could see the sidewalk and the dim streetlamps.

"Maureen Sullivan, now where are you girl?" She spoke out loud, just to hear a familiar voice. "You're just like your father. Always late."

She peered into the blinding snow, looked both ways along the avenue. There was no traffic at all on the street. The parishioners had left; even their tire tracks had been almost obliterated. Grace walked to the end of the high porch and looked around the corner of the Cathedral. There were cars on Church Drive but none of them was Maureen's. She could see lights in several of the brownstones and that cheered her up. She wasn't alone. That was the answer! She'd walk down to the rectory and find out what what had become of Maureen.

But the priest was probably counseling the girl, Grace reminded herself. Well, she wouldn't want to barge in on them. The priest would need time with that one, she thought, and smiled to herself. Well, she could stand a little cold weather if it meant he could make Maureen see reason. She offered up her suffering to the Blessed Virgin. A little extra grace never hurt, she knew.

Then Grace had a better idea. She would go around behind the church and find Maureen's car in the lot. It would be warmer inside the car, and Maureen would come there as soon as she left the Father.

Clutching the iron guard rail, Grace Keller carefully descended the stone steps of the Cathedral. The ice was treacherous and all she needed was to fall and break a bone. That was a constant fear of hers. But if she fell now, she'd freeze to death in the snow. "Maureen, you little twit, where are you?" she said aloud.

She followed the sidewalk down the north side of the Cathedral, toward the parking lot. The walk hadn't been shoveled and Grace had to struggle through some drifts. This was a shame, she thought, getting angry with the Monsignor herself now. The pastor had slowed down a lot, she knew. She could understand that, at his age. But couldn't he see that his people did their jobs?

Grace had almost reached the side door near the sacristy when the headlights pinned her. She halted, shielding her eyes, puzzled by the long, black automobile that had swung into the parking lot. And then she remembered what Maureen had told her, the stories of old bag ladies being snatched off the city streets.

"Maureen!" she said aloud, a small cry for help. Then she rushed for the sacristy door, fighting the drifting snow. The Monsignor might be there, she frantically thought, still changing from his vestments. Please, dear God, let him be there.

She turned the knob and pushed against the heavy wood. The door swung open. She was safe. Then someone grabbed her shoulder from behind. She swung out, tried to hit the man with her missal but a hand seized her mouth and she was muffled into silence.

Grace Keller could smell the dampness, the putrid odors. She opened her eyes and looked straight into the hanging light-bulb. Blinking, she tried to move. Her whole body hurt. She couldn't lift her arms. They had tied her down, left her to die in some damp place. She tried to turn her head, to see. She was lying on something slick and cold and she began to tremble, to cry out loud for her niece.

But it was her own fault, she knew. She should not have stayed in MacPatch, not after everyone had died or gone away. Oh, Lord, she had done this to herself. Going off on her own, being too independent

After Jimmy had died. Oh, Jimmy, if only you had lived. If only you had come back we would have married, had a family of our own. And the farm. You wanted that farm, remember? We had talked about it, moving out there once the war was over, once you had come home again.

"Maureen!" She called the name and heard it echo. Where in the world had they taken her? Oh, they wouldn't hurt her, not an old lady. It was just for fun, a game or something. Grace

Keller could hear voices coming, but they were muffled. Even so she felt better. She wasn't alone. They hadn't just abandoned her in this strange wet place.

"Help me, please?" she shouted. The approaching voices fell silent.

"Oh, Maureen, where are you, dear?" she began to sob in her misery. Her thoughts whirled without reason. Jimmy, you said you'd be careful and you weren't. You let them kill you right there at the very end, just when you should have lived. You had me, Jimmy, and didn't I love you like you wanted, even though we both knew it was a sin?

"Maureen, my child, help me, dear God!" Her voice echoed off the high ceiling, rang in her own ears.

"Now, Agnes, quiet there." The voice broke through her ranting. Calmed her. She looked back, tried to see. For a moment she thought of asking why they didn't even know her name, and then the pain jabbed her throat and she gasped, unable to speak, to whisper Jimmy's name, to ask God's forgiveness for her sins.

Jamie heard the doorbell as he came in the back entrance, his boots and jacket covered with snow. The chimes rang urgently, repeatedly, as if someone was in trouble, and he ran straight through to the foyer without even taking his coat off.

The curved windows of the front door distorted the image, but Jamie recognized who it was. Undoing the three locks, he threw the door open.

"I'm sorry," he said. "I was down the street, shoveling a car out for a neighbor, and I just got back."

"It's my aunt," Maureen exclaimed, leaning against the house as she panted. "I went to pick her up...I was late, I guess...now I can't find her anywhere." Maureen's face was raw from the cold.

"Have you asked the Monsignor?" Jamie asked, stepping out again into the cold.

"I can't get inside the Cathedral; it's locked." Maureen talked in a rush, hurrying him back to the church. "There aren't any cars left in the lot."

Ahead of them, Jamie could see Maureen's footsteps, in

the snow. He saw where she had circled the Cathedral, and how she had come back a second time to try the front doors. They went up to the front door, and Maureen pulled at the heavy iron ring that served as doorknob.

"See, it's locked!"

"I have keys," Jamie answered soothingly.

"But she can't be inside!" Maureen protested. "They wouldn't have locked up if she were inside."

"Clarence locks up immediately after Devotions. The Monsignor is afraid of the church being robbed."

". . . But he would have seen Aunt Grace!"

"Maybe not. It's a big church. She could have been off praying at one of the side altars." As he talked, Jamie unlocked the doors. He hoped he was right.

Without lights, the vast Cathedral was ominous. Maureen was too frightened to move beyond the entrance, to leave the scant light that penetrated from the doors they had left open.

"Wait here," Jamie said, whispering, "I'll turn on some lights." He sounded furtive, as if he were doing something illegal.

The Cathedral swallowed him at once. She saw his shadowy back moving up the aisle toward the altar, and then he was gone. Alone, she was even more afraid. The church was full of distorted shapes, flickering red vigil lights, and strange sounds. It was as if the empty Cathedral had its own life, was breathing deeply, laboring under the weight and age of old brick. Maureen felt the building press in on her, smothering her again in the mantle of the faith.

Stop self-dramatizing, she told herself; this old pile has no more power than you give it. Feeling better, she thought about Aunt Grace. The woman was always trying to get along on her own, to show Maureen she didn't need her. When Maureen hadn't appeared, perhaps Grace had tried to walk home.

Maureen had a momentary vision of the old woman struggling through the snow, and realized she had to leave for Pierce Street immediately. There was no time to waste. Afraid to go looking for Jamie, she called his name softly. There was no answer. She had to make a decision. She would leave for Pierce Street right away and ring the rectory later to let him know she was all right. Again she called, louder this time. When there was still no answer, she stepped purposefully from the vestibule into the darkness beyond, and into the arms of the waiting man.

She knew at once that he was smaller than she, thinner but stronger. His arms seized her about the waist, pinning her hands to her side, and drew her into an embrace.

She could feel his mouth at the nape of her neck, could feel his breath against her flesh. The man stank. Then the Cathedral lights blinked on and she saw her captor: a man with bad teeth and a day's growth of gray beard. He pulled her back into the vestibule but kept his fierce hold on her, his tiny eyes bright with pleasure.

In a sudden motion, Maureen raised her arms and broke his grip. Before he could recover, she raised her knee and caught him fully in the groin. He doubled over as, enraged, she swung her heavy shoulderbag, catching him flush on the side of the face. The man went sprawling.

He was old, she realized, over sixty, yet she couldn't stop herself from attacking. The rage and anxiety she had built up from living alone in the city, from always being on guard against strangers, burst out and she struck again, kicked him with her foot. The toe caught the man low in his stomach, sank into the softness of his abdomen. He slid across the floor, retching his dinner onto the marble.

"Maureen! Damn it, stop!"

She looked toward the altar and saw the young priest running, waving her off with his arms, and she backed away from the old man, thinking wildly: What is wrong here?

"It's Clarence," Jamie shouted, reaching the sexton, helping him to get up.

"Clarence?" she said faintly.

"The church sexton, Clarence Farrell. Who did you think he was?"

"He grabbed me in the dark. How was I to know?" She wheeled away from the priest, grabbed hold of a holy water font to steady herself.

There were tears in her eyes and she felt put upon, as if she had been falsely accused. Father Ignatius helped the weeping old man inside to a pew, speaking gently to him, and in spite of her own bewilderment, Maureen was touched by the kindness of the priest. She had not realized he could be so caring.

"I thought she was robbin' the church, Father," Clarence explained, gaining his voice. His accent was that of the city, the hard edge of someone raised by the river's edge.

"Of course you did, Clarence. It's all a mistake. I didn't think you'd be here, not with the lights off. It's my fault, really." He turned toward Maureen and saw that she too was crying. It hurt him physically to see her in tears.

"I'm sorry," he said quickly. "I didn't mean to yell at you." Jamie moved nearer and touched Maureen's arm. He could feel her shivering.

"Where's my aunt?" Maureen asked, pleading. "Make him tell you where my aunt is."

Jamie went back to the sexton. "Clarence, when you locked up the Cathedral, did you notice anyone waiting in the vestibule?"

The old man looked up, as if confused at the question. "No one's inside when I lock up," he said.

"Grace Keller?" Jamie prodded. "Do you know Grace Keller, Clarence?"

"Of course I do. We went to Saint Apollonius together. My big brother, he was in the same class with her." Clarence sat up, recovering, speaking as if he had everything under control. "I locked up like I always do after the Devotions. There wasn't anyone inside the church. I'd know that for sure. I watch out for those bums. They come out of the park, you know, Father, when it's cold like this. They smell up the church, if I let them hang around. I keep them all out." He flexed his shoulders, as if to show his resoluteness.

"Was Miss Keller with the Monsignor?" Jamie asked next.

The priest was endlessly patient with the old man, Maureen thought, asking questions as if he were dealing with a child, and then she realized the sexton was indeed retarded.

Oh, Lord, why was she standing here listening to this? He hadn't the slightest notion of what had happened to her aunt.

"Father Ignatius, I have to leave. Aunt Grace isn't here. I'm going to walk over to her house. Perhaps she went home with one of the other women. Lately she gets confused. Sometimes she forgets what we've agreed on. . . ." Maureen's voice faded away. She was thinking of Grace, of how old she had become within the last year. It had been like watching a family photograph fade before her eyes.

"I'll go with you," he volunteered.

"That's not necessary. It's only a few blocks. I'll telephone you when I get there."

"You'll be all right?"

"Father, I'm out on these streets every day of the week." She smiled briefly, kindly, to show she knew he was concerned. "Why don't you search a few blocks in the other direction?" she suggested. And then quickly, as if she wanted to get on with it, she picked up her bag and went out, striding across the marble to the north transept entrance, her boots striking the floor like gunshots.

"She's someone you know, Father?" the sexton asked.

"That's right, Clarence." It wasn't necessary to explain; it didn't matter to the old man. "We won't be bothering you again." Jamie smiled and patted the sexton on the back, tried to reassure him. "Once the vestibule has been cleaned up, you can lock the doors again and go home."

"I didn't do nothing wrong, did I, Father?" A new worry was reflected in his eyes and he cocked his head.

"No, Clarence, you did your job fine. Remember to turn the lights off, please."

Jamie left by the north door and started searching. He covered Church Drive, then went toward the park. As he'd expected, he saw no one, not even a set of fresh footprints. When he got back to the rectory the phone was ringing, and he picked up the office extension.

"Saints Peter and Paul. Father Ignatius."

"Jamie, I can't find her." The fear in Maureen's voice pressed against his ear like an ice cube. "I've called the police, and they, of course, know nothing."

"You're at her house?"

"Yes. I've also spoken to Mary O'Connor, her best friend. She saw Aunt Grace at Devotions. They talked on the steps afterward. Mary wanted Aunt Grace to go home with her but Aunt Grace said no, she had to wait for me or I'd worry. Oh, God, Jamie, what have I done? I've killed that poor woman,

I know." Now there were tears. Jamie could hear her turn away from the phone to sob.

"Maureen, we have friends at the police station, parishioners. I'll call. They'll get the force out tonight. I'll telephone His Eminence. He can get extra men assigned. If we search door-to-door, perhaps—"

"Search door-to-door? My aunt is seventy-three years old, Jamie. There's no way she could be alive out on those streets, or huddled in some doorway. My aunt is dead, Father. She's been murdered, just like all those other old people down here by the river." She was sneering now, mocking his good intentions. "She wasn't some shopping bag woman, but that doesn't matter. She was old, just like them, and someone killed her on the steps of your Cathedral."

"Maureen, please don't give up!" He was pleading, as if to someone suicidal. "You can't be sure she's dead. They haven't found her. Please hold on until I call the Cardinal." He spoke loudly, tried to be heard over her sobbing.

"You do that, Father Ignatius," she answered, still gasping with tears. "Call his Eminence and ask him some questions for me. Ask him why he doesn't do something about the tenements the Church owns, all those SRO apartments. Ask him why he evicted the Poor Clare nuns and closed down their shelter for old people. Ask your friend that, Jamie. Ask him why the old and poor aren't safe on the streets of Saints Peter and Paul!"

Jamie turned off the lights in the office and walked back through the house. He was too upset to sleep or meditate. He thought of getting dressed and going uptown to see Hanlon or McDonough. The idea of getting away from the rectory cheered him.

In the study he paused and impulsively picked up the remote switch for the television. The set blinked on without sound and Jamie spun through the channels, catching a few glimpses of basketball, a movie, a talk show, while searching for the weather report. After talking to Maureen he had called the police himself. No search could be mounted, the lieutenant had told him, until the storm was over.

It was too early for the news or weather. He settled on a

channel and saw they were showing a movie, a western. The camera was slowly panning across a river gorge, then the high rocky mesas of the far west. He kept watching, feeling the landscape before him, anticipating the next rocky plateau before the camera reached it. His ears were ringing. A sharp, shrill single note filled his eardrums, grew within his head. And now his body weight shifted. He lost sense of where he was and he felt as if he were effortlessly floating. The television image blurred and a bright burst of color filled the room. He was trembling, but he felt no fear.

The Apache Kid rolled over in the mud and vomited. He had been too many days at the *tulipi* party, had drunk too much *tiswin*, and now he could not stand. Pulling away from his own vomit, he turned over on his back. That slight movement left him nauseated and dizzy, and he could not at the moment remember where he was.

He was thinking only of his first raid, of how his father, Togo-de-Chuz, had taught him to run with his mouth full of water, so that he would learn to breathe through his nose. Air through the mouth made one thirsty, which in the desert meant death. He thought of his father and his heart ached.

The Kid stopped his memories and opened his eyes. He could hear the soft voices of women outside the smoky wickiup. The cloud of *tiswin* left his mind, and he thought: I have killed a man. Killed the bastard who killed my father.

He found his feet and shouted to the other scouts, ordering them to come, to ride back with him to San Carlos. It was time, he told them, to speak with Al Sieber.

The Chief of Indian Scouts pitched his tent below the Agency, away from the troops, and it was there that the Kid drew rein. Sergeant Toney was passing and the Kid stopped him, saying in English, "Tell the Chief I want to see him." The other Indians pulled up beside him, lowered their rifles across their ponies and waited. A crowd formed at once, Apaches carrying rifles, and troops: They made a half circle behind the scouts, stood back and waited quietly in the dying afternoon light.

"Where have you been?" Diaz asked the Kid, speaking in Apache. The Mexican spoke good Apache and good English so the Agency employed him as an interpreter, in spite of his well-known contempt for the Indians.

"We have been off and have killed a man at the Aravaipa," the Indian said.

"Sorry to hear that, Kid," the small Mexican sneered, then stepped back from the nervous ponies. "Guess you'll be sorry, too, when the Chief finishes with you. He's been out for two days looking."

"It is no matter of yours nor of the Chief's. It is our affair and no one else's." He said it flatly, in Apache, without emotion.

The Mexican grinned and nodded. "That may be, all right. It doesn't matter to me whether you kill ten Indians a day or a dozen. But now they say it's not an Indian you killed."

"Hello, Kid," Al Sieber said, pushing through the circle of bystanders. To Diaz he said nothing. He despised the man and would have run him off the Agency if he had not been needed as a translator. Sieber spoke only a few words of Apache, and though the Kid had learned some English, the other scouts knew nothing of the language.

"Hello." The Apache Kid did not look at the Chief of Scouts. He had pulled his black sombrero down so Sieber could not see his eyes.

For a moment Sieber stood quietly, watching. He had known the Apache Kid for eight years, since he had found the young brave near the town of Globe. He had taught the boy English, brought him into the Army as a cook. He had raised his army rank to sergeant after the Big Dry Wash fight, then to first sergeant when they both had gone to Mexico with General Crook in '83. There wasn't an Apache scout in the Arizona Territory that Sieber knew better than the Kid, and now he realized he did not know the Kid at all.

"Get off that mount and give me your rifle," Sieber directed.

"Yes, Kid," Diaz said in Apache, knowing Sieber would not understand him. "Or will you tell the Chief that this is your affair and no one else's?"

Ignoring the Mexican, the Kid swung off his pony and handed over his rifle. The other scouts moved uneasily on their ponies, watching Diaz.

"Now your belt." Sieber took the rifle and laid it on a chair outside the tent flap. "All the others," he said, speaking to the line of Indian scouts. "Your rifles. Put them on this chair. And your belts."

Diaz translated the order, then, without being asked, he stepped forward and made a show of collecting the rifles.

"Sieber says that these will not be returned to you," he told the scouts in Apache, "until you have been punished for this killing."

"It is not we who have killed," one scout protested.

"You did not stop the Kid. You ride with him, don't you?" Diaz asked, silencing the scout.

It was quiet then before the tent, quiet in the whole Indian Agency. The silence made the ponies nervous and they backed up, dividing the crowd.

"Do you have anything to say, Kid?" Sieber asked in English.

"I am not educated like you and therefore can't say very well," the Kid began in his halting English. "God sent bad spirits in my heart, I think. You know that all people can't get along in the world. There are some good people and some bad people amongst them. I am not afraid to tell these things because I have not done very much harm. I killed only one man whose name is Rip, because he killed my father. That is all I have to say."

The Apache Kid stepped away from Sieber. His head still hurt from the *tiswin,* and he wanted only to sleep, to let the bad spirits leave him.

So it was a white man he had killed. Sieber shook his head. He couldn't believe he had been wrong about the Kid. The Indian before him was dressed like an other Sierra Blanca Apache: loose-fitting gray cotton shirt; short, loose trousers; black army boots. His hair was long and unbraided, held back from his black eyes with a strip of buckskin tied lightly around his forehead.

Yet the Kid wasn't just an Indian. Sieber had trained him, adopted him, practically. He had taught the boy how to use a firearm and how to sight a rifle. And already the Indian had saved his life, when they had gone after Geronimo in Mexico. But he wasn't a white man, Sieber reminded himself. An Indian couldn't be trusted. Even the Apache Kid, the best scout he had ever seen. Because of this killing there would be trouble again, between the Apaches and the army.

"All right, come with me," Sieber said, gesturing toward the Agency. Without waiting, he started up toward the army post. For a moment the Kid hesitated, then followed after.

"What of us?" one of the other scouts shouted after them.

The Apache Kid did not answer, nor did he know. He shook his head and kept walking up the hill.

"I'll tell you what will happen," Diaz said in Apache. He knew Sieber would be too easy on the Kid and he wanted to frighten the others. "You will be sent to Florida, just like the Chiricahuas who were shipped from Bowie Station. That is what will happen to you, to all of you, for riding with him!"

Hearing him, the Kid halted on the hillside and turned back.

"What is it, Kid? Diaz, what did you say to them?" Sieber asked, walking back to the tent and confronting the translator. When the Mexican did not answer, Sieber looked again at the Kid, in time to see the Indian signal the others to rush for their rifles.

Sieber reacted at once. Jumping forward, he shoved the Kid back with his left hand, then reached for the Scout's carbine.

"Look out, Chief," someone yelled, "they're going to shoot."

Sieber broke for the safety of the tent, throwing the carbine ahead of him through the open flap.

Shots were being fired. Two carbines went off, quickly, over Sieber's head as he dove forward, rolled inside. He grabbed his own rifle from beside his bed and kept moving, running for the back entrance to the tent. More shots were fired. The bullets tore through the canvas, punctured the tin ceiling.

By the time Sieber reached the back flap, the Kid had mounted up and was riding past the opening. Sieber shouted for him to stop, then fired a warning shot, but the Kid did not halt. Leaning low over his pony, he looked back and returned fire. The first slug caught Sieber, broke his leg and knocked him backward. The Chief tried to fire again, but the Kid blew the carbine from his hands, caught him a second and third time, then rode out of the Agency, leaving in a pool of blood the man he had called his friend.

• • •

The image faded, the memory drifted. Jamie felt his consciousness returning, felt the pricking sensation of his own skin. He was aware once more of his breathing. Of his life. He swallowed and his mouth was as dry as desert dust.

Then he shivered from the sudden cold of the study. The movie was over and the next show, a police drama, was on the air. The clock over the fireplace said five after ten. He had been in the study for over an hour. Unaware. Lost. Feeling the heat on his dark skin, feeling the powerful pony beneath him, as familiar as his own body. In the darkened room, he raised his hand, studying the palm as if to make sure of his own flesh. It was as if his body was another country and he was a stranger to himself.

CHAPTER TEN

December Twenty-ninth, Morning
Feast of Saint Thomas of Canterbury

"What do you think you've got here?" the detective asked Jamie. He was in his early fifties, a short, fat man, poorly dressed. His overweight was recent and his wardrobe had not caught up. His stomach spilled over his belt like a piecrust.

Jamie shook his head.

The detective made a fist, then opened his fingers wide. "You've got nothing. You've got a hysterical woman over there at the Community Center. One of those do-gooders. She lost her aunt. Okay. A tragedy, I know. If only she'd been on time. All that bullshit. Excuse me, Father." He shook his head.

"But then she starts with this conspiracy stuff. And she's got nothing. A couple of tramps, old bums disappearing. Believe me, it happens every winter. I'm telling you the truth, Father. You've got nothing."

"Her aunt wasn't nothing, Lieutenant." Jamie could feel his own anger building and he clenched his teeth. They were standing in the cold entranceway of the rectory, between the two sets of cut-glass doors.

The detective sighed, looked martyred. "Look, Father, that

woman is in the city somewhere. She was an old lady; her mind went. The niece said as much. She probably got on a bus last night and went uptown. She's probably wandering around someplace, maybe out in the suburbs. She'll turn up. We got the word out to all the precincts." He made it sound reasonable, even routine.

"Maureen Sullivan says it fits a pattern. Elderly people have been disappearing—and more than a few." Although privately he agreed with the detective, he found himself pressing Maureen's argument.

The man waved his hand in dismissal. "Sullivan! The girl's got her old man's imagination." He hitched up his pants, tried to stuff his white shirt back into his trousers. "We'll find the old lady, Father, don't you worry. Maybe she's out in one of the malls, you know, wandering around. If she looks presentable they won't say anything to her. We've got a one-three-six out on her now. She'll turn up."

Jamie could see the detective was not going to accept any new interpretations of the case, not now anyway. "Well, thanks for coming by, Lieutenant," he said, trying to sound appreciative.

"Call me Matty, Father. Everyone does. Matty Joyce. I'm not a big one for titles. And how's His Eminence, Father?" The detective talked as he buttoned up his overcoat. He was missing two buttons.

"I know the Cardinal myself, you know. We met when I lived down here in MacPatch. I was in uniform then, Father. This was my first precinct. We used to walk a beat then, in them times. It was me, Father, that the Cardinal called."

"Called when?" Jamie put his hands in his pockets, trying to keep warm until the bundled-up detective decided to stop chatting and leave.

"That night, Father. When we found you on the church steps."

"Oh!" Jamie smiled automatically, as he had learned to do. Through the years he occasionally met people who had been part of that night, or had cared for him as an infant. Although there was no way he could remember them, they all looked at him expectantly, and Jamie never knew what to say. Did they all feel somehow responsible for his life?

Now, to Matty Joyce, he said, "I guess I should thank you."

Again the wave of dismissal. Then the detective moved closer. "Tell His Eminence that Matty Joyce is working this case." And then he winked, opened the storm door and stepped outside. Jamie had not shoveled and the detective's boots tramped down the snow on the top step.

"Lieutenant . . ."

"Matty, Father. Nothing highfalutin'."

"Regardless of whether she eventually . . . turns up, I think the parishioners are upset about Miss Keller just disappearing. The old people especially, and they, as you must know, are really the main constituency of Saints Peter and Paul."

"Don't worry about a thing, Father. I'm asking the precinct captain to beef up the patrol around the Cathedral, especially during Devotion hours." He flexed his shoulders. "And my partner—he's out today with the flu, but Bobby, Bobby Murphy will be around to get everyone's statement." The detective grinned. "It's a formality; you know."

"Thank you, Lieutenant. You've been very helpful." Jamie tried to keep his smile from looking forced.

The detective waved good-naturedly as he walked toward his car. "Remember now, tell the Cardinal. Tell him you talked to Matty." He paused at the car, his hand already on the door, and shouted back, "Tell him Stinko is on the case. He'll get a kick out of that." The fat detective laughed at his own childhood nickname.

Jamie stepped back quickly into the warmth of the foyer. The cold ran up his spine, and he shivered as he clapped his hands to warm them. They all want to be remembered to the Cardinal, Jamie thought; they all want a bit of recognition. And His Eminence would come through. He'd ponder the name for a moment, work it around his memory like a sliver of glass. His mind was jammed with such information, but he could always retrieve it. Like a politician, he used names and past associations like hard currency.

Jamie glanced at the wall clock. Time to dress for the trip uptown. Time to see His Eminence and tell him about the disappearance. He swung around the first floor newel post and climbed slowly to the third floor. He wasn't looking forward to telling the story.

Opening the bedroom door, he stepped into his small monastic world. The bare, white-walled room. His few possessions. Again he took a certain pride in how little he owned. The way of Christ, he thought, forsaking the world's goods. He pulled his black cassock up over his shoulders and as he did his eyes caught the Duccio.

He felt the chilly wind off the valley, smelled the eucalyptus trees. There was a crowd coming. Oil lamps burned in the distance, came down from the walled city. And he knew. He heard the soldiers, the babbling mob. He knew. They were coming for him. What would he do?

The image faded. He was shivering in the small white room, his skin burning as if with fever. He grabbed the corner of his desk and took several quick, deep breaths. His heart kept racing, all out of control. It was over, he told himself. He was James Ignatius, a priest in MacPatch. He changed his clothes without ever letting his eyes return to the Duccio.

"Matty Joyce . . . Stinko Joyce!" The Cardinal gave a satisfied nod. "A good man, Matty. We don't have to worry then, not with Matty looking for her." The Cardinal sat on a corner of his massive desk. He was wearing a custom-made black suit that had been tailored to undertake his large frame.

For a moment he seemed to ponder the problem. Then, abruptly, he stood, changing the subject, putting the disappearance of Grace Keller behind him.

"Look here, Jamie!" he said excitedly. "Look here!"

Going around behind the desk, he unrolled a set of architectural drawings, pinning down the corners with a paperweight and books.

Jamie glanced at the legend on the artist's renderings. "Saint Monica's . . . What is it, Your Eminence?"

"A brand new parish, Jamie. We're breaking ground in May. The governor is coming. I promised him two tickets to the Notre Dame–USC game." He tapped the sketch. "It's a beauty, isn't it?"

"I thought the archdiocese was facing bankruptcy." There was no sarcasm in Jamie's voice. He simply didn't understand.

"We don't have to worry about Saint Monica's losing money. I spoke to the Senator's office on Friday. The Pentagon is about to award Wenzel Brothers another contract. An experimental solar defense system. That means they'll be expanding by next fall, transferring management and engineers from their California plant."

Again the Cardinal tapped the drawings. "Saint Monica will go into the Thompson–Berlew development in Country Club Hills. Those families coming in from Santa Ana and Anaheim will be buying houses there, and they're used to new facilities. A place of worship where they don't have to worry about rats running across the pews."

His Eminence looked across at Jamie. "What do you think, son?" His smile was broad, expectant.

Jamie shook his head, stalling for time. "Spectacular," he replied, not looking up. The new church, he thought, looked like an airport terminal.

The Cardinal leaned over the desk. "It's going to be the finest church in the archdiocese. A real revenue-producer." He stood up, tucked in his red sash. "And next fall, I know who the new pastor at Saint Monica's will be. We need a young man who can work with those new families. A young priest with fresh ideas."

The Cardinal rolled up the plans again, then pushed them to one side. He wanted to wrap it up now, Jamie knew, then get on to his next appointment.

"Well, son, how about it? Hilda Windmiller will need a parish after we close the Cathedral. What about taking her with you? She'd love it out there in Country Club Hills." He waited, still smiling, expecting Jamie to reply.

"Your Eminence, you know I'll go where I am assigned. It's my duty, and my wish, but. . . ." This would be difficult, Jamie realized. He had never disagreed with the Cardinal before, but this new proposal stunned him. He felt as if he had been hit with flak. He was too young. It wasn't what he wanted. "I really don't think I'll be able to wrap things up at the Cathedral until late spring."

"Fine! Fine! No problem. We haven't even broken ground yet, remember? The summer is plenty of time for you to come aboard."

"Your Eminence, this is very flattering, but am I the right man for that parish? I'm not at all experienced—"

"You've had a year with O'Toole, and you more or less run things, isn't that the truth? You've learned the ropes; you know what it's like to be in charge."

"Your Eminence..." Jamie took a deep breath. "It's just that I don't want to be a pastor. I don't want to start dealing with a Holy Name Society, and running bingo, and managing a convent full of nuns." He shook his head. "That's for an older man, someone more settled in the system, I should think." He looked as if he were in pain.

The Cardinal laughed, the deep, rolling roar of a big man. Stepping around the desk, he slapped Jamie on the back. "Of course it is, and I'm damn glad to hear you say it. I didn't send you off to Rome for years so you could babysit some church out in the boonies. I've another thought in mind, a much bigger project, and I want you to head up the executive committee."

Jamie stared at the Cardinal. He couldn't imagine what was coming next.

"A national effort, Jamie," His Eminence whispered, smiling. "A new venture. The Confraternity of Catholic Principles. A Roman Catholic response to the Moral Majority, with a cable network all its own." He began to pace the office, speaking quickly, explaining.

"There's no reason why those Protestants should be carrying the banner of righteousness in this country. Not while I'm around, anyway. And this will be easy to organize.

"We begin with the Catholic societies that already exist—Legion of Mary, Holy Name, etcetera. We can also bring in some women's clubs, bowling groups, small outfits like that. Then we go for the Knights of Columbus. They'll be a little tough, those fellas. Mostly because they didn't think of CCP themselves. But it's sound, Jamie. That's the beauty of it. Good Catholics across this country want something like this—a focal point for their anger and outrage at the world we live in, all this media crap we're being forced to swallow. And TV is the place to fight them. You turn on the set today and there's some slick guy from New York or California selling you something, or trying to corrupt your mind with garbage. If you can get five or six million Roman Catholics boycotting these trashy movies, TV programs, newspapers, and what have you, we'll make them sit up and pay attention."

He stopped pacing and stood before the younger priest, looking him in the eye. "I'm counting on you, Jamie," he said firmly. "I'll appear on the tube and supply the spiritual direction. The on-air talent, so to speak. But I need a first-class executive director. A good friend, a priest I can trust, turn to, and who can develop the CCP into a strong national organization, a powerful lobby in Washington. We'll drive the Moral Majority back to the Bible Belt."

Jamie smiled and nodded, then eased away, taking one of the leather chairs near the coffee table.

"It's very ambitious, your Eminence. But won't it be expensive? Staff, computer, direct mail, all that. Not to mention the cost of the cable. How do we pay for it—from Saint Monica's collection plate?"

"Fat chance," the Cardinal laughed. "No, we'll sell real estate. Besides the Cathedral buildings, there are at least six other inner city churches that should go. We won't dump them all on the market at once, of course. But over time, we'll divest." He took the chair opposite Jamie. Even seated, he still dominated the office.

"But, Your Eminence, those parishes' schools are full. Not the Cathedral's, of course, but they're turning kids away at Saint James and Trinity."

"Not Catholic kids!" The Cardinal's voice rose, turned angry. "Those grammar schools are full of blacks and poor whites from Appalachia, those West Virginia people living near Grant Park." The big man shook his head. "Look at the figures, Jamie. I have. Less than sixteen percent of our grammar school students are Catholics.

"Sure the schools are full They're full because the parents downtown won't send their kids to public school. But that's not our responsibility; that's the mayor's!" His thick palm swept through the air, as if to show he wanted the whole issue cleaned away.

"Those parishes are tearing us apart, and even their pastors know it. Ask Joe Branch at Trinity. He wants out of there. Not every pastor is like your Tommy O'Toole."

The Cardinal paused, smiling now, amused. "I called Tommy today and he gave me this long song and dance about how attendance was up last Sunday. Of course, he didn't want to say how much, but when I pressed him, it turned out to be 'two hundred or thereabouts.' That's for all four Masses! Jamie, my boy, that Cathedral holds a thousand, and in my day you couldn't get in the door for the twelve o'clock. The man's a fool, Jamie. He won't give up. When the time comes we're going to have to drag him from the altar."

The Cardinal returned to his desk, dropped into his thick-cushioned chair.

"According to my projections," he continued, jotting down a note with his Mont Blanc fountain pen, "we should be able to announce the Confraternity of Catholic Principles next fall. By then—thanks to your hard work—we'll have generated enough capital." He stopped abruptly and looked at Jamie.

"You see the simple beauty of this, don't you, son? By using cable, we go directly into the homes of Catholics. We bypass all those priests and bishops across the country. Virtually overnight I can create a national effort, without having to massage a lot of egos who, you can bet, would want a percentage if I went through their diocesan structures."

He tipped back again in the big soft chair. "And what am I selling?" He smiled. "Nothing really. Just fundamental Catholic principles. The basic stuff we all were raised on, all of us who were fortunate enough to be around before the Vatican Council. And on Sundays, I'll offer a Latin Mass on cable." Grinning, he slammed his fist on the desk top. "That alone is worth two million subscribers."

"And you're the fella I need most of all, Jamie." The Cardinal pointed the fountain pen at the priest. "As you say we can't buy a cable network with indulgences. Once this damn weather breaks, I'd like you to start getting around town more. Drop into Trinity, for example, and look over their books. Then Saint James. I'll call ahead for you, clear the way, so to speak, but let's work out a schedule of closings. I'd like to be out of downtown no later than fiscal year '85."

"But Your Eminence . . ." Jamie spoke nervously, intimidated by the breadth of the plan and the Cardinal's enthusiasm for it. "What will happen to the Catholics who are still down there? When it was just the Cathedral closing, I assumed the parishioners could go over to Trinity, or some other downtown church. But now . . ." He shook his head. "Where will they go to Mass on Sunday?"

The Cardinal shrugged. "There's a bus service, Jamie. A train system. They can come uptown or cross the river to Spring Valley." He raised his hand, motioned for the young priest to remain silent. "Now I won't hear any more of this. Those people should have been smart enough years ago to get the hell out of MacPatch. I can't—I won't!—maintain a lot of big, drafty churches for a handful of diehards. They just have to move with the times. As I am!" He pounded the desk top.

"Cable networks aren't going to be up for grabs indefinitely, you know. We've got to move now. And it will work. I can see it already: a good Catholic family somewhere out on the farm, too far from any church, all gathering around a TV, one of those giant Sony screens they have now in bars for football games. That family will see and hear a Latin Mass broadcast from right here in our Chancery. We can make this city the new Jerusalem of America, Jamie. So don't talk to me about a handful of slumdwellers. In the grand scheme of things, they're not important. We have more important work to achieve."

He lowered his voice, appealed again to Jamie.

"Now, can I count on you, son?" He made it a question, but the answer he expected was clear.

"I'd like to think it over, Your Eminence. Pray about it."

The Cardinal raised his eyebrows. "You surprise me, Father Ignatius. When you wanted no part of Saint Monica's, I thought you understood. It's an electronic age we're in. If we don't bring the Church into it now, then we won't have a church at all in fifty years. We'll be back to the catacombs, a handful of true believers meeting in a hole in the ground."

Jamie did understand. The CCP was an enormous, big-league project. It would cap the Cardinal's career and he wanted Jamie to help, to share the most exciting challenge of his life. He would be angry if Jamie refused, but even worse, he would be wounded.

Jamie owed it to him, he realized. The Cardinal had taken

care of him all his life. Now it was Jamie's turn to repay some of that kindness. It was time for Jamie to think not of himself, his desires, but the Cardinal's hopes.

Jamie reached out to take the Cardinal's hand, to kiss his ring and show his submission to His Eminence's wishes, and the Cardinal, smiling, clasped Jamie's hand in his.

"Fine! Fine!" The Cardinal was delighted, smiling. "Now let's get to work." He came around his desk and began walking toward the door with Jamie.

"I'll get on the phone with Joe Branch about opening Trinity's books. And Pat Partin at Saint James. Call me tomorrow and I'll give you the lineup."

As they reached the front doors of the Chancery the Cardinal's secretary and chauffeur materialized from nowhere. The Cardinal did not acknowledge them, just beamed at Jamie as he slipped his arms into the overcoat the monsignor held up for him.

"I'm passing you the ball on this one, Father. You're smart. You're ready. I know you can run with it."

And then he was gone, out the doors and down the wide curving steps of the Chancery, off to his limousine for another meeting. From the doorway Jamie watched as the Cardinal descended. His footsteps on the marble sounded light and snappy, like a Broadway tune.

CHAPTER ELEVEN

December Twenty-ninth, Evening
Feast of Saint Thomas of Canterbury

"And now do you believe me?" Maureen asked. Her voice was like a knife moving slowly across his open palm. "We were right about old people disappearing. Whatever you say about the street people, you know Aunt Grace didn't go south to a warmer city."

"Yes, we know that much," Jamie admitted. He had come to her apartment to offer comfort, but that wasn't what she seemed to want. "This detective may be right, though. She could be dazed somewhere, wandering around an empty shopping center."

"She's been missing since last night, Jamie. My whole family—all my brothers and sisters, and friends of theirs and mine—have spent eight or ten hours searching. She isn't alive. Not now. Not in MacPatch. Your Altar Boys got her—or someone else did."

Maureen looked away. She was sitting on a cushioned bench built over the radiator in her kitchen. She looked haggard, as if she hadn't slept, and her ebullient self-assurance was missing.

She seemed like a different woman from the one he had met on Christmas Day.

Yet in the warmth of the kitchen, wearing jeans and a man's blue cotton shirt, with her black hair down and her feet bare, she looked younger, and to Jamie, more beautiful.

"If you knew these people as I do, you'd help me," she said, raising her head to look at him directly. "You think they're out of it, that they don't have any idea what's happening, and that's simply not true. They may not remember it all at once, but the pieces come floating back. They know."

"I believe you, Maureen," he said uncomfortably. "But that's not the point. They tell you their friends are gone, yet they can't say what has happened to them. We can't find any bodies. That's why I don't buy a conspiracy."

"Tony remembered what happened. I told you this already—how an old man, Tony, came in and told me his friend Joe was gone? Well, he was frantic. He hardly ever comes to the Center, but in the last several days he's been in a half dozen times. And each time he comes, he asks me if I've seen Joe.

"Well, one of those times he mumbled something about a car, and how he shouldn't have run away and left Joe like that. I asked him what he meant, but he just rambled on. The next day, though, he remembered some more about it.

"He and Joe were going into the park with a bottle of wine Joe had just bought—"

"Where do they get this money for liquor?"

"Panhandling. Or maybe someone just gave him money out of kindness, thinking he'd buy food. At times they will, but mostly they just buy booze." Maureen spoke matter-of-factly. She didn't criticize or condone her clients; she just accepted them as they were.

"Anyway, he and Tony were just at the park entrance, the one with the gothic gates, when a car pulled up and a man called them over.

"Tony was frightened and he didn't want to go, but Joe did. The car was black and you couldn't see in the windows, Tony said. He ran into the park alone and hid in the bushes. He didn't come out again till he heard the car pull away, and when he did, Joe was gone."

"Maureen, that's not any kind of proof," Jamie answered,

trying to be gentle. "Maybe the driver just gave Joe a few bucks and he took off to spend it."

"No." Maureen shook her head firmly. "First of all, the park block is very long. Tony doesn't move fast, but there's no way Joe could have been out of sight before Tony got back to the gate. And there was the bottle. Tony remembered that: the bottle of wine was smashed against the curb. Joe never would have done that."

She looked at the priest expectantly. She wanted him to acknowledge her evidence, to join her, but he couldn't. Instead he said neutrally, "Maybe you should tell this story to the police."

She snorted. "I did. Matty Joyce was very patronizing. I think he subscribes to the raging hormone theory of female behavior. Besides, if I'm right, that means problems and Matty Joyce doesn't like problems—unless they involve a payoff for him. And that's why I need you, Jamie. The police won't take this seriously but you've got credibility. They can't just shrug off someone from the Cathedral."

It wasn't fair, Jamie thought. She trusted him, was counting on him to be different, to respect her people. But the Cardinal had drawn the line and he couldn't cross it.

"I'd be glad to help, Maureen," he began. "But I'm not sure how much I can do. I just learned I'll be spending more time uptown, at the Chancery. The Cardinal has this plan—"

"Fine!" She didn't let him finish. "The Cardinal's plans don't interest me."

"I'm sorry, Maureen."

She shook her head and sighed. "It's not your fault, Jamie." She felt sorry for the young priest. He had no life of his own, only what the Cardinal decided for him. He could not have saved Aunt Grace. Only she could have, by moving out of MacPatch and taking Grace with her. She bent her head and rested her cheek against her knees.

In the small apartment kitchen she was less than six feet away. If he stretched he could reach out and touch her bare feet, which were smooth and very white, the toes long and elegant. He wasn't used to watching women, but now he found himself alert, aware of details, like a painter, or a spy.

"I have big feet," she commented, seeing that he was staring.

"You have beautiful feet," he whispered. He tried to go on, to make a joke to ease the moment, when he saw that her eyes were wet and she was blinking rapidly.

"Maureen!" In two steps he had reached her and she allowed him the space beside her on the windowseat. When he touched her shoulder she buried her face in his black clerical shirt and sobbed.

Tentatively, Jamie wrapped her into his arms, pressed her against his chest. He could see their reflection in the window, see the long black sleeves of his shirt holding her. He felt her smallness, the fragility of her shoulders. Her long hair was soft in his hands and when he stroked the back of her head, his fingers moved as if across silk. He had never embraced a woman who wasn't old, and the strangeness of it, the excitement, left him breathless.

He tried to forget his feelings for her. Her sobbing was from deep inside and each one wrenched her body, as if a hand were reaching down, grabbing hold, and ripping out her insides. He stayed with her, held her tightly. When she had finally sobbed herself into exhaustion, she pulled away, saying quietly, "Thank you, Jamie."

She glanced up at him quickly. She could still feel her cheek pressed against his cheek, feel his heart pounding in her ear. Oh God, she thought, feeling a surge of guilt coming, like a tidal wave from far out at sea.

As if he sensed her thoughts he went to the kitchen table and sat down with his cup of coffee. The moment was gone. She was safe now. It had all taken place like a card trick and she wasn't really sure how it had been done, what had actually passed between them.

"What?" he whispered, noticing her smile.

She shook her head.

"You're feeling better?" he asked, finding nothing else to say. The intimacy had left him light-headed, as if he had been suddenly shot into space.

Again she nodded. She still sat perched on the radiator, watching him over her knees, hiding her full face.

"I guess I better go. It's getting late." He waited for her to object, and when she didn't, he stood up slowly, feeling foolish.

His leg bumped the leg of the table, spilling the coffee.

"I'm sorry!" He was too big, too awkward for the small kitchen, he thought, and in that instant he felt a chilly wind, smelled oil lamps burning. He reached out, as if to grasp his impressions and make them real.

"Jamie!" She jumped from the windowseat and took hold of him. "Are you all right?"

He nodded. "Yes, I'm okay. I think."

"What's the matter? Do you feel sick?"

He shook his head. "Do you remember what I told you about meditating? How I sometimes witnessed events . . . scenes from somewhere else?"

"Of course I remember. Is that what happened just now?"

"Yes, but not a real trance, just a flash. It's a scene I've been in before, though. It's always the same: I seem to be in an olive orchard. There's the smell of eucalyptus, and I can hear people coming toward me. It's cold and I can smell oil torches." Jamie shook his head and shrugged. Only then did they both realize she was holding his hand in both of hers, clutching it as if they were lovers.

"Sorry," she whispered, withdrawing her fingers.

"There have been others as well," he said, as if to hold her attention with his strange occurrences. In one of them I was an albino boy who became a slave catcher in Africa. One of the natives I was tracking turned out to be my twin. Nothing about it makes sense," he added helplessly.

"Of course not. Dreams don't, unless you're Freud." She smiled, hoping to make him feel better.

"Have you ever been in therapy?" he asked.

"Yes, at one time. It was very good—for me, at least."

"Maybe that's what I need."

"Have there been other . . . trances? Nightmares?"

Jamie nodded.

"Like what?" she asked, curious now, but then said, "Or is it too painful?"

"Yes, in some ways. What's upsetting is that, in these trances I always seem to act in inhuman ways. Why do I dream that— because that's how I'd really like to be?"

Because you feel guilty about what the Cardinal has you

doing, Maureen thought, but she did not say it aloud.

"Perhaps it would help you to talk about it," she said. "Relieve the pressure, so to speak."

She saw the fear in his eyes, but he sat down again at the table and she joined him.

"The first one really frightened me," he said, beginning slowly. "I had it when I first got back to MacPatch. I was some sort of medical person at Auschwitz, and I seemed to have the job of stripping women and shoving them into gas chambers. These trances are hard to explain. They're not like a drama, where you watch yourself do something. I'm doing it, not seeing it. I'm actually stripping the women. I can feel the clothes in my fingers. I can hear them screaming. . . .

"Then I'm watching them through a peephole. It takes about half a minute before they begin to fall, tumbling down on each other. Later I go into the chamber, and they are all dead. Smeared with their own excrement."

He stopped for a moment, too upset to speak. It was like living through the trance once more, remembering it all again.

"Is that the end?" Maureen probed.

"No. There's more . . . Another time I'm involved with some sort of experiment on a prisoner. I'm looking through the observation window of a decompression chamber, watching to see how long it takes for the man's lungs to rupture. He goes mad first, starts pulling out his hair, then tears at his face with his nails, as the pressure builds. Then he beats his head against the wall, screams, tries to stop the pressure against his eardrums . . . He died, too. They all die. . . ."

"There are others?"

Jamie nodded. "Tests in ice-water tanks. Freezing prisoners to see how long it would take to kill them. We wanted to find out how to save our soldiers in case their ships went down in the ocean, or up near the Arctic Circle. It was Himmler himself who suggested that we use women to warm up the test subjects, so we took prostitutes from the camp brothel and used them. It was a simple experiment, really."

His tone was changing, Maureen noticed. He had started to speak quickly, to snap off the words like a soldier in authority. "We found out soon that one woman warmed a frozen man faster than two women. I attributed this to the fact that with no one else present the woman's personal inhibitions were avoided and the woman clung more closely to the chilled person."

"And how many persons did you test, Doctor?" Maureen asked. The priest was sitting in the chair, agitated and impatient. Now she was frightened. The personality change was striking.

"Perhaps four hundred. But only eighty or ninety died of the freezing. Others, of course, died later, in other experiments."

"Died how?"

Jamie shrugged, looked off. He was trembling.

"We needed skulls. We had skulls of almost all the races, but not of the Jewish race, and now we had our opportunity. It was fairly simple. We killed them in the gas chambers with cyanide salts, then we had the fresh bodies. The first females I saw after the gas chamber were still warm. There were traces of blood about their noses and mouths, but they were perfect specimens."

"Please, stop," Maureen whispered. She could not listen any longer. She got up from the chair, as if to stop him by force. The young priest had come back to himself. His face was pale, his expression anguished. He looked like a man who was dying of guilt.

"See," he whispered, helpless himself.

"Oh, God," Maureen sank back into her chair. "Do you have to live through that often?"

"Not that one. Some of the others are just as bad, but some of them are more ambiguous."

"Did you read about those concentration camps somewhere? You might have been so affected by the stories that you suppressed them—and then later . . ." Maureen stopped. Jamie was shaking his head.

"You said you knew my story—how I was left by the Cathedral and grew up at the orphanage with the nuns." He smiled wryly. "Do you know what my first word was?"

Maureen shook her head, already fearful.

"Jew." Jamie shrugged. "Not Mommy, or even Sister, but Jew. The nuns couldn't explain that one. They talked about it for years afterward."

"I'll agree that was unusual. But it doesn't seem a very direct connection."

"Well, there were other things. Tae Kwon Do, for example."

"What do you mean?"

"I first became interested in martial arts back in the seminary. A group of us got a class going, but I was the best student, by far. The instructor couldn't believe the moves I made even during the first class."

"You were a natural. Lots of people pick up a sport exceptionally fast."

"No, it's more than that." He shook his head. "After a few classes I was better than the teacher. It seemed odd, but I didn't think that much about it till I got back here to MacPatch. In one of my first trances, I was an aristocrat in ancient Korea. My whole family was dedicated to protecting the king, and we passed the skill of Tae Kwon Do from one generation to the next among ourselves. My grandfather taught me my art.

"Well, in that trance I found myself running through the palace at night, from one dark interior to the next. I'm able to pass the palace guards, of course, because I was the Emperor's most trusted defender.

"But when I reach his bedroom—where he's alseep with one of his concubines—I assassinate them both, without a qualm. I can see the king's astonishment as I leap across the room, then I smash his face in with my bare foot.

"That's the end of the trance. But I come out of it knowing, somehow, that I escaped from the palace. But my whole family—grandfather, parents, brothers, and sisters—are put to death because I killed the king."

"Jamie, this is the same pattern as the Auschwitz trance. Tae Kwon Do is something you already know about. Your subconscious just appropriated it."

"I don't see it that way. I think the answer is reincarnation."

"Oh, Jamie, you don't believe that, do you?"

"Why not? You're studying life after death at the Center. Resuscitation, I think you called it."

"The phenomenon I'm concerned with—was concerned with—was near-death experience, not reincarnation. Do you really believe that you were a martial arts killer in ancient Korea, or a doctor doing experiments on Jews during the Second World War?"

"That I don't know. I don't know why I have *any* of these trances."

"But you can't believe in it. I mean, you're a priest."

Jamie was shaking his head. "The Church has no reason to condemn reincarnation; it's not in conflict with any Catholic dogma. Early Christians believed in the pre-existence of the soul. You went to Catholic school; remember Origen from religion class?"

She nodded. "Vaguely. A theologian of the first or second century."

"Right. He believed that all spirits were created blameless. Eventually man would sin, of course, but his soul would be punished through successive lives. By the time the world ended, every soul would have returned to its original perfection."

"You're leaving out one fact," Maureen said. "The reason I remember Origen is that he was excommunicated for being a heretic."

Jamie nodded, agreeing. "Yes, at the Fifth Ecumenical Council. But what no one remembers today is that the Pope— Vigilius—wasn't at that Council. The Byzantine emperor, Justinian, controlled the Church then and he was the one who condemned the teachings of Origen."

"Jamie, I can't debate you in theology. I don't know enough. But you can't pretend that the Church has ever accepted reincarnation. Or even tolerated it."

Jamie shrugged. "What's a heretic anyway? Just someone who is able to choose, rather than blindly believe. And what did Saint Paul write, in his first epistle to the Thessalonians? 'Test all things: Hold fast that which is good.' So maybe I'm a heretic. But I have to believe that my soul lived before. It's the only explanation that makes sense to me. I mean, I'm the one who has lived through these strange trances."

Maureen shook her head. "I'm too much a westerner to accept an idea like that."

"But it's a western idea, too! All the Transcendentalists were reincarnationists . . . Emerson, Thoreau, Hawthorne."

"They were Protestants," she answered, smiling.

Jamie burst out laughing. "Oh, well, in that case forget it. Those Protestants are such romantics, they'll believe anything."

"Very funny. The point we're arguing is that you, a Catholic priest, are not at liberty to believe it."

"But I am!" Jamie leaned forward eagerly. "All of us— Catholics, Protestants, Buddhists, Jews—we all instinctively believe two things. One: that the soul is real, and separate from the body. And two: that sometime in the future we will all be rewarded or punished in accordance with how we've behaved on earth. That's the basis of our morality, right? Well, the doctrine of transmigration satisfies, to some degree, both of those instinctive beliefs."

"All right! All right! Believe what you want. It's your soul." She smiled again, amused by his determination to win the argument.

"Then you'll help me?"

"Help you do what?"

"Find out who I am."

"How could I do that?"

"You've studied psychology. You've done research on afterlife."

"Jamie, I told you: Near-death experiences aren't what you are talking about."

"I realize that. But I want a scientific investigation into what I'm experiencing. I need someone to help me induce trances, to be there when I come out of one, and question me afterward."

"Jamie, I'm not qualified."

"Yes, you are. You're perfectly qualified. Anyone with training in clinical psychology knows how to hypnotize people."

"I don't hypnotize. I could put you into a light trance state. But I won't."

"You have to." He sat back. "What else am I going to do?"

"See someone else. A priest trained in psychology. There was a priest at my college, Father Tahney. He's a Jesuit who has his own psychiatric practice."

Jamie smiled. "I can't go to a priest. He'll think I'm crazy."

"You are crazy," Maureen replied, smiling back.

He looked at her. "Do you really think so?"

"No. Of course not."

"Then what are these trances? This life in the twilight zone?"

Maureen shrugged. "I have no idea."

"Aren't you even curious to find out?" He was smiling again, flirting almost.

"Curious, yes, but not interested. Jamie, I don't want to start messing around with your psyche."

"Mind or soul?"

"Come again?"

"Psyche. It means both: mind and soul."

"Mind. You can worry about your own soul." She glanced up at the clock on the kitchen wall. "Jamie, you'd better go. It's late."

"Do you mind my stopping by? I didn't mean to talk about myself all night."

"No, of course I don't mind." She smiled. "These are bad times, especially alone."

"No Michael DeSales to turn to?"

"That's right. No Michael DeSales. How did you know about him anyway?"

"Your Aunt Grace told me. She stopped me after Mass one morning, asked me to persuade you to move uptown so you could have a boyfriend again."

Maureen laughed, but Jamie could see her eyes misting over. She and Grace had looked out for each other, he thought. Now Grace wasn't there anymore.

"Do you ever see him at all?" he asked, to keep her talking. And also, he wanted to know.

Maureen shook her head. "It wasn't the kind of relationship that had an afterlife."

He saw on her face that the thought of Michael hurt her, dredged up too many memories. For a moment he was almost jealous of her pain. He had never let anyone mean that much to him. Probably no one ever would. A priest lived alone and died alone. That was a given.

"Thank you for stopping by," she said, walking with him to the door.

"They're predicting more snow tonight," Jamie said, trying to delay his departure with conversation. At the doorway he fussed with his parka, made a production of wrapping his scarf around his neck.

"Won't it ever stop?" Maureen asked. "We can't keep the Center warm as it is. Most of the residents spend the day wrapped up in blankets and they're still shivering from the cold."

Stepping into the hallway, Jamie felt the draft of wind, the outside world. He didn't want to leave the shelter of her apartment, the warmth of the rooms, the warmth of her. He thought of his room at the rectory, the bare white walls, the mat on the floor, the books stacked up on planks and bricks. He was portable in life, like a nomad. Until he met Maureen, he hadn't known how lonely he was.

"Into the cold," he said, pulling himself together.

"Thanks for stopping to check on me," she said. "I'm fine now."

Jamie nodded, slipped on his blue wool cap. Saying goodbye was a skill he had never learned.

"Call me," she asked, like a girl saying goodnight after a date, and closed the door. He started to leave, then stood a moment in the hallway, listening as she bolted the door, locked herself away for the night.

CHAPTER TWELVE

December Twenty-ninth, Night
Feast of Saint Thomas of Canterbury

Maureen poured herself a small glass of Irish Cream and took
it with her to the bathroom. Then she moved in her portable
TV so she could see it from the tub. She liked to watch the
news while she soaked in the bath before bed.

It was her nightly routine in winter, one of the luxuries she
had discovered since she had begun to live alone. She had
never had a chance to command her own space before—not
growing up in a houseful of kids, nor when she shared a house
at college with five other girls, nor with Michael.

Michael. She wished Jamie hadn't brought him up. Set her
off on her memories.

Maureen set the glass of Irish Cream on the wide shelf
behind the old-fashioned tub, and stripped. The oversized cotton shirt she pulled off without bothering to unbutton it. Then
she peeled off her jeans and stuffed them and the shirt into the
wicker hamper. It was full to overflowing and that depressed
her. It meant spending two hours in the drafty launderette on

LaClade where she always felt out of place, being the only young, white person there. She missed Michael then. He had always done their wash, sparing her the hassle of street dudes coming on to her.

She had always told Jamie she felt safe on the street, but she didn't really, not among people she didn't know by sight. And in the project off LaClade the faces were always changing. People moved in and out, rootless and homeless, and without work.

Naked now, she sprinkled bath soap into the hot water, then stepped in, eased herself down, submerging her long body. It was a short tub, without enough room to stretch out, but it was deep enough to make her feel safe and warm. The TV faced her silently. She had forgotten to turn it on, and now she was too lazy to climb out again and do it. She slid down into the tub, dipped her hand into the sudsy water and gently rubbed a bar of soap. She was remembering how Michael would come into the bathroom and wash her body gently, when from the next room she heard the rocking chair creak.

Her hand stopped in the warm water. The chair moved again, just once, as if someone was testing its balance, or brushing it as he walked past. She heard it creak again, then there was silence.

She held her breath. There were no footsteps. No other sound from the bedroom. The apartment was locked up, that she knew. She had checked both doors herself and made sure the chains were in place. She never undressed without making sure.

The footsteps made her heart jump. She heard them distinctly, several quick steps in a row, as if someone were crossing the bedroom. She knew the sound, had made it herself walking barefoot on the hardwood, and in that instant she realized what had happened.

Someone had gotten into the apartment during the day, when she had checked in at the Center. He had hidden there in the bedroom closet, back behind her summer things. Oh, dear God, he had been there all night, waiting for the priest to leave, hiding in the dark, waiting until now, until she had taken off her clothes. He had already seen her naked, seen her image reflected off the full-length mirror on the bathroom door.

He could hear her, would hear her step from the tub, and then come at her when she was still dripping wet, standing helpless on the bath mat. She made herself splash the water, as if she were still unaware of him, still bathing peacefully, while her eyes searched the small room for something sharp, something she could drive up and into his heart, killing him at once, before he could touch her.

There were cuticle scissors in the cabinet, small thin ones. She could conceal them in her palm, let him come close, embrace her, then plunge them in. He wouldn't think. He wouldn't suspect.

She stopped moving her hand in the tub. Her fear had chilled the water. She heard nothing now from the bedroom. He could have gone into the kitchen. He would feel safe now, would feel the apartment was his.

Maureen pulled herself up from the deep water, careful not to splash. The water sucked at her ankle as her foot cleared the bath. She did not look toward the open doorway. Her heart would stop, she knew, if she saw him standing there, watching her. It was safer not to look. Reaching back, she splashed the water again. If he were listening, he might think she was still in the tub.

She saw herself for a moment in the cabinet mirror. The terror had registered on her face. Her eyes were huge and her skin was aflame, as if she were not getting enough oxygen. She forced herself to take a breath, a short, shallow one. Then another. Her hands on the mirror were trembling. She wouldn't be able to pick up the scissors, much less control them.

With clumsy fingers she jabbed at the shelves, scattering all the little bottles and old lip glosses. They showered down onto the washbasin, spilling pills and tablets onto the tiles and into the tub.

Where were the scissors? She swept her hand across the top shelf, convinced it was too late. She felt him behind her, ready to seize her. Her fingers found the scissors and she spun about, the tiny blades poised to pierce his eyes.

The doorway was empty and the bedroom beyond was dark. The only light was the small patch cast on the floor by the bathroom. Maureen could see the end of the brass bed and not much more. But she had turned on the lamp at the head of the bed, she knew. She always did. She never slept in the dark.

Oh, dear God, she prayed. He was crazy. He did not want to just rape her. He wanted to make her suffer as well. Her knees buckled and she dropped to the bathroom floor, curled up on the small thick mat, arms now wrapped tightly around her body.

The footsteps again crossed the bedroom, moving erratically, as if he were not sure of where he wanted to hide. He was doing this on purpose, she decided. He realized she had heard; he was having fun with her fear.

She curled herself tighter on the mat. She would not let him see her naked. She would not just give herself to him. She could still fight, and knowing that gave her a surge of courage. She regripped the scissors, slipped her fingers into the eyes of the handle. All she had to do was take a swing and the blades would slash his face. He'd have to break her hand to disarm her.

Still she waited, huddled on the mat. He did not cross the bedroom again, or come toward her. She had tried to mark his progress, to remember where the last sound had been, but in the silence she had lost her bearings.

She waited. Listened. Her breath had stopped choking her. She could hear beyond the pounding of her own eardrums. Water was dripping slowly into the full bathtub. It made a slow steady plunk, as if falling from a great height. She could hear traffic from the street, an occasional car stopping at the corner light, then skidding on the icy intersection. Her upstairs neighbor was home. She heard the muffled sounds of his television set.

She could scream, Maureen realized. Her neighbor might hear her. He might come to help, or call the police. But the man would move fast if she screamed. He would have to kill her then, if only to stop her screaming. She'd be dead before they could break down the door.

The rocking chair moved again, only once. Then the springs of the mattress squeaked. He was sitting on the bed. That made her feel better; at least now she knew exactly where he was. Cautiously she rose from the mat and took a step toward the door. She would not cover herself with a towel. Let her nakedness be a weapon to distract him, to give her a moment longer to lunge.

But after the first step she could not force herself forward. She hadn't the courage to just step nude into the bedroom, as if unsuspecting. Again her knees weakened and she reached out to brace herself. She was in the doorway, her body framed in the bathroom light, when she saw him.

He was sitting on the mattress, waiting like an obedient child, his hands in his lap, and his head down. He did not look up when her figure blocked the bathroom light.

"Jamie," she whispered, still too frightened to understand. "Jamie, why did you come back?" From a hook in the bathroom she grabbed a white terrycloth robe and held it to her breast.

"Jamie, what do you want?" she asked, moving closer. He was dressed as he had been earlier, in jeans and a black collarless shirt, but now he was crying, and the face he raised to her was in torment. His suffering wrecked Maureen. The fear melted off her heart and she raised her hand in an ancient gesture of consolation.

In that moment his eyes met hers, beseeching her for something. Sinking down beside him, she took him in her arms and he clutched her as if he were about to drown. She felt the pressure of his body, felt his strong arms tighten about her.

Then his lips were on her neck, his breath hot behind her ear. The comfort they were sharing had turned to passion, and, frightened, Maureen broke his hold on her, jumped up, and spun around to confront him. But the bed was empty. The room was empty. He was gone.

"Jamie?" She said his name aloud, to reassure herself that he was real, that he was there with her. But he was not. He never had been there, she realized; at that moment Father James Ignatius was safe at home, with the Monsignor, on Church Drive. As that knowledge sank in she began to tremble.

She had imagined the footsteps, the creaking chair. She had imagined the figure on her bed, the sensation of his arms around her. She had sent the priest away, and her subconscious had called him back again.

Frantic now, she threw on her robe and rushed through the apartment, turning on lights, dispelling the darkness of every corner. Then she turned on the radio and spun the dial until she found an all-night call-in show. She needed voices, even those of cranks and insomniacs. For the next six hours, until early morning, she sat in the windowseat of the kitchen, listening to strangers rage about the unions, city snow removal, and Adolf Hitler.

He stood in the shadows of the train station, hidden among the long rows of lockers, and watched the clock over the information booth. At eleven the bathroom attendant went off duty. At eleven they'd begin to come out of hiding.

Already he had spotted a few of the women, hiding in the telephone booths near the locked newsstand. Another, an old man, had crawled under the wide wooden waiting room bench, made a bed of cardboard, and pulled under the seat with him his broken pieces of luggage, his shopping bags full of possessions.

For a moment he thought of starting immediately, of getting that dipsomaniac first, but that would have required some effort and strength. He'd have had to get down on the cold marble floor and coax the man from his shelter. Besides, the tramp was drunk, disoriented. He wouldn't be able to make him understand.

He glanced back at the clock. Eleven. Still he waited, a little anxious now, worried that something might go wrong. He kept scanning the vaulted station, watched for stragglers rushing to catch the last train out of the station, or neighborhood people cutting through the building on a short cut home. He couldn't be seen. He was too easy to recognize.

Two railway detectives came up from the tracks, locking the gates behind them. They were talking loudly, laughing. In the vast empty building their voices echoed, ran the length of the marble floor and bounced off the walls. He stepped back farther in his niche between the lockers, hiding like the street people, ducking the police.

The detectives kept moving, going, he knew, for a coffee break on the second floor of the station. He reached into his overcoat pocket and fingered the vial of chloroform.

The woman attendant came out of the bathroom, let the wide wooden doors bang behind her. She moved slowly, an old woman herself, heading for the bus stop beyond the station. Few lights were on in the building; she disappeared in the deep shadows. He waited, kept scanning the exits and entrances, alert to possible trouble.

The shopping bag women were picking up their belongings, heading for the lighted bathroom. They moved slowly, weighed down by their bundles. Also there was no need to hurry. The bathroom would be theirs until the morning, when the attendant came back on duty.

For the next few hours they were free to undress, to wash their clothes and bodies. They would dry themselves off with the hand dryers, then spread papers inside the cubicles and sleep curled up around the toilets until daybreak.

He waited, gave the women time to wash themselves, dry their hair, and get rid of the lice. He didn't like handling them when they were so filthy. It was bad enough having to touch them at all. Sometimes they were strong enough to resist, to give him trouble. He fingered the chloroform again. Then he took out his gloves and slipped them on. The gloves were unnecessary. He didn't worry about fingerprints, they would never matter, but he didn't like touching old flesh.

One last look. The huge station was silent, empty now. Stepping out from the lockers, he crossed the marble floor, hurrying as if for the last train. His footsteps tapped quickly, like a code.

He had done this before and knew what to expect when he barged into the bathroom, waving and shouting, raking his keys across the metal doors. The old women scattered in six directions, bolting past him back into the station. Like mice in a cupboard, he thought, they dashed for a hole in which to hide.

All but one. As always, there was one too old to escape, too disoriented to react. She rose from her bed of newspapers and held her ground, ranting unintelligibly and snarling like a trapped animal.

"There! There! Everything is all right, Agnes. Don't trouble yourself." He took the woman by the wrist, clamped his glove around her brittle bones.

She paused, cocked her head, took in the man's clothing, his benevolent smile. He could see what she was thinking: that she was all right. He wasn't a cop. He wouldn't bust her head.

She turned her face up to him and he saw the ulcerated skin, the bruised lips. The woman had been beaten recently. The sores would not heal.

"Come! Come!" he said gently, but she made a fuss, wanting her brown bags, the battered piece of luggage she had roped together with twine. He waited, helped her with the rag pile of belongings. There was no reason to use force. No need for the chloroform. She was one of those who came quietly.

He picked up one of her bags, hurrying her now; and grabbed her by the elbow. She was a short, squat old woman, bundled up in two overcoats, several sweaters, men's trousers. Her thick feet were stuffed into laceless men's shoes, but she could barely walk. The shoes were too small and her feet were swollen. She began to cry and complain as he rushed her across the marble but he ignored her protests. Holding her arm firmly he propelled her forward, rushing her from the station and out into the snow where the limousine waited on the deserted side street.

Toward morning Maureen went to bed. It was light enough for her to feel safe turning off all the lamps. As the heat began to rise the radiators hissed and clanked, and that familiar sound reassured her too. It told her that everything was back to normal.

She stretched out her body, cramped from the windowseat, and pulled the warm quilt up to her chin. She was exhausted, but even now she could not sleep. For hours she had dwelled on what she'd seen, reconstructing every moment and every detail. And she was sure now she hadn't imagined it. Yes, she was deeply shocked by Grace's disappearance—by Grace's death, she forced herself to think—but this was more than just a hysterical reaction.

Maureen glanced at the clock on her night table. Soon it would be late enough to call. She closed her eyes, wondering what Jamie would say when she told him where he'd been seen that night.

CHAPTER THIRTEEN

December Thirtieth, Morning
Feast of Saint Sabinus and Companions

Jamie's eyes were still closed as he picked up the receiver, catching the phone on its first ring.

"Hello?" His own voice woke him.

"Jamie!" Maureen sighed. "Thank God it's you. I was afraid I'd get the Monsignor. I'm sorry I'm calling so early, but I had to catch you before you left to say mass."

"Maureen, what's happened?" he asked. Her voice was unsteady and she was speaking in a rush. They must have found her aunt, he thought at once.

"Last night...after you left...." She began slowly, hesitantly. "I was taking a bath, and..."

As he listened, Jamie moved around his desk and dropped into the chair, propped his cold bare feet up against the window radiator. He looked out along Church Drive toward the end of the street and the vacant lots. The snow had stopped falling, and it was light enough for him to see several blocks west, toward the river. Jamie realized then that he had a clear view

143

across the empty fields to Maureen's brownstone apartment.

When she had finished speaking he was silent for a moment. "I don't understand," he said at last. "What's your interpretation of all that?"

"What's my interpretation? Christ, I was frightened out of my mind. I thought I was having some sort of psychotic episode because of worrying about Aunt Grace. But I wasn't. You were there! On my bed. I touched you."

"Maureen, I wasn't." He had to protest, feeling somehow violated by the accusation.

"Where did you go last night, when you left here?"

"I went home," he said immediately. "Where else? It was late."

"And what did you do?" she continued.

"I don't remember," he said irritably, adding, "And I have the right to call my lawyer."

"Did you meditate?" she asked.

"Yes, why?"

"And you reached this fourth level, the one you described to me?"

"Yes . . . but . . ." he answered slowly, seeing he was being cornered.

"And what happened?"

"Nothing. I mean, there was no trance. I didn't remember another life. That's usually the way, you know. I don't go into a trance every time I meditate."

"Well, there's got to be some connection, something to explain how you appeared last night."

"But how could I?" He watched the lighted windows of her apartment as if looking into her eyes. "Once I got home I didn't leave the rectory."

"Maybe you didn't have to. There's something called an energy field. I'm not sure how much you know in this area, but it's been documented. The Russians have done a great deal of research. All of us, all humans, project our feelings, our emotions. But some of us can do it much more powerfully, more tangibly, than others. For example, it is now thought that poltergeist phenomena—you know, objects flying around a room—are more likely to occur when young teenage boys are present. Their unresolved sexual energy creates an atmospheric charge in the room that causes the furniture to move, and glasses to break."

"But none of that has anything to do with me. Even in my past lives I haven't turned up as a furniture mover." He spoke lightly, trying to make her laugh.

"You were here," she repeated. "I saw you. You held me. I felt your heartbeat. I mention the poltergeists because I think there may be a connection between what happened last night and all that . . . suppressed sexuality of yours." She stopped. It had become too personal, too close to what she did not want to discuss.

"Are you afraid, Maureen?" He kept watching her apartment, sensing that she, too, was at the window, looking back across the empty lots.

"Yes, I'm afraid not to do something. This has to be resolved, Jamie, for your sake as well as mine."

"What might happen?"

"I don't know. Anything. You could hurt me."

"Maureen, this is going too far. If I have all the suppressed sexual feelings you say I have, then why would I hurt you?"

"Come on, Jamie, you know that answer. Even at Rocklands they must have taught you about sexual aggression."

For a moment Jamie did not respond. He knew what she meant but he was hurt by her suspicions. Then he simply repeated, "I won't hurt you."

"I believe you, Jamie. At least, I believe that that's how you feel."

"But?"

"But I'm not sure you're always in control."

"You mean I'm dangerous. Or I could be."

"Perhaps. As you said yesterday, all the trances you've experienced show you doing something evil, criminal."

"Maureen, that's enough," he interrupted. "You come up with some far-fetched psychedelic theory to prove that I was in your room last night when there's a much simpler answer. I didn't see you in *my* room. I didn't feel you in my arms. This is your fantasy, Maureen, not mine." His voice had risen in his anger and he stopped abruptly, afraid the Monsignor would hear him.

"I thought of that," she admitted. "I've had sexual fantasies before. Elaborate ones, in fact, with dialogue and great costumes and terrific settings. But, Jamie, I never went into a trance over one. I was always in control."

"So you're convinced it's me. Even if I agreed, which I don't, what would we do about it?"

"Just what you said yesterday: work on it. Together."

"You mean regression?"

"Yes. If you're suppressing something, that may be the way to bring it out. I'll put you into a light trance state, work you back in time, then try to let your subconscious release the recollections you experience. In the trance you won't be able to protect your ego, shield yourself from what's painful or embarrassing."

"Like sex," he noted.

"Yes. Or whatever. It may not happen all at once, in the first regression, but eventually we should learn something."

"Will I find out why I'm so attracted to you?" Jamie tried to say it lightly, but she didn't respond. "Well, Maureen, will I?" he pressed, now wanting to know.

After a moment she said quietly, "The regression may explain your feelings, Jamie, but not mine. Call me later."

The telephone clicked and disconnected and slowly Jamie replaced the receiver. His eyes did not leave her apartment building. He heard Mrs. Windmiller down in the kitchen, smelled the bacon she was frying for his breakfast. Then the scent turned bitter in his nostrils, and he knew there was wood burning on the wintry day. Eucalyptus, he thought; he knew the medicinal smell. And then Maureen's window was gone and he saw he was on a dusty path, moving uphill through an orchard of olive trees. His feet were in sandals. A woman was on the path above him. She turned to speak in anger. Her lovely face moved from shadows to torchlight and he knew he was in love with her. Then he was in the rectory again, staring across the lot to Benton Place. But the image lingered—her pale face framed by the stark and twisted winter olives—and he caught it, held it fast, like a possession.

The pastor's bedroom door was open. Jamie tried to pass it quickly, as if he thought the Monsignor was already down at breakfast, but O'Toole was in wait for him.

"Good morning, Jamie," he called, waving him into the bedroom. The pastor had built a blazing fire and pulled his chair right up beside it. The heat was stifling, and Jamie compromised by standing in the doorway.

"Good morning, Monsignor. I'm just on my way over to say the seven. I'm running a little late this morning," he added pointedly.

"Good, good," said the pastor absently. "Jamie, do you know what feast day this is?"

Jamie shook his head.

"The Feast of Saint Sabinus. Do you know Saint Sabinus, Jamie?"

"No, I'm afraid that one slipped by me." Jamie fidgeted in the doorway. He hated this, when O'Toole got him on some tangent.

"They aren't teaching the lives of the saints at Rocklands?" The Monsignor looked up from his book, sighting on Jamie over the top of his reading glasses.

"Since Vatican II I don't think they feel hagiography is quite as important."

The old man shook his head. "Pity. Well, I think you should pick this stuff up on your own. You can't tell when the lives of the saints will come in handy. They're a practical thing to know. You might find yourself on a quiz show or the like. And, naturally, they're an inspiration to us.

"There's a book I found recently, saw it advertised in the Sacred Heart Messenger. It's called *Families That Followed the Lord,* all about the lives of over one hundred and fifty brothers and sisters from all over the world who joined religious orders. I should make a note of it; it would make a good sermon, particularly during Catholic Family Week."

"I'd like to see that book myself, Monsignor." Jamie backed away from the doorway. "But I have to go now—seven o'clock already, you know."

"Wait a moment! Don't be in such a hurry. All you young fellas, rushing about, listening to no one. I want to read you this." The old priest flipped through the pages of the book. "It's about Saint Sabinus... 'In the year 303 the cruel edicts of Diocletian and Maximian against the Christians, were published. Whereupon the Governor of Umbria ordered that the hands of Sabinus be cut off; and his two Deacons, to be scourged, beaten with clubs, and torn with iron nails.'"

The old priest kept reading, holding the book at arm's length and peering down at it, as if suspicious of its contents. Jamie glanced at his watch. He was so late now it didn't matter. They ought to discontinue the early Mass anyway, he thought. It had been scheduled so that Catholic businessmen on their way uptown might stop off and receive Communion before work. Now there were no businessmen left in MacPatch and the early Mass was an anachronism.

The Monsignor looked up, finishing the account, and smiled. "The book is called *A Saint for Each Day*, Jamie." He held it up for inspection.

"I'd like to borrow it sometime," Jamie responded quickly, hoping to cut off the old man.

Monsignor O'Toole placed the book carefully on his night-stand and tapped it lightly. "It will be here when you need it. And when is your feast day, Jamie, by the way? We should have a small celebration."

"On May eleventh, Monsignor."

The old priest shook his head. "No, no, that's James the Less, first Bishop of Jerusalem. You were named after Saint James, brother of John, the son of Zebedee. I remember. There was a great to-do about it when you werre christened. The Cardinal insisted that you be named for James the Greater, the first of the twelve apostles to give his life for Christ. He was beheaded by Herod Agrippa, you know. And when he died, his body was miraculously transported from Jerusalem to Spain. Now his shrine at Zaraguza is a favorite of pilgrims all over the world."

The old priest tapped the book on his desk. "It's all here. Read it, Jamie; you should know your patron saint. I'll have Hilda make you a feast day cake. On July twenty-fifth. Angel food." He grinned at his small joke, then looked up at Jamie, as if suddenly surprised to see him. "Now what is it, Father? What do you want? You'll be late for morning Mass, son, hurry on now."

"Sorry, Monsignor." The old man's mind was cut off again,

but Jamie was relieved to be dismissed. "I better hurry." He waved good-by to the pastor, then bolted down the last flight of stairs. July twenty-fifth, he thought. He wouldn't be at the rectory in July, nor would the Monsignor, or Hilda. By then there would be no Saints Peter and Paul.

The black man was waiting when Jamie came off the altar into the cold, empty sacristy. He was a big man wearing a blue parka, and his hands were deep in his pockets. Jamie's step faltered and he glanced down at the solid gold chalice he was carrying. For a second he considered running back onto the altar and yelling for help. But before he could decide the black man spoke.

"Father Ignatius?" he asked.

Jamie nodded, too nervous to speak. The big man stirred and straightened. He was even taller than Jamie had first realized.

"Father Ignatius, my name is Robert Murphy. Detective Robert Murphy." He withdrew one hand from his pocket and displayed a gold badge. It was lost in his huge pink palm.

Jamie grinned with relief and embarrassment. "You gave me a start there. I mean, I'm not used to seeing anyone in here."

"Especially a black man big enough to play college center?" Robert Murphy smiled. He had watery brown eyes and a sad, sleepy expression. "When you're my size and color, you get a lot of peculiar reactions. I hope it's okay, my being in here." He glanced about the large room, taking in the walnut cabinets, the marble sinks. "I thought it might be against the rules, but your janitor said it was okay."

For a big man, Jamie thought, the detective had a softness, an innocence about him, and Jamie liked him at once.

"That was Clarence, our sexton. No, it's fine. No holy of holies back here." Jamie set down the chalice and slipped the chasuble over his head, then quickly took off the alb. Beneath the investments he was dressed in jeans and a Notre Dame sweat shirt.

Robert Murphy grinned. "That's quite a transformation. I guess I never thought priests wore, you know . . ."

"Street clothes?"

Murphy laughed. "Those are not what I'd call street clothes. Not down here."

"What are they, then?" Jamie looked down at himself. He took a certain pride in his casual, nonclerical image.

"Oh, those are a white dude's clothes." Murphy shook his head, smiling, amused by the priest's earnestness. "It's not your fault, Father. I mean, Pine and Olive isn't exactly your territory."

Jamie shrugged. "I must look okay to somebody. I've been here since October and never been mugged."

The big detective nodded, smiling in his sleepy way. "You will be. It's part of the life-style. One is either a mugger or a muggee. Wear a white collar; it's safer."

"I'm not so sure," said Jamie, annoyed to be thought naive. "These days churches are robbed and vandalized. Priests get killed in their own rectories, their own beds."

"And people—old ladies especially—keep disappearing."

Jamie nodded. "You know about Grace Keller, then?"

"That's right." A thin smile touched the black man's face. "I'm on the case with Matty Joyce."

"Partners, huh? And how does Matty Joyce like that?" Jamie asked. He opened the walnut closet and began hanging up the alb and chasuble. He handled the old, worn vestments carefully, with respect.

"He doesn't much," the detective said. Now he was grinning. "We try to keep out of each other's way, work both sides of the street, so to speak."

"Down here, I guess, that has its advantages." Jamie washed the ciborium as they talked, then dried it and placed it in the Aumbry, the small cupboard for the sacred vessels.

"It doesn't hurt. At times the Lieutenant needs an interpreter."

Jamie paused and looked around the sacristy. Everything of value was put away and locked up now, as per the pastor's orders.

"I've been going around taking statements, talking to people," the detective went on.

Jamie nodded. "Lieutenant Joyce said you'd be coming around." He folded his arms and leaned back against the marble washstand. The two men could have been talking about sports.

Murphy nodded. He had taken out a small notebook and flipped it open. His eyebrows were long and fine, like a woman's, and gave the only expression to his sleepy face. When he spoke, they moved dramatically, like a gesture.

"I spoke to Maureen Sullivan. You know, the woman's niece. She said the two of you had gone out looking for Miss Keller together?" He spoke slowly, carefully, as if he weren't sure of what he might say openly to the priest.

"Maureen came by the rectory after Devotions, when she couldn't find her aunt." Jamie filled in the details of the story, and it wasn't until he stopped talking that he realized Murphy's slow, hesitant approach was an investigative technique: He forced people to speak up, to grow tired of his diffidence.

The detective still had his notebook open, but he hadn't jotted anything down. His eyes had never left the priest's face, and Jamie found himself wondering if he had said something wrong, something to contradict Maureen's statement. The detective's coolness made Jamie nervous, made him keep talking, as if silence would somehow indicate guilt.

Finally the detective had heard enough. He raised his eyebrows, and at that slight gesture Jamie stopped speaking in mid-sentence.

"The lady—Miss Sullivan—she filled me in pretty much about this, Father. How you searched for the woman and didn't find her."

Jamie nodded dumbly.

"She mentioned these kids..." Murphy glanced down at his notepad "...these Altar Boys, from the orphanage over there on LaClade. She said you two had a bit of a run-in with them, a couple nights back." The detective waited, eyebrows raised again, forming accent marks over his sleepy eyes.

"I think they were the Altar Boys. I mean, I have no idea who else they could be, but they did have ski masks on." Jamie moved away from the marble washstand. He wouldn't let this cop rivet him to one spot.

"Miss Sullivan thinks they might be somehow involved in all this...." The detective let his sentence trail off, waited for the young priest to conclude the thought.

"Connected with her aunt. Yes, I know."

"And the other disappearances as well."

Even though he had spotted the technique Jamie couldn't resist it. "You mean the street people Maureen claims have disappeared?" Jamie shook his head. "I just don't know. The Altar Boys is just a teenage gang. You must know that. They're mean, but I doubt they're killers. I belonged myself when I was that age."

"You an orphan?"

"Yes. I spent my first fifteen years at that orphanage."

"Me, too. An orphan, that is." The detective smiled. "I'm from Chicago originally."

"I was wondering actually where you picked up that Murphy." Jamie grinned back, slapping the black man's upturned palm. All at once he felt at ease.

"There used to be this fighter when I was a kid, Irish Bob Murphy. A tough son of a bitch, but you know how kids are. I wanted to be just that tough. Took the name myself when I was eight or nine."

Jamie had his coat on and led the way to the side door of the sacristy.

"How about some coffee, Lieutenant? We can talk back in the rectory. Have you had breakfast?" His fear of the man was gone.

"Thanks, Father. Sometime I'd like to, but right now I got to get moving." The big man kept grinning, laughing as he shook his head. "That's one thing about orphans; you find them in the damnedest places." He stepped ahead of Jamie, walked out into the winter morning and down the short steps to the parking lot. "Especially, they're out causing trouble, running in gangs. I belonged to the Vice Lords. We were real mean. The Chicago cops don't know it but they still have a few unsolved 346's in their files that I had something to do with." They began to circle the old Cathedral, walking through the deep snow toward McCarthy Boulevard.

"How did you get out of there?" Jamie asked, always curious how someone else had survived an institution.

"Basketball. Sure helps to be born tall, and with a nice soft hook shot. I got picked up early, off the streets, more or less. For a city league; you know. A prep school called Saint Andrew's—Episcopalian—they gave me a full scholarship, a place to live on campus. You know Chicago?"

Jamie shook his head.

"Far north side. Nice. Trees and everything. Sheeit, I thought I had died and gone to heaven. Then I got a ride to Northwestern for college. How 'bout you? How'd you break out?"

"The Cardinal. It's an old story down here in MacPatch— I'm surprised Matty Joyce hasn't told you. I was found over there on the church steps by our Cardinal, raised by the nuns and brothers at the orphanage, then went on to the diocesan prep school. That's the preparatory school for the priesthood, and, well, one thing led to another." Jamie smiled, slightly embarrassed that his life had been comparatively easy.

"That's nice," Murphy said, sounding impressed. "So now you're back home, you might say."

"Yes, in a way." Jamie glanced away, kept himself from explaining about the closing of the parish. He didn't want the detective to think badly of him.

"You do much with the orphanage?"

"Sure. I mean, I try. The brothers have their own programs, naturally, but I teach a few courses, help out where I can."

"Make any IDs on the kids that hit on you?"

"I haven't tried," Jamie said, startled by the sudden segue back to business. "Actually I've stayed away since then. I did speak to Brother Raymond. He's the Headmaster. He said he would investigate."

"I've spoken to Brother Raymond. He's come up with nothing. Miss Sullivan is afraid they did to her aunt what they did that night to you and the old man. Or worse. At least, she thinks that's a possibility."

"I don't know." Jamie shook his head. "That's hard for me to believe. We wreaked some havoc, sure, when I was a kid, but we never killed anyone, harmed them."

"You've got a different dude in those places today, Father." The black man spoke softly, like an older, more experienced brother. "I see it every day, see what teenagers are capable of doing to each other, much less strangers."

They reached the detective's car and paused. McCarthy Boulevard had not been plowed and Murphy was parked at an angle several feet from the sidewalk. On the wide empty street the car looked abandoned.

"Say, I was meaning to ask you back there," the detective said. "About those robes you wear...?" Again the question slipped off, the thought not completed.

"Vestments," Jamie answered.

"Yeah, vestments." Murphy grinned. "I see you lock them up after your service."

"We do here in MacPatch. I guess that's usual in city churches. The vestments are silk and expensive to replace. Also, of course, to us they're sacred. We wouldn't want them stolen and treated sacrilegiously. As you may have noticed, Lieutenant, there's a lot of crazy people out on the street. So we lock up our valuables."

The detective nodded, fell silent.

"Why?" Jamie pressed. He knew Murphy's question wasn't idle.

"But there are ways to get hold of vestments, and clerical garb in general?" he asked.

"Of course. I buy my things in town here, at a religious store."

The black man nodded as if satisfied. Then he stuck out his hand and Jamie shook it. "Thank you, Father Ignatius." He smiled. "Let's shoot a few baskets sometime." Then he stepped off into the deep snow, plowing his way back to his car.

Jamie stood on the empty sidewalk, watching the detective start his car, then move off slowly. Murphy waved but Jamie only nodded good-bye. He was remembering himself as an Altar Boy, stealing the holy vestments because they made the midnight raids much scarier. What was their nightly ritual now, he wondered. And what did Murphy suspect about them? Or, he suddenly realized, what did Murphy suspect about him?

CHAPTER FOURTEEN

December Thirty-first, Morning
Feast of Saint Sylvester I

Maureen's sofa wasn't long enough for Jamie to stretch out on, so she rearranged the cushions on the floor and threw in two pillows from the bed. Then she gestured for him to lie down and he obeyed, but cautiously, as if the big stuffed cushions might conceal a bed of nails.

"You have to relax first," she told him, then sat down just behind his head, in the classic analyst's position: close enough to hear, even if he mumbled, yet still out of his range of sight.

"I'm sure this will be very much like the meditation you do now, this centering prayer. We'll begin by getting you to let your body go. Start by closing your eyes. Let the relaxation from your closed eyelids flow from your forehead like a warm, relaxing liquid.

"Don't struggle. Don't push away your feelings or thoughts. Just let everything go, float away in this golden warm liquid."

Maureen sat quiet for a moment, looking to see if Jamie was really following what she said. His face still seemed tense, wary. It was obviously hard for him to give up control, to turn himself over to her. Meditation was something he did alone. Now he had to trust someone else.

"Let's begin with your feet," she began again. "Tell your toes to let go, to relax. And now your arches, your heels. Speak to them, let them relax. Talk to your legs, your calf muscles and shins, think how wonderful it is to get into bed, to let go, to fall deeply asleep. Follow your body, speak softly to your hips, thighs, your lower back. From the waist down your body is falling off to sleep, to rest.

"Keep moving up your body. Go to your ribs and chest, tell your heart to calm; follow the soft current of warm liquid from vertebra to vertebra, all the way up your body.

"Now your arms. They're so tired, so heavy. See how the sweep of warm, golden liquid flows down the length of each arm, touches the fingers. Let both arms sleep, rest.

"And your head. Let your mouth relax, let all the pressure leave your mind. Every part of your body is now relaxed. Your body is falling through space, falling gently, turning with the currents, falling through the warm liquid of life."

Maureen was speaking softly, not whispering, but letting her voice fill the quiet space in the room. He needed to trust her. He needed to let himself go.

"Jamie, we're in a shoreless sea of golden light. The river of warm liquid has widened and spread out across the world. We are moving quickly, freely beyond time, beyond our own bodies. You are at the center of this sea, and safe from earth and everyone's demands on you. I want you to get comfortable with this freedom, something you have never experienced before.

"Jamie, I want you to follow me, to listen as I slowly count to ten, as I take you into yourself. And though you'll be deeply asleep, your mind will be alert, and you'll continue to hear my voice, to follow my direction.

"If this is what you want, Jamie, if you are comfortable and ready to continue, then lift the finger of your right hand, signal me your wish."

Maureen waited for her voice to take the long journey through the layers of his sleeplike state. Then the finger of his right hand jerked, lifted up momentarily. He was ready.

"Listen, Jamie, follow my count. One . . . two . . . three . . . You are traveling deeper and deeper into the sea, dropping through the warm liquid. Four...five...six...You are so, so tired. Seven...eight...nine...ten...You can hear only me, my voice, and nothing else as you pass through time."

Maureen paused a moment, waited for him to make the long journey with his mind, then softly asked, "What is your strongest image? What do you see?"

"Cobblestones. I see a cobblestone street...I'm walking on it, no, actually I'm running." He broke off, as if afraid.

"Go on," Maureen encouraged, "tell me more. What is the street like? Look around. Describe it to me, Jamie." She fell silent to let him collect his thoughts, to push his memory back through all the years, to find out what had been so important to him then that he could not, today, let go of the image.

"I'm running on a narrow, cobblestone street. The buildings on both sides are high and brownish-looking, ocher really. The street, or path, whatever it is, is deserted. I think it must be midday. The siesta perhaps. Above me, between the high narrow walls, I can see a brilliant blue sky. It is warm, but cool in the shade between the buildings."

"Where are you? Do you have a feeling of what country you're in?"

"This is Spain. I am in Zaragoza, and I'm running down a side street toward the Castle of Aljafería."

"Do you know why you're running, Jamie?"

"I am not called Jamie. My name is Jaime." He was breathing hard now, as if laboring from an uphill run.

"Why are you running, Jaime?" Maureen asked again.

"I'm late. There's an *auto-da-fé* in the open square before the castle. Everyone is here. I had a cow to care for; she was calving. I was up with her all night."

"What is an *auto-da-fé*?"

"A burning. There's always an *auto-da-fé* on feast days. And today is the feast of the Blessed Virgin. Last night there was a procession through the streets. I could see the torchlights from across the river."

"What is being burned?"

"A heretic." Jamie shook his head. "I don't know who. A woman, I think." He moved a little restively on the cushions, and Maureen saw that perspiration had broken out on his forehead. Perhaps she should stop the regression, she thought. She could see he was suffering already. But the mystery of these lives was causing him incalculable pain. They had to go on.

"What about this *auto-da-fé*? Tell me more. What happens? Do you know?"

"Yes, we have many in Zaragoza, now that the *Santa Hermandad* is here. In the morning the heretics are taken from their cells and given their *sanbenitos,* the sort of black habit they wear on their last day. And then a procession is made.

"First come the halbardiers, then the cross of the parish, all shrouded in black. Next come the penitents, then more halbardiers, and the families of heretics. Also the effigies of heretics who have escaped. They, too, will burn. Next the officials, and the important families of Zaragoza, and behind them the banner of the *Hermandad*."

"What is it like, the banner? Can you see it?"

"It's a green cross on a black background. To the right of the cross is a branch of green olive, showing the Church's mercy, and on the left is the sword of justice."

"And that is all of the procession?"

"Yes, except for the inquisitors themselves. They follow everyone else."

Of course, Maureen thought. These were the days of the Inquisition—the Holy Brotherhood, the *Santa Hermandad*. "And who is the chief inquisitor?" she asked.

"The saint." Even in his prone position Jamie bowed his head in deference to the name.

"Who is the saint, Jaime?"

"Fray Tomás de Torquemada." When Jamie said the name of the Great Inquisitor his body jerked involuntarily on the cushions, as if struck with a blow.

Maureen leaned forward for a moment, waiting to see if the sudden blow would destroy his concentration and pull him back again to reality. Still in a deep stupor, the young priest wiped his face with his sleeve, but did not wake. She sat back and said, "Go ahead, Jaime. Tell us more about the procession."

"It moves through the street, moves slowly, for there is a very great crowd and the streets here are narrow. It winds through Zaragoza until it reaches the open plaza before the Castle, where the stage is set up. One of the priests reads a sermon and gives the crowd the oath of allegiance to the Holy Office. And then the sentences are read out from the pulpits on each side of the stage. Each penitent, as his name is called, comes forward and remains standing while the sentence is read."

"Why are you upset, Jaime? Do you know one of these penitents?" Maureen asked, watched Jamie's reaction. Each sentence was a struggle for him, as if he had developed a high fever. She would stop now, she thought. Remembering was too difficult for him, too dangerous.

Jamie shook his head. "I don't think I know anyone. But I am late. I have missed the morning procession. Now I am in the plaza, but I'm exhausted from the running and I cannot get near the stage. The crowds have come in from the surrounding villages. It is like a festival, with games of chance, dances, food and drink for sale. I have to push my way forward to hear the Grand Inquisitor."

"Tell me, Jaime, what is he saying? Try and get close enough to listen."

"They are reading charges—the Grand Inquisitor has quieted the crowd and is reading." Jamie paused, turned his head slightly as if straining to hear. "'We, the Inquisitors against heretical depravity and apostasy in the most noble city and Archbishopric of Zaragoza, by virtue of authority apostolic and ordinary, have examined a lawsuit pending before us, between the honorable Diego Ortiz de Angulo, prosecutor of this Holy Office, and the accused criminal Marina de Guevara, native of the city of Zaragoza, as to the validity of an accusation by the prosecutor, who claims that the accused has committed heresy and apostasy against our Holy Catholic Faith in the following matters and instances:

"First, that in speaking of the wicked heresiarch Friar Martin Luther, Marina de Guevara stated and affirmed that Luther spoke well on the subject of confession: that men need confess only to God and not to the priest. When she was reproved and told that the Church teaches the contrary, Marina de Guevara remained in her Lutheran error.

"Second, when a certain person said Luther was a terrible heretic, Marina de Guevara replied that not everything Luther said was bad, as for example when he said there should be no statues and pictures, that one should worship only God and the

Holy Sacrament, that images were for the simple and not for the judicious. She also asked what difference there was between the statues in use today and the idols used by the pagans. Being told that the pagans worshiped their images as gods and Christians worshiped them because of the saints in Heaven which they represent, Marina de Guevara remained in error.

"Third, a certain person told her that the images of Our Lady of Guadalupe and Montserrat had performed miracles. Marina de Guevara said she did not believe a word of it. A certain person told her of the miracle Our Lady had performed in giving Saint Ildefonso a chasuble with which to say Mass, and that a later Archbishop who insisted on saying Mass with it, had blown up. Marina de Guevara replied that the whole thing was a joke."

Jamie stopped.

Maureen waited a moment, then spoke quietly, so as not to break the spell in the room. "Is there more?"

"Yes, but it is difficult to hear. The crowds are pushing. They have been standing in the sun all morning." Jamie twisted his body, as if shouldering through the mob in the hot Spanish sun. "The Grand Inquisitor is still speaking. He says that there is more. He says that Marina de Guevara has lived with a man not her husband in the town of Calatayud. If this is true, the law allows the Inquisitor to burn her without further trial."

Jamie paused, his eyes fixed on the distance, his lips slightly parted. He was watching something intently and Maureen waited; she would not question him.

"The Inquisitor asked the woman if the charge was true," he burst out. "Then she laughed—at the Inquisitor!—and said the Holy Office was a sad case if all its spies had not learned a truth known by the entire town." Jamie laughed too, as if glad that the woman had gotten her own back. Then he quieted down, listening closely again.

"The Grand Inquisitor has raised his arms for silence. The guards have seized the woman, and forced her to her knees before him. Her crimes of heresy can be forgiven, he says. When the others go to the stake she can appear on the scaffold as a penitent only, witnessing their deaths barefoot and bareheaded, with a wax candle in her hand. But to win this mercy she must do penance.

"What is the penance?" Maureen's heart jumped as Jamie shouted the words, bellowing as if he had to be heard above a crowd.

"Now they are all shouting," he went on. "All but the prisoner. She has not asked what her penance is to be.

"The Inquisitor has ordered silence again. He says that to win mercy she must abjure the man. And must abjure *de vehementi* their child, the sinful symbol of their crime."

Maureen saw the terrible choice that was laid before the woman: to die a hideous death by fire, or to utter a renunciation that would just as surely destroy her life.

"Look! The woman is speaking." Straining to hear, Jamie reported Marina de Guevara's words: "'Fray Tomás, as you well know, the man is dead. I cannot put from me that which I have not. My son I have, and I will not renounce him. Our child is proof there is no God, no evil but the evil of you priests.'

"The crowd is roaring, cursing her, calling upon God. The Inquisitor is striking her...." Jamie choked on his tears and stopped speaking. Resting his head on his drawn-up knees, he rocked back and forth gently as he wept.

"They burned her?" Maureen asked gently.

Jamie nodded, his eyes still closed. "They dragged her off, then...burned her in the high noon sun. I ran from the plaza before they put the torch to the faggots, but I could smell the burning flesh for miles. I tasted it in my mouth forever, from that day, until I died an old man."

Maureen crept forward, knelt down beside him and whispered in his ear, "Who is she, Jaime?"

Jamie shook his head, unwilling to speak.

She asked again, "Who is she, Jaime? Your mistress? Are you the man, not her husband, with whom she lived?"

"No," Jamie answered, his voice very faint, as if it were coming from the Middle Ages. "She is not my mistress. Marina de Guevara is my mother. I am her bastard son."

"It's all true," said Maureen. "It makes sense, every bit of it. You're an orphan. You have no mother, and you feel ashamed of not having one, but at the same time you want to believe that she would never have given you up except under extreme duress. You know that she abandoned you, but you want to believe that she never renounced you in her heart. You're ashamed of being a bastard, so you envision her as proud of her child and contemptuous of the church's morality." Maureen stopped to sip her tea. She was sharing the sofa cushions with Jamie, and they both sat up, backs propped against the couch.

"Yes, but it's more than just psychologically true, Jamie said. "I mean, it really happened. It was so clear, so vivid. I was Jaime. I felt those cobblestones under my sandals. I knew the procedure for an *auto-da-fé*."

"You studied the *auto-da-fé* at the seminary—probably the whole inquisitorial process."

"Never! Believe me, subjects like that do not receive emphasis in the Church these days."

"Then you read about the Inquisition in general history courses. Lots of people remember Torquemada was the Grand Inquisitor. I mean, he even came up in courses at Our Lady of the Snows."

"Why are you resisting this? You're the parapsychologist."

"It's because I've had training that I am cautious. Dreams are clues, blueprints even. But they're not history."

"This wasn't a dream, Maureen. None of my trances—or whatever they are—have been dreams. I'm sure of that."

"Oh, really? Why are you so sure? You're a priest. Why are you so anxious to believe these are glimpses of past lives, when reincarnation goes against your religious beliefs?"

"I've already told you, your idea of Catholicism is too narrow. Just because Eastern ideas haven't filtered down to the level of Our Lady of the Snows doesn't mean the Church condemns them."

"Okay," she answered, "so reincarnation is as western as John Wayne. Tell me this: Since you behave so despicably in most of these trances, why claim them as your previous lives? Nazis, slave dealers, renegade Indians—why set them up as your spiritual ancestors?"

Jamie shrugged. "If that's my karma, I don't really have any choice."

Maureen groaned. "All right, what's that supposed to mean?"

"Don't you know about karma—the law of cause and effect?"

She shook her head. "No, not really. I've heard of it but I couldn't define it. Nor could ninety percent of the people who use it, I suspect."

Jamie laughed. "Well, I can. Karma is the Sanskrit word for action. It means that every time someone acts—whether it's a physical act or a mental, psychic one—he creates an effect that comes back to him, either in this life or another."

"But Christians don't believe that."

"The Hindus and Buddhists do," Jamie answered, "and there are millions of them. They believe a person amasses karma in each lifetime. He does good and evil every day, and each of these actions returns, not within one lifetime, but over many lifetimes. We all carry these deposits of good and bad karma with us, from one world to the next, and they come back to us as obstacles or opportunities. And we keep being reborn until all our evil karma is eliminated."

"So evil karma is equivalent to the punishment we receive for sins," Maureen said.

"No," Jamie shook his head. "To Hindus and Buddhists, at least, this is not a question of sin. They believe God exists in all things, good and bad, but he exists to different degrees. There is only Light and less Light, and the purpose of karma is to teach a person to want the Light."

"But what about forgiveness?" Maureen asked. "I do something bad; presto, I create bad karma. Okay. But then, if I'm a Catholic, I go to confession and get absolved. Good-bye, karma. Right?" Maureen smiled, knowing that this time he was cornered. "Jamie, confession is one of the seven sacraments. If you repent, you're forgiven. If you don't, you get punished. If you don't buy that, it's time to turn in your cassock."

Jamie nodded, agreeing. Then he raised his head and she saw the sadness in his eyes, such a sudden, profound sadness that it shocked her. It was as if he were dying before her eyes.

"Don't you see?" he said. "Unlike the Hindus, I do believe in sin. And I believe these lifetimes are my punishment."

Maureen put her teacup down. "Why would you jump to that conclusion?" she asked.

"Because the trances have a pattern. You've told me so yourself. In each of them I do something violent, or at least cowardly. In this last one, I ran away and left my mother at the stake. But either way, violence is the common theme."

"That's a big generalization," Maureen argued. "You may have had hundreds of lifetimes you haven't even glimpsed yet which were filled with peace and serenity. Who knows, the next regression we do may reveal you were with Schweitzer at Lambarene."

Jamie smiled. "In your previous life you must have been a cheerleader. Why would you even conduct another regression, when you know you don't believe in this one bit?"

"Because you were here in this room the other night, and I want to know why. That's all." She shrugged, looked off. The winter sun had come out and warmed a patch of glowing red and blue in the center of the worn Oriental rug.

"Oh Lord," said Maureen, exhausted suddenly by the tension of the meeting. Standing up, she stretched toward the ceiling, then reached down to touch her bare toes. The rug was warm when she touched it and on an impulse she lay down, turning her face toward the heat like a cat.

"This is so nice," she said, not opening her eyes. "I hardly ever see this place in daylight, much less lie around here."

Jamie did not answer. Her eyelashes were thick and black against the pallor of her cheeks; her lips were red. "You're very beautiful," he said, carefully. It was like speaking a second language; each word had to be premeditated.

Maureen heard, but did not look up; she lay motionless, her eyes closed, encouraging him with her silence. She wanted him to say these things to her; she wanted the words, as if they were talismans.

"When I first saw you at the Center on Christmas, I was overwhelmed. You looked so strong and full of life. I thought you were . . . magnificent."

"Please, I wasn't."

Jamie sighed. This was so hard. As a priest he rarely expressed emotion. Parishioners did not want to listen, they wanted to be heard. Even with each other priests were distant: circumscribed, careful, and controlled.

That was the price of independence, he believed, the price of standing apart as other men's confessor. In return God would give him solace, but God would not give him friends. Especially not women friends.

"Well, this is my problem, not yours," he said. He would let her escape from this conversation, not pin her down.

"It's mine, too, Jamie." Maureen sat up now, but with her back to him. "You couldn't have come here last night all on your own, I mean, this force of yours, whatever it is—it couldn't have come here without my consent, without my subconscious desire for you. I drew it out of you, like a magnet."

For a moment neither one said anything. They sat on the living room floor, Maureen studying the window, Jamie studying her back.

"It scares me," he finally admitted.

"Me, too." Maureen smiled, though he couldn't see. "These feelings always do."

"I guess. I haven't thought of that. I'm scared in another way as well. I'm afraid I might hurt you."

"Hurt me? Why?" She spun around on the rug, sitting back on her heels as she confronted him. "Oh, because of your 'pattern'? Jamie, listen. I know I said that myself on the phone the other day. But I really can't believe you would. When I found you sitting on my bed the other night there were tears in your eyes. You were like a child in pain."

"But the others. The African, the Apache, the war criminal, the Korean. Maureen, I've always been a killer. Perhaps I still am. It just hasn't emerged yet."

"Stop it! Don't talk that way. You're imagining this; talking yourself into it." She jumped to her feet as the telephone rang. It startled her like a gunshot. "Oh, God!" she said. "It's got to be Karel at the Center. I forgot to call and say I wouldn't be in until noon."

But when she picked up the receiver and said hello, it wasn't the Center calling.

"May I speak to Father James Ignatius," a man said.

"I'm sorry, you must have the wrong number," she said at once, automatically. She didn't want anyone to know Jamie was there with her. It was irrational, silly. More guilt from her childhood.

There was a moment's pause, then the man responded. "Miss Sullivan, I know the Father is in your apartment. He has been with you since nine-forty this morning. My name is Lieutenant Robert Murphy. We talked earlier . . . remember?

Now tell the priest I wish to speak to him. Please."

Maureen dropped the receiver onto the bed. It fell gently into the thick quilt, muffling her voice as she went back to the bedroom door and spoke to Jamie.

"Father Ignatius, it's for you." She waited until he reached her, then whispered, "It's Robert Murphy, the detective. I said you weren't here, but he said he knew you'd been here all morning."

Jamie grinned at her concern. "Don't worry," he said, slipping past her. "We don't have a Grand Inquisitor. You won't burn at the stake for this."

She kept busy while he talked on the phone. She picked up their cups and saucers—for some reason she wanted the living room returned to order—then went into the kitchen and began to wash them.

"He wants to talk to me again," Jamie said, appearing in the doorway. "He's outside right now. His car is parked at the corner." Jamie was talking quickly, nervously. "You know, I came into your building this morning the back way."

"Ask Murphy why you're being followed."

"I have a pretty good idea." He had left his parka on the kitchen chair that morning. Now he put it on and zipped it up.

Maureen waited, watched the young priest. "Which is?" she prodded.

He did not look at her.

"Jamie, come on. If you know why they're following you, tell me."

Jamie looked at her finally. She saw then the fear on his face.

"It's about your aunt," he said, trying to meet her eyes. "I'm sure they think I killed her."

CHAPTER FIFTEEN

December Thirty-first, Morning
Feast of Saint Sylvester I

Both detectives were waiting in a black LeMans at the corner of Benton Place. Matty Joyce had left the engine running and when Jamie slid into the back he pulled out with a jerk and started up Jefferson, toward the precinct headquarters. For a moment neither of the cops said anything, and Jamie waited them out.

"We got a problem, Father," Matty Joyce said, as he stopped for a red light. He kept glancing at Jamie, using the rear view mirror to spot the priest in the back seat.

Jamie said nothing, and when the light changed the detective resumed driving without pressing him. Joyce proceeded slowly, cautious on the icy street, and in no real rush. When he didn't turn right onto Grand, Jamie realized they weren't heading for police headquarters.

It was a brilliantly sunny day and there was little traffic downtown. Few of the side streets in MacPatch had been cleared, and even on Jefferson Avenue there was room for only one lane of cars. Jamie looked out through the front window, uphill toward the center of the city. The low winter sun was bouncing off the windows of the uptown high-rises and Jamie looked away. The sun hurt his eyes. He thought of the albino boy in Zanzibar.

"We got a problem here, Father," Matty Joyce said again.

"That's what Lieutenant Murphy suggested," Jamie answered, then sat back. He would let the two of them get started without his help.

The black man turned sideways to look directly at him, but before he could speak, Matty Joyce went on. "Bobby here has been looking into these alleged disappearances of bag ladies." In the mirror, his quick eyes flickered over Jamie's face, as if checking for a reaction.

"That Maureen Sullivan might have something," Murphy added, as if admitting a mistake. "There's a lot of talk out on the street." He gestured toward the neighborhood. Jamie glanced out the side window, toward the bleak row houses off Jefferson. At each corner, outside a Seven-Eleven or in front of a liquor store, a few old black men were gathered, bundled up in overcoats, grouping together to share a bottle. At several corners fires had been started in trash cans and the old men circled the heat, stamping their feet in the deep snow.

"Someone really is killing them?" Jamie asked.

The black cop nodded.

"And you think you know who it is?" Jamie was frightened, just asking the question.

The cops were silent a moment and then Matty Joyce cleared his throat. "They say it's a priest, Father. Some priest in a black limousine."

"I don't drive," Jamie blurted out. "I don't even have a car." At once he felt foolish.

"No one is accusing anyone, Father," the black man replied, speaking softly. He looked as if he had just woken up.

"Of course not, Father." Matty Joyce smiled then, a crack in his round, smooth pumpkin face.

"That's the problem," Murphy continued, still in the same low voice. Listening to him was like following a melody. "A lot of loose talk down here in MacPatch. People are full of stories—you know, eyewitness accounts. That sort of bullshit; 'scuse me, Father. But you got to know that in the black community, I mean the hard-core poor people, there's a lot of paranoia. The man is always coming down on them."

Matty Joyce took up the story. "Now you get a rumor like this going in the Project, where you don't have a lot of Catholics. You know, just Baptists like Murphy here. And pretty soon everyone believes that the priests over at Saints Peter and Paul are doing them in. They might not say it in so many words. And, after all, no bodies have been found—"

"But Grace Keller was Catholic," Jamie interrupted.

The Lieutenant ignored him and finished the sentence. "—but people are definitely disappearing. Old people, black people, drunks, bag ladies. Folks living in cardboard shelters by Montesi lot, and in those tin shanties down in the pilings under the expressway. They're gone, Father. Gone." He raised his eyebrows, and his glance in the rear-view mirror was a challenge.

"And a priest is killing them," Jamie answered.

"Someone dressed up like a priest," Matty Joyce added quickly. "We know it isn't a *real* priest. I mean, you know how you look, Father. No offense meant, but you don't go much for the black suit, white-collar routine. You know, the outfit. This guy probably looks more like a priest than you do." The detective grinned, showing his bad teeth.

"The priest getup is the ploy," Murphy went on. "It lets the man get close to the victim, establishes a sense of trust. You wouldn't expect a priest to kill you, now would you?"

Jamie shook his head. He felt immensely relieved. He would have to telephone Maureen and tell her he wasn't a suspect. He glanced out the front window, wondering now where the cops could be taking him.

They had left MacPatch and gone straight up Jefferson Avenue, past the Salvation Army outlet and the endless, shabby rows of secondhand stores and used-furniture shops. Now they were in the new downtown district. Here the streets had been plowed and the snow hauled away. The Shop-and-Ride commuter bus had turned the corner ahead of them. People were filling the Mall, waiting to cross the light at the next intersection. The First National Bank clock said the temperature was fourteen degrees at eleven-thirty-five. Almost time for lunch.

"Where are we going?" Jamie asked. They passed the Mall

and Matty Joyce slowed the car, then turned left.

"To the Chancery, Father," Joyce answered. "His Eminence asked us if we could pick you up."

For a moment Jamie was surprised. He wasn't sure what he was being told. "You mean you report directly to the Cardinal when a Catholic is a crime victim?"

Matty Joyce glanced at his partner, but the black man stared out the window. "Well, sort of, Father. We brief him, you know, sometimes . . . when it seems important. You know, His Eminence and I go way back. I told you that, right?"

Jamie nodded. Now he understood. He also understood that Robert Murphy didn't like it much. "And how did you know where to find me?" he asked.

"Ah, well, we didn't actually," Joyce answered, looking in vain again to Murphy. "But . . . the Cardinal . . . he told us."

"I'm not spying on you. Don't be so touchy." His Eminence continued signing his correspondence as Jamie paced the Chancery office.

"Then how did you know where to find me?" Jamie demanded.

"Matty Joyce gave me a call yesterday. He's got this daughter who wants to attend Catholic University. She's interested in theater, Matty says—"

Jamie stopped pacing. "You're having me followed, aren't you?" he broke in. He was shaking his head in disbelief.

"Jamie, that's a dangerous area down in MacPatch." The Cardinal tipped his leather chair back, opened his arms wide in a gesture of innocence. "I happened to see Matty in September, at a K. of C. function, and I asked him to sort of keep an eye out for you. Now there's nothing wrong in that, is there?"

"So Joyce trailed me from the rectory to Maureen Sullivan's apartment?" He was furious at himself for not having noticed the cop car on the empty streets of MacPatch.

The Cardinal was smiling, amused by Jamie's reaction.

"Jamie, I spoke to Hilda this morning. She told me where you went, and when Matty stopped by here earlier, I told him."

"I didn't tell Mrs. Windmiller where I was going."

"My son, don't you realize that rectory housekeepers always

know what we're up to... who we're fucking."

That stopped Jamie, pinned him, as if with a lance.

"Your Eminence, I'm not, as you would say, *fucking* anyone."

"Of course you're not, but you're thinking about it." The Cardinal kept smiling.

"Your Eminence, I'm—"

"Come on, Jamie, don't lie to me. I've known you all your life. I knew you were thinking of sleeping with that girl before you did. And why wouldn't you consider it? She's a real looker. Reminds me of her mother, Peggy. All those Keller girls were lookers. Great dancers as well. We used to go uptown to the Park Plaza for tea dances. I was still in college then, hadn't taken the plunge, so to speak. I didn't start at Rocklands until the summer of 1950. Me and the Koreans; we took the plunge together. Anyway, we'd go uptown on Sunday afternoons and dance in the main ballroom of the Plaza. It was quite a room then. You've never been to a tea dance, have you, Jamie?"

"I can't dance, Your Eminence. I never really had the opportunity."

"Well, tea dances are a thing of the past. Went out of style with the big bands." The Cardinal leaned back again in the leather chair, tipped it back while he enjoyed himself, remembering.

"There was a gang of us, all nineteen and twenty. The Keller girls, Liam Sullivan, Tommy Quinn, myself and that little dago fella, Al Conti. His father owned the deli at the corner of Pine and Ward. Al became an accountant, a CPA. He lives in Springfield now. Peggy Keller had her eye on little Al. She always liked those Italians."

The Cardinal stopped, stared across at Jamie. "Now what was this all about?"

"How Maureen Sullivan was a real looker." Jamie had to smile, amused in spite of himself at the way the Cardinal could disarm him with long, rambling reminiscences.

"Oh, yes, that Sullivan girl. Now what about it, Jamie? Are you prepared to keep the vows you just made in Rome?"

"Your Eminence, I haven't broken my vows and I don't intend to." He tried to sound forceful, as if the issue had already been decided.

"Really? And what about the sin of lust, my boy? Even if you haven't slept with her, can you say you haven't wanted to?" The Cardinal let Jamie squirm a moment longer, then said good-naturedly, still smiling, "You wouldn't be a normal young fella if you didn't notice a good-looking gal. I don't want a bunch of fairies in my diocese. Christ, they're worse than the skirt chasers." He shook his head, then turned to the stack of letters, signing his name over and over as he talked. The geniality had gone from his voice. He was again the Cardinal, the final authority.

His pen scratched quickly over the thick, embossed stationery. "I've been asked to speak at the Convention of Catholic Law Enforcement Officers in San Diego next week and I want you to fly out with me.

"This is the type of organization we want to get associated with early. I want you to meet these people and let them get to know you. They're a good bunch, those cops. Right-thinking people. For one thing, they still respect authority. Church *and* state.

"Bill Vicars just got back from Rome so I'll have him fill in for you at the Cathedral. Besides, your work must be almost finished. Why don't you pack up your things and move in here at the Residence? I'll want you to get an apartment soon, someplace where we can give small dinners. In the meantime, though, it's best if you're here."

"But Monsignor O'Toole—"

"I'll have another word with him. Tommy keeps resisting me, keeps telling me how things are turning around there." The Cardinal shook his head. "The old guy is being tougher than I would have guessed. We never heard a damn peep out of him for twenty years, and now when I tell him the Cathedral is closing, he's a tiger. Keeps saying he can cut expenses."

"Your Eminence, I thought, given the Monsignor's age— he'll want to retire in a year or so—that we could keep the rectory open. And I'll stay on, you know, to look after the place. I can commute to work up here, but we'll still have something of a presence in the parish. We could open a small chapel on the first floor of the rectory, for the old Catholics who are still living there."

The Cardinal stopped signing letters. He looked up, frowning at Jamie, baffled to find himself invited over old ground.

"Jamie, there isn't going to be a Catholic presence in MacPatch. I'm selling off everything, that whole block of brownstones; you know that."

"Well, what about just during the interim?" Jamie could feel his arguments slipping out from under him, like his feet in soft sand.

The Cardinal watched the young priest pensively, then shook his head, slowly, deliberately. Finally he remarked, "She's really got her hooks into you, huh, son?"

"Your Eminence, that's not true!" Jamie's voice rose. He began to sweat.

"Bullshit!" The Cardinal capped his gold-nibbed pen and set it down. "I'm getting you out of MacPatch just in time."

"Your Eminence—"

The Cardinal raised his hand, waved Jamie into silence.

"Enough! Pack up your things. I'll telephone Tommy and tell him. Don't worry, I won't say anything about Sullivan. Reassignment, that's all. He'll appreciate your leaving. You made him uneasy anyway with your bookkeeping."

"Your Eminence, you're basing this decision on the wrong assumptions. You don't—"

"My decisions are not subject to your review!" The Cardinal seemed as amazed as he was angry. "You took a vow of obedience, Father Ignatius. Or is that one inconveniencing you as well?"

Jamie backed off as the Cardinal rose to his feet. In his red flowing robes, he was formidable, even threatening. But when he spoke it was in a soft, reasonable tone.

"Now don't disappoint me, Jamie. I have a future planned for you. A grand and good life in the service of God, and I don't want you to throw it all away on some fool woman with a good, but really not significant, cause. I have much more planned for you, son, much more in store." He smiled gently. "You belong to the Church, Jamie, now and forever. And you belong to me."

That afternoon Maureen took the short cut to work. Plunging through the cold, deep snow of the park, she thought how the last week had changed her whole outlook. For the first time, she was thinking that the park route was dangerous, a wide open space in which she could be mugged without anyone's noticing. But now she no longer cared. A part of her felt reckless, even aggressive. She willed someone to come at her; then she could get even, pay the world back for Aunt Grace.

She would walk home through the park as well, she decided. Even if she got back safely it would make her feel better to have taken the risk.

"Oh, Maureen, we didn't expect you at all today," the Director said, spotting her as she came through the door. "Are you okay?"

Maureen nodded, then unwound the long wool scarf from around her face and mouth. "The cold was making me crazy at home," she said when she could speak. "I'd rather be down here and busy."

Her tiny office was off the main lounge, the warm place where street people congregated to sit quietly, watch TV, or doze. Most days Maureen made a point of circling the lounge as soon as she arrived, chatting if she had time, or sometimes just saying hello. The men and women were lonely, she knew, hungry for a kind word or some recognition.

And often she enjoyed their company. Not all the homeless people were disoriented or depressed. Some read the news every day and had interesting opinions. Some were energetic and funny, just like Aunt Grace. Talking to them was often a lift, but not today.

Today she couldn't take it. She headed straight for her office, ignoring the patient figures lined up against the walls. She had paperwork to do. Correspondence.

She was at the office door when Tony caught up with her. She heard him behind her, shuffling across the wide lounge with the characteristic hitch in his step, and she stopped wearily, braced herself. She did not feel like handling anyone else's problems.

"Missy," the old man whispered, glancing about. Everything in Tony's life was conspiratorial.

Maureen's resistance softened at the sight of him. Tony wouldn't look at her, she knew. Like all the battered street people he lived in fear, and to confront anyone directly, to look up into her eyes, was beyond him. It was a skill he had lost irrevocably.

"Yes, Tony," she asked, though she knew already what he wanted to say. "What is it?" She smiled encouragingly.

"You ain't seen Joe, have you, Missy?" He shuffled about, keeping his distance. He knew he smelled and he didn't want to offend her. Of all the people at the Center, she was the only one he trusted enough to speak to about Joe.

"I'm sorry, Tony, but I haven't. I told ... some people. They're looking for him. But you'd know best where Joe is, Tony. You'd know where he hangs out. Have you looked there?" There was always the chance that something would jog his memory, that he'd tell her something else he'd seen. Yet as she spoke, she wondered if the old man was understanding her at all. His face did not register any comprehension.

"I can't find Joe," he mumbled, backing off further, shuffling nervously.

They were all like that, Maureen knew; too afraid to stand still.

"Oh, I'm sure he'll come back soon," she said, giving up for the time being.

"Joe, he can sing and dance," Tony said next, unexpectedly. "He especially likes to sing." The old man grinned, and now he looked up at Maureen, feeling safer when he talked about Joe. "I seen him out on the street. Me and Joe, we were going up to the park. Joe, he had this bottle and we were going to sit in the sun. It's nice there in the park. The cops leave you be once it gets cold." Then he turned sideways, looking through the front windows of the Center at the park across the street, forgetting what he wanted to tell her.

Maureen already knew about the disappearance. But Tony had forgotten that; the day he'd told her about Joe was lost, like all his life, in the dim world of memory.

"Tony," she said, pulling him back to the present. He stood there dumb, trying to recall what it was he wanted to say. It was about Joe, he knew. Joe was gone. Where was his buddy?

"Tony, why don't you get yourself a warm cup of coffee?" she suggested gently.

Tony nodded, slowly crossed the wide lounge to where a

coffeepot and cups were set out for everyone. Another person in trouble, she thought, dressed in rags, feeble and lost, walking out of her life. She couldn't take much more of this, Maureen realized. The cold weather and snowstorms, and all these help-less, homeless people. She needed to get away from MacPatch.

Yet she couldn't leave. Her aunt was missing and very possibly dead, snatched from the stone steps of Saints Peter and Paul.

Maureen fingered her stacks of paperwork. This was not where she ought to be, she realized, not here, not behind a desk while Aunt Grace was lost. What if the police were right, she thought. Suppose Aunt Grace was wandering the streets, or was trapped somehow in one of the abandoned tenements. She had to keep searching, Maureen decided, and buttoning up her tattered fur coat she walked out of the Center, back onto the streets of MacPatch. As she left the telephone began to ring, and she let it.

CHAPTER SIXTEEN

December Thirty-first, Evening
Feast of Saint Sylvester I

"Oh, it's you." Maureen was surprised to see him in the hall-way. The safety chain was still on and she looked out at Jamie through the narrow opening.

"Happy New Year," he said. He stood with his hands in his pockets like an errant schoolboy, waiting for her response. "Busy?" he asked.

"Busy? No. I'm just cooking some fish. Come in." She shut the door for a moment to unlatch the chain, then opened it again.

Now Jamie could smell the fish baking. "I telephoned this afternoon, here and at the Center." He stepped around her and came into the room. Although he had been there just that morning, he felt like a stranger again. "I didn't know if you'd be home, New Year's Eve and all."

She shook her head. "No partying for me. I just don't feel like it."

"Are you okay?" he asked, unzipping his jacket as he fol-lowed her into the kitchen. She was wearing a soft-looking pink velour top, black corduroy jeans, and the cheap black cotton flats that were imported from Taiwan.

"Yes, I guess. Tired, that's all. I spent three hours wandering around MacPatch looking for Aunt Grace again." She sounded totally despondent. "Would you like anything, a New Year's drink?" She tried to pick up her spirits for him.

"No, thanks. I have Devotions later." He sighed, looked off. He had come to tell her about the Cardinal's insistence that he move uptown, but now, in her presence, his courage was slipping away.

"Well, what happened?" she asked.

"Happened?" he said nervously. How could she know about the conversation at the Chancery?

She stared at Jamie for a moment, then said, "Jamie, don't you remember? The police came here this morning and took you off. You said they suspected you of killing Aunt Grace. It's preposterous, I know, but what was it all about? My God, did you forget all that already?"

"I'm sorry." He gestured, as if apologizing. "I *did* call. It was nothing really. I mean, I was totally off base. What seems to be happening is that someone is dressing up like a priest—you know, wearing a collar and the black suit—and, well, the cops now think maybe these people really are disappearing." He looked sheepish, and away. "I'm really sorry I forgot; I meant to tell you, but I've got a few things on my mind."

"You see?" Maureen crowed. "I told you. I told the police. Well, it's about time they're taking this seriously. Thank God." She sighed, as if suddenly exhausted from carrying the weight of all that knowledge herself.

"They just wanted me to know. The word is out on the street that it's a priest, I mean, someone dressed like a priest, and they're worried about some kind of reaction from the local people."

"Don't be silly. It's not a priest, and the people in MacPatch know that. They know the score." She turned toward the stove. "Well, finally, we're going to get somewhere." Her spirits were picking up now. "Jamie, really, would you like something . . . coffee?"

"That's all right, Maureen, don't bother. I just came to see you for a few minutes."

She reached for the coffeepot and turned on the sink water. "It's no trouble."

"I've been nothing but trouble since we met," he said. Now he was the one who sounded depressed.

Maureen paused and looked over at him. His exhaustion showed in his face, in his eyes.

She nodded softly, then said, "You're right, actually."

"I'm sorry."

A small smile broke on her lips. Jamie had to look away, brace himself. He wanted to hold her in his arms and comfort her. He wanted her to comfort him.

"I'm sorry, too," she said. "Half of our problems were caused by me, not you. I was the one who dragged us out into that snowstorm, for example."

"The trouble I'm talking about goes beyond snowstorms."

She kept quiet, knowing what he meant.

"Maureen?" He was behind her, whispering.

"Don't touch me," she said instantly. The empty coffeepot slipped from her hands and bounced on the linoleum.

"Why don't I do this?" he said. He took the can of coffee from her, then bent down to retrieve the pot.

"I feel so stupid," she stated, beginning to pace the kitchen. She hated the cat-and-mouse, the innuendoes, the masquerade of romance. She had never been good at the whole elaborate game of courting. "I wouldn't be acting so strangely," she blurted out, "but all I can think of is taking your jeans off."

At that, Jamie dropped the coffeepot, spilling the container of grounds.

Maureen burst into giggles. "God, we're a pair!"

Jamie knelt down and began to sweep up the coffee with his hands.

"Here, let me." She dug into a corner cabinet and produced a whisk broom. "Go try again, okay?" She knelt down beside him.

"All you can think of, huh?"

"Please, Jamie, don't make fun." Carefully, concentrating, she began to sweep the dry grounds into a mound. He stayed next to her. She could feel his breath on her cheek, smell his body. "I'm sorry I said anything. Sometimes I say foolish, unthinking things and make a fool of myself."

"I don't mind," Jamie answered, and then he thought of the Cardinal, of his warning.

"You should mind. I should mind. God, this is stupid." She stood up and carried the coffee grounds to the trash can. "Don't you have Devotions?"

"I have time." He stood up, but kept away from her. Thinking of the Cardinal had chilled him.

"Well, there's enough fish . . . I mean, if you'd like to eat dinner beforehand."

"That would be great! Thank you." He smiled, pleased. Then he began to relax, felt the tension leaving his shoulders. He would have to leave, but not right away.

"No funny business?" she asked, eyeing him.

"Like what?" He kept smiling, kept flirting.

"You know what I mean," she said impatiently.

"Okay. No funny business."

She nodded, and he could see her relax as well. Her shoulders softened, and she let out her breath. Now he felt guilty, realizing how much pressure he created.

"You can help me peel the potatoes," she continued, walking back to the sink.

"Idle hands," he said helpfully.

"That's right. I'll use a knife; you can have the good peeler." She pulled out the center drawer of the table and found the peeler, saying, "Get to work. We'll each clean three small ones, unless you're especially hungry, and then slice them into that pot of cold water."

"You know, in the orphanage—"

"Yes, I know. In the orphanage you were always the one who had to peel the potatoes." She smiled at his predictability.

"Well, it's true," he said meekly.

She allowed herself a quick sideward glance at him, then turned away and impulsively opened the refrigerator. Staring at the cluttered shelves, she let the cold air cool her down. This was silly, she realized, letting his simple presence get to her. She shut the door and returned to the potatoes, keeping her back to the priest as she worked.

"Voilà the potatoes." He moved the pot to the kitchen counter. "What do I do with them now? You're Irish. You must have some secret recipe." He felt immensely happy. He liked this, being with her in the kitchen, preparing dinner. He loved, he realized, the domesticity of it: the warm room, the simple chores, the smell of trout baking. "You know, this must be what it's like being married," he said out loud.

"Easy, Jamie. That's the kind of talk that gets you in trouble." Maureen could feel her resistance caving, slipping away like shoreline against the tide. She glanced up at the kitchen clock, concentrating, not letting his presence disturb her. The trout had been cooking ten minutes. She had sautéed the mushrooms in butter and already added them to the baking pan. In another ten minutes they could eat.

"I left the potatoes too late," she said. "We better just hash brown them. Can you do that, Father Ignatius?" She glanced at him challengingly. "Or weren't hash browns on the menu at the orphanage?"

"No, at the seminary," he responded. "Cut them into cubes, combine with yellow onion, peeled and minced, add salt, pepper, etcetera, and brown in a heavy skillet for six minutes or so. Form a pancake."

"Very good!" She smiled, oddly impressed by his knowledgeability. Michael DeSales had been uninterested in food and unwilling to make an effort. She found that she was having a good time cooking dinner with Father James Ignatius.

"I didn't know priests could cook," she said, smiling as she handed him the iron frypan. "Better not let the Cardinal know; he might revoke your housekeeper to save the archdiocese more money."

She thought Jamie would laugh but he didn't. "Don't sulk," she said, after a moment.

"I'm not," he answered, turning the potatoes rapidly in the skillet. The sound of hot oil sizzling filled the quiet room.

"Yes, you are; you're mad because I said something inappropriate about your peerless friend."

"All right! Enough! Let's not start this again." He shook the heavy skillet over the heat, banging the burner.

"Fine." She came closer, slipping on two padded oven mitts. "Move, please. It's time to take the fish out."

"Look at me," he said, blocking her passage, standing before the oven door.

"Jamie, you'll make me burn it!" She let the frustration register in her voice.

He reached over and turned off the stove, still not moving. "Look at me," he whispered. "You haven't looked at me since I walked into this apartment." Reaching out, he gently lifted her chin, forcing it up until until her eyes met his. She did not resist but held herself stiffly, as if daring him to make something of a look.

His eyes were plainly blue. But now, up close, she saw that they were gray as well, their color the same smoky sky as her favorite Wedgwood.

As if he sensed her defiance melting, he released her chin, then caressed her cheek, brushing it gently with the backs of his fingers.

"Jamie, stop!" she asked. "Now I've looked at you, okay? So let me serve dinner." She pulled at the oven door, trying to force him to step back, but instead he banged the door shut with a knee and caught her.

"Jamie, I warned you!" She tried to wriggle free, but the anger was gone from her voice, and her arms were draped limply over his shoulders, her hands still encased in oven mitts.

Jamie ran his hand up the nape of her neck into the thick black hair, seizing and trapping her. Her mouth, when he kissed it, was hard and resisting, her lips scissored closed. Still holding her against him he lifted her an inch and backed her up against the white refrigerator. Captive now, she felt his hands smoothing the velour of her shirt, then slipping beneath it. She was not wearing a bra and her breasts filled his open palms.

"Oh," she moaned, dizzy with pleasure. His warm fingers crossed the globes, brushed her nipples. "Please, Jamie, stop," she begged. Then, gathering her own willpower, she pushed at his chest and broke away, gasping.

"Maureen, I'm sorry." He leaned against the kitchen table. The tips of his fingers felt as if they had been singed.

"All right, you've got to go," she ordered, then left the kitchen and walked toward the front door.

He stopped her halfway across the living room, grabbed her arm as if he were a drowning man.

"Please," he asked. Maureen did not answer. He released her arm and she moved toward the door again. This time he seized her, held her square shoulders. "Maureen," he whispered.

"Don't do this to me," she said.

He tried to pull her into his arms, but still she would not budge.

"Maureen, I would never hurt you," he said.

"Come on, Jamie," she answered. "Both of us know better, right?"

"But this isn't just me," he argued. "You said you were attracted to me, too."

"My God, of course I am. You're gorgeous. But that's got nothing to do with it." She sighed and moved away again. "If I actually slept with everyone who attracted me, I'd be dating everyone from Teddy Kennedy to the driver of the eight A.M. crosstown bus."

"But you do think I'm good-looking?"

"Jamie, don't be such a jerk, okay?" She had her hand on the doorknob.

"I'm sorry, but no one ever called me gorgeous before."

"Well, it's not something you whisper in confession." She turned to the door, began to unbolt the locks, slipped off the chain.

He reached out and slammed it shut again.

"Jamie, don't try to be tough with me. You'll ruin everything."

"Everything? What do you mean? We don't have anything, much less everything."

"We have a friendship. At least I thought we did."

"I want more."

Maureen kept shaking her head. "Father, we have already been through this—"

"All I think about is you," he interrupted. "You're on my mind all the time."

"Make a good act of contrition."

"Maureen, please. Don't be such a smartass."

"You bring out the worst in me, Father Ignatius." She leaned back against the door and crossed her arms. Her expression said she was bored and impatient.

He stood a moment watching her, trying to pull his emotions together. He wanted to grab her, kiss her sullen mouth, but at the same time he wanted to slap her. Her cool resistance thwarted him, and for a moment he lost the boundary between anger and desire.

"Go to hell, then!" he said, and left the apartment, his heavy boots clattering down the stairs to the street.

Maureen did not move. At that moment she lacked the strength. From downstairs she heard a distant slam and, knowing he was really gone, she pulled herself away from the door. A draft of cold air from the hall swept around her bare ankles, chilling her, and she forced herself to shut the door, lock it, and replace the safety chain.

Then she leaned back against the door, trying to place the odd feeling that was dominating her emotions. It was a minute before she realized that it was fear. Jamie had frightened her. She did not know the man at all.

There were only a handful of people at Devotions, but Jamie wasn't surprised. Word had gone out in MacPatch that Grace Keller had disappeared from the steps of the Cathedral, and that others were missing too.

Jamie hurried through the Devotions, eliminating nothing but speeding everything up. He led the rosary, preached a short sermon, and sang the English version of a Latin hymn. He didn't want to discourage those who'd attended by keeping them out late. At the conclusion he came down off the altar and walked down the central aisle, turning to the right and to the left as he gave his blessing. It was not until then that he saw Robert Murphy, looming in the shadows of one of the pillars.

"Making the novena?" Jamie asked, nodding to the detective over the heads of the last few parishioners. Jamie wished them goodnight and ushered them out, watching from the front steps for a few minutes until everyone had disappeared down the dark, snowy streets. Then he began to lock up.

"You do nice work," the black man said, giving the priest a hand with the heavy iron doors. "Where's your main man? Isn't this his job?"

"Clarence? God knows. He tends to forget these nightly chores. But that's okay. He works hard enough, keeping this old place clean." Jamie led the detective back inside and up the side aisle, checking confessional boxes along the way to make sure no one was hiding inside.

"You hear people's sins in here, right?" Murphy asked.

"It's called the Sacrament of Reconciliation these days. Less threatening than penance or confession." Jamie smiled and gestured toward a confessional. "You can conceal yourself behind a grille or sit face to face with the priest. The face to face way is what we call the modern form. Most of the young people prefer it." They began walking again, toward the front of the dark church.

"What if a person, you know, comes in here and confesses a murder? What if—"

Jamie grinned, knowing what was coming next. "It's called the seal of confession," he said, interrupting. "It goes back to the time of Saint Augustine, about 400 A.D. If a penitent confesses a murder, the priest is forbidden to indicate in any which way that he has knowledge of it."

"What if he's called to testify?"

"Doesn't matter. If the priest is put under oath, he must say that he neither knows nor has any information. The Church does not consider that perjury. Hitchcock made a whole movie about this, Lieutenant. Montgomery Clift plays a priest who hears a murderer's confession. When the police come around asking questions he doesn't tell them anything."

"What happens then, he gets subpoenaed?" asked Murphy.

"No, Lieutenant. He gets arrested for the murder. He's innocent but no one believes him."

Murphy nodded. "Tough spot," he commented. "So, in other words, I couldn't ask you in front of a grand jury if you know anything about Grace Keller? Assuming she's been murdered, that is."

By now they had reached the altar. Jamie did not answer until he had closed the railing behind them, then genuflected before the Blessed Sacrament.

"That's right, Lieutenant," he said, leading the black man into the sacristy. As he walked he slipped the chasuble over his head, giving himself a moment to fight off the panic.

"But I'll do this much for you," he went on. He kept disrobing, taking off the alb and amice. "Without breaking the seal of the confessional, I can tell you I don't know anything about the murder. No one has confessed to me or asked for absolution." He was stripped down now to jeans and a gray sweater. The sweater was old and had a small hole at one elbow. He had had it since high school; it had been donated to the orphanage.

Murphy grinned, surprised again how the young priest dressed under his finery. "You sure don't look like clergy, Father; I've got to say that again."

"Clothes don't make the priest, Lieutenant."

"I guess not, but they make a killer, that's for sure."

"You mean this guy who dresses up as a priest?"

Murphy did not respond, but only asked, "Tell me about Clarence. He's a bit daft, right?"

Jamie nodded as he locked up the vestment closets. "He's what they once called simpleminded. But he's a kind, gentle guy. He's been with Saints Peter and Paul, I guess, all his life."

"He's not a killer then?"

"Clarence?" Jamie spun around. "My God, Clarence is too, too. . . ."

"Retarded."

"Yes, retarded," Jamie paused. He was putting on his parka, ready to leave. "Why would you single him out?"

"Does Clarence drive a car?" Murphy asked next, ignoring Jamie's question.

"I have no idea. He wouldn't have been able to pass the written exam."

"He might still know how to drive, license or not."

"You don't have anything, do you?" Jamie said. "I mean, you're just fishing."

The black man smiled sheepishly, as if he had been caught outright.

"And you, Father, do you drive?"

"No—though I can, if necessary. I don't have a license, either."

"This parish . . . do you have an official car, one of those long, black Continentals?" The detective smiled.

"The parish did have a car, but it was sold off before I even came down to MacPatch. I'm not sure who purchased it; I can find out for you."

The black detective kept nodding, absorbing the information without reacting to it. He did not write anything down, and he seemed almost bored with the details, but Jamie was learning that the detective discarded nothing.

Jamie snapped off the lights and opened the outside door of the sacristy. "More snow," he announced, sounding defeated.

"The worst winter we've had since they began keeping records, I hear." The detective followed Jamie out, then stood aside as the priest locked the rear door and shook it, making sure it was secure.

"You'd think that with all this snow, we'd find our man," Murphy remarked, leading Jamie toward the corner of the parking lot where he'd left his car. "You know you'd expect some tracks to be left in the snow. But these people, they're just vanishing, like they were airlifted out."

"New snow, I suppose." Jamie shrugged. "But are you really sure anyone is disappearing, besides Grace Keller?"

Murphy lifted his eyebrows. "Two days ago, on West Pine, we found this abandoned homemade shelter. A tin makeshift lean-to, you know, built up against the alleyway. Everything intact, and no one around." The tall man shook his head as he found his car keys and inserted them in the door.

"So I've been going by there, checking it from time to time. But no one's using that tin shanty. Odd, don't you think?" He seemed barely able to keep his sleepy eyes focused on Jamie, yet still he kept watching, waiting. Jamie felt like a trout being played with by a fly fisherman.

"So you assume he or she is gone," Jamie answered. "Missing, presumed dead. No body. No trace of any body." He filled in the facts for the detective, then took a short cut. "It isn't Clarence, Lieutenant. Believe me, he couldn't pull it off."

The detective slipped into the car, lowered the front window, and slammed the door. A shower of dry snow blew into his face, caught in his hair and his eyebrows like dandruff. "You're probably right, Father. You know, I saw that Hitchcock movie. Name of it was *I Confess*." Waving goodnight, he pulled slowly out of the parking lot, his tire tracks marking the way, like evidence.

• • •

Inside the rectory, Jamie pulled off his boots and stripped down to his shirt. It was too hot in the building even for a sweater, which told Jamie that the pastor was home and watching television. He tried to come in quietly but the Monsignor had heard him.

"I'm back here, Jamie," he called. "How did the Devotions go?"

"Fine, Monsignor, just fine," Jamie responded, walking back to stand in the doorway of the study. The pastor was watching *Wild Kingdom,"* listening to Marlin Perkins talk about sea lions on the Farallon Islands.

O'Toole nodded, but his eyes stayed on the screen, where the sea lions played on the California rocks. He was sitting in a high-back wing chair that made him seem smaller. To one side of the chair was a tray of food—potato chips, nuts, cheese, a bowl of soft candies—as well as a small bucket of ice cubes and a glass of bourbon. The Monsignor seemed settled for the night.

"Looka there!" O'Toole pointed at the screen. "They're like great big puppies, aren't they?" he said, smiling. "Do you watch this program, Jamie?"

"No, Monsignor, I don't. As you know, I don't catch much TV."

"This is the best thing on. Except for some old movies. Spencer Tracy was on last night, one of those Pat and Mike films with Hepburn. Great show. She played a professional golfer." He laughed, recalling.

"Well, I'll be saying goodnight, Monsignor. I have my office to say."

The old priest sat up and looked around the high wing of his chair. "You had a good crowd, I guess, on a night like this." He was smiling, waiting for Jamie to agree.

"One of the better nights, Monsignor," Jamie said vaguely. He couldn't spoil the pastor's evening by admitting they'd had so few people in church.

"I think we're at the beginning of a religious revival here, Jamie, an upswing. I was telling that to His Eminence. Once we get over this terrible weather, I expect a real upsurge." He dropped a maraschino cherry into his bourbon and dropped out of sight behind the wing.

"I hope so, Monsignor," Jamie replied, withdrawing quietly from the study. It was pointless, even cruel, to argue. O'Toole had so little time left in MacPatch, he thought sadly. And he himself had even less.

Jamie headed upstairs to his room, moving silently in his stocking feet through the dark. At his bedroom window he looked across to Maureen's apartment. It had stopped snowing and the moon had come out. In its light the hard, glazed snow sparkled as if diamonds had been scattered across the burnt-out empty lots.

Maureen's building was dark, he saw, but there was light in her windows. Jamie thought of the binoculars downstairs, an old pair of heavy military glasses that he had seen one day in the office cabinet. He could go down and get them. He swallowed. His mouth went dry, thinking of her, and he wondered how women behaved when they were all alone.

With the cuff of his shirt he wiped the condensation from the cold glass and stared hard across the lots, trying to see beyond the curtains of her windows. He thought he could pick her out, one shadow among all the shadows in the room. And then her shadow moved, and he was sure. She crossed from room to room, and to his distant eyes, her gliding figure looked like mist, like a woman wrapped in gauze. Like a woman in a shroud, he thought, like the figure who had appeared to him at night.

Tony hurried. It was late, after eight, and he liked to be off the street by then, before the downtown traffic thinned, before he became noticeable on the street.

At Grand Avenue he ducked into the railway entrance. He could take the underground walkway across the intersection, then come up inside the station. It was a route he had taken before, that time when he was running away from the police.

At the top of the stairs he hesitated and let a rush of people pass him. They gave him a wide berth, afraid he might grab at them, afraid they might accidentally brush against him. His stink, he knew, repelled them.

From the top of the stairs he squinted into the darkness, looking for the gang of kids that hung out there below the intersection. Usually they stood by the locked bathroom, selling dope to commuters, but sometimes, when bored or broke, they'd pick out a tramp or shopping bag woman and toss them for money. It had happened to others, he knew. It had happened to him.

Tony descended slowly, keeping close to the railing, watching, ready to run back onto the street. He pulled up the layers of clothes at his waist. He was wearing three pairs of trousers, all beltless, and that made it difficult to run, if he spotted the Altar Boys. People wouldn't help, he knew. They'd rush past, looking away as the kids corralled him, herding him into the wet corner of the tunnel. Then they'd pounce on him, strip off his clothes.

But tonight Tony was safe. No one waited at the bottom of the cold stone steps. He kept moving, hugging the wall, dragging his bad right leg. He did not look at people but turned sideways, kept his head down, moving with a slight hitch, like a hunchback.

He was all right, he knew, if he kept moving, stayed with the thick flow of people heading toward the trains. In the midst of the crowd he was lost, almost invisible, the way he liked it.

At the bank of lockers against the far wall, he stopped and stepped out of the traffic. People got out of his way, halting abruptly to keep from encountering him. It made him feel better, feeling for a moment some power over other people's lives.

He glanced back, looked to see if any cops had spotted him at the lockers. His belongings were here, packed away in two of the deep tin boxes, and he couldn't be too careful. The cops would take everything he owned, the bastards, he mumbled out loud.

At the end of the row he knelt down, fished out the keys from his pockets and opened the lockers, pulling out stuffed shopping bags, dumping the contents on the floor, then searching through the piles of rags.

"Okay, buddy, outta here!" A uniformed cop banged his nightstick on the metal lockers.

Tony scurried around on his knees, looked down the length of the row. "Shit," he mumbled, grabbing for scattered clothes.

The cop stayed where he was, blocking the exit. Tony hurried, shoving back the clothes into the two shopping bags. The cop would come get him, Tony knew. Come down the aisle swinging that nightstick.

"All right, all right," the cop kept complaining. His voice was weary, as if he had had to deal with this too often.

Tony was almost finished now. He stuffed his cooking utensils into the bags, retrieving his tea kettle as it bounced away on the marble floor, pinging like a pistol shot.

"These lockers aren't for your kind. Hear that, buddy?"

The cop was above him now, a big man with flat feet. He spread his legs for balance, giving his fat thighs space, then he poked Tony with the butt of his nightstick. He kept his distance, too: Everyone knew these bums would give you their lice.

Tony stood and, clutching his bags, edged around the cop. He kept his face hidden. It was better that way. He didn't want a cop remembering him. And he watched the man's right arm, watched to see that it didn't jump up and take a swat at him. Just to be mean. Just for the fun of it.

"Keep out of here!" the cop yelled. "Understand, Charlie?" He prodded the tramp, poking the butt of his nightstick into his ribs.

The cop followed him to the end of the aisle. He kept the nightstick jammed into Tony's side, holding him like a speared fish.

"I'll bust you next time, buddy. Stay away from them lockers. People don't want your garbage near them. You'll get your cooties on their suitcases." The cop laughed, remembering the childhood name, then he dug the stick deeper into the tramp, and pushed the old man against the metal lockers.

People had gathered, a crowd of the curious as well as travelers waiting to get to their lockers. They stood back, watching, as the fat cop escorted the tramp away. He was all right now, Tony knew. The cop wouldn't beat him up with all those people around.

The cop slipped his nightstick into the old man's back, nestled it against his kidney, and shoved. "Okay, off you go. Get out of here," he ordered.

Tony yelped and stumbled forward. He kept his head down and kept moving, following the flow down the ramp, through the gate and to the trains. He was like a log being swept along on a river's current.

At the bottom of the ramp he spun away from the people and ran back along the parked train and into the tunnel. Then he slowed, and collapsed against an empty car, exhausted from fear. There were no lights here, except the high, dim ceiling bulbs that ran the length of the long tunnel. He looked around. No one had followed him. He was safe, hidden away among the parked trains until morning. He stood, picked up the two bags and kept walking, moving farther away from the busy end of the platform.

Tony walked for several hundred yards, keeping to the inside edge of the platform, away from what light there was in the tunnel. He was on the lookout for maintenance crews. They stored equipment in the tunnel and sometimes they'd surprised him at night, roused him from sleeping.

But mostly he was left alone, safe for the night. He had lived for five years in the tunnel. It was warm and roomy. It was home for him.

Tony stopped at the end of the tunnel, where the last cars were jammed against the rock foundation of the train station. Here there was a large cavernous space that Joe had found years before and showed him. They had both kept it secret from the other street people. Kept it for themselves.

He paused to make sure no railway workers had wandered down that far on the open platform. Hearing nothing but the distant rumble of trains leaving the station, he set down the heavy shopping bags and settled in for the night.

The tunnel hideaway gave him everything: a bed made from layers of cardboard boxes; hot water from the steam pipes; food from the parked train's dining car—soups and crackers, soda and tea bags, all tossed off the train as garbage. In the ceiling was a low-wattage bulb which he replaced with a brighter one he carried. His hundred-watt bulb shed enough light to read by, and enough to keep the rats away from his makeshift bed. And the tunnel cave was warm. Steam from the station pipes kept the underground temperature over eighty. Tony could undress, tap into the safety spigot, wash himself and his clothes, dry his things on the hot pipes.

He dug into one bag, sorting about in the clothes, papers

and books until he found the light bulb. Then he climbed up
on the trash cart and replaced the tunnel light. The new bulb
brightened the platform like a searchlight. He could see now;
he could get organized. Tony grinned, happy with himself and
his good fortune.

First he got out his bed, pulled the flat thick cardboard from
its hiding place over the wide steam pipes above the platform.
He had more belongings tucked away above the steam pipes,
in the crevices of the concrete foundations, and these he took
down as well: a coffeepot, two tins cups, a saucepan, and a
few battered spoons. All had been scavenged from garbage
cans in restaurant alleys, and he placed them neatly on a big
railway equipment box that he used for his table and chair.

Here he could sit, curl up his legs, and read newspapers.
He had two papers today, complete morning and evening edi-
tions that he had found in the bus station. He liked to read. He
liked to keep current, to know what was happening in the city,
in the world.

That was something he'd been missing since Joe disappeared. He missed having someone around to discuss things
with. He lifted Joe's cup from the cranny and turned it in his
fingers. Tony had been with Joe when he found it. They were
working the alley behind Third Avenue, going from house to
house, searching the garbage left out for the morning trash
trucks.

It was a kid's cup, with lions and tigers enameled all over
it. Joe had held it up, laughing at his good luck, yelling over
to him. Tony smiled, remembering his buddy. He missed Joe's
company. Carefully he replaced the small battered cup in the
crevice.

He'd keep the cup, keep all of Joe's things. His friend would
be back, Tony knew. They couldn't hurt Joe. "Can they, Joy-
boy?" he said, jumping down off the square metal container,
talking out loud, keeping himself cheery. It made him feel
better, having his voice bounce off the curved tunnel ceiling.
He felt as if he were with a crowd of people, sharing a good
time. He laughed out loud, then listened fast to the echo. It
was almost as if Joe was with him, laughing while they shared
a warm bottle.

Tony laughed again out loud, his breath whistling through

his broken teeth. He shook his head, kept chuckling, amusing himself. He stopped. He felt like dancing. Joe liked to dance. At times, coming back to the railway station late on a summer night, Joe would stop, step out into the empty street, and begin to dance, to shuffle up the street, to shout out crazylike.

"The son of a bitch," Tony said out loud. Now he was crying, the tears rushing down his cheeks. He couldn't feel them, didn't know he was crying. "Poor goddamn Joe," he said out loud. "Those sons a bitches!" His angry voice rolled along the tunnel. He tried to keep dancing, shuffling from one edge of the platform to the other, but now that Joe was gone Tony couldn't hear the imaginary music. He stumbled, almost fell. His legs hurt. His back, too. But he kept dancing, breathing hard, trying to do it right, the way Joe had showed him. "Is this right, Joe?" he shouted.

Tony fell against the metal container, exhausted, dizzy from the effort. "Jesus H. Christ," he whispered, gasping. He straightened up, wiped his runny nose with his sleeve, hitched up his trousers, pulled himself together. It was late and he was hungry. He was always hungry, but that day he had found half a ham-and-cheese sandwich and three pizza crusts, all fresh, all less than a day old. He grabbed the coffeepot off the metal container and carried it to the end of the tunnel, where he cracked open the valve on a hot water pipe and filled the pot with boiling water.

Moving back to the metal container, he opened his can of coffee and carefully poured two spoonfuls into the pot. It was then that he heard the footsteps. A single person, coming slowly down the length of the tunnel. It was a man, Tony knew, soft steps, like he was wearing slippers. Not a cop. Cops were always afraid in the tunnel, Tony knew. They made a racket banging their nightsticks against the walls, as if to scatter the tramps like rats. Nor was it a railway worker. They came in pairs or small work gangs, never alone.

The footsteps stopped again, paused, moved slowly around one of the thick, square concrete support pillars of the platform. Tony glanced around at his small setup: the bed of corrugated cardboard, his bags of belongings. The tiny room he had claimed at the dead end of the tunnel. Nowhere to run. The parked trains were locked. He was trapped.

The coffeepot slipped from his nervous hands, banged against the metal container. More footsteps. Running now, rushing down the tunnel. Tony backed away and slipped down into the corner, caught there between the train and the edge of the concrete platform. He pulled his heavy cloth coat over his head and curled against the cold cement floor, making himself small. He had done this before, in the park, disguised himself as a dirty bundle of rags and refuse. He held his breath and listened.

The man had reached the end of the tunnel. Tony listened as he picked up the coffeepot, heard the metal scrape against the equipment box. There was more light, and it circled the tiny space. A hand-held lantern, Tony guessed. The man searched his bed, walked over the thick cardboard and off again onto the cement, still circling. Tony heard him kick the shopping bags, the soft punch of a leather shoe against paper.

Tony kept his face turned away, buried in the folds of his coat, not breathing. The man moved away from the shopping bags, came closer. Again the soft steps. The smooth slippers. A toe nudged him, poked his back. Tony flinched at the pain when the toe struck his kidney.

"Now, now."

The voice was reassuring.

"Get yourself up from there," the voice said, encouragingly.

Tony rolled over on his back, shielding himself with his raised arm and looked up. He was staring into the bright ceiling bulb.

"Please," Tony whispered. "Don't hurt me. I'm gone. I'll get myself out of here."

"Sure. Sure." The man was still encouraging.

Tony relaxed. He knew the streets. He knew whom to fear. People's voices gave them away. This man was all right. Someone from the Center, he thought, someone with a hot meal to offer.

"Here, let me help you," the man said. A gloved hand reached down, grabbed Tony beneath the arms, lifted him off the cold cement.

Tony did not resist. He didn't have the strength; besides, he was in safe hands. He smiled, laughing at his fears. Joe would have liked that—the way he had tried to hide, to get away. He was grinning, telling the story to Joe in his mind, when the blow caught him behind the ears. The club sank into the soft, old flesh and Tony's head jerked up, as if his neck had snapped, the blood gushing into his mouth.

The killer turned Tony's head aside and let the old man bleed on the concrete platform. He would deal with the blood later, open the hot water taps and wash that end of the tunnel. He glanced around the small space, taking into account the cardboard bed, pots and pans, the shopping bags of raggy clothes. He'd remove it all, that trash, and when it was cleaned away, there would be no record of the old man who hung dead in his arms.

Maureen was awake at midnight, remembering yet again how Jamie's hand had felt, when she heard the knob of the back door rattle. She sat up, startled into alertness, and wondered if she had imagined the sound. She could go into the kitchen, check the lock, she thought, and then, without more preliminary, the rattle was followed by a muffled thump. Another thump, and Maureen identified it: It was the sound of someone's shoulder thrown against the wood.

Maureen rolled across the bed, grabbed the small Princess telephone and dialed 911. She did not raise her voice or rush the information as she told the police dispatcher that her apartment was being broken into. She kept thinking to herself how calm she was, how sensibly she was behaving. The dispatcher said the police would be there within five minutes.

She hung up the phone, then jumped off the bed and ran quickly, lightly, to the bedroom door. She was barefooted, but still wearing the jeans and velour shirt she'd had on earlier. She reached the bedroom door and closed it just as the back door gave way, shoved open. He was in the kitchen now. Quickly she turned the latch, locking herself in the bedroom.

He might just leave her alone, she thought. If he wanted the TV or the typewriter, rather than jewelry, he might only ransack the front room and not bother her. But maybe it wasn't just one person. Maybe, she thought with a sharp stab of fear, it was the Altar Boys, come to even the score because she'd gotten them in trouble. Robbery wouldn't be enough for them; they wouldn't be satisfied until they'd terrorized, maybe even raped her.

Maureen glanced back at the telephone. She could call Jamie. He lived close enough to reach her apartment before whoever it was could break down her bedroom door. She moved away from the door, her bare feet softly creaking the floor, and picked up the phone. There was no dial tone. The receiver in the other room had to be off the hook. Then she heard heavy breathing, like an obscene phone caller, and realized that someone was on the other end, listening as she tried to call out. Maureen dropped the phone and it slammed on the floor, ringing involuntarily.

Someone knocked on the door, and said something, but the voice was muffled and unintelligible. Maureen did not answer. Whoever it was shoved against the bedroom door. It would give, she knew, and much faster than the back door had. Maureen ran into the bathroom, then ran out again. Grabbing a straightback chair, she dragged that back in with her. She locked the bathroom door, then wedged the chair under the knob, creating a little barricade.

Maureen heard the bedroom door give way. The old lock popped off and the frame splintered. Now they were in her room. She heard breaking glass and thought of the perfume bottles on top of the dresser. It sounded as if someone had swept a hand across the dresser top, sending them all flying.

She slid to the floor, pulled a bath towel off the rack and stuffed a thick fold into her mouth to keep herself from screaming. Then faintly, as if from far uptown, she heard a police siren, and she made herself focus on that, straining to hear if the wailing was growing, coming closer. The siren ebbed and flowed, seemed to come near, then faded. She could not tell if it was coming to save her.

A body slammed against the bathroom door. The wood panel swayed, buckled slightly, but held. The back of the chair was wedged tighter under the doorknob. The police siren again. It was approaching. She could hear it turning onto Jefferson at the end of the block and coming down the short street to her apartment.

There was more than one squad car and the sirens played a chorus in Maureen's ear. The fear left her. She sank down, exhausted from tension, but knowing she was safe.

Someone was knocking on the door now, pounding as if

persistence would persuade her to open it. Why weren't they running away, she wondered. Didn't they hear the police outside, the car doors slamming?

It wasn't the Altar Boys, she realized; they'd have tumbled out the front door by now, or headed for the roof. No, it was some single, determined intruder, someone crazy enough not to mind being caught. He could still break the door down, she realized. When the police arrived, they might have missed saving her by seconds.

Terrified all over again, Maureen scanned the bathroom frantically. The tub was useless; not even a shower curtain to hide behind. The hamper, the toilet, the sink—there was a tiny spot there, not safe, but hard enough to reach that dragging her out might cost a few seconds.

The man was shouting now but Maureen barely heard him as she squeezed herself under the sink, pulled her legs into the tight space. She was crying, her head pressed against her up-drawn knees, her palms over her ears to block out his voice.

"Open the door! You've got to open the door!" he was yelling, pleading almost, and through her tumult Maureen slowly realized that the voice was one she recognized.

"Jamie!" she cried. She had only wished for him, thought of calling, and now he was here to save her. Scrambling from the hiding place, she wrestled the chair free and flung the door open.

"Jamie!" she cried again, laughing and crying with relief. "Where is he? Did you see him?"

Jamie did not answer. He towered above her, his body tense, his blue eyes inflamed. And he was all alone.

It had been Jamie all along. As she formed the thought she ran, through the bedroom and into the kitchen, running out the broken door and toward the policemen pounding up the back stairs.

As she ran, she yelled to Jamie, "Get out of here! What's wrong with you? Get out of here!"

Then the police were all around her, swarming into the apartment, their heavy boots stomping through all the rooms.

"Ma'am?" The officer who approached her was young, twenty-two or three, she guessed. "Ma'am, how did he get away? Where did he go? There's no one here."

CHAPTER SEVENTEEN

January First, Morning
Feast of the Circumcision

"Why did you try to kill me?" she asked.

"Maureen, I didn't," he sighed. "Once I left your apartment last night I didn't go back." They were sitting alone in the Reconciliation Room of the rectory. He had returned from saying the New Year's Day morning masses and found her waiting.

"What about the doors, then? And the broken perfume bottles? You think I keep fantasizing that you're in my apartment, but I didn't fantasize two splintered doors, and neither did the cops who showed up."

"Did you give them my name?" he asked. He thought of Robert Murphy, of how he would receive that news.

Maureen shook her head. "Of course not. There was no point. Even last night it was clear that you weren't yourself; you were so emotional, so violent. You even looked like a different person."

They both sat silent for a moment, wondering what it all might mean. Then Maureen said, "I believe you, you know. I have to. When the cops checked the apartment they found the front door still locked. If you had really been there, you couldn't have escaped any other way."

"Yet you insist you saw me."

"Because I did—just like the last time."

"Oh, I remember: the poltergeist theory."

"But Jamie, it makes sense!" She was excited now, pursuing a new train of thought. "If it's sexual energy that creates the apparition, or whatever you want to call it, then last night was a perfect time for it to appear. After what happened in the kitchen, you know—" She stopped talking, embarrassed at having to discuss how they had parted.

"Yes, I know," he said. "But if I really wanted to get at you, why didn't I just materialize in the bathtub? Why bother starting on the back stairs and battering my way in?"

"I don't know," she said. "You disappeared fast enough when you wanted to. Maybe the answer is that simple: that you wanted to use force. You wanted to batter. You were acting as much out of anger as desire."

"But why would I be so angry with you?"

"Jamie, you know you were angry when you left. You told me to go to hell."

"Maureen, come on. I was frustrated, yes. And angry; I admit that. But not enough to come back four hours later and break two doors down."

"Maybe you weren't yourself," she said. "I said you looked like a different person, and maybe you were. Suppose you went home and started meditating. And instead of just seeing a past life, some part of you started acting it out."

"Still there is no reason why I'd be after you, in particular," he objected, then stopped suddenly, as if a new thought had seized him. Maureen waited.

"It's because you were there," he said slowly, drawing out the thought as he spoke.

"Where?"

"In my past. Yes! This one recollection keeps coming back to me. We're on a path together, in an orchard of olive trees. You're up ahead of me and you turn to say something. You're angry."

"That sounds like me," she said.

"It's a winter's night, but the path is lit by torches. We're moving in and out of shadows as we walk, and your face is in profile. You look absolutely beautiful and you turn to me, say something." Jamie stopped, shook his head, unable to recall more than a snatch of the memory.

"Do you remember anything besides the lighting?" she asked. "Can you pinpoint the feeling between those two people? Are they enemies? Is that why they're angry?" There was an intensity to his voice, a sureness of what he recalled that made her feel this brief memory was important.

"No, they're not enemies, they're lovers. I'm sure of that," he said. "Maureen, I'm positive she's you," he went on excitedly. "Remember the day we met, on Christmas? Even that day I felt a bond between us, something more than just a strong attraction."

"Soul mates?" offered Maureen dryly.

"Yes, if you want to call it that."

"And you think that is what keeps drawing you back to me, even in your trances?"

"Well, don't you think so? It makes sense."

"Who was I, then?"

"I just don't know. In the trances I never hear your name."

"In your trances do you ever remember anything similar to that—fragments of memory that might come from the same time period, the same life?" Maureen asked eagerly.

"Yes, one. I'm in a garden and I wake up. I see a crowd of people coming. There's a cold bitter wind—at least I feel cold—and I can smell eucalyptus burning.

"Then I see a crowd of soldiers and people dressed in robes. They're coming into the garden and I stand up, walk through the olive grove to meet them. And somehow I realize I'm in danger and I begin to run away, up the hill through this olive orchard. And that's all I know."

"For now," emphasized Maureen. "But each time you undergo a regression you seem to see more, understand more. It's as if whatever is in there is gradually coming out, is being revealed to you."

"So you think we should try again."

Maureen nodded. "Are you willing?" she asked.

"Are you?"

"Jamie, it's not my past lives we're confronting."

"No, but you're linked to me; we know that now."

Maureen shrugged. "Well, let's find out if I am."

"When do you want to do it?"

"Any time. Are you free right now?"

"Yes. Monsignor O'Toole is saying the last Mass." Jamie sighed, then added, speaking softly, slowly, "If there's a demon living in my memory, I've got to find it. Whatever is haunting me, I've got to face it, or I'll never have any kind of peace with myself."

"All right, Jamie," she said. She laid her hand on his, wanting to comfort him. "Where shall we work? Where do you have your most vivid recollections?"

"My bedroom, always."

"Will we cause a scandal if I go up there with you?"

"I think I've already caused all the scandal possible, thank you. Besides, if we try to do it here, someone will come in, ring the doorbell."

Maureen slung her bag over her shoulder and walked toward the foyer. At the door Jamie stopped her.

"Maureen, are you afraid?" he asked. "Of me, I mean."

Maureen studied the young priest, then shook her head gently and started for the stairs. In a way she had told the truth: It was not Jamie Ignatius she feared, but the secret that was waiting in his memory. The first time she had seen his apparition in her room, the figure had been sad and desperate. The second time it had come in anger. They had to unlock the secrets of his past. The third time he might come to kill.

His bedroom did not surprise her. She liked the monastic look of the stark, white walls, and simple makeshift furniture. It was severe, but beautiful in its way, she thought, especially that morning with the low winter sun filling the windows, flooding the white interior with sunlight.

"Good!" she pronounced, looking about as Jamie tugged off his running shoes, then went to the corner and unrolled his bed mat. Maureen walked to the desk and set her purse down, then looked out the window. She saw at once that her apartment was directly opposite, across the empty lots, and suddenly she felt doubtful, as if she might have misjudged him after all.

"I really didn't watch you," he said, seeing her stand fixed at the windows. "I thought of it, but I didn't."

Maureen nodded. At least he was being honest, she told herself; at least he wasn't lying to her. She turned away from the windows and asked, "Ready?" She tried to make herself sound positive.

"Let us begin with the garden. You wake to see a mob coming, and you can smell the eucalyptus fires from the city. . . ." Maureen's voice trailed off. She was sitting at the desk, out of Jamie's line of sight, and he was stretched out on the mat, his arms at his sides, his legs pulled up. He had used meditation techniques to relax himself and had quickly, easily, moved back in time. Now she was hoping that she could guide him, that her suggestion might bring to the surface the particular memory they were seeking.

"It is cold," Jamie responded softly, "and I am sleeping against a rock, between Peter and the two sons of Zebedee. I wake up and hear the crowds coming out of Jerusalem. They cross the Kidron Valley and move toward the grove of olive trees.

"This is an angry mob, I know. I can hear their voices, and I am afraid. I get up and walk away from the others, up the path."

Already, Maureen noticed, Jamie had begun to sweat, to twist nervously on the mat.

"How do you know it's you they're angry at?" she asked.

"We were warned. Jesus knew there might be trouble from the priests."

Maureen's eyes widened, but she tried hard to keep the surprise from her voice. "And you leave Jesus and the others?" she asked calmly.

"Yes, I leave them," he whispered.

Maureen kept quiet; she let Jamie find his own way to explain what happened next.

"Peter is asleep, and so are the others. Jesus is farther below us, in a grove of olive trees. He loves that spot."

"And you? Where do you go when you leave them?"

"It is better to avoid trouble, especially at Passover. I told them that. So I run up to the ridge, to the top of Harha-Zetim.

As I run I think that I will cross the valley and go into the city from the north and hide somewhere until morning, until the mob has all gone home."

Jamie began to labor on the mat, to breathe deeply as he ran.

"The ridge is high and almost bare of trees. I know I can be seen; it is a clear, cold night. I do feel safer, though, away from the others, but then I see...."

"See what, Jamie?" Maureen asked, pressing him now. She leaned forward in the chair, whispered over him.

"There are more soldiers and priests. They have crossed the valley bridge and are coming down the ridge toward me. They're blocking the path."

"Jesus! Jesus the Nazarene!" Their voices rang out into the cold, clear night.

The priests were old; he shouldered his way past them without trouble. He would not go into the city, he decided. He would hide out in the desert. She could join him there. How simple it would be for both of them, he thought—away from Jesus and his sermons, away from all the people who followed them from town to town, hanging on his words. The Gospels. The good news. The son of God. Why did he call himself the Messiah? Why did he have to antagonize the priests?

"Jesus. Jesus of Nazareth!" the priests kept shouting, following him across the ridge.

He was sure they had come directly from the Sanhedrin, the council, where they had worked themselves into a fever. In spite of all their spies, they still thought Jesus was political, a radical who'd use the holy days to rally the Jews against the Romans.

They were wrong about Jesus, he knew, but right to be afraid. Jerusalem was filled with Jews at Passover, and any spark might start the rioting. Jesus had been warned, but he wouldn't go into hiding. Well, now there would be arrests. Now there would be trouble, and he did not intend to be the one shut up in a Roman jail for weeks.

"Jesus...? Are you Jesus of Nazareth?" The soldiers were there now on the path, backing up the priests. They thrust torches into his face and called for witnesses. He could smell the burning oil, and beyond the circle of flame light he could hear the high priests shouting, declaring that he was the one. He was Jesus of Nazareth.

They would take him away, he knew. There was no need to go down into the olive grove and search; they needed only the leader, the so-called Messiah.

Jamie shook his head, protesting. The torch so close to his face was searing.

"I am not Jesus Christ," Jamie shouted.

A protest began behind him, the priests shouting that they knew him; he was lying. The soldiers looked around at the high priests, demanded to know who was telling the truth.

"Arrest him!" the old men kept shouting, pressing in tighter, anxious to seize someone, anyone. Caiphas, the chief priest, had warned them that at least one of the Nazarenes had to be arrested and charged with inciting revolt. Otherwise, he had lectured at the council, "If we let Jesus go on like this, the people who don't know any better will call him the Jewish king. Even if it goes no further the Romans will hear of it. They will come and destroy both our holy places and our nation. Find us one man and save us all."

"My name is Judas Thomas," Jamie kept shouting, trying to be heard over the hysterical old rabbis. In the hot, flickering flames of the oil torches, Jamie saw the confusion in the soldiers' faces. They were short, brutal men, simple in their logic. And they hated Jews, he knew. All Jews. But they hated especially the high priests, the hectoring old men who pestered them, kept complaining of abuses. This he knew also.

Seizing on their uncertainty, he pulled loose from the soldiers who held him and grabbed one of the torches, held the flame up close to his face, showed himself fully in the yellow, smoky light.

"I am not Jesus of Nazareth. My name is Judas Thomas. If you have been told to bring back Jesus, then you had best look further. You have the wrong man."

Jamie had silenced them. For a moment, the handful of priests stood mute, puzzled and unsure what to do next.

"Let me see," another voice announced. Someone was stepping forward, pushing through the tight crowd of soldiers and priests. "I ate Seder with this Jesus, and the others."

Jamie sighed. It was all over. He was safe. He raised the

torch, held it high so as to see who had spoken.

"Judas," he whispered, "Judas Iscariot."

Judas Iscariot stepped forward and kissed Jamie on the cheek, whispering as he did. "They want him, Thomas. And if not him, then one of us."

Jamie lowered the oil torch. "He means no harm, Judas." Jamie shook his head, weary of the long days, of the three years he had spent with Jesus, traveling through all the regions of Judea.

"Where is he, Thomas?" Judas asked, keeping his voice low.

Jamie shook his head, unwilling to be specific. They knew Jesus was in the garden, but perhaps Peter would get him out before they reached the grove.

"Tell me, Judas Thomas, or I will say that you are he."

"He means no harm," Jamie answered, "and you know that, Judas. You know they all call him a fool. They call us fools, for following him. Can't you persuade the priests to leave him be?"

"I cannot," Judas answered. "It is too late for that." He, too, sounded weary of it all. "I can only save you. They want one of us, Judas Thomas. They want one as an example to those who talk of Jesus as the Messiah." He glanced up at Jamie, his face still deep in the folds of his night cloak. "Do you want to take his place, Judas Thomas? I will tell them it is you who calls himself the Son of God." He was smiling. Jamie could see a white flash of teeth in the dark, hidden face.

Jamie glanced away from Judas, looked down the long ridge toward the grove where he had left Jesus praying. It had to stop, Jamie realized. Only trouble would follow if the high priests let him keep preaching, trouble from the soldiers, from the Roman governor. Jamie turned back to Judas and said, "He knows the council has met. He warned us. He knows that Caiphas wants him arrested. What will happen if they take him?"

Judas shrugged, "What do you think? The usual. He will be beaten like a common criminal, then sent before Pilate."

"For what? For saying that the kingdom of heaven is near? Judas, you and I both know that hermits wander in off the desert almost daily, claiming the end is near. The people of Jerusalem laugh at them, they don't send them before the Ro-

man prefect." Beyond them, in the dark night, the priests began
to shout, to call for a judgment.

"Pilate will decide," Judas said, putting a stop to the debate.
"Pilate will give him forty lashes, Judas Thomas, that is all.
That will appease the high priests and Caiphas. After the holy
days they will turn him loose, when all the visiting Jews have
left the city."

Jamie nodded slowly and Judas turned to the priests and
soldiers, to tell them Jamie was not the man.

"Wait!" Jamie whispered quickly. "Judas, I will go in his
place." Forty lashes . . . a simple beating from the soldiers, but
Jesus would not survive it, Jamie knew. As alike as they seemed,
he was much stronger. Jesus was too gentle for such punishment.

Judas lifted his eyebrows. "Thomas, if you do this there is
no going back. I cannot identify you now, then change my
story later."

"I won't ask that of you," said Jamie. "This is the best for
everyone." And then he saw her.

She had come across the bridge, come searching for him
after the Seder, when he did not return to the city. Now she
stood in the first ring surrounding him, her pale face shadowy
in the torchlight. She had seen him grasp Judas's arm, knew
what had been decided.

"Judas Thomas, please," she begged. She stepped forward,
beseeching him.

She wouldn't understand, he knew. She had stopped believing in Jesus, had left them after Galilee. On her last night
before departing she had come to him, and by the dawn, holding
her in his arms, he had promised that he, too, would come to
Jerusalem. He had served Jesus; he deserved his own life, a
life free of the desert, the long journeys, the endless talk of
salvation and deliverance from Rome.

Now she was here to claim him. But he couldn't go. He
would do this last thing for Jesus.

"I must," he told her gently. "It only means a few days of
prison."

"Then they are right when they call you a fool," she answered angrily. Without a word she turned and started back to
the bridge, the soldiers parting and laughing as she passed.

"Just once more!" he called, and when she didn't turn, he ran up the path after her.

She was above him on the path, and when she turned, her hood fell away to reveal hair as black and fine as Herod's ceremonial silks. She turned only halfway, as if he were unworthy of her full attention, and her face was like a pale half-moon against the cold night sky.

"You must choose, Thomas," she said angrily. "You cannot have me and Jesus too—even if he is your brother."

Then she was moving again, and he was compelled to follow her. The soldiers made as if to stop him, when Judas Iscariot spoke out. "I have talked to this man. He is not Jesus, he only looks like him. He is Judas Thomas, the brother of Christ— in fact, his twin. We must look further for the traitor, here in the garden." Then, motioning the crowd to follow, he started down into the grove of olives, leaving Thomas and his woman to climb the long high ridge that led out of the Garden of Gethsemane.

". . . You are coming up from having dived deep into the sea. As I count you are rising slowly, through warm liquid toward the light . . . ten . . . nine . . . eight . . . seven. . . ."

Maureen counted in steady cadence down to zero and then she fell silent. She sat quietly, letting Jamie take his time. It was like watching a new lover wake, she thought.

Jamie raised his hand and touched his forehead, tentatively, as if testing if it were really there.

"Tired?" She smiled and slid down on the floor facing him. She was wearing jeans and a turtleneck of rich blue wool, knitted by her Aunt Grace. Her black hair, whch needed a washing, was pulled back in a single thick braid.

"Exhausted."

"It can be like that. Sometimes, though, people are elated."

Jamie looked up and she saw that he was shocked. "Maureen, don't you realize what that regression means? I could have saved him, but I didn't. I let them kill him."

"We all did, Jamie. It's straight from the third-grade catechism: by our sins, past and present, we all killed Christ. Jesus died for our sins, remember?"

"But he was my brother. My twin brother," he repeated in a whisper, as he realized fully the implications of the regression.

"You weren't, Jamie. Jesus never had a brother. Judas Iscariot betrayed him for thirty pieces of silver. It's in the Bible." She spoke angrily, but it was the Church she was hostile toward, not Jamie. They had done this to him, she knew; they had destroyed him with their dogma, battered him with guilt. Jamie had never had a chance, she thought. He had been destroyed from the moment they found him on the steps of Saints Peter and Paul. The Jesuits were right. If they were given a boy till he was seven, he would be theirs for life.

Jamie shook his head. "It may not be in the New Testament, but Christ did have a brother. An identical twin, named Judas Thomas."

Maureen frowned. "I don't know what you're talking about."

"There was a set of gospels—called the Gnostic Gospels—that was suppressed by the early Church. According to them, Jesus Christ had a brother. And the brother was a twin."

"A metaphor, like the Mystical Body. We're all Christ's brothers." The ease with which she argued, after all these years, surprised Maureen. She thought she'd forgotten most Church teachings, but apparently her subconscious was a cesspool of religious instruction.

"No, it's more than a metaphor," Jamie said firmly. "Judas Thomas wrote one of the several accounts that make up the Gnostic Gospels. He was a disciple, just like Matthew, Mark, Luke, and John—but he was also Christ's brother."

"Then why haven't I ever heard of him? Or of that whole set of gospels, for that matter?"

"Because they were buried," he explained. "In the first century after Jesus died, some Egyptian monks buried a copy of these gospels in the Nag Hammadi cliffs near their monastery. The cliffs were a gravesite, and no one really went digging around in them until 1945, almost two thousand years later. That's when they were discovered: thirteen papyrus books, bound in leather.

"It was clear from the start that they were the real thing, and they were sold on the black market in Cairo. Later some were even smuggled to the United States. But it wasn't until 1955 that a religious historian from the Netherlands flew to

Cairo and deciphered them at the Coptic Museum.

"When he had finished translating, the very first line read 'These are the secret words which the living Jesus spoke and which the twin Judas Thomas wrote down.'"

"But I don't understand," Maureen said, intrigued by the story. "The early Christians worked so hard to spread the story of Christ. Why would they have suppressed Judas Thomas' account? Especially if he really was Christ's brother."

"Politics," Jamie answered. "Immediately after Christ died, there were a lot of sects of Jesus-worshipers. They had a lot of beliefs in common, of course, but a lot of differences, too. The Gnostics, for example, were in touch with Buddhist philosophers, whose writings came to them in Egypt via trade routes. And that was okay for a while. But eventually, after a couple of hundred years, the Church got very big and a power struggle was inevitable."

"And the Gnostics, obviously, lost."

Jamie nodded. "Around 200 A.D. the Church first became an institution resembling the one we know, with bishops, priests, deacons, and established tenets of faith that had to be accepted by all believers. All other forms of Christian teaching were excluded, and the people who practiced those beliefs were denounced as heretics and expelled."

"Including the Gnostics."

"Including the Gnostics. We didn't know much about what they believed until this Arab found the thirteen papyrus books. Bits and pieces of gnostic manuscripts had been found over the centuries, but it wasn't until the Nag Hammadi text that we could really study them."

"So the Gnostics were excommunicated for teaching that Jesus had a brother?"

"No, the split was more philosophical than that. The Gnostics believed that we can learn to know God by knowing ourselves. That's where they got their name: 'gnostic' comes from 'gnosis,' the Greek word for knowledge. But orthodox Christians—and Jews as well—believe that God is separate from humanity, and essentially different."

"So out went the presumptuous Gnostics."

"Right. Of course, as Catholic doctrine evolved it became impossible for the Church to admit that Jesus might not have been an only child; that the Blessed Virgin might have borne other sons. So even now the Gnostic Gospels are not recognized or welcomed by the Church."

"Nevertheless, you choose to believe them." It was a statement, not a question.

Jamie shrugged. "I find it impossible to ignore them. Especially now, after what I learned today."

Maureen sat watching Jamie for a moment, wondering how best to approach him. She didn't want to upset him, or make him stop trusting her, but she had to help him confront his problem. The power of Jamie's mind was extraordinary. However deeply disturbed he was, his mind had the power to create phenomena that could reach others and affect them. He could hurt her, she realized, even without wishing to, and he could hurt himself. He might, she was beginning to fear, want to hurt himself.

"Jamie," she said softly, "stop a moment and think this through. Aren't you bending these regressions to fit your gospels, to make some kind of transcendental connection for yourself? You know about these Gnostic Gospels. You've studied them, and now they appear to confirm your recollections. We can fool ourselves so easily, Jamie."

He was shaking his head. "These aren't dreams that I'm making up for my analyst. They aren't works of fiction. I know they're true. I know I once lived those lives, in Germany, Arizona, Africa, Spain, all of them. They don't frighten me. I can accept my own reincarnation. But... it's what they all mean."

"What do they mean, then?" she asked. Let it all come out, she thought. Let him face his own fears.

"They fit a pattern. In each life I've failed people close to me, people I was responsible for. I've let them die, or sometimes I've even killed them. Jesus was the first, the betrayal that began it all."

"And you're still being punished for it," Maureen concluded, finishing his argument. She clicked her tongue, exasperated with him. "Jamie, you'll only hurt yourself by thinking this way. You have to stop."

"Stop? I can't stop my trances. I can't stop being attracted to you."

Maureen nodded, signaled that she understood, and stood. "I have to leave," she said. "It's getting late. I'm due out at my sister's this afternoon." She was on her feet, had picked up her coat and slipped it over her shoulders like a cape. She did everything with such an economy of effort, he thought. He wondered if all women were that way: neat, economical, efficient.

"There are more questions to answer, Maureen. Will you help me? Come back and do another regression?"

She shook her head. "No, I'm sorry. It's too dangerous."

"I don't care."

"Too dangerous for me, Jamie. You've already linked me in your mind to this mystery woman in the garden."

"But I loved her," Jamie said, following her to the bedroom door. "Why is that dangerous?"

"Jamie, don't you see?" she said. "You love her but you hate her, too. She's the one who made you choose. You tried to kill me for it once. I can't give you that opportunity again."

Without waiting for him to respond, she opened the door and started down the narrow hallway. Despite his confusion, Jamie said nothing as they walked. The rectory was silent; sounds carried. Maureen led the way downstairs, as if she knew her way.

At the first floor, outside the Reconciliation Room, Maureen stopped again to dress for outdoors. She pulled red leg warmers over her jeans, then tucked the pants into blue ski boots. She could have been preparing for an Arctic trek.

"What next?" Jamie asked. "What will you do now?"

He stood with his hands in his back pockets, a slight smile on his face, as if he were resigned to being abandoned.

"I'm not sure," she said. "Probably move uptown, just as Aunt Grace always wanted me to. But please don't worry, Jamie. Given time and distance—" she hesitated, then went on. "And given a change in my receptiveness toward you, I don't think we'll have any more problems. No more midnight visits." Maureen had her hand on the inside door, the one with the cut-glass windows. "I can't believe this," she said, smiling wryly. "Here I am, thirty-two years old, and still running away from the Church. You guys just don't let go, do you?"

"And what about me?" The smile had left Jamie's face and

his eyes were dark with doubt. "Am I dangerous—not just to you, but to everyone?"

They looked at each other wordlessly. Unspoken, the thought of Robert Murphy hung between them. Grace Keller. The missing street people.

"Please, Jamie, go see the Jesuit I told you about. He'll help you." Maureen pushed open the door and stepped into the vestibule.

"But it's you I need. Only you can help me. I've led all these unholy lives until now. Maybe I can change, now that I am a priest. But I need you to help me. Only you. You were there at the beginning." He followed her outside into the snow, standing on the top step in just his short-sleeve clerical shirt and jeans. "God wants you to help me understand what I have to do."

"Don't drag God into this, Jamie!" Maureen went down the steps to the sidewalk. White wet flakes were catching in her wool cap, melting like tears on her cheeks. "Leave the past alone, Jamie, mine and yours. We can't change who we are, what we have become." She turned away, began to trudge down Church Drive, heading home.

"But it won't leave me alone," he shouted after her. "Nor you, Maureen. It's trapped inside of us. And if we don't bring it forth . . ." He stopped, feeling foolish and afraid his shouts would be overheard.

Maureen did not stop walking. She did not turn at the sound of the heavy rectory doors closing behind him. But she had heard.

"If we do not bring it forth," she thought, then finished for him—"it will destroy us."

CHAPTER EIGHTEEN

January First, Afternoon
Feast of the Circumcision

"If there's a point here, I'm missing it," the Cardinal said. They were upstairs in the private rooms of the Residence, watching the New Year's Day football games. The Cardinal would look at Jamie only between plays.

"A delay, that's all. It's been all straightened out." Jamie spoke quickly. He was sitting on the edge of a chair, keeping his eyes on the TV screen.

"A delay caused by your involvement with that Sullivan girl?"

"Not involvement, Your Eminence."

"Well, what the hell would you call it?" the Cardinal interrupted. Another play, another glance at Jamie. "I tell you to pack your things and move up here, but nothing happens. When I call you on it, you say there was something you had to work out before you could move. With O'Toole? I ask. No, you answer, with Sullivan. With *Maureen!* In short, you disobeyed my orders because of that woman. 'Involvement' strikes me as the charitable way of putting it."

"It's complicated, Your Eminence. Maureen is a psychol-

ogist, and she and I have been working on something. I'm not
sure I can understand it, much less explain it."

"Try," the Cardinal shot back. He glanced at his watch,
then pulled himself up from the deep, cushioned chair. "Come
with me. I have to dress for a mayor's reception. You can tell
me while I shave." He led the way through the upstairs rooms
to his bedroom and bath at the back of the huge Residence.
Jamie followed obediently, as he had often done before, when
he was home from prep school or the seminary and he'd spend
an hour alone upstairs with the Cardinal, just the two of them,
talking like father and son.

"This really doesn't make much sense, out of context,"
Jamie said next, building up his defense before beginning the
story. He had wanted to keep everything from the Cardinal, at
least until he had a plan, but now he saw that was impossible.
The Cardinal was angry now, would be angrier still if Jamie
tried to feed him an obvious alibi. Telling the truth would
almost be a relief, he thought. Perhaps the Cardinal would even
know what he should do.

The Cardinal pulled off his collar and began unbuttoning
his black shirt. They reached the large bedroom and the Cardinal kept walking, on into the bathroom, stripping down to
his white tee shirt. He dumped the black shirt into the hamper
and opened the medicine cabinet, took out his shaving brush.

"I'm still waiting, Jamie." An edge of impatience showed
in his voice.

"It has to do with reincarnation. And the Gnostic gospels."

The Cardinal grinned at himself in the mirror as he lathered
his face with shaving cream. "You know, Jamie, you were
always an odd one about your reading. Remember, I told you
when you were out at Rocklands: Avoid the esoteric. The
problem is that you never developed a good healthy appreci-
ation for sports."

He reached out and turned on the hot water. The faucets
were gold and they sparkled in the bright bathroom light. "It's
my fault, really. I should have taken you out more, got you
on the golf course when you were still a lad."

His Eminence began to shave. "Now get on with the story,"
he said out of the side of his mouth, pulling his skin tight for
the razor.

"I don't know really where to begin."

"Start with telling me why you've been trying to get into this girl's pants."

"Your Eminence, I haven't—" In the mirror, Jamie could see himself blush.

"Then start with this apparition you saw. The old tramp that looks just like you."

"I didn't tell you that!"

"I have more than one set of eyes and ears down there in MacPatch, Jamie." The Cardinal continued to shave. "Now hurry it up. Good Lord, I'd think you were planning to lie to me the way you're hemming and hawing."

"The Gnostic Gospels . . ."

"Yes . . . Yes . . ." With his free hand, the Cardinal encouraged Jamie, gestured for him to get going.

"It's really the story of my karma," Jamie said, beginning.

The Cardinal watched Jamie in the bathroom mirror as he told the long, rambling story. It was not a neat account, with a beginning, middle, and end, but a disjointed collection of incidents, improbabilities.

The Cardinal kept still for all of it, even the hallucinations, though it hurt him to realize how sick the boy was. He had seen it happen before to priests, good men, young men, so committed to God that they let themselves be torn to shreds with guilt. In his own time, in the seminary days at Rocklands, there had been an underclassman, an Italian kid from south St. Louis, who had crucified himself over the long Easter vacation. Nailed his hand to a closet door in his room, bled to death in the empty dormitory. Well, he would not let that happen to this boy. Not to Jamie. He was lucky, at least, to have caught on this early. It would've been some scene, he thought: Jamie on the road for the CCP, telling some Catholic congressmen over breakfast about the shrouded figures in his basement.

His Eminence splashed warm water on his face and then toweled himself dry. He would be late for the mayor's reception, but now it no longer mattered. Going to the young priest, he wrapped his arm around Jamie's shoulders and walked him back into the bedroom. "Jamie, I want you to stay here. Starting tonight. Don't go home. I think you've been carrying too much of a load down there in Saints Peter and Paul. You need a few good days of rest. You'll feel better, I'm sure." He felt old, seeing how sick Jamie was.

"Your Eminence, I'm okay, really."

"Of course you are." He patted Jamie on the shoulder, had him sit down at the end of the bed. "Think of your time here as a short retreat. Time for yourself. A chance to get yourself right with God." The Cardinal smiled encouragingly, as if he were discussing a holiday, a few days in the sun. "Here's a grand idea. A good friend of ours has a place down in Boca Raton. It would be good if you could get away for a few days in Florida, get some sun. You look awfully pale."

"I don't have anything with me...." Sitting on the bed, exhausted and emotionally wrung out, Jamie didn't want to struggle. He liked the idea of staying at the Residence. It would be like old times, like being a boy again.

"Don't worry about that. You can borrow some of my things, and the sisters will get you anything else that you need." He wrapped his arm around Jamie's head and hugged him briefly to his chest. Jesus Christ, he swore to himself, why hadn't someone told him this was happening to the boy? O'Toole was out of it himself, of course. But Hilda was on the spot, taking care of Jamie every day. Why hadn't she seen that he was behaving strangely?

He thought then of not spending the evening as he'd planned, of not leaving the boy alone, even for a few hours, but he had to go downtown, it was important. "I'll be home later, Jamie," he said, "and we'll have a chance to talk. Go take your old room. I'll call the kitchen and have Brother Adrian bring you something to eat. How would you like that?" He spoke gently, like a parent trying to coax a sick child.

Jamie nodded. It did feel good to be here again, to have the Cardinal making all his decisions, caring for him.

"I'll telephone Monsignor O'Toole—" he began.

"No, don't worry about a thing. I'll call him myself. You go off now and get some rest."

At the door of the Cardinal's bedroom, Jamie hesitated. "If it were just me, Your Eminence.... If I were the only one who ever witnessed these experiences, I wouldn't be so sure they happened. But Maureen saw me in her room. I didn't even know about the apparitions till she told me."

"Now don't worry yourself, Jamie." The Cardinal spoke quickly, trying to stop the young priest from dwelling on his obsessions. "We'll talk later." He kept smiling, speaking positively, as if by good words and smiles he could alter Jamie's mood.

"I'm in love with her, Your Eminence. At least Judas Thomas is. So why did I want to kill her?" The terror had returned to his voice.

The woman is driving him mad, the Cardinal thought. Carefully keeping the anger from his voice, he said, "It's okay, Jamie. It's all right. We'll talk about it later."

He would have to call Doctor Bartlett that evening, have him stop by the Residence while he was out with the mayor. It would be dangerous to let Jamie struggle too long with his nightmares.

With a sigh, the bag lady dropped her bundles in the doorway of the liquor store. Her left knee gave out and she staggered, fell against the heavy iron grating of the display window. Lights had been left on in the store, and the liquor in the bottles shimmered. Her mouth watered, seeing the amber colors.

"Oh, good God, what the hell," she mumbled, her eyes fixed on a bottle of J&B Scotch. She liked Scotch best of all. It was a good drink. Strong. A fifth of Scotch and she wouldn't care about the cold, wouldn't worry about sleeping in a doorway. She grinned in pleasure at the thought.

But it had been years since she had had a bottle of Scotch, years since she had even remembered what it tasted like. She drank wine now. White wine. Red. Rosé. She pressed her face to the cold grating, scanning the shelves. The big, gallon jugs she liked were not on display.

"Jesus Christ," she said out loud. Her lips hurt from the cold, from the thought of a drink. "Oh, shit," she cried, leaning back against the locked doors. Her whole body ached, from the weather, from the deprivation. One drink, she thought, one little gulp of wine and she'd be well again.

"Oh, fuck!" She stumbled along the sidewalk, tripping on her own shopping bags, and began to shout, to scream incoherently, banging her fists against the metal grating. She had a momentary vision of knocking down the grating and breaking into the store, of filling her bags with whiskey, Scotch and bourbon, French wine.

She broke off shouting and laughed into the cold night. Her voice rang out on the empty street, bounced off the dark storefronts. She was alone. She began to calm down. She could not stay here, she knew. Her body told her that it was too cold to be outside, not without a bottle to warm her blood.

She leaned forward, balancing herself against the brick wall of the building, and picked up her bags, four bundles that she had tied together with twine. She hated the bundles. They were like an albatross around her neck, a curse. She was never free of her belongings.

Straightening, she collected her strength, tried to think which way to walk. Down the short street and across the park was the quickest way to the bus station, but she was afraid of the park after dark, afraid of it during the day as well.

She'd walk along LaFayette, then down Pine. It was a longer, but safer, route to the station. Once there she could stay till morning, till the cops sent her back out into the weather.

As she moved from the shelter of the building she was struck at once by a blast of cold wind off the river. Bending her head against it she pushed forward, as a black limousine turned off LaFayette and into the short, deserted side street.

Head down, the bag lady did not see or hear the car. It drove quietly past her, then paused, waited, as she inched her way up beside it. Only then did she stop, look up, but then it was too late. She couldn't run; she couldn't get away. The chloroform-soaked handkerchief was up against her face, pressed against her nose, and she struggled only briefly, then was dumped with her bags of belongings on the carpeted floor of the limousine.

The car moved slowly away from the curb, taking care not to skid on the ice. At the corner it paused for the stop sign, then turned onto LaFayette and went west, downtown, back toward the river and the heart of Saints Peter and Paul.

"Through this holy anointing may the Lord in his love and mercy help you with the grace of the Holy Spirit," he whispered, giving the bag lady the last rites before he killed her.

She lay on his makeshift table, a wide plank of coffin board covered with a rubber sheet.

"May the Lord who frees you from sin save you and raise you up." He moved around the old drunk, anointing her forehead and hands. "Father, your Son, Jesus Christ, is our way, our truth, and our life. Our sister entrusts herself to you with full confidence in all your promises. Refresh her with the body and blood of your Son and lead her to your kingdom in peace. We ask this through Christ our Lord."

The woman began to mumble, twisting on the flat board, as she came to again. Setting aside the small book called Rites of Anointing, he picked up the disposable 25cc syringe and broke open the pre-package of lidocaine, the local anesthetic used in hospital emergencies to slow down a patient's heartbeat. Printed in red on the label was a reminder that the lidocaine had to be diluted in 500 cc of glucose solution. But he did not dilute it. It was late and cold and he worked quickly now. His bare hands trembled as he filled the syringe with one gram of lidocaine in 25 cc of fluid, enough for one massive slug that would kill the woman quickly, quietly, in less than forty seconds.

The syringe was ready. Seizing the woman's arm, he pulled up the layers of old clothes to expose her bare, skinny arm. Then quickly, as expertly as a nurse, he jabbed the bag lady's arm with the lidocaine, filled her blood with the toxin, then stepped back and watched for half a minute while she died.

The old woman's arm slipped from the table, and she began to convulse, to shake on the makeshift table. Her eyes opened, popped open, then the gray iris rolled up into her head, and the pupils flashed into sight.

He reached out and carefully drew down the lids. It made him feel better not to see the white. Later he would prepare the eyes. He knew the procedure: place a thin, circular pad of cotton wool under each lid to compensate for the sinking of the eyeballs into the socket. Then apply massage cream to the lids. That kept them drying, and glued the lids together until he had had a chance to inject fluid and harden them into position.

But now he only moved away from the corpse and knelt down before the small altar he had built, to say out loud the closing prayers from the sacrament of Extreme Unction: "O

Lord, hear my prayer, and let my cry come to you. Hide not your face from me in the day of my distress. Incline your ear to me: in a day when I call, answer me speedily."

His voice echoed from the damp stone walls, came back to him down the dark hallway. He recited the prayers faster, rushing to finish. It was late. He would be missed.

Returning to the body, he began quickly to strip off her clothes, tossing each layer aside. These, and her bundles of bags, he would burn later. By morning nothing of the woman would remain, nothing that would link her to him.

Backing away again from the body, he studied the woman as he put on gloves and a rubber gown. She was syphilitic, he saw at once. The tissue on her right thigh had already degenerated, leaving a patch of yellowish, fatty muscle exposed. He would have to inject the thigh with a cavity fluid before he started, then wash her with bichloride of mercury.

Now he was ready to begin. He worked first on the old woman's joints, breaking down the stiffening muscles, delaying rigor mortis until after he was finished. First the fingers, then the wrists, flexing, bending and rotating her arms, legs, and head, softening all her limbs.

When the body was flexible, he turned her on her back, straightened her arms and legs, then shoved a block of wood beneath her head so that her face looked down toward her feet. He injected cavity fluid into the thigh, washed her with disinfectant spray, and began to work on the mouth.

He hated this job. The lower jaw had fallen open when she died and now it hung loose. He pushed hard against the body, dug the heel of his palm into her chest. Under the pressure, a final gasp of breath escaped the lungs. He seized the back of her neck and lifted. Her head rolled back and he dropped a few ounces of formaldehyde and germicide into the gaping mouth. He let the liquid swirl around for a few moments, then slip through the larynx and trachea and into the lungs.

He lowered her head to the block of wood again and cleaned out her nostrils, packing them with balls of cotton. Then he threaded his curved suture needle and hooked it into the muscle tissue at the base of the bag lady's lower gum. From there, he slipped the curved needle through the fatty septum of the nose. Then into the flesh between her upper lip and gum. Next, up into tl left nostril, across to her right, and pulled the thread tight. .ier jaw snapped into place. Holding the lower jaw in position with his little finger, he knotted the thread inside her lower lip.

There was more that he could do—pack the mouth with cotton, position the lips—but the woman would never be on display. No one would ever see her again, except for him.

He left her, crossed over to the damp wall where he kept his gallons of embalming solution and poured out a half gallon of formaldehyde, borax, and alcohol into a pail, which he carried back to the makeshift embalming table.

To get at the roof of the armpit, he extended the dead woman's arm at a right angle from the body and turned the palm upward. He searched for the artery and vein, midpoint between the collarbone and the elbow, and with a sharp Z-blade scalpel made a two-inch incision just below the woman's flabby upper arm muscle. Then, using a broad-tip forceps, he dissected the fatty and fibrous tissues until the artery was exposed.

He plucked the bluish axillary vein clear of the artery and the cluster of large nerves, then slipped two ligatures around the vein and tightened the lower one.

Embalming was becoming routine to him now, his speed and technique improving with each new venture. He could see the difference in the appearance of the bodies when he finished, and he took a certain pride in that.

He cut the vein halfway through with a pair of straight scissors and inserted the vein tube, pushing it up several inches until it got caught beneath the collarbone. He held the tube steady with one hand as he lifted the elbow, and with a little manipulation the tube slipped through, into the right atrium of the heart.

Next he tied a second ligature to hold the tube in place and gently milked the blood toward the heart with his fingers. He inserted a short artery tube into the lower end of the arm and tied it in place, and pushed the rubber catheter into the upper end for several inches and made it secure. She was ready now for the injections.

He picked the syringe off the work table behind the corpse and sucked up a bulb of embalming solution from the pail. He filled the lower arm first. It took two bulbfuls before the back of the hand and the forearm veins bulged out with fluid, and he kept stroking the arm upward, away from the hand, coaxing the blood that remained in the veins back into the torso.

The fingers had not firmed up; they were still distorted and white. Even in death, the old woman had poor circulation, he thought, and filling the syringe again, he jabbed the fluid into the tips of her fingers, using this local injection to firm up her hand.

He went back to the torso, injected another eight pints, and watched carefully until the cheeks became fuller and her eyeballs hardened. She looked, he saw, better now than she had in life.

He injected the body at all six of the normal points, moving around the table as he cut into the carotid, axillary, and femoral arteries, pausing only long enough to drain the thick blood through the tubes and into the pails. When the embalming fluid had been spread throughout the old lady's body, he pulled away the tubes and closed the incision with the suture needle and twine.

There was still one final task. He cut a small incision in her abdominal wall, two inches above the navel, and slipped in a ten-inch trocar, guiding the sharp point into the right atrium of the heart. Then he turned on the small motorized aspirator to suck out the remaining blood.

He did the stomach next, the bladder, the cecum and the colon. When her torso was clean, he used the trocar again, this time to inject the fluid, twenty-five ounces of concentrated cavity solution, moving the trocar point around the viscera as he did so and leaving a thick layer on top of each organ so that afterward the fluid would filter down. Then he pulled out the trocar and closed that incision.

A real undertaker would do more, he knew. A professional would wash the hair, scrub the hands, and buff the nails. He would apply lipstick, cosmetics, and dress the body again, cutting the clothes up the back and slipping them on. But he had no time and there was no need. Besides, he wouldn't put those filthy clothes back on this woman, not after all his work. She had never been cleaner, more perfect. He smiled down at the sight of how restful she looked.

"No more cold nights," he whispered, "no more DT's and binges. You're home now. Safe at last. You're home with God." Then he bent and lifted her up, off the table, and used all his strength to carry her into the dark passageway where he placed the body in the rocky side of the ancient riverbed, slid her into her rock-walled tomb.

The music was blaring so loudly that at first Maureen didn't hear him. She always turned the stereo way up when she did housework, and tonight her job was particularly difficult: straightening up the mess Jamie had caused when he rampaged through the apartment. She was scrubbing at the perfume that had dried on the bedroom floor when she thought she heard the doorbell. She listened closely another moment, then dashed into the living room and turned down the volume. Now she heard it clearly, someone ringing and a man's voice saying her name.

The voice was familiar but she could not place it immediately. Whoever it was was trying hard not to disturb her neighbors, trying not to draw attention to himself.

"Yes," she said, standing just behind the door. The ringing stopped. "Yes, who is it?"

"Maureen, this is Jamie's friend. Your father's old friend. Please open the door." He did not say his name. The voice was pleasant, kind, and Maureen recognized it then. It was a voice from her past, from her childhood in the big house on Jefferson Place. She removed the chain and opened the door.

The Cardinal was older, certainly, but he looked much the same as when she had last seen him up close, the same broad, tough shoulders, the same steel-blue eyes. He was dressed in a black suit, carrying his hat in his hands, and it gave Maureen an odd sense of daring to keep him standing on her doorstep.

"Yes?" she asked.

"Well, hello, Maureen." The big man smiled and reached out, touched her arm affectionately. "Do you have a few minutes, my dear?" He spoke politely, but there was no question in his voice.

"It's very late, Your Eminence. And I am...busy."

"Ah, well, indeed it's late. But the matter I've come about is very important...I was downtown myself at the mayor's, and I did want to talk to you. About Jamie. I'm concerned about the young man, Maureen, and I was hoping you might help me."

Maureen spotted the subtle shift of responsibility, the Cardinal's way of involving her in his problem.

"He's told me all about you, Maureen," he said, as enticement.

She hesitated a moment longer, but there didn't seem to be much choice. Annoyed at having let him take the first round, she stepped aside and let the Cardinal enter the apartment.

"Good Lord," he exclaimed, scanning the room, seeing the damage.

"Jamie, Your Eminence," Maureen answered, closing the door.

"Yes, he told me. Not Jamie, but this apparition, is that right?" He looked at Maureen skeptically, as if they were two adults discussing a child.

"Yes, it is, Your Eminence," she said, but it was hard to meet his eyes. Immediately he had attacked her weakest point, the idea she'd had the most trouble accepting.

"Don't do this to the boy, Maureen. Earlier tonight he told me the whole crackbrained story, all these trances and regressions and apparitions. I'm telling you, I'm worried. He's troubled in his mind, and he doesn't need you going along with him, egging him on."

"I'm not, Your Eminence." She heard herself sounding defensive and stopped to reorganize. It was so easy for him to make her feel she'd misbehaved. "I agree with you that Jamie is troubled. And I've suggested that he see a therapist, a Jesuit at City College. But don't deceive yourself, Your Eminence. These apparitions are real. It's a phenomenon that's rare, but not unheard of in parapsychology."

"Parapsychology!" The Cardinal waved his arm, gesturing for silence. "Now listen to me, Maureen Sullivan. We don't need a shrink, either of us, to explain what's bothering Jamie. Just look at this Garden of Gethsemane nonsense. It's not God that's driving him crazy, it's sex. It's you, making him feel he's got to choose. Well, take it straight from me, there'll be no choosing going on here. You're to leave the boy alone, Maureen. Starting now. Tonight."

Maureen felt the old sense of shame creeping over her again—shame and powerlessness. The Cardinal knew just how to evoke it; all priests did. It was the memory of Eve, the guilt of having made alliance with the serpent. The priests would never let it rest. To them, women were tainted and troublesome; useful in some ways, but only when they were too old to cause problems. Well, she wasn't that old yet.

"Jamie is not a boy, Your Eminence," she answered back. "He's my age, thirty-two. And I am leaving him alone. I haven't laid a hand on him. But I won't stop seeing him. I won't stop being his friend."

Maureen folded her arms and hoped for a reaction. The Cardinal knew how to mask his feelings. It was what he had been taught at Rocklands, practiced as a parish priest, perfected as a Catholic politician. Still, his blue eyes flashed a moment's awareness, a quick quiver of anger.

"Your parents would be sick if they knew about this, young lady." He spoke softly, mournfully, as if his concern were all for his departed friends. "I knew them well, of course. I don't think you'd remember, but I spent a good many Sundays with your family."

"I remember." Maureen kept her arms crossed, waited him out.

"He was a fine man, Liam."

"No, he wasn't. He was a dreamer, a loafer. You know that. He used my mother like an indentured servant so he could sit home reading all day."

The Cardinal nodded as if agreeing. "He should have been a priest. The man had a craving for theology, the word of God. He would have been a fine Church scholar."

"And he would have saved my mother a lifetime's suffering if he had."

The Cardinal said softly, "No, Maureen, you're wrong there. I knew both your parents before they were married. We were kids together. She's the one who kept him from the Church. However she might have suffered later, she made her own bargain with Christ. She stole Liam Sullivan from the priesthood."

"As you think I'm stealing Jamie?" She was almost speechless with her rage.

"Yes. I think you'd like to."

"Bullshit, Your Eminence."

This time there was no reaction. The Cardinal crossed the room and sat down in the most comfortable armchair. He was still wearing his black wool overcoat, but he had unbuttoned it, and pulled the dark scarf away so that the Roman collar showed.

"Let me tell you a story, Maureen."

"Please, Your Eminence, it's late. And I'm really not interested in more stories of the old neighborhood." She put her hand on the doorknob as if ready to see him out.

"You have the time," the Cardinal answered flatly. "Besides, the story isn't long, and it's important."

Feeling slightly foolish, she drifted away from her stance at the door and came toward him. She would have to sit down and listen, but as a compromise she merely perched on the arm of the sofa. If the Cardinal noticed, he said nothing.

"In this parish, before you were born, there was a young man, a good Irish Catholic, the only son of a wealthy family. The boy secretly wanted to be a priest. Nothing else in life, just a pastor in a little parish in the city. But he came from a prominent family and they had other, more important, ambitions. They wanted him to go into politics, to run for Congress, maybe even beat Joe Kennedy's sons to the White House.

"Now, of course, these ambitions clashed, and a compromise was worked out—with the help of the Cardinal, I might add, Dan Cardinal Farley, who died, God rest his soul, in 1949. The compromise was that the boy go to Notre Dame, and after graduation, if he still wanted to become a priest, well, the family would relinquish its claim on him.

"Families in those days, Maureen, were much stronger than they are today, and fighting your father was a bold step. The young man suffered a good deal, agonizing over his vocation.

"Still, when he finished college he went off to Rocklands. But his father wasn't convinced, you see, and he felt—not unreasonably—that his son really didn't understand life. There were no girls at Notre Dame then and the boy had hardly ever dated; mostly he went out in big groups to the basketball games, the local tea dances, but he had never taken any girl seriously, and he was very pure.

"After the boy actually entered the seminary the father seemed to relent. The Korean War was about to start and no one in America knew if it would last as long as World War II. The father figured that even being a priest was better than getting drafted.

"It was a sad time for MacPatch then. The neighborhood was changing. It had been an Irish stronghold for generations, but when the fellas came back from Europe in '46 and '47 they moved away from the river, the old houses, and bought into the suburbs, and the blacks started arriving from the South, moving into the old brownstones, turning them into tenements. And there was his son, working with these people, treating them as if they had a right to be there. I think it drove the old man slightly crazy.

"He was sixty-three at the time, ill with lung cancer, and all the pain made him malicious. God had stolen his son from him; well, he'd steal him back. Oh, he was bitter; he was going to outfox God." The Cardinal smiled, as if amused by the strange revenge.

"The family had always had servants and they were usually German girls, even during the war. The mother, who was Irish herself, felt that German girls were cleaner, more dependable than greenhorns from the old country.

"There was a young girl from Germany, a survivor of the war in Europe, that the father came across somehow. A shy child, lovely, still in her teens and without a family. He brought her to the house, but she had very few household skills, so she really was only a ward, a companion, and she spent her time fussing over the old man. And in time they became co-conspirators."

The Cardinal paused. He could see that Maureen was impatient, so he went directly to the point.

"What the father did was promote an affair between this young girl and his son. He encouraged the girl, lied to her, really, about his son, and offered her the security of the family and its fortunes. Produce a baby, he told her, and the wealth of the family would belong to her and her child."

The Cardinal shrugged. "She was an attractive woman. The young seminarian was inexperienced. She simply seduced him." He smiled. "And the young man loved her. They loved each other, really, in their own way, but the man wouldn't give up the Church, not even when a son was born."

The Cardinal had Maureen's attention now. She had stopped gazing off and was watching him, following the story closely.

"The woman killed herself after the birth. The young man would not marry her and she had no legal claim on the family. She was not emotionally strong, not after having been a child in Germany during and after the war."

"And the child?" Maureen asked.

"An orphan. No one would claim the infant. The old man had hoped to force his son into accepting the responsibility of a family, but he wouldn't. Without his son, the old man had no use for the grandchild."

"Jamie," Maureen said softly.

The Cardinal nodded.

"You didn't find him on the steps of the Cathedral."

"Not really, but he was abandoned. No one would claim him."

"And Jamie's father? Who was the young Irish priest?"

"I think you can figure that out, Maureen."

The admission knocked the wind out of her. "Does Jamie know?" she asked.

The Cardinal shook his head. "It was safer, of course, if he didn't. It was safe, too, for me."

"Then why tell me? You must know I'm no friend of yours."

"I want you to help me, Maureen, as your father helped me thirty-two years ago."

Maureen stared at him. For once he had really taken her by surprise.

"It was Liam who saved me. When Jamie's mother died, I went a little crazy myself. But Liam helped me pull myself together." The Cardinal was not looking at Maureen, but kept staring off, as if into the past.

"I loved the woman. I did . . . but it all happened so fast, the night she had the baby. It was such a different world then . . . much more frightening to have a baby but not a husband. And, of course, she was a foreigner, far away from her family, speaking only a little English. Anyway, it broke her. She brought the child to me right after he was born. I was at the rectory for Christmas and she came there. Rang the bell."

He stopped speaking for a moment and looked down, as if trying to regain control, then he went on, slowly and carefully, evoking all the details.

"It really was Christmas Eve; that part of the story is true. I was out in the kitchen at the time, having a cup of tea. We were getting ready for Midnight Mass, and I wanted to have a bite to eat before beginning my fast. You remember how we couldn't eat before Communion in those days?

"She must have realized I was home. I don't think she would have left the child otherwise. . . . She rang the bell and ran. Ran to the river, disappeared in the snowstorm. I opened the foyer doors and there he was in the snow, bundled up in blankets, blankets from my bedroom back home. And a note was pinned to the blankets. 'Ihr Sohn,' she had scribbled—'your son.' The baby was blue, freezing. She had given birth to him in her room at the house, then came out into the cold, carried the child to me. Later, I found the bloody sheets still on her bed—"

"Stop! Stop! Please!" Maureen had begun to cry.

Behind her the Cardinal went on, still speaking slowly, softly, as if caught in a trance of memory. "I went to your father then; he was the only one I could trust, who understood me, really. . . . Everyone thought of Liam as being impractical, lost to the real world as it were, what with his talk of theology, the ways of knowing God, all that . . ." the Cardinal smiled, recalling, ". . . but Liam understood things better than most of us. He told me to say nothing, to turn the child over to the nuns, and he made up the whole story, right down to my finding little Jamie under the statue of Saint Ignatius. He believed in details, the verisimilitude."

Maureen spun around, enraged. "You bastards!" she whispered.

"No, Maureen. Young, yes, and foolish; scared, certainly. The way Jamie is today. That's why I won't let you destroy him. I'll protect him, the way your father once protected me."

"Get out of here!" Maureen demanded. She stood her ground, pointed toward the front door. "You have no say over my life, not any more. Take your corrupt story, your corrupt life out of here."

"But I do have control over your life, Maureen; I still do."

He kept his voice down. "One telephone call from me and you'd be out of work. The mayor won't ask any questions. He's a man of the world; he understands."

"Get out of here!" she said again. But his threat had calmed her; here, at last, was something she could deal with. And as the rage left her, a simple thought began to form: What if it wasn't true? What if he'd created a story he knew would overwhelm her, would make her believe his tie to Jamie was stronger than hers, would leave her feeling guilty for the role her father played?

Look, he was saying, your dreamy father was no saint; in fact, he was no better than I was. She'd been a fool to believe him, she thought...and yet it had sounded true. Her father had been a great one for verisimilitude.

The Cardinal stood, but buttoned his coat very slowly. He could see the girl was unsettled. Now was no time to rush.

"I don't want Jamie hurt," he said again. "And I can see that you don't either. You're not even part of this, not really. You're just back here for a term, doing research, trying to finish your degree. It's interesting work, I'll say that. The Church is interested in afterlife experiences, did you know that?"

He paused for an answer, and she shook her head, weary now.

"Yes, indeed. Why, at Notre Dame they're funding research on it right now. You should look into it. Perhaps I could write you a letter, it being my alma mater and all."

"No, thanks, Your Eminence. My focus of interest has shifted. But I appreciate the thought."

He was nodding, his forehead furrowed. "Yes, you've done great things at the Center. Of course, the scope there is so limited. No money to expand; barely enough money to keep up. Jamie told me your idea of using the Cathedral buildings. That won't work, of course. No, I'm afraid there's not much future for your work here in MacPatch." He paused, as if a thought had just come to him.

"Of course, other communities are taking this more seriously. The Lubow Foundation, in New York, is staffing a pilot project right now, but they're having trouble finding people with experience."

"That surprises me, Your Eminence," she interrupted. "In MacPatch alone there are a number of good people; in New York City there must be hundreds."

"Good caseworkers, yes," he answered. "But this program will require a wider range of abilities—a combination of fundraising, public speaking, street work, etcetera. To make this project work they need people who know how to get things done—people like you."

He looked at her appraisingly. "Everyone is watching this project. If it's successful, it will mean support from a lot of other foundations and corporations. It could make the housing and rehabilitation of the homeless a going venture, rather than a lost cause, which is what it is now. Of course," he added casually, "given their staff problems, the project may very well fail—in which case, all that new funding will evaporate."

How had he gotten her into this spot, Maureen wondered. He was presenting an option that was truly insidious, because it served everyone's purposes, even her own. She wanted to get away from Jamie, and she wanted to fight for the homeless. She had even heard of the Lubow Project; had thought of sending them a résumé. Because the Cardinal was right: Local efforts like the Center were doomed unless money started coming from sources besides the government.

She hadn't sent the résumé, partly because New York was unappealing, but also because she hadn't thought she had a chance. Now she had the job, if she wanted it; no application necessary. There was only one rather childish reason to refuse: because the Cardinal wanted her to accept.

He was knotting his scarf now, taking elaborate care with it while the pros and cons raced through her mind. Her conflict was so clear, he could almost see it written on her forehead. But as much as she hated him, she was too practical, too dedicated, to resist, he thought.

"It's late; I'd better let my chauffeur get home to bed," he said, walking to the door. She wouldn't capitulate now, right on the heels of denouncing him. So he'd give her another opportunity. "Why don't you call me at the Residence tomorrow? Jamie is there now, you know, and I can fill you in on how he's feeling."

"Thank you," she answered.

"Oh, you're welcome, my dear. As I said, I know you only want what's best for him."

"I do, Your Eminence. But that's not what I meant. I want to thank you for taking me to the top of the mountain. I've never been tempted by Lucifer himself before. It was really quite a show."

The Cardinal's expression hardened. Maureen watched his eyes, saw the blue-gray turn steely. Jamie had those eyes, she thought suddenly, feeling a moment of doubt. Or was that just a coincidence?

"I see I've overestimated you, Maureen. I would have expected more respect from a Sullivan."

"No guilt trip, Your Eminence. It won't work. I'm not my father's daughter; I don't think the clergy are above it all. In fact, from what I've heard tonight, I'd say you were up to your elbows in it."

She expected him to get angry, to scold her for talking that way, but his face was closed and calm. It was as if he had written her off, placed her firmly beyond the pale of those that mattered, like an excommunicated soul.

"And how did you lose your faith, Maureen?" he asked. "Some young friend in college?"

"No, it was much easier than that. I did it on my own. I didn't need anyone's help."

"Something you're proud of, it seems." The Cardinal stepped out into the hall. "That's why you enjoy this vengeance you're taking on the Church."

"Your Eminence," she sighed, "I'm not taking vengeance. I don't plan to help the Church or hinder it. I really and truly don't want anything to do with you people."

"And Jamie?" the Cardinal asked.

That was all he wanted, Maureen realized. He wouldn't give up till it was settled. A deal made. He wanted her out of Jamie's life. She wondered what he would do next to stop her. Have her legs busted? The apartment torched? Or send the Altar Boys to gang-rape her in LaFayette Park?

"Just leave Jamie to me," she said sweetly, closing the door as she spoke. "I think you'd make a perfect grandfather."

CHAPTER NINETEEN

January Fourth, Afternoon
Feast of Saint Titus

Jamie hesitated in the doorway of Maureen's tiny cubicle. She didn't see him; she was busy going through the drawers of her desk, cleaning out her things. He tapped lightly on the partition and she glanced up, looked surprised.

"What are you doing here?" she asked. "I heard you were installed at the Residence."

"Time off for good behavior. Plus I wanted to see you. I stopped by your apartment and the guy upstairs said you were moving out."

"I almost have, except for my books and a few big things. I'm staying with my sister out in Spring Valley, and her husband is going to drive the station wagon in to pick up the rest of my stuff, maybe tonight." She gestured around her office. "I'm leaving the Center as well."

"You're leaving the city altogether, then?"

"Yes, I'm leaving." She started on another desk drawer.

"But everything is unresolved."

"Not for me it isn't."

"Maureen, I need your help."

She swung back in her swivel chair, tipping away from the desk. "Your Cardinal came to see me. He tried all kinds of threats and bribes to keep me away from you. I thought he was going to call down Michael the Archangel to slay me."

"It's none of his business," Jamie answered, taken by surprise.

"It doesn't matter. He's right, really. I thought about it all night and decided the sooner I move away the better." She wouldn't mention how the Cardinal had threatened to call the mayor about her. Since she had to move on anyway, she preferred to do it on her own, without a dismissal on her record. What really galled her, though, was the thought of the Cardinal congratulating himself on having run the little lady out of town.

"Where are you going?" the priest asked.

"No dice, Jamie; you're the last one I'd tell." She had filled her briefcase and now she zipped it closed.

"But what if I have to reach you?"

"You won't. Once I'm out of MacPatch I think your life will calm down. You know: lead us not into temptation. Without a receptive partner, I'm not sure you'll be able to project the apparitions."

"He actually went to see you?" Jamie said, as if only then realizing what she had said.

"Yes, late Saturday night. He said you were at the Chancery and he was worried about you." She made herself stop. She would tell him everything in a moment, the Cardinal's whole tale of love and suicide, and that would be unfair to Jamie. Unlike her, he would probably believe it.

"He frightened me to death, arriving after eleven, knocking on my door. I'm all nerves as it is." She moved around the desk and picked up the briefcase, straining under its weight.

"Let me," Jamie said, taking it from her.

She gave him the briefcase and stepped quickly by him into the main room of the Center. It was after one and a bright winter sun was shining in the storefront windows. There were a dozen or more old people in the large open space, sitting at tables and up near the windows, basking in the warm, direct light. Someone had put on a few scratchy albums, Guy Lombardo tunes, and two women wearing sweaters and coats were foxtrotting together in the middle of the floor.

Maureen kept walking. She wanted to make a quick getaway, with no painful farewells to the people she was leaving behind. She pushed open the front door and stepped into the bright cold day.

"He thinks you're overwrought, overworked, and oversexed, and that it's all my fault." She felt freer to speak, now that they were in the open air.

"Don't believe it, Maureen. This started before I even met you." He followed Maureen to her car, the two of them clambering over mounds of frozen snow at the curb. Maureen unlocked the driver's side and got in, then reached across and unlocked the other door for Jamie.

"I hope it starts," she said, turning the ignition key. "Every time I park I have to wonder if this baby will ever move again."

"So you're bringing me along so I can push?"

Maureen smiled. It was silly, but she liked being kidded by Jamie. "Where do you want to go? I'll drop you anyplace but the Chancery. If the Cardinal sees you in my car, he'll have me arrested for kidnapping."

"Church Drive, I guess. I have to pick up my things at the rectory."

She glanced over at the young priest. He was staring straight ahead, as if caught up again in his troubles.

"I wanted to tell you that I'd talked things over with the Cardinal, but now you already know that," he began. "This morning he said that he's arranged for me to see a shrink—a good Catholic layman, he calls him—and to make a retreat in Boca Raton. He's already booked my flight."

"Boca Raton! I didn't know they were building retreat houses in Florida resorts now."

"Well, His Eminence has good friends in Florida, a married couple who are on a board with him. I'll be staying with them, rather than at a conventional retreat house."

"More good Catholic laymen," Maureen answered, amused.

"That's right. Anyway, I'm leaving tonight."

"Tonight!" Maureen slowed the car and turned onto Church Drive. "The Cardinal sure works fast."

She stopped the car in front of the rectory and they both sat quietly for a moment, thinking about the imminence of his leaving.

"There's just no escaping for you, is there?" she said. "Short of just chucking the whole thing, I mean. And you'd never do that."

"Sometimes I think that if I left the Church I'd bleed to death," Jamie said, managing a smile. Then he twisted in his seat to look at her. "I'm not crazy, Maureen, am I?" he asked. He sounded so helpless she wanted to embrace him, to comfort the priest as if he were a child in the world.

"No, Jamie, of course you're not." Maureen turned sideways behind the wheel. He looked so sad, she realized. His blue eyes were dark, like jars filled up with sorrow. "You're not crazy and you will feel better as soon as you begin work with the therapist. You must believe me."

"I do. I want to. But why won't you stay and help me?"

"I can't, Jamie." There were tears in Maureen's eyes. "It's too dangerous, for both of us." She looked away, looked out the side window, toward the rectory. After a moment she realized that someone was standing in the window. She saw the white curtain move, as if stirred by a draft.

"Someone is watching us," she said. Outside, in the bright cold day, she was not frightened, just annoyed that she was being spied on.

Jamie glanced back over his shoulder. "I doubt it. It's probably the Monsignor checking to see who's out front."

"Jamie, quit defending them. They're always out to manipulate and control you, but you won't see it."

"All right, come in with me."

"No, I don't want to go in there."

"We could do one more regression. One more before I leave."

She shook her head, her eyes closed tightly.

"Maureen, you won't be here when I get back," he whispered. He was like a college boy, trying to coax a girl into his apartment.

She shook her head again. "No, I'm afraid."

"Maureen, please look at me." Reluctantly she did. "We're near some kind of answer now; I can tell. The trances and regressions are coming closer to our lives. Please help us both."

Impulsively, she reached out and turned off the ignition. She would not be like all the others, she told herself. She would not run away, let him down.

"All right, Jamie, let's see what is hidden in your past." She nodded toward the rectory. "But first let's see who's hiding behind those curtains."

Jamie peered from the foyer into the parish office. The door was open, but if the Monsignor had been there, he had exited quickly.

"See?" Maureen commented. "If it was all so innocent, why did he clear out when he saw us coming?"

"It could have been Mrs. Windmiller," Jamie replied. "Dusting. In fact, it probably was; she always works in here around this time. I'll go ask her."

He gestured toward the front parlor, the formal room where Maureen had first visited before the New Year. It seemed to her like a million years ago.

"Why don't you wait here?" Jamie suggested.

"No, I'm going with you."

"Okay, come on," he laughed, "you can hear the testimony yourself." He led the way back to the kitchen, calling out to let Mrs. Windmiller know that he was home.

"Father Jamie!" The housekeeper came away from the sink, drying her hands on her apron. "I was so worried this morning. You weren't here for breakfast and the Monsignor said he hadn't seen you—" She took hold of the young priest as if to embrace him, and then she saw Maureen.

Maureen realized how it seemed—the young priest disappears all weekend, then wanders into the rectory on Monday morning with a woman. She saw the resentment build in the old woman's eyes, the quizzical frown: Who was this girl, why was Jamie with her? Maureen knew then who Hilda Windmiller really was. She knew then that the Cardinal had lied to her.

"Mrs. Windmiller, I'm so sorry," Jamie was saying. "I've been with the Cardinal, up at the Residence. He was supposed to notify the Monsignor, but I guess he didn't. Or maybe the Monsignor just forgot. You know he isn't himself these days."

"And she?" Mrs. Windmiller moved her head slightly, indicating Maureen without ever looking at her.

"Oh, yes. This is Maureen Sullivan, Grace Keller's niece. You knew her mother, Peggy, I think."

Jamie waited for Mrs. Windmiller to react, to start fussing over Maureen as she always did with him. But the housekeeper only nodded. "Yes, and her father, too," she said.

"I promised Maureen some of your delicious coffee," Jamie hurried on. He, too, had felt the sudden chill in the kitchen. "And do you have any apfeltorte? Maureen, this lady makes the greatest German pastries. I keep telling her we could fund this parish forever if she would just open the Cathedral Bakery. Right, Mrs. Windmiller?" He hugged the small woman to him, which brought a smile to her round, pink face, but still the atmosphere was strained.

Mrs. Windmiller began to take down the cups and saucers, while Jamie went to the refrigerator for the milk. He was comfortable in the kitchen, Maureen saw. She guessed he probably spent a good deal of time there, with the attentive housekeeper.

"Is the Monsignor here, Mrs. Windmiller?" Jamie filled the creamer as he spoke.

"Yah, he's upstairs, as always." The small woman was slicing a banana bread, making him a special treat.

"I better let him know where I was," Jamie said, thinking out loud. He was out of the kitchen at once, as if escaping from the tension.

"Can I help you, Mrs. Windmiller?" Maureen asked, breaking the new silence in the room.

"No, thank you." The housekeeper kept her back turned, froze Maureen out.

Maureen bit her lower lip. This was stupid, she told herself. She would not let this woman think she was trash.

"I'm not your son's mistress, Mrs. Windmiller."

"What? What is that?" Mrs. Windmiller stood motionless, but would not look around.

"You heard me. You understand. I haven't slept with your son. I'm not going to steal him from the priesthood."

Mrs. Windmiller looked around now, studied Maureen for a moment. The anger had disappeared from her blue eyes. She just looked old and very tired, as if exhausted from the years of carrying the secret, of trying always to be inconspicuous and submissive. Maureen felt nothing but compassion for her. She must have wanted never to see the Cardinal again. Yet she had worked her whole life for the Church, just so she could be near her son.

"His Eminence told me," Maureen said softly.

The older woman nodded, understanding. Then she said, "But I'm not Jamie's mother. If the Cardinal said I was, then he has told you wrong."

Maureen nodded, smiling sympathetically. The woman had not chosen to release her secret and she would not; Maureen saw that as fair.

"No, do not smile. It is true. I do not lie. Jamie is Greta's boy. His Eminence's father, Mr. Corrigan, brought Greta to America. At first that made me happy. The war, you see, had made things very hard at home. The bombings. People starving. And Greta, she was so young. My little sister. . . ." The house-keeper turned back to the sink and wiped her eyes.

"I'm sorry, Mrs. Windmiller. I'm sorry that I said any-thing—"

The old woman raised her hand, gestured that she was all right. "It is something you would not know. No one knows."

She whispered, still in tears. "It was this kind of winter. Much, much snow. There was no doctor at the birth, just me. They wanted to keep it all a secret." The housekeeper sighed; she shrugged. "My sister was so foolish. She was in love with him. He said he would not marry her, that he could not. But Greta did not believe this. She told me the sight of his son would change his mind.

"After the birth I tidied up and made them both comfortable. Then I went down to make beef tea. Greta needed to get back strength. The house was large; I heard nothing in the back. When I returned upstairs, Greta was gone and the baby with her."

"She went to plead with him," Maureen said. The scene was taking form, more awful than she had even thought.

"I cannot say," said Mrs. Windmiller carefully. "He swore she left the boy and never let him know. Perhaps that is the truth."

"But Greta disappeared?"

Mrs. Windmiller bent her head. "We never found her. Afterward, someone said he thought he saw her by the river. It was frozen, but she could have walked until she found a patch . . . somewhere that she could break through. No one found the body. The river stayed frozen almost until April, I remember. Each day I waited for the sun, for the spring, so it would thaw. . . ."

"Oh, Mrs. Windmiller, I'm so sorry." Maureen had begun to cry. She could feel the tears on her cheeks.

The old woman shrugged. "I am sorry, too. I am sorry all these years. It is my fault, you know. I should have taken better care. My Greta, she was only seventeen." She turned back to the coffee, took a filter down from the cabinet.

There was no more to say. Maureen turned, left the kitchen, hurried toward the door. She would leave, she decided. It was foolish to become even more involved. What other terrible secrets were to be learned at the Cathedral?

Jamie intercepted her in the foyer. He skidded down the last few steps as she reached the doorway.

"Maureen! What is it? We were going to have coffee."

"Please," she asked, "let me leave. I'm sorry. I'll call you."

"What's the matter? Did Mrs. Windmiller say something? Is that why you're leaving?"

"I'll call." She broke past him and went through the doors into the snow. Jamie followed, grabbing a parka.

"Maureen, you said you'd do a regression with me. Upstairs."

She stopped and put her hands in her pockets. It was true; she had promised. Then she glanced up at the rectory and shook her head. "I don't think we'd make it past the first landing," she said.

Jamie looked back over his shoulder. Both of them were watching now, the Monsignor from his second-floor bedroom, Mrs. Windmiller downstairs in the office. This time they were in the open, not even trying to hide, as if they had a right to be checking on him. As if he were a child who might be in danger, or dangerous. And waiting for him uptown was the Cardinal, his plan of action all mapped out, with the help of his "good Catholic laymen."

Suddenly Jamie felt oppressed, hemmed in, as if a net were closing on him. He looked back to Maureen.

"Take me with you," he said. "I don't ever want to go back in there."

CHAPTER TWENTY

January Fourth, Early Evening
Feast of Saint Titus

"I want you to imagine a time tunnel," Maureen began. Her stripped-down apartment was not a comfortable place to work, but she and Jamie had untied the rolled-up rug and pushed cartons aside so the rug could lie flat again. Now they were both stretched out on it, Jamie on his back with a folded bath towel under his head.

"The time tunnel stretches back into antiquity, to when you first walked this earth. We are going to count to fifteen and then you'll come out of the tunnel, and you'll be in Jerusalem, at the time that you last saw your brother. All right. Fifteen . . . fourteen . . . thirteen. . . ."

Maureen did not rush through the numbers. "This is a long journey," she had explained, "and you are passing through many lifetimes, going toward the time that your soul was first born into our world." She reached the final numbers, "Three . . . two . . . one . . ." and said next, "now tell me where you are, and what is happening to Jesus."

"They took him to Annas."

"Who is Annas?" Maureen asked, leading him along.

"The father-in-law of Caiphas, the high priest of Jerusalem. He was appointed by the Roman procurator, Gratus."

"And what next? What happened to Jesus?"

"They bound his hands and took him before the High Council—the Sanhedrin—and condemned him to death."

"But why, when you thought they would only whip him?"

"Judas lied to me; they always meant to kill him. They had heard about what he had said in the temple: that we had to give Caesar his due, but that God was higher than Caesar. They said that was treason, and since he himself claimed to be the Messiah, he would have to die for it."

"And was he, Judas Thomas? Was your twin the Messiah?"

Jamie moved uneasily on the rug. The question troubled him, Maureen realized. Belief in Christ as the Savior encompassed everything he lived for as a priest. His mind was struggling with the truth, the final truth of his life. She found that she too was holding her breath.

"Tell me, Judas Thomas, what do you believe? Is your twin brother God?"

"When he was taken in the Garden we went to hide with Mary Magdalene, the woman and I. Mary lived near the Via Dolorosa, a small apartment above the wall of the Old City. I hid there like a woman until the third day."

Maureen let him ramble. He had to explain himself in his own way.

"It took only a few hours. He was arrested at night, then condemned by Pilate and executed." Jamie shook his head. "He was buried in a tomb that Joseph of Arimathea owned. It was a new one, cut into rocks."

"Did he speak the truth, Judas Thomas? Was Jesus really who he said?" She watched his reactions carefully. She had to be sure she did not push him too far.

"He was not to be killed. It was only that Judas lied to me; I never thought that he would die."

"He did die, Judas Thomas. But did he rise from the dead, did he climb out of the tomb?" She got to her knees and bent over him, whispering, "Tell me, Judas. Tell me what happened. You are safe here. They won't come. I have hidden you in my rooms."

"Mary went there after the Sabbath to anoint the body," Jamie began. "I did not tell her of meeting Iscariot on the ridge above the Garden, nor how they took me at first for Jesus. Mary said the others knew about Iscariot, said that it was he who had brought the soldiers. Peter told her that Judas came into the Garden and embraced Jesus, and then the soldiers seized him. Peter had sent word by Mary that I should hide, stay away from the Ecce Homo, Pilate's judgment seat, and from Golgotha, where the execution was to be. The others were afraid for me." Jamie stopped, as if choking on his shame. Then he went on. "When Mary got to the tomb, she found Jesus gone."

"Then you believe your twin had risen?" She knew she would have to stop soon. Jamie's body was wet with sweat.

He shook his head and did not answer right away. Perhaps, Maureen thought, he had reached his limit. His memory might not allow him to search further, to drag more tragedy up into his consciousness.

"The body might have been taken, I thought. Grave robbers were very common. I thought, too, that Peter and John, the others from Galilee, might have taken the body at night. Jesus had always preached that he would die and be resurrected. They could have hidden the body away, I thought, to make us all believe. I assumed the resurrection was a fake, a trick to keep us believing that Jesus was King of the Jews."

He spoke again. Each sentence was being uttered in pain, as if flesh was being torn from flesh. Maureen could see how he had suffered, carrying the terrible guilt of his disbelief.

"But the body was not found. Nor was it a deception."

"You're sure, Judas Thomas? How do you know?"

"Because of the shroud, his burial shroud."

"Yes?"

"Joseph and Nicodemus had wrapped the body in the way required by Jewish law. They bound the hands and feet and placed the *sudarium,* the handkerchief, about his face. Then they wrapped the body in one sheet of clean linen, as the Law requires when a person has been executed by the state. But it was close to sundown on Friday, and some of the ritual had to be left till after the Sabbath. They had no time to shave his head and beard, nor to wash away the blood and anoint him.

Instead they simply placed spices around the body, to keep it sweet and pure until Sunday, when Mary and the other women could return and complete the rituals."

"But by then he was gone."

Jamie nodded. "Mary brought me the shroud, the *sindon*, which had been left behind in the tomb. It was stained with blood—blood where his heart had been lanced, blood from his hands and feet."

Jamie stopped again. He gestured, as if he wanted to say more but had lost the power to speak.

"What else, Judas Thomas?" Maureen pushed. "What else about the shroud?"

"His image. It was burned into the linen. His face. My face," Jamie whispered. "That was no trick. It was a miracle."

Maureen did not speak. Quietly she got to her feet and went to sit in the bay window. They had been talking only a few minutes, she realized, but she felt as exhausted as if she had been wrestling with him physically. They both needed to rest a little, and then she would bring him out of the trance.

"I kept the shroud," Jamie continued without prompting, speaking slowly, as if he were listening to a foreign language and translating the meaning of the words. "We were afraid, all of us, and many were ashamed, but I most of all. Because of the woman, I had left him to face the soldiers all alone. I left Jerusalem that day, and left her, too. I went to Jericho, then into Jordan, following the valley, as we had the week before when we came out of Galilee. I could have traveled faster, by cutting over the hills of Samaria, but the Samaritans hated Jews. I stayed in Jordan, then went north to Syria, and took the shroud to the city of Edessa, to King Abgar. I was safe then. Even Caiphas could not find me there."

And then he was silent.

"Who is this King Abgar? Do you know what all that's about?" Maureen asked, after Jamie had recovered from his trance.

"I know there's a legend about King Abgar," he answered. He was sitting up now; had joined her in the bay window. "The king lived in Edessa, which is now in Turkey, but at the time of Christ was in Syria. After many years of rule he was stricken with leprosy and he despaired of his life. Then he heard about a healer-teacher in Palestine and he wrote, asking Jesus to come and cure him.

"The legend is that Jesus wrote back, promising to send a disciple, and after Jesus' death a disciple did travel to Edessa, bringing with him a holy cloth imprinted with the Savior's image. At the sight of the cloth Abgar was cured, and the Christian faith was established in Edessa."

"How much of that is really true?"

"Well, it's a historical fact that Abgar did rule Edessa, and that he was converted soon after Christ's death. And a holy image of Christ was associated with the conversion.

"But when Abgar died his son brought back paganism and persecuted the Christians who persisted. There's no more talk of a shroud until five hundred years later, when a cloth bearing an image of Christ was found in Edessa, hidden away in a niche above the city's gates. The assumption is that the Christians hid it rather than let the pagans destroy it. The cloth became famous and in 944 the Byzantine Emperor, Romanus, decided that it belonged in Constantinople, the center of eastern Christianity. He actually sent a general to Edessa to retrieve it, which the general did, and the shroud was installed in Constantinople, where it was referred to as the *Mandylion*, an Arabic word meaning veil."

"And that veil was the same shroud Christ was wrapped in?"

"Many people think so. The Byzantines certainly did; they started modeling all their pictures and statues of Christ after the image on the shroud. Before the shroud was rediscovered in Edessa, there had been no agreed-upon image of what Christ looked like. He was depicted as bearded and clean-shaven, long- and short-haired. But once the shroud was found, everyone, including the Byzantines, portrayed him as looking like the face on the *Mandylion*. They obviously believed it was authentic."

"Since I never heard of the *Mandylion*, I assume it eventually disappeared."

"Right, around 1200, and afterward nothing more was heard about anything like a cloth bearing the image of Christ until what we call the Shroud of Turin turned up in France a hundred years later. It was brought there by the Knights Templar, who presumably seized it during one of their crusades in the Holy Land.

"The Templars never displayed their shroud, but a lot of rumors grew up around it. People wrote of the Templars as idol worshipers, because they worshiped a mysterious 'head' at their secret initiation ceremonies. These initiations always took place near a model they constructed of Christ's tomb, and each new Templar was given a white mantle imprinted with a red cross symbolizing Christ's crucified body. Initiates were also given one glimpse of the 'supreme vision of God on earth.'"

"The missing shroud."

Jamie nodded. "Which brings us back to Abgar of Edessa. He saw the shroud; he was cured by its powers, or so the legend goes. And I was the one who brought it to him, out of Jerusalem."

"Judas Thomas took it, Jamie, not you. Look, what you call past lives may be creations of your subconscious, brought on by this great struggle in your mind about your real father and mother, about who you are in *this* life."

"How can you ignore these regressions, Maureen? They set a pattern of betrayal, and now we see what it all goes back to. You think my subconscious could be that concerted? That detailed?" Jamie pulled himself up to his feet. He, too, was exhausted, tired from the intensity of his recollection.

"I can ignore them because there's no proof. There's no connection—now, in this world—between the Jamie Ignatius I know and any of these other 'incarnations.'"

"There's one. I think I saw him."

"Saw who?"

"My twin."

Maureen sighed. "You mean the tramp out in the snow, the one you saw on Christmas morning? It's your subconscious, Jamie," she insisted. "You're creating this phantom. You won't admit it, but you feel guilty that you're an orphan, guilty that your mother wouldn't keep you." Maureen stopped. She was tempted now to tell it all, to let him know it wasn't he who should feel guilt about his birth. And yet she hesitated. The secret was not hers to tell.

Jamie picked up his parka, slipped it on.

"Where are you going?" she asked quickly.

Jamie started to say home, then realized he did not have one any longer.

"The rectory," he answered.

"Why?"

"I have to pack."

She didn't believe him. He didn't want to go back there; had asked her to take him away from there. She crossed the room to stand beside him, and felt the fear pouring off him like waves of heat.

"Jamie, don't, please."

"Don't do what?" He would not look at her.

"Don't go back there to the rectory and meditate. Don't try to find out more."

"You said it was only my subconscious." He moved around her, went toward the apartment door. "But you saw someone, too, Maureen, who looked like me."

"Now I'm not so sure." The fear was like a knife at her throat. "Don't go to Boca Raton. Stay here. Stay with me. If this tramp is in MacPatch, we'll find him."

He had to choose, he knew. Maureen wanted to protect him from his past, help him pretend there was no sin, but only guilt. He could stay with her, and hide, but he knew it was no use.

He had never told her of the figure wrapped in gauze and linen that came at him through the darkness of the brownstone. He thought then of the last time, of the face he had then seen. The face that was his own. He shrugged, looked at Maureen. There was only one choice now.

"I must go back to the Cathedral," he said.

"You're doing this to yourself, Jamie."

The young priest shook his head. "There is a reason why I have to meditate."

"What is it?" she demanded.

"I know who wants me."

And then he left her.

Maureen kept busy. She kept packing. She wanted to get out of MacPatch for good. She wanted to keep herself from thinking what might be happening to Jamie at the rectory, upstairs in his cell, his bare white bedroom.

Well, she couldn't go until the books were packed, ready in cartons for her brother-in-law. Some of the books were old, textbooks from college, and some of them belonged to Michael. But she had no time to sort them now. Swearing under her breath she began to work furiously, pulling volumes off the living room shelves and dumping them into the cardboard liquor boxes.

She was almost finished when her fingers grabbed one book—an oversized book, slipped in horizontally so that it lay flat across a row of others. She pulled it out and checked the spine: The book was called *Decision on the Shroud of Turin*.

Maureen did not remember buying it or owning it. Perhaps it was Michael's, she thought, packed inadvertently when she left him. Or it could have been lent to her by a friend, and then forgotten.

She stopped packing, leaned against the shelves and quickly scanned the copy on the inside cover. She slowed down when she read: "In 1978, a team of 40 American scientists made an attempt to solve the mystery of the Shroud of Turin. They went to Italy and spent five days examining the cloth with the most sophisticated analytical equipment available. Their scientific analysis, combined with archaeological and Bible studies, concluded that the Shroud of Turin was the burial shroud of Jesus Christ."

Maureen opened the book and flipped through the stiff pages, stopping at the insert of color photographs taken by the scientists. She read more details of their study, how digitized computer photos had enabled them to see details in the Shroud image that could never have been perceived by the eye or captured by conventional photography.

She kept flipping the pages, not looking at the pictures, just reading the blurbs beneath them. Under one photograph it said, "Scientists discovered that the density of the image varies according to the distance between the cloth and the parts of the body underneath it. Because this distance can be measured mathematically, they were able to create a three-dimensional image of the man buried in the Shroud."

She skipped to the next caption, still not looking up at the set of photographs. ". . . The scientists were able to use this three-dimensional image to construct a fiberglass statue of the man buried in the cloth. . . . At the Jet Propulsion Laboratory, they used computers to search the face area for the tell-tale signs of an artist's hand at work. The picture showed that the image of the face came from the body underneath and not from a brush moving from side to side."

Maureen scanned the next few captions: "Advanced photographic process called isodensity enhances subtle details. . . . The beard is turned up, indicating that a chin band may have been tied around the head to keep his jaw closed in death." She kept flipping the pages, kept reading bits and pieces. "The bloodstains on the Shroud are real blood . . . nail wound in the wrist and feet indicate that the man was crucified. . . . Blood seeped into the crevices of the linen fabric. . . . Microscopic examination did not find any painter's pigments on the cloth. . . . Scientists have concluded that the Shroud image is not a painting. . . . The scalp punctures, scourge wounds, shoulder chafing, and side wounds—all visible on the image—are consistent with additional punishment inflicted on Jesus of Nazareth."

Maureen turned to the last color page. It showed a computer photograph of the face of Christ, a composite picture gained from all the information obtained by the scientists and their space-age equipment. It was the face in the Shroud of Turin. It was the face of Father James Ignatius. It was Jamie.

CHAPTER TWENTY-ONE

January Fourth, Night
Feast of Saint Titus

Detective Murphy, dressed in trousers two sizes too big for him and an overcoat that was too small, fed another piece of scrap wood to the oil can fire. He stamped his feet in the snow and turned around, warming the backs of his legs before the makeshift fire.

He was too big, he told himself again, too menacing looking. His size scared people off. This was his third night on the street, the second night he had stood, a clear target, near the entrance of LaFayette Park. Robert Murphy watched the street, looked both ways, alert to any sign of a black limousine.

He could be at home, he thought. He could be watching HBO, having a beer, sitting down with his wife. "Sheeit," he said. He hadn't made love to his wife in a week. His jawbone hurt and he talked out loud to himself, a little worried that the freezing air would damage his vocal cords unless he kept using them.

The trouble was that the grab bag of used clothes—the coats and sweaters and long pants—were not enough. They were

255

threadbare and full of holes. He should have worn long un-
derwear. His wife had told him that. "Sheeit," he said again.
His lips ached and he grabbed the end of his wool scarf and
tucked it up over his mouth and nose.

This was stupid. Matty Joyce had been right. "I ain't going
out there at night and play decoy, freeze my ass just to stop
someone killing off shopping bag ladies. Forget it, Murphy!"
The short, fat cop had unbuckled his pants and tucked in his
shirttails. "It ain't worth the effort. The truth is, the city is
better off without that element. This guy is doing us all a favor,
Murphy."

The tall black man hunched his shoulders, tried to seem less
conspicuous. The killer would pick on the meekest first, he
knew, those least likely to fight back. The detective bent his
legs and crouched down behind the fire, scanning the park for
anyone who might be casing him from the shrubbery.

The park was the answer, he realized. That was where the
bodies had to have been concealed—dropped into the pond,
left under the ice, or stuffed into the thick bushes. Now the
bodies were frozen, covered up with snow, but in April they'd
begin to find them, when everything started to melt and the
dogs caught the scent.

He moved again, positioned himself so he could see the
avenue. There wasn't much traffic on the downtown streets: a
few local cars, a few heading toward the river to catch the
Fourth Street ramp for the bridge, and of course the Pimp-
mobiles, long pink and red Caddys. But no sign of what he
was looking for. Another half hour, he thought. Another half
hour and he'd give up, climb into his car across the street, and
go home. Rochelle would be up, watching TV and waiting. She
always waited up when he worked late. The detective grinned,
thinking about getting home. The bed would be warm. Rochelle
would be warm. "Goddamn!" he swore out loud. And then he
spotted the limo.

Impulsively Maureen ripped out the computer photograph
and folded it into her jeans pocket. Then she grabbed her old
fur coat and ran from the apartment. It wasn't until she was
outside on the snowy sidewalk that she realized she didn't have
her car keys.

It was faster anyway, she decided, to walk—to cut across the empty lots to the rectory. During the summer she would never go into the lots, or even walk nearby. They were infested with rats, rodents living among the rubble and the trash. Yet now, under four feet of snow, the landscape looked inviting and serene.

She ran across the side street and cut into the first lot, heading toward the dark rectory. One hundred feet into the open field she knew she had made a mistake. The weeks of heavy, blowing snow had left drifts several feet high amidst the rubble. Yet she kept pushing forward. Running. She had to hurry. She had to show Jamie what she'd found. She stumbled forward in the snow, swore, then picked herself up, slowed down, gained control. It was better not to rush. Better just to walk, plow ahead one step at a time.

Maureen could see the rectory. A light was on in Jamie's third-floor room. It encouraged her, seeing the high beacon, knowing which way to head. Still, the snow was deceptive, treacherous in its whiteness. A storm was sweeping in over the river and the dark night was losing what little visibility it had had. She had been lost this way before, skiing out west once with Michael. They had been caught in a cloud at the top of a mountain—a whiteout, skiers called it—and she had had no idea where she was in the world. She remembered her terror. She bent her head against the swirling snow, pushing harder. Already her face was numb, bare to the driving wind.

Jamie flipped off his bedroom light, stood a moment while his eyes adjusted to the darkness, and then he began the meditation. He made himself as comfortable as possible on the mat, bent his knees and pulled his bare feet up, closed his eyes and concentrated on his body, letting each part settle deeply onto the floor.

He was in a rush now, but he forced himself to be calm, to take it slow. He began by letting his consciousness drift off, let it search for some safe harbor of his memory. He pictured his consciousness as a spotlight, a searcher, and he moved with the beam of light. He waited. He did not concentrate. He knew the beam of light would find the shrouded figure where it waited for him.

Jamie wanted the figure. Wanted to confront the apparition. Only that way could he learn what his twin sought, and why he was appearing in the night. This time, Jamie told himself, he would not run.

He began to visualize the apparition. When he had conjured up its picture, he concentrated on it, as in the Centering Prayer he had concentrated on the name of Jesus. He thought of doors opening, one after the next, leading him back in time. He let his consciousness pass through them freely. He was no longer afraid of the darkness beyond each doorway to his past.

In the dark bedroom Jamie's eyes snapped open. He was not succeeding, he realized; he was still himself, still in the rectory. He could feel his heart beat against his chest, feel his own prickly hot skin.

The winter moon was out. Its pale light filled the room. Jamie turned his head slightly and found the Duccio. He kept his eyes on the painting, concentrating now on the kneeling Christ in the Garden of Gethsemane. He began to pray, asking for the courage not to fail, as he had failed before, in all his lifetimes on earth.

"Lord Jesus Christ, have mercy on me," Jamie whispered. It was the prayer from *The Way of a Pilgrim*, the classic Russian book on meditation. The pilgrim, Jamie remembered, was a Russian peasant who wanted to be holy, to obey Saint Paul's dictum: Pray unceasingly. But the peasant was a simple uneducated man; he could not imagine how to do such a thing. So he spent his whole life searching, till he came upon a holy monk who taught him the simple prayer.

"Lord Jesus Christ, have mercy on me," Jamie said again, then again, calling upon the divine name with his lips, his spirit, called upon him with his heart.

He kept repeating the name of Jesus, kept repeating the simple prayer, until he was no longer praying, not with his lips or his mind. The prayer was part of his breath. He could touch the words with his tongue, feel the phrase in his bones. His whole body was wrapped up inside the humble request: Lord Jesus Christ, have mercy on me.

Then he felt the presence of the shrouded figure. Felt it afar off, felt it coming toward him. He listened to the heavy footsteps as they climbed, coming to find the one who was calling.

Now Jamie was afraid. He couldn't help it. He tried to keep praying, but his concentration was gone, and he heard only the heavy footsteps approaching. He was going to die. He was going to be punished. His fear was like a rat eating away at his insides, devouring his resolution. His head fell back and he lay, exhausted and panting, on the bare floor of his bedroom.

Outside in the hallway, the slow steps halted again before his door and he waited for the knock, the three soft raps calling him to serve.

The limousine passed the detective and kept going, heading slowly toward the river. When it reached the corner, it hesitated. The light was red at the empty intersection, and the long black car paused, then made a quick U-turn and came back up the avenue, on the park side. Murphy's side.

The detective tightened the wool scarf across his face, and moved so he was behind the oil can, in the shadows of the flames. He reached inside the layers of coats and sweaters and felt the butt of his service revolver. It made him feel better, relaxed him.

Well, it would be over soon. He'd make the collar, close out the case. He could call Rochelle from the station, tell her he had got his mark.

The limo paused and slid gently to a full stop near the icy curb. He was tense, waiting. They were watching him, debating, making a decision on what they saw: a tall, slumped-over drunk warming himself by an oil can fire.

"Come on, goddamnit," he swore silently. He pulled a pint bottle from his coat pocket, pantomimed drinking from it, and tossed the bottle away. He heard the limo door open and slam shut, and he turned slightly to see who was coming at him in the snow.

He had been right. It was the sexton coming across the sidewalk, stepping down the narrow path that led to the park's stone wall. Out of the corner of his eye Murphy could see how the old man dragged his bad leg. It left a mark in the new snow.

Then the sexton was standing next to him, warming himself at the fire. The detective mumbled, moved away.

"Easy there, pal," Clarence said, following.

Murphy kept shuffling away, kept mumbling. His face was bent down, away from the sexton.

"How about another drink, pal?" Clarence asked, approaching.

Even in the frigid air the detective could smell the chloroform. Christ, what amateurs, he thought. He and Joyce would take a razzing when the story of this collar got out.

He took a deep breath of night air and held it as he stumbled against the sexton, letting the man cup his nose and mouth with the cheesecloth soaked in anesthetic and folded into a white handkerchief.

He let the sexton help him out of the park, across to the parked limousine. Clarence let him breathe, forgot to keep the chloroform up tight on the nose. But the detective didn't resist. He went passively, tensing up only when the sexton opened the back door of the limousine. Now the light would go on, Murphy thought. Now he would see the face of the killer.

But the light did not go on. It was not until the man in the back seat said "Good evening" that Murphy realized who it was. He had expected the young one, the blond with the strange, haunted eyes, and when it wasn't he felt bad, realizing he had been wrong. He pulled out his revolver and said quietly, so as not to alarm the older man, "I'm sorry. I'm really sorry about this." And then he read him his rights.

Maureen was crying. The tears were briefly warm, then they burned. She turned away from the blowing snow, walked backward against the wind, but the drifts were too deep and she stumbled over buried rubble, the bricks and concrete of the old houses that had been wrecked, burned out and abandoned.

She pulled herself together, tried to orient herself once again. This was taking too long, she realized. Somehow she had gotten turned about. In the driving, blinding snow she was lost, circling endlessly in the big, open lot. She raised her hands to her face, blew hot air into her palms. She could not feel her breath, nor bend her numb fingers.

"No!" She tried to scream, to make some protest, to hear her own voice. She forced herself to look up, to open her eyes and squint into the thick, blowing snow. Nothing. She could see nothing beyond a few feet. The world dissolved into white, as if it were the end of the universe.

For a moment the wind shifted. Paused. The night was suddenly clear and she spotted the Cathedral, the huge, looming shape. She wasn't turned around. The Cathedral was directly ahead of her. She had only strayed further down the block, closer to the church's back parking lot.

She was less than a hundred yards from the sidewalk and the corner. There were cars parked at the curb, blanketed under inches of snow, and at the end of the street a traffic light blinked from red to green, signaling silently to the empty intersection. She stepped off again, tramped toward the safety of the Cathedral.

The rapping on the door was soft but insistent. Jamie covered his ears, but still he could hear it. He scuttled away from the door on his knees and cowered in the corner. He opened his mouth to scream, to summon help, but he couldn't. His cry was a tiny yelp, the sound of an animal trapped in a strange house. He turned his face into the corner, flattened his cheeks on the white plaster walls. This was his bedroom, his home. Nothing bad could happen to him here.

The rapping stopped.

Perhaps there had been no rapping, Jamie told himself, just his mind playing tricks. There were no footsteps, no shrouded figure at all, only a psychotic episode, or some sort of hallucination. He was only going crazy, he thought with relief. He embraced that thought, as one would a close friend.

Yet now he heard the footsteps again, and they were crossing the hardwood floor of his bedroom. Jamie closed his eyes tight, pressed his face to the plaster. He felt the heat of the figure, felt it burn his body, singe him, as if he had stepped too close to flame.

Not a word was said.

Jamie pushed himself from the wall. He could not see the arms of the figure, folded beneath the burial cloth, but still he knew it was beckoning him to follow. Jamie knew. It was time, and with eyes averted he followed the shrouded shape from his room.

His heart was pounding but he felt a sense of peace. In the

wake of the figure he drifted down the narrow hallway, down through the dark house. Jamie touched the wooden banister, felt the smooth varnish beneath his fingers. He needed this tactile contact. It told him that he was still alive.

Doors were open, had been thrown wide, as if the house itself had been abandoned. Jamie easily followed the figure, down flight after flight and back through the building to the cellar entry. It, too, was unlocked and stood open, though surely it had not been left so by the Monsignor.

He did not stop. The shrouded figure led the way and he felt the fear begin once more. A sliver of uneasiness crossed his heart, left him breathless. At the top of the cellar stairs he stopped, held up.

The shrouded figure had reached the bottom of the steps, turned slowly. The weeping face beneath the linen cloth looked back, looked up, as if from the entrance to its own sepulcher.

Father Ignatius began to prepare himself for death. Passing through this door he would pass into another life, condemned to his strange odyssey until his sin had been forgiven.

"Tell me, what about the bodies?"

The priest smiled. "Embalmed them." He seemed pleased with his achievement.

"Really? And then what?" The detective chuckled, oddly amused by the situation. These two, he thought, had one-way tickets to Cloud-Cuckoo-Land.

"Then we stored them, so to speak." The limousine was in motion now, Clarence at the wheel, the detective and his prisoner in the wide back seat.

"Where's that, Father?" Murphy was surprised; he wouldn't have expected them to plan so carefully.

"At our Cathedral, would you believe? Clarence here, God bless his soul, found the place." The priest took his time, as if wanting to get it all correct. "He was in the basement of the rectory. We were having this rat problem at the time—you know how it is down here close by the river—and when he broke through a basement wall, searching for the source of our problem, he found this old tunnel to the Cathedral."

"An underground tunnel?" The black man grinned again. He was having a hard time containing himself. This was going to make a great story at the precinct. Already he could hear himself tell it.

"Yes, rather amazing actually. I was surprised. I did some research and discovered it was quite common in the old days, before they laid pipes for the city water, to use the streets as burial plots. It's all limestone down here by the river. Very fine for burials."

Lieutenant Murphy glanced through the glass partition. Clarence had turned off McCarthy onto Church Drive. Ahead of him, the detective could see the old Cathedral, the empty parking lot. The sexton had misunderstood him, had not driven directly to the precinct. Murphy was not surprised. Neither of the murderers realized they had been apprehended.

"You'll have to tell Clarence to turn around, Father," Murphy said softly. "We've gone the wrong way." The detective took pains to be nice to the priest. The man was beyond censure anyway.

"Yes, I see that he has. Creature of habit, I'm afraid. Sorry. But since we're here, would you care to see the burial place? It's really quite impressive. I mean, we've done work with it, Clarence and myself; we've fixed it up." He watched the detective, looked eager.

"Sure, why not. I'll have to see it anyway." He could call the precinct from the rectory, have them send over some uniforms and a lab unit. If it was really grisly, they'd have to rope off the whole block, snowstorm or not.

Maureen had reached the sidewalk when she saw the black limousine go past her, smooth and silent as a shark in deep water. The sight of it paralyzed her. It was the car, she knew immediately. It was the car the street people had seen.

She followed after it at once, stumping through the snow, struggling to keep up, trailing the limousine down the short street to the parking lot of the Cathedral.

It could be taking a short cut, she thought, driving across the parish property to reach the Project beyond. She tried to pick up her pace, to turn the corner of the Cathedral fast enough to see which way the car went. Yet when she had circled around the back of the Cathedral, she saw the black limousine was still there in the lot. It stood quiet, motor off, and it was, she realized, empty. Even in the blowing snow Maureen could see the footprints, the three sets of prints that left the car and went up the stairs into the sacristy.

Her first thought was that she'd been wrong. It wasn't the mysterious limousine, just a car belonging to the Church. The Cardinal had a limousine, as did the old Cathedral. She remembered as a child seeing her father brought home in it, after High Mass on Sunday, or from Holy Name Society evenings. Later, when he had begun to drink too much, the Cardinal would send him home from uptown in the Chancery car. Nothing strange about a limousine at the Cathedral, she decided.

Still.

A small tear in her theory made Maureen pause. She looked around, studied the footprints in the snow. The tear lengthened, like a rent in a bolt of cloth. One of the people had been dragged from the car—she could see where the shoe had scooped out the thick snow.

She followed the deep footprints up the stairs and tried to open the sacristy door. It was locked, as she had expected it would be. She beat her fist against the thick wood, but no sound, she realized, would echo inside the Cathedral.

She stepped back and looked up to see if any lights were on inside. If they were, the high stained-glass windows of the North Transept would be glowing. But the church was dark. Silent.

There was another set of doors at the North Porch, toward the front of the old building. Maureen climbed down the sacristy steps and went that way, hugging the stone wall of the Church where the snow was lightest. She would try those doors, she decided, and then the front. If she couldn't get in, she'd go back to the rectory and find Jamie.

Jamie! God, she had forgotten him. But her quest was as important as his—in this life, anyway.

The North Porch door was set back, out of the wind, protected slightly by the flanking wings of the portico. Maureen climbed up the stone steps and leaned against the heavy wooden door, briefly thankful that she was out of the driving wind for a moment. But she didn't pause very long. She took her numb hands from the sleeves of her coat and tried the huge iron door pulls. Her fingers would not close on the heavy iron rings. She could feel nothing, not even pain in her cold fingers.

"Oh, Christ," she said out loud, beginning again to cry. "Help me," she pleaded, struggling to lift the thick rings. Even if the door wasn't locked, she couldn't open it. She didn't have the strength left in her. She needed help. She needed Jamie.

She pulled herself up, stuck her freezing hands into the sleeves of the fur coat, and built up her courage to step back into the snow, to make one last effort at the front of the Cathedral. Then she would go find Jamie, get him to come with her to see who was inside.

And then the huge wooden door swung back, swung open. Maureen stood poised at the threshold. "Hello?" she asked, speaking up, staring hard into the deep darkness of the cavernous Cathedral.

No one moved. No one spoke from the shadows.

"Hello?" Maureen raised her voice in frustration. She shouldn't go in alone, she knew, remembering the last time when the sexton had grabbed her.

"Clarence?" she asked.

The heavy door moved slightly, as if blown open wider by the wind. This was silly, she told herself. She wanted to get into the church. She wanted to find who had been in the limousine. Besides, she told herself, she knew the Cathedral, had attended Mass there all the days of her childhood. It wasn't some kind of haunted house. She wasn't frightened by the house of God, she told herself, and resolved, she boldly stepped forward, out of the snow and cold wind.

The darkness engulfed her at once. She was blind for a moment as her eyes adjusted to the black depth of the building. Then she heard the old hinges creaking. With a sudden rush, the big door slammed shut behind her.

"Wait! What is it?" she cried, spinning around in the darkness. And then she was grabbed.

"The Archiepiscopal Crypt is here," the priest said, leading the way. "All the cathedrals have a place to bury their bishops. We have a dozen buried with us." The priest flipped on the light in the small vaulted crypt. "Bishop Farley is here. He was our pastor when I was a boy."

The detective had not seen this room before. Built under

the high main altar, the crypt was only eight feet deep, and nearly that wide. He could stand in the middle and touch both sides. The walls were faced with marble slabs each two feet thick.

"There's room for twenty prelates of the Cathedral," the priest continued. "I've asked to be buried here. I've already had the inscription prepared. Frank Cummings did it, an old stonecutter from the parish. Do you read Latin, Lieutenant?"

"No, can't say I do." Murphy followed the priest toward the rear of the crypt, looked where he was pointing.

"That's a shame. Latin is an especially beautiful language for burial inscriptions. Mine says: *Qui natus olim e Virgine Nunc e sepulchro nasceris*. It's a sixth-century Easter hymn. 'Once was Thou born of Mary's womb. And now, new-born from out the tomb.' That's important to remember, Lieutenant. We may die and be buried, but we rise again—new-born. Beautiful." The priest sighed with satisfaction.

"Father, it's late. Can we get on with it?" Murphy glanced around for the sexton, but the old man hadn't followed them down into the crypt. Damnit, he thought. It made him nervous, not having both of them in sight.

"Oh, yes, of course, you must see the rest. I'm really quite proud of it." He pushed against the small back door of the crypt and a slab of marble gave way, leading into another room. The priest turned on a light as he stooped and entered.

"No one had any idea this existed. That door into the crypt was sealed off from this side. We always assumed it was simply decorative, not functional at all. Then when Clarence accidentally discovered the tunnel from the rectory, I discovered this . . ." He stopped, turned on an overhead light, a low hanging light-bulb attached to a construction cord.

Murphy could not see the length of the underground cavern. The single bulb lit up only one small section: a table, shelves of bottles, and large white plastic pails. The room was narrow, only as wide again as the crypt and honeycombed with niches carved high on the walls.

"We had to make do," the priest said, almost apologetically.

The detective stepped forward, still puzzled by what he was seeing. The chamber was damp, musty, and stank to high heaven. He identified the pungent, irritating odor of formaldehyde. Of course, he thought, the embalming fluid. It reminded him of the smells in the county morgue.

The room smelled also of wet cement, of powdery concrete mix. He saw that concrete had been poured recently, that there were stacks of red firebrick sealing off half a dozen of the narrow enclaves carved into the rocky walls. And then he identified the other odor: that of decomposing flesh.

Behind him, the priest said softly, as if in reverence for the dead, "We call this our catacomb."

It was not dark in the cellar, not completely. The shrouded figure ahead of him illuminated the way. Jamie felt as he had during his trances and regressions, felt he was slipping back through time, following a tunnel of light. The cellar was damp and freezing cold, but he was oblivious to his surroundings. The shrouded figure consumed his attention, filled his mind. He followed obediently. He knew, in the calm, certain way of dreams, that he had left the house he knew and started down a narrow passage. This was the way of death, he thought, his soul passing from one world to the next.

Suddenly the dream was over. Jamie realized, with bewilderment, that his feet were bare, and he was standing in inches of cold water. He was fully aware; the dream, the trance, the shrouded figure were gone. He had come downstairs and into the basement without shoes. He was awake, and aware now of danger in the darkness.

There were no lights, no shadows, no hint of gray or the soft glow of the figure. Jamie reached out and groped for the wall, found the bare limestone. He kept feeling with his hands, exploring. Turning, he could see behind him into the full basement, and he realized then where he was—it was from here, from this passage, that the Monsignor had emerged with the case of wine that day.

Jamie tried to straighten up and realized he couldn't. The passageway was tight, wide enough for only one person. He took another step forward and his foot splashed in the cold seepage water. He took another step, felt his way forward.

This was stupid, he told himself. Go back. Get out of this dark hole. Yet he kept walking, pushing forward, following where the shrouded figure had led him. The passageway narrowed, tightened. The cold stone brushed his face and he bumped his forehead on overhanging rock.

The light found him. He was peering into the hopeless blackness when the light materialized, like a star coming out at night.

Jamie moved toward it eagerly. He was safe, he told himself. He kept his eyes fixed on the pinpoint of light, afraid to blink. Perhaps it was an optical illusion. Still, as he crept forward the light spread, widened like a lens, and Jamie saw he wasn't mistaken. Then he heard the voices. Distant and soft. People were conversing, but the words were not intelligible.

Jamie stopped, a dozen yards from the end of the tunnel. He had lost the feeling in his feet, and now he was stumbling with each step, but that was not why he had hesitated. It was not rescue that lay ahead, he realized. He tried to summon up his courage. Ahead of him was what the apparition had led him there to find. The secret that had roused the shrouded figure from its tomb.

"Why, Father? Why?" Murphy looked into the eyes of the madman.

"Is it better, my son, to let them suffer in the cold, without shelter or the price of a simple cup of coffee? How else was I to care for them? The Sisters of Mercy are gone, the convent is closed. We couldn't afford to keep open the soup kitchen.

"Oh, I know what you Protestants think—that the Church, the Vatican, has all this money. Statues with feet of gold. Well, by God, I don't have any. And how can I run this parish without funds? We haven't the people. They're gone, moved to the suburbs, left us behind with the colored. Baptists, every one.

"Besides, all these poor people received the last rites. No one dies until he or she is prepared to meet God. *Nunc e sepulchro nasceris*. New-born from out the tomb."

"How many, Father?"

"How many what, Lieutenant?" The priest seemed puzzled. His mind had drifted off.

"How many did you kill? Cut open down here and stashed in what you call your catacomb?" The detective found his voice rising, a rage toward the insane man building inside him.

"Oh, I have no idea. Two dozen, maybe more. I don't keep count. That's not the point. We're doing you a favor, Clarence and I, cleaning up the streets, getting rid of these old bums—useless drunks, the whole lot of them."

"And Grace Keller?"

"Oh, a tragic circumstance, Lieutenant. She saw us—Clarence and myself—when we were bringing one of those bodies back after Devotions." He shook his head, then shrugged. "A pity. But, you know, they say Grace was already a bit senile."

The Lieutenant turned back to the charnel house, the catacomb that ran the length of Church Drive. Crazy, he thought; madmen. He thought of Matty Joyce. He would have to tell Matty, and that thought upset him more than finding the priest in the back seat of the limousine.

Murphy looked around once more to see if there was any evidence he ought to confiscate immediately. But the catacomb would keep, he reasoned. It had remained a secret all these years; it could remain so for a few more hours. None of these bodies were going anywhere.

"All right, Monsignor, let's go to the precinct," he said, turning back to the old priest.

From the corner of his eye the detective saw something, saw the old man raise his hand, reach out as if to slap his face. Murphy took one step back, then realized, too late, that the priest wasn't going to strike him. Hidden in his fingers was a medical syringe. Before Murphy could react the fresh needle jabbed his pupil, pierced like a hot wire deep into his retina, hurt him like a dentist's needle finding a live nerve.

Murphy's hand jerked up involuntarily, knocked the Monsignor's arm aside. But O'Toole's hand still gripped the syringe, and the thin, delicate needle plucked out Robert Murphy's sleepy brown eye, ripped it like an oyster from its shell.

Murphy screamed. Grabbed his face. The blood squirted out from between his fingers and sprayed into the catacomb. He swung out wildly at the old priest, tried to smash him in his rage, then frantically fumbled with his left hand for his revolver. He'd kill the fuckin' bastard, Murphy thought. Blow his crazy head off.

Then the revolver was forgotten. Murphy could feel the blood of his body pumping up to his head, feel it gushing from the empty socket. He grabbed the slippery eyeball, dangling against his wet cheek, sprung loose from his head like the eye of a broken doll, and tried to squeeze it back into his face.

Then his legs gave out. He dropped to his knees, doubled over. The Monsignor was at him again. Murphy felt the swift, painful jab below his ear as the needle plunged into the thick muscles of his neck. He grabbed the old man's hand and knocked him off balance, then ripped the syringe from his neck and threw it away. The lidocaine splattered against the stone wall. The detective sat back on his heels, reaching out wildly, trying to lay hands on the murderous old man.

Monsignor O'Toole backed off, kept away from the black man's grasping hands. He was confused, upset. The others had been so easy. He had felt them fall asleep in his arms. But this one had to be finished. O'Toole rushed around the makeshift table. He needed something hard, something to hit the man with, and he spotted the paschal candle holder, went for it at once.

The candlestick was too heavy. It stood three feet high and had a solid brass base. O'Toole couldn't lift it over his shoulder, but if he used it like a baseball bat. . . . He dragged it back around the embalming table and came at the kneeling detective from behind.

Murphy heard him, flailed out blindly. His long arm struck the low-hanging light bulb, sent it swinging wildly. O'Toole ducked calmly out of its path. Then, lifting the candle holder only inches, he swung upward as hard as he could, caught the man on the side of the face, where his eye still dangled from its socket. Murphy screamed and doubled over, but did not go down.

The old priest was desperate now. He had to kill the man at once, before he stood up, before he got away.

The Monsignor swung the paschal candle holder backward, two-handed, and hit Murphy again. The heavy metal crushed the detective's left cheekbone. As Murphy toppled forward, his face struck the stone floor and bounced slightly. O'Toole kept at him, moving around the twitching body to get a good clean shot at the black man's head. His arms were exhausted but he made one more effort. Lifting the heavy brass as high as he could, he let the square base come down directly on

Murphy's cranium. Then he did it again.

O'Toole leaned on the candle holder, panting. Without even looking at him, he knew the detective was dead. O'Toole knew the smell of warm fresh blood. The other odor was less familiar, but he had read of it: the semen-like smell of human brain.

"Clarence, it's me!" she screamed. After the first seconds of terror, of blind struggle, she had recognized him, known him by his smell, that odd chemical odor she had smelled the first time he'd seized her. Knowing it was Clarence calmed her down a little; as soon as he recognized her, he would let her go.

"Clarence," she cried again, "it's me, Maureen Sullivan." Her voice bounced off the high nave of the Cathedral, echoed down the dark, empty aisles. He had his arm wrapped around her chest, was dragging her up the side aisle toward the main altar.

"Clarence, don't you remember? I'm Jamie's friend. Father—" His arm around her throat cut her off. She couldn't speak, could barely breathe, and from then on she offered no resistance as he propelled her past the side altars, past the velvet-curtained confessionals.

Maureen was almost unconscious by the time they reached the front. She hardly knew where she was, but the heels of her boots scraped across marble and then he was dragging her up steps. That meant they were on the altar. From the corner of her eye, Maureen could see the flickering red light of the sanctuary lamp suspended from the ceiling.

Knowing where she was encouraged her. Soon he would release his grip and she could turn and face him, explain who she was. The poor old man was so simple he did not realize what he was doing wrong. The Monsignor had turned him into an attack dog, pouncing on anyone that came near the Cathedral.

But he did not release her. Instead, he pulled her back behind the altar, and then they were descending a flight of steep marble steps.

At first Maureen was baffled, not knowing where they could be. And then it came to her—the crypt. She had never been down there, though she knew that it existed. Every cathedral had a crypt for burying its bishops. But why was Clarence bringing her there now, in the dark, with no one around?

Truly frightened now, she fought for consciousness, fought to gather up her strength. At the foot of the steps Clarence stopped for breath and she seized her chance. Drawing up her feet, she thrust them forward suddenly, breaking his hold on her, and she stumbled away, fell flat against the cold marble wall.

For a moment they eyed each other in the dark. Maureen crouched, bracing herself for his rush. But he surprised her. Instead of trying to grab hold again, he only straight-armed her, shoving her back against the slab of marble. The slab gave way and she tumbled into the dark beyond.

The odor hit her first: the thick, strong chemical, mixed with the reek of something rotten. Gagging and choking, Maureen covered her mouth, cupped her nostrils to keep from breathing the foulness. Something was dead, she thought. But she couldn't think what could be big enough to cause so overwhelming a stench.

If only she was able to see better. She tried to run back into the crypt but Clarence blocked her, shoved her back, and she stumbled further into the dark room.

What she saw came to her in waves of recognition. She saw it all in slow motion, the way the mind works, slowing down the images, protecting itself from excruciating knowledge. The single dangling lightbulb was swinging in a wide arc, its harsh glow moving like an erratic searchlight.

Maureen saw the black man kneeling, his eye dangling grotesquely from its socket. Behind him the priest wielded the candlestick like the sword of an executioner, and the black man crumpled, slipped out of sight beyond the table as the candlestick came down again, and again.

Screaming, Maureen covered her face and turned away. When she lowered her hands she was facing the wall opposite, and the lightbulb sailed by again, bringing into sight the thin slots cut into the limestone.

Maureen saw then the catacomb, the aged graves and crumbling bones, skulls and skeletons left in the high-tiered limestone wall. The eyeless, fleshless faces stared down at her as the high floating bulb kept sweeping the damp walls.

She tried to scream again, yet she knew the roar of fear was caught in her throat. Her eyes followed the beam of light, hypnotized by its course. The light pinpointed the priest. He was coming toward her, circling the table, carrying the heavy candle holder. His face was white by the naked bulb, his eyes wild in his head.

The swinging light reached the opposite wall. More grave slots were cut into it. Some were cemented up with bricks and mortar, but others had been swept clean, stood empty and ready. Still others were exposed and occupied. In the brief, glancing light, Maureen saw more remains, bones fallen to the rocky floor and shattered, bony cadavers and bodiless skulls. The empty eyesockets met her gaze.

She could see rats in among the decaying bones, saw the heavy rodents nimbly scramble from the sudden beam of light. They crawled on noisy claws across the empty tombs and stared down at her appraisingly, their tiny eyes glittering in the dark.

Then the light was switched off and she was lost in total darkness. She thought of the Monsignor beside her in the dark, and she lost control of her fear. The cloth that closed over her face was almost a relief: one deep, panic-stricken breath and all the bodies disappeared.

Jamie knew there was no turning back. The apparition was giving him his chance, he knew—the chance to change the pattern of his lives, the chance to act for good. If his courage failed him now, the chance might never come again.

As if to warn him, the light in the distance wavered. It disappeared, then appeared again, as if someone were closing a door and opening it. His chance would not last forever, the light seemed to say. It could disappear at any moment.

Jamie set off again. His bare feet reached higher, dryer ground, but the tunnel was even more cramped. He had no idea how far he had walked, or where he was under the ground. Yet he knew that he would not die. The shrouded figure had not delivered him to death on this strange, labyrinthine path.

The flickering light spread its glow. The passage widened now and Jamie realized he was nearing the tunnel entrance. There was a room of some kind beyond.

Moving carefully, silently, he stepped through the opening.

A single exposed bulb hung from the ceiling. In its harsh light Jamie saw the scene: the old priest, bloodstained, bending over a table; the big black man, his skull crushed, his body stripped of clothes, stretched out on the rubber sheet.

Maureen gagged as she returned to consciousness.

The cheesecloth had slipped off her nose, leaving only a handkerchief tied around her head, jammed between her teeth. Slowly she absorbed what had happened, became conscious of her body. She was lying on her side. She had been bound hand and foot, her legs bent up to meet her hands, and she was squeezed into a tight space. There was little light, but she could see enough to choke with fear.

She was encased in her own catacomb, her face pressed against the rock, her lungs full of limestone dust that she could taste. Lifting her head as high as she could, she looked around. Over her shoulder she saw that the slot's narrow opening had been loosely bricked over. In that instant Maureen knew she had been left alone to die.

Panicking, she drew a deep breath to scream, and her head filled immediately with the stench. All around her, she knew, were the dead old people, the tramps and bag ladies, all of them rotting into the high stone walls of the catacomb.

Christ. She wouldn't die like this. Carefully, she drew two shallow breaths. Then she twisted her body to test the rope. The pain shot up her spine and bit like a wooden wedge into the base of her head.

Those bastards.

Leaving her to die, by inches, in the catacomb. If she didn't go mad first. She moved her head slowly, tested how far she could maneuver. But it was hopeless. She was too big for the old niche, and they had had to pack her in, her face flat against the limestone, her feet an inch from the brick.

Maureen's head ached from the chloroform. Aunt Grace was here, she realized, that feisty, sweet woman dumped here like so much garbage. The tears came then, flowing from the corners of her eyes straight back into her hair. And then she heard the shout.

• • •

"You!" Jamie shouted. He lunged toward the Monsignor and stumbled, his bare feet so numb from the seepage that they barely supported him.

The old man spun around, startled, and Jamie saw the scalpel in his hand.

"Get out of here. Get out! This is none of your concern." He came at Jamie, handling the long scalpel like a switchblade.

Jamie waited for the old man, watched him, stepping slightly to his right and giving himself room, as he had been taught somewhere in time. He could feel his body calming down, cooling out. He kept his eyes drilled on the old man's. The eyes would tell him when to move. He had learned it well, the art of Tae Kwon Do. His grandfather had taught him well.

Control your mind, his grandfather had said. You control your body with your mind. Cold, hot; happy, unhappy: you decide. So in training, a mind that's clear makes a body that's strong.

The Monsignor was raving as he came closer. "Saint Michael the Archangel told me, Jamie," he shouted. "Defend Saints Peter and Paul. He helped me, as he helped Daniel against the King of Persia."

It was the kick that he relied on. The kick is more important than the punch, his grandfather always said. You must train your kick a thousand times.

"Jamie, please listen, boy," O'Toole was begging.

Jamie moved. He raised his left knee above his belt, pivoted off his right, twisting his hip as he stretched the cocked knee. He was aiming for the old man's shoulder, not wanting to kill him, and he felt his bare heel slam into the soft old flesh, snapping the Monsignor's collarbone.

Jamie raised his hands as if in prayer, bowed to his unconscious victim, and whispered the words of Lao-tzu. "The conqueror of man is powerful, the master of himself is strong."

Maureen held her breath. Jamie had come to her, come to save her. She pulled again against her bindings and once more the violent pain numbed her body, left her gasping.

He would not find her, she realized. He did not even know she was there. Again she struggled, shifted in the tight space. She had to reveal herself some way. Make a noise. She tried to calm herself, took small, shallow breaths. If Jamie left now she would die.

Again she tried to move, and this time her booted toes touched the brick. Perhaps that was it. Her legs were bound, so she could not kick, but if she moved her whole body her boots might move the loose-stacked bricks.

Concentrating, trying to consolidate her force, Maureen thrust her body backward, enduring the excruciating pain. The bricks gave way only slightly and she gasped, lay trembling from the effort.

Jamie. Please, God, let Jamie know. Let him look around, see the new brick. She tried to think where he might be below her. She couldn't hear him. She heard nothing from the other side of the brick wall. Once more, she told herself. One final try.

Father Ignatius knelt down beside the fallen priest and gathered him gently into his arms. He would have to carry him back through the tunnel to the rectory and get help. The Monsignor in his arms, Jamie circled the table, averting his eyes from the dead detective. He remembered Murphy's strength and gentleness. Dear God, he thought, what had happened here? He had just stepped into the tunnel when, from behind him, he heard a door open and shut. Still holding the Monsignor, he stopped, glanced back into the long, shadowy room and saw Clarence come out of the darkness, come limping forward with a load of fire brick. The sexton looked as startled as Jamie.

"Clarence! It's you. Thank God." Jamie stepped back into the shadowy catacomb. Only then did he realize how frightened he had been, how afraid to be alone in the tomb.

"Clarence, where does that door go?" he demanded. The passage was so tight in places he would have had to drag O'Toole behind him. If Clarence had stumbled on a better route, it might mean he could get help sooner.

"Into the crypt" was all Clarence said. He was staring at Jamie wide-eyed, as if bewildered by what he'd walked into.

"It's okay, Clarence," Jamie whispered. "This is a shock to me, too. But we can go now."

"Monsignor . . . ?" Clarence said, focusing on the old priest hanging limp in Jamie's arms.

"He's okay, Clarence. He'll be all right. Now open that door and let me out through the crypt." Slowly Clarence bent, as if to set down his load before obeying. And then a loose firebrick tumbled down the catacomb wall.

Maureen kicked out again, before her body could register the pain. Her booted toes slammed into the brick and another broke from the wall. She kicked again, crying with the pain, and this time her boots broke through, sending more bricks tumbling and laying bare her grave.

Even in the dimness Jamie recognized Maureen's boot, realized at once she had been walled in alive. Now he spun around to Clarence, knowing what the firebricks were, and why the sexton was carrying them to the hidden tomb.

"You, too!"

The old man's eyes went wild in his head. His friend, the Monsignor, was hurt, maybe even dead, and he fired one of the bricks at the head of Father Ignatius.

Jamie ducked. The heavy brick flew over, harmlessly, but the old man kept throwing, picking bricks off the floor and tossing them wildly across the catacomb.

Jamie kept backing away, turning to shield the Monsignor with his body. A red brick caught his back, hit him beneath the shoulder blade. Jamie winced and lost his grip on the old pastor. He stumbled to his knees and dropped the unconscious priest, then rolled away, kept moving, not giving Clarence a stationary target.

Then he regained his feet and assumed the Tae Kwon Do attack position. Abandoning the bricks, Clarence ran to a bundle of clothes beside the embalming table and began to tear through them.

Jamie approached him across the floor. The poor, hopeless soul, he thought, another victim of MacPatch. And then Clarence pulled back from the pile of rags, Murphy's service revolver in his shaking hands.

Jamie moved at once, jumped forward, turned and kicked,

all in one, smooth, swift motion. His right bare foot kicked out, caught the old man flat against the face. From where she lay Maureen saw nothing, but heard the sound of breaking bones, and a sharp, clear "snap."

Clarence's head popped back, hung lifeless on his broken neck, and Jamie's loud attack shout echoed off the high, cavernous walls of the catacomb.

CHAPTER TWENTY-TWO

January Fifth, Before Dawn
Feast of Saint Simeon Stylites

The Monsignor was crying. He sat in the wing chair before the television set, his thin pink face turned into the fading fabric, his hands clutching the broken collarbone.

"Give him a drink for Chrissake, Jamie!" the Cardinal said, motioning to the young priest. "And what about you, Miss Sullivan?" He looked across the study to where Maureen stood, her back to the bookshelves. She shook her head.

"Well, make a drink for me then. If she doesn't need one, I do." The Cardinal had just returned from the catacomb. He had gone down alone, entering through the cellar passage and exiting through the crypt. When he emerged into the Cathedral he had descended slowly from the main altar, then knelt at the railing for a long time.

"Did you give Clarence the Last Rites . . . after you killed him, that is."

"Yes, I did," Jamie replied. "He died at once; he felt no pain. Or at least less pain than he caused all those poor, homeless people."

Good for you, Maureen thought, watching the two priests. Don't let him get you on the defensive.

The Cardinal made a quick turn of the small room and then stopped in front of Jamie, planting his feet apart as if to block any attempt to escape. "Now what in God's good name were you doing down here all this time, that only now you realize this crazy old fool was killing people—not just a few either—and burying the whole lot under our Cathedral? Tell me, Jamie, where were your eyes, your common sense?" He was shouting at the young priest.

Jamie shook his head, began to fumble for an answer. "I never suspected, Your Eminence; it's true. I wouldn't still, except for the shrouded figure. It came and got me, brought me to the catacomb."

"Oh, please, don't start that again." The Cardinal waved his hand in disbelief.

"Do you want me to call the police?" Jamie asked.

"Don't do a goddamn thing," His Eminence shouted. "Enough has been done over there to set the Church back into the Middle Ages. The two of you. Jesus Christ!" He kept pacing, circling the old pastor a few more times, then abruptly he stopped and leaned over the high back of the chair. "Tommy, tell me now," he said softly, "what automobile did you use?"

"Ours. Here at Saints Peter and Paul." His eyes brightened at the question.

"But you said you sold off the limousine."

The Monsignor grinned, "I lied a bit about that, Frank."

"But why did you take those poor folks off the street like that?" He was whispering, as if hearing the old man's confession.

"The expenses. I couldn't keep things going here, and those bums were stealing me blind. Stealing from the poor boxes, taking the vigil light money." He began to cry again, suffering from the pain in his shoulder.

"But, Tommy, killing all those people . . . what did it accomplish?"

The Monsignor's head snapped up and he said quickly, "It was a start. Without them this parish could be the way it used to be—you know, when we were lads." He stopped, as if he had lost his thought, then he smiled and said good-naturedly, "Do you remember Sister Pamphilus? Remember the time you put the snake into the Alms Box, and she found it right before summer vacation, and you had to wash out the church all summer. Do you know who told her you did it?" His eyes were bright with amusement.

"It doesn't matter, Tommy, that's a long time ago now—"

"I told her! I told her!" The thin old man was grinning.

The Cardinal stood up slowly. He was exhausted, broken by the evening. "Drink up, Tommy. Finish off that whiskey and go up to bed. We'll have a doctor here soon to take care of that shoulder of yours." He smiled kindly at the old priest.

"You're not mad at me, are you, Frank? I was only, you know, trying to help out. They were dead weight, Frank. Just bleeding us dry. Do you want to see the books? We haven't a cent to our name, and the fuel costs going sky high." He began to weep again, uncontrollably.

"There's nothing to worry about, Tommy. Easy there. Don't you worry now about Saints Peter and Paul." He patted the Monsignor on the back and helped him stand.

"Does the doctor who's coming know about all this?" O'Toole asked fearfully.

"No, Tommy, it's our secret."

The Monsignor nodded, then started off. At the doorway he brightened. "I was just reading the other day about Saint Agnes. I think I'll do something special this year on her feast day. She's a saint we don't think about much. And here my dear mother was named after her." He nodded, making his point, then went along the narrow hallway toward the front, bracing himself against the wall with his good arm.

"Pour me another of these, Jamie, would you, like a good lad?" The Cardinal held out his tumbler to Jamie, then sank down into O'Toole's seat. Unlike the old Monsignor, he filled the chair.

"Do you want me to put through the call now?" Jamie offered, handing him the Scotch.

"What's that? What did you say?" The Cardinal had closed his eyes, appeared to be dozing.

"The police," Jamie answered. "Do you want me to get things started?"

The Cardinal looked up, alert now, and stared at Jamie as if he had said something shocking.

"This isn't the time to go running off at the mouth," he answered.

Jamie glanced at Maureen, who still stood back against the bookshelves, watching them. It had been a terrible night, and the next day and weeks would be worse, he knew, once the story got into the papers and on television.

"Your Eminence," Jamie began again, "there must be someone you'd like me to contact—your secretary, or Monsignor Pettit at the press office? A statement will have to be made. The more information we can present at once, before the reporters start getting involved . . . I think—"

"I think! I think!" The Cardinal leaned forward angrily, one elbow leaning on his knee. "You're not thinking at all, Jamie." He waved the young priest into the other armchair.

"How many people know about this situation?"

Jamie shrugged. "Just us." He stared at the Cardinal, frowning.

His Eminence stared off across the room. He finished the second drink, quickly and in silence, then said, "And that's the way it will be."

"Pardon me?" Jamie leaned forward, not sure he had understood.

"No one need know, beyond us." And now he looked up, locked Jamie's eyes with his own. "This is a Church matter, Jamie."

"Your Eminence—" Jamie gestured, looking toward the old Cathedral. "People have been murdered, buried down there. And Monsignor O'Toole . . . the man is out of his mind." Jamie stood, frightened by what they were discussing.

"I'll handle Tommy. We'll send him off to Saint Jude's, the downstate retirement home. They've a special section for the mentally incompetent—no different, really, from where the state would send him."

"Your Eminence, I'm not saying the Monsignor belongs in jail. You're right; he'd never even stand trial. But there are at least two dozen bodies over there. You can't really believe—"

"Bag women, Jamie, and old bums. No families or friends

to worry about, to make a fuss over missing relatives. I'll say Mass myself for them, and you can assist me."

"What about Murphy?" Jamie said it conclusively, as if he'd won.

The Cardinal nodded, momentarily considering, then said, "Well, that's unfortunate, but it will have to stand. He disappeared on the job, became part of this string of unsolved murders. I'll speak to Matty Joyce, have Catholic Charities do something for his family, even though he wasn't RC."

"My aunt was, Your Eminence." Maureen Sullivan spoke up, still motionless against the bookshelves.

The Cardinal looked surprised, as if he had forgotten she was there.

"She'll have a proper Catholic burial, Maureen. We'll say a special Mass for her. Don't forget, she is in consecrated ground." He glanced back and forth between the two young people. "Hasn't there been enough tragedy? Do we have to cause more pain and scandal by labeling Tom O'Toole a mass murderer?"

The Cardinal shook his head, answering his own question. "It's my fault, really. I left him down here too long, that was it. The riots scared all his old friends off to the suburbs. He must have snapped then—not, you know, that he wasn't always a little soft in the head. Liam Sullivan said it years ago: 'Tommy and his saints for every day.' That was always his idea of religion."

"I killed a man myself, Your Eminence. I can't just let that go."

"Clarence, that old fool! He's as guilty as O'Toole, if you're wanting to pass out blame. Besides, it was self-defense; he would have shot you with Murphy's gun. No, the answer is to level that Cathedral, close off that catacomb once and for all. Seal it off forever, and those poor unfortunate people with it."

"No! We treated those people as if they didn't exist; that's why O'Toole killed them. We can't go on treating them that way now. We owe it to them; we can't betray them any longer."

The Cardinal glanced at Maureen, then back at Jamie. If they decided to go to the police together he couldn't stop them. The archdiocese would become notorious, a byword. O'Toole, that nutbar, would be packed off somewhere and he himself would take the blame. He'd never see his cable network that was sure.

"All right, Jamie . . . Maureen. I accept your criticism, your concerns. I have ignored the changes in this parish, and I'll try to do something about that." He spoke rapidly, trying to find solid ground on which to build his case. "I *will* do something about it. But the first step is to keep the Church clean in all this."

"No."

The Cardinal studied the young priest. There was no over-ruling the boy, he saw; Jamie had come into his own that night. There was the look of the true believer in his eyes.

"I was led to the catacomb, Your Eminence," Jamie said. "Three times the shrouded figure came to find me, tried to make me follow, to discover what O'Toole was doing." Jamie shook his head. "Some justice must be given. We're just as guilty as he is—not of killing them, of course, but of wishing them out of existence. Denying their claim on us. We've got to admit that, no matter how much good we try to do afterward."

"Jesus, Mary and Joseph, let's not have any more of that." The Cardinal sank back in the wing chair, but kept his eye on Jamie. "Do you want me to throw away everything because of your nightmares? Your midnight visions? Jamie, you're not a saint, and MacPatch isn't Lourdes. One word to the public about your shrouded figure ghost and it's good-bye to the CCP and all the good that network could have accomplished. Dear God, Jamie, they'll pack you off to St. Jude's with O'Toole, and ruin me as well. The Vatican won't stand for it. Jamie, you can't do this to me. You can't do this to yourself."

The outburst silenced Jamie. Once again he was filled with his own doubts. Perhaps he had never really seen the figure. He remembered how it had disappeared down in the passage.

He glanced at Maureen. She had always doubted his trances, the regressions. She had said he was suffering only as an orphan, a man starved for more knowledge of his origins. And the Cardinal was right. O'Toole was mad and Clarence was dead. The killing had been stopped. Perhaps it was better to leave the dead in their tombs and turn now to helping the living.

He looked over at Maureen. "I dreamed it all, didn't I?" he admitted.

"No, Jamie, no," she cried. She could see the Cardinal was winning. From the pocket of her jeans she pulled the forgotten photograph and handed it to Jamie.

The Cardinal looked on, frowning. The young priest unfolded the color photograph, looked down at the face in the Shroud of Turin. Looked down at the image of himself.

"Those lives are true, Judas Thomas," she said softly.

Jamie nodded, then silently handed the photograph to the Cardinal. No longer was he in doubt about what he should do, about what was right. He looked at His Eminence.

"This is who came to me tonight and led me to the catacomb," he said.

The Cardinal fingered the glossy paper for a moment, read the caption beneath the computer photograph. Then deliberately, in a show of contempt, he tossed the page aside. It drifted to the carpet.

"Jamie, it's time for you to listen." He rose from the deep chair. Now he wished he had not had the Scotch. He needed a clear mind to do what he had to do next. But when he began to speak he found he was cold sober, certain that this was the only way to save himself, the archdiocese, and Jamie. He had to save Jamie, at all costs, even by telling the terrible truth.

"My son, you're not anyone's twin brother. You're not the reincarnated Judas Thomas, if there ever was such a person in the first place. That isn't what you believe. It isn't part of our religion, our way of life. But you are troubled, Jamie, that I can see, about your life here in MacPatch.

"You know, son, that all your life I have been with you, caring for you everywhere, always, ever since your days with the nuns at the orphanage. There's a reason for that, and the reason has been my lifelong secret."

The Cardinal paused, but Jamie didn't ask the question. He just stood waiting, his eyes raised to the Cardinal's.

"You know the story I always tell about finding you on the Cathedral steps. Well, it's true enough, but it wasn't the Cathedral exactly. I found you here, outside the rectory, and Jamie, I did know who your mother was. I knew her well, in fact . . ." The Cardinal looked away as he told the story of Jamie's birth, the death of Jamie's mother. He couldn't look into the eyes of his son.

"So perhaps you'll understand now," he concluded, "when I say you can't let these delusions break you. You're my son. I won't let this happen."

"But I don't believe you," Jamie said. He walked to the far end of the room, as if wanting to put distance between them. "I don't believe any of it." He reached out and grabbed the back of a chair. His hands were trembling. "Does my silence mean that much," he demanded, "that you'd lie to me about who I really am?"

"I'm not lying, Jamie. I wish to God I were, but . . ." The Cardinal turned slightly, nodded to Maureen. "Am I, my child?"

For a long moment Maureen did not answer. Jamie wanted his father, she knew; would do anything to please him. She would report the murders to the police herself, but without Jamie no one would believe her. The Cardinal would "have a word" with Matty Joyce and she would be labeled a trouble-making social worker, wrought up over the disappearance of her aunt. Why should she have to tell the truth, she asked herself. Why should she play fair when the Cardinal didn't?

She saw His Eminence watching her. He was alarmed now by her silence; he must have guessed what she was contemplating.

Maureen enjoyed his nervousness. But for her the burden of lying was too great. When she spoke she looked not at the Cardinal but at Jamie.

"He told me the same story the other night, when he was trying to get me out of town." She spoke as if the Cardinal were not in the room with them. "I didn't believe him either, not at first. I thought he was trying to manipulate me. But then . . . Mrs. Windmiller . . . earlier today she told me the rest of what had happened to your mother. She was her sister. She wasn't lying."

Maureen couldn't keep talking; she couldn't keep looking into the sad blue eyes of the young priest.

Jamie nodded but did not speak. No one spoke in the quiet study. Jamie moved to where the photograph of the Shroud of Turin lay on the carpet and carefully, lovingly, he picked it up, folded away the sad image and slipped it into his shirt pocket.

He looked over at the Cardinal, looked at his father. Now

he knew the truth, Jamie thought, of this lifetime as well as the others. Jesus died for our sins; that he had been taught. But he, Jamie, had died again and again for his own, for the terrible sin of forsaking his brother. He would not forsake his brothers any longer.

That was why his soul had been reborn into the world; that was why the shroud had come to him, to see that his brothers would be cared for. This time he would not betray them—not even for his father.

"No, Your Eminence," Jamie spoke up. "No, Father. I won't let you hide this. God won't let us. This is our parish, these were our people. We must do God's work, Father. We have to."

Maureen watched as the Cardinal looked back at Jamie, saw the older man finally nod, acquiesce. She walked out then, went past Jamie and out of the rectory and left the two priests alone, left the father and son to each other.

EPILOGUE

July Twenty-fifth, Afternoon
Feast of Saint James the Greater

The Cardinal waited. It was his turn now: the mayor had spoken, Rabbi Frisch from Beth Israel, Karel Chase from the Center, and Liam's daughter, Maureen. The Cardinal waited, glanced down along the dais, then out at the crowd, smiling.

What a motley collection, he thought: bag ladies mixed up with Sisters of St. Clare, social service types, reporters and TV people, and all the blacks, browns, and yellows of MacPatch. Jamie's people. Oh, Jamie, my dear boy, where are you today? He felt as if his heart would break. Shut down. Explode. Cardinal Dies Dedicating Center for Homeless. He could see the headlines. Jesus Christ, what a way to go.

He cocked his head, looking out over the cloister of the old convent. It was a bright, sunny day, perfect for a game of golf. Well, all he had to do was wrap it up: Say a few words, lavish them with praise, then get the hell out of MacPatch. Maureen Sullivan and her crew could have it all. Good riddance.

His Eminence coughed into his thick hands and said, "Now who would have believed, back in the dead of winter—in the middle of our troubles—that we'd be here on this lovely July day, to dedicate the Robert Murphy Center for the Homeless . . . honoring, as we all know, the memory of that fine man who gave his life to help the poor, the old, the forgotten people of this parish and our city."

The Cardinal paused, looked down at Rochelle Murphy, nodded to her solemnly. She was a good-looking colored woman, he thought. She'd be all right. Young. Attractive. Well off now, too, with the police pension, the Catholic Charities donation—the guilt money, Maureen Sullivan had called it.

"And who of us can forget the tragedies of last winter, the tragedies that bring us all together today?" The Cardinal went on, picking up his pace. "And which of us would want to forget? For it is out of such tragedy and sorrow that hope appears. That is our belief, as religious people, concerned people: that out of such sickness we can learn new lessons, see our duty more clearly.

"No, we must not forget. Yet it is the fate of men—God's fate for man—that faced with such atrocities, man has always been able to see what is right, and do it. It is in that spirit that we come together. To atone for the evils of one man's madness by protecting others. The people Robert Murphy died to protect. The least protected people of our city."

The Cardinal paused. Looked out over the summer garden. Held all their attention with his silence.

"Two people would never let us forget." The Cardinal shifted slightly, found Maureen at the end of the long table, brought her into range, as if sighting her with a rifle. "I want to thank them today. First, Maureen Sullivan, who has dedicated her life to the old neighborhood, her neighbors."

The applause broke around Maureen, who nodded back at the Cardinal coolly. She thought then of Jamie, as she often did. He stayed in her mind, especially now, what with the opening of Murphy Center.

They had made a mistake. They should have decided to write, to keep in touch. It would have been easier. They could have let the attraction between them change and grow. Become something else. Something more. Now she clung to her memories of the short time they were together. In love. She smiled at that. Yes, she had been in love with him, more so than ever with Michael DeSales. She could not really remember what Michael looked like. But not Jamie. His face was locked into her heart.

"The other person who had so much to do with the Center is not with us, I'm sorry to say. And yet I'd like to thank him. . . ."

Maureen's head snapped up. Of course he would say something about Jamie. How could he not.

"Our former assistant pastor of Saints Peter and Paul, who like Maureen Sullivan made the necessity of this Center apparent to me."

God, she thought, he certainly knew how to make a silk purse out of a sow's ear. He had weathered the entire scandal, made a virtue of necessity, and now was organizing a national coalition to help the homeless.

"Father James Ignatius. . . . Many of you are familiar with the young man. Knew him."

Maureen looked out over the crowd. What did they really know, she wondered. She spotted Hilda Windmiller sitting several rows back, next to a group of nuns. She had telephoned Maureen and asked if she could come in from her post at Saint Monica's for the dedication.

"That would make me very happy," Maureen had said. "And Jamie too, I'm sure." But even Hilda, his mother's sister, knew nothing of what had really happened.

"It is appropriate that we dedicate this Center today, on July twenty fifth, the feast of St. James the Greater. Some of our non-Catholic friends might not know, but James the Greater was the first of the twelve apostles to give his life for Jesus.

"A true disciple, as our own Father Ignatius is a true disciple. We tried to keep the young man among us, among the people of MacPatch. But Father Jamie left us behind to tend the flock while he took his love to other people in other lands."

Maureen could hear the sadness in the old man's voice. The pain. Now, she thought with some pity, he was paying for his sins.

"Father Ignatius requested that work, asked my permission to carry it out. I regretted losing Father Jamie, but . . ." The big man shrugged.

He was going to cry, Maureen thought. He was going to

break down before this crowd of strangers. Maureen, too, could feel her tears welling up. The man had lost everything. He had lost Jamie. Lost his son.

". . . but we keep in touch, Jamie and myself. We write." The Cardinal had pulled a letter from inside the folds of his cassock. ". . . and his letters, I must tell you, give me courage, help me with the burden of my responsibilities here in the city."

He held up the white pages. "He wrote recently about the Murphy Center, about the work of Maureen Sullivan, the years she has spent struggling to get those of us uptown to listen. . . ."

The Cardinal had shifted toward her once more.

Oh no, Maureen thought, don't say anything personal, not now, after all this time.

"And what he wrote about Maureen he writes for all of us— you who live here daily in MacPatch, and all of us up here on this dais. And he was writing about himself as well."

The Cardinal slowly unfolded the stiff pages.

"Father Jamie was speaking of the people he serves now, the homeless of another land. And it struck him that we are all homeless souls, orphans in life, trying our best, failing, trying again to do better. Until, he says, quoting from Aeschylus, 'In our sleep, pain which cannot forget falls drop by drop upon the heart until, in our despair, against our will, comes wisdom through the awful grace of God.'"

The Cardinal looked up, looked at her. There were tears in the old man's eyes. She could feel the tears in hers. Jamie wouldn't write, she realized, but he had wanted her to know. He was all right now. He had survived. His soul was rested.

December Twenty-fifth, Morning
Feast of the Nativity of Christ

Father James Ignatius stood in the open window of his bedroom and watched the rain clouds cross the desert. The clouds had been in the far highlands for weeks, growing, spreading, darkening the horizon to the north of the mission compound. The face of God, the local people called the storm. The angry face of God.

Jamie smiled. Rain on Christmas. It was a good omen in

the desert. Then he said out loud, to no one, "Christmas. Bah, humbug!" And stepped out into the bright African morning.

Outside, in the shade of the porch's thatched roof, Jamie could feel the cool breeze of the approaching rain. After so many hot months, no summer rains, a whole year of dust, the moist breeze felt like an embrace.

The parched soil had yielded no crops that year, and hordes of refugees—Gallas, Anuak, and Nuer, the tribes of southern Ethiopia—filled the mission compound. Every night more of them came in from the desert, sat waiting patiently in the dust to be fed and cared for by the foreign missionaries. Every morning Jamie would find new people, but all with the same starving faces, the same distended bodies. Their hollow eyes pleaded for enough food to stave off starvation that day. The missionaries tried to give it to them.

Jamie stepped off the porch and felt the sudden heat of day. It was not yet seven and already the temperature was in the hundreds. Stepping off the wooden porch he felt his sandals sink into inches of dust. Across the compound he saw that the children had already gathered for Mass, but stood waiting outside the church till he arrived. The church had no doors, no walls even, but they would not enter it before him, out of respect. They would not even speak first, greeting him only with smiles until he had recognized them in Amharic.

"Tenastelign," Jamie said. "May God give you health." He saw these children every day; they were all orphans of the drought, being raised by the missionaries. His favorite was the little girl called Kelemwork, "Black Gold."

"Iski! Indemin aderu?" the children shouted back. "We're fine, thank you. How did you pass the night?" They parted before him, giving Jamie a clear path into the church.

Jamie stepped inside, feeling cooler now that he was out of the sun. He could smell the small fires around the compound, smell the morning coffee. Already he could see the refugees lining up, waiting in the heat for the coffee and some portion of *dabo,* of bread. Sometimes he waited in line too, chatting with the people about the homes they had had to leave, eating what they ate. Today, however, he was fasting; he would drink only water that day.

The wood they were burning was eucalyptus. Jamie sniffed

it on the air and as always—as he had every day since he had come to Africa—he thought of Maureen. He wondered if it was snowing that Christmas morning outside the Center.

Snow. He was surprised that he missed it, as he was surprised that he missed MacPatch. He had known he would miss Maureen Sullivan.

"*Abate!*" Kelemwork was speaking to him, covering her mouth with her hands, calling him father in Amharic.

"Yes, *abebetch*. Yes, my flower. *Tadess?*" Jamie smiled, asking the little girl what was happening.

"*Shamagile,*" she whispered. Jamie turned where she was looking and there he was, an old man slumped down on the floor in the corner, half hidden by the wooden pews.

The *shamagile* wore only a scrap of cloth for clothing, no shirt, no sandals, not even a *shamma*, a piece of white woven cotton. Even the poorest of refugees, Jamie had learned, had a *shamma* to wrap around his shoulders in the cold desert nights.

The crowd of children began to whisper among themselves, to push forward to see, and Jamie said quickly, "*Zim bal!*" telling them to keep quiet.

It was unusual for a refugee to wander into the church, Jamie thought as he went to him. Most of these Ethiopians were Moslems. Perhaps the man had gotten lost during the night. There were so many sick people now that the nuns and nurses had set up tents beyond the school, filling the playing field with those beyond hope of saving. The mission could offer only shade and a cot—not much, but at least a place to die, and a burial.

As he moved through the pews toward the old man, Jamie saw that he did not know him. That was not surprising. He worked most of the day in the segregated quarter of the mission, among the lepers, and this man was not one of them. Probably he was new and would have to be brought to the nurses to be tagged.

Jamie emerged from the pews and approached the *shamagile*. It was then that he saw the elephantiasis, the hideous lymphatic obstruction. Below the knees both of the old man's legs were the size, shape, and texture of an elephant's. Jamie had seen the disease before in Africa, once unforgettably. Taking the *littorina*, the little train, from Addis Ababa to Dire

Dawa, he had looked out the window at Awash Station and seen a man carrying his enlarged scrotum through the marketplace in a wheelbarrow.

Still, this was a rare sight in the desert, especially at the mission hospital. How far had this man come? Jamie knew by looking at him that he couldn't have walked more than twenty yards a day, moving his tree-trunk legs one or two steps an hour, supporting himself with two poles cut from the hard wood of the baobab tree.

"*Ebako*," the old man whispered. "Please."

Jamie knelt beside him, took the old man's head in his lap. The *shamagile*'s lips were as dry and cracked as the parched soil; there was no saliva in his mouth. The flies had found his face, however, and they swarmed around the tear ducts of his eyes, searching for moisture. The old man was too weak to lift his hand and brush them off. Jamie recognized the eyes.

"*Wuha?*" asked Jamie. He called to Kelemwork to bring some water.

The old man shook his head.

"*Dabo?*" Jamie said. He saw now that the old man was close to death, but he could give him one last meal.

With great effort the old man nodded toward the little altar, whispered, "*Maskal, esti.*"

For a moment Jamie did not understand the man's Amharic. Then he realized it was the cross he wanted. The old man wanted to go up front where he could see the crucifix, the large carving of Christ crucified that hung above the altar.

His dying wish, Jamie realized. The old man had somehow managed to drag himself across the desert, to reach the mission so he could die there. This was unlike the Ethiopians, even the Coptic Christians from the north. Often families would take their dying relatives out of the mission hospital, bring them home to die in their own villages.

Jamie slipped his arms under the man's shoulders and lifted him easily. Even with his distended legs the man weighed nothing. The drought, the famine, his sickness had left only skin and bones.

"*Amesegginallehu*," the man said, thanking him. Even in his pain he was polite and formal, Jamie thought, as all Ethiopians were.

Jamie carried him to the front of the church, set him down gently and stepped quickly to the altar. He opened the tabernacle and took out the silver ciborium, opened that, and lifted out a thin wafer of Holy Eucharist. He moved quickly, realizing now that the man had only a few minutes more of life. Jamie had seen enough in the mission to know how quickly and silently death came.

Again Jamie knelt beside the dying man. He held up the wafer and prayed in Amharic, "This is the Lamb of God who takes away the sins of the world."

"*Getoch,*" whispered the old man. "My Lord." With his last strength he raised his head to receive the sacred wafer.

"Lord, I am not worthy to receive you, but only say the word and I shall be healed." Jamie placed the small, flat disk of unleavened bread on the Ethiopian's tongue.

The *shamagile* opened his eyes and looked up at the priest, as if the host had prolonged his life, given him a moment longer. And then he spoke suddenly in Aramaic, the language of the Holy Land, speaking to the priest for the first time since they had parted on the high ridge of the Garden of Gethsemane. "Forgive me, Judas Thomas," he whispered. "Forgive me for deceiving you."

Jamie stared down at the dying, deformed old man. How many lives had he lived? Into what worlds had his soul been born to pay for his sin?

"*Egzier ystelign,*" Jamie whispered in Amharic. "May God give to you the rest he has given me."

The man slumped back dead in his arms. Jamie knelt for a moment longer, then picked up the Ethiopian, carried him outside. The sun blinded him at first, as it had the albino boy, and then he felt the rain. The storm clouds had reached the mission, begun to sweep across the dusty compound. From the church and all the mission buildings people ran into the pouring rain. Jamie could see doctors and nurses, priests and nuns coming out to turn their faces up into the downfall, to bless themselves, thank God for answering their prayers. Food would grow now, the cattle would live, the refugees could return to their scattered villages.

In the church behind him, Sister Mary Margaret began to play "Adeste Fideles." The Christmas music carried across the compound, its chorus picked up by the faithful in the dust of the desert mission. Jamie thought of Maureen Sullivan, of his father the Cardinal, of the homeless people who would not die this winter in the snows of MacPatch.

"Merry Christmas," he whispered, joining the moment of thanks. Then he lifted again the last body of Judas Iscariot, and carried him across the rainy compound, uphill to the Coptic graveyard under the wide candelabrum trees, carrying the last body of his brother disciple to his final rest.